The baying of the hounds was louder now, and the dogs were so close that the fleeing elves could almost smell the fetid scent of their fur and feel their frenzy. They were like humans, these dogs, hunting not for food and survival, but for the sordid pleasure of the kill. They crashed through the underbrush on massive paws, slavering like moon-mad wolves as they closed in on their prey.

The elven leader shot a grim look over his shoulder. All too soon, the hounds would have them in sight . . . and the humans would not be far behind.

Songs and Swords
Elaine Cunningham

SILVER SHADOWS

Songs and Swords • Book III

Elaine Cunningham

SILVER SHADOWS

Cover art by Alan Pollack
First Printing: January 1996
Library of Congress Catalog Card Number: 00-190756

9 8 7 6 5 4 3 2 1

UK ISBN: 0-7869-2022-X
US ISBN: 0-7869-1799-7
620-T21799

U.S., CANADA, ASIA, PACIFIC, & LATIN AMERICA	EUROPEAN HEADQUARTERS
Wizards of the Coast, Inc.	Wizards of the Coast, Belgium
P.O. Box 707	P.B. 2031
Renton, WA 98057-0707	2600 Berchem
+1-800-324-6496	Belgium
	+32-70-23-32-77

Visit our web site at **www.wizards.com/forgottenrealms**

To Marilyn and Henk,
just because.

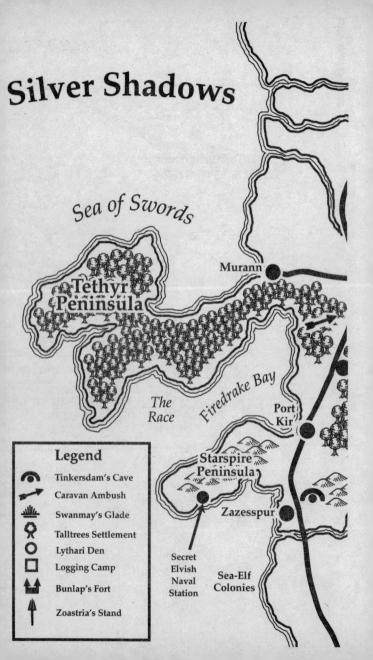

Silver Shadows

Sea of Swords

Tethyr Peninsula

Murann

Firedrake Bay

The Race

Port Kir

Starspire Peninsula

Zazesspur

Secret Elvish Naval Station

Sea-Elf Colonies

Legend

Tinkersdam's Cave	
Caravan Ambush	
Swanmay's Glade	
Talltrees Settlement	
Lythari Den	
Logging Camp	
Bunlap's Fort	
Zoastria's Stand	

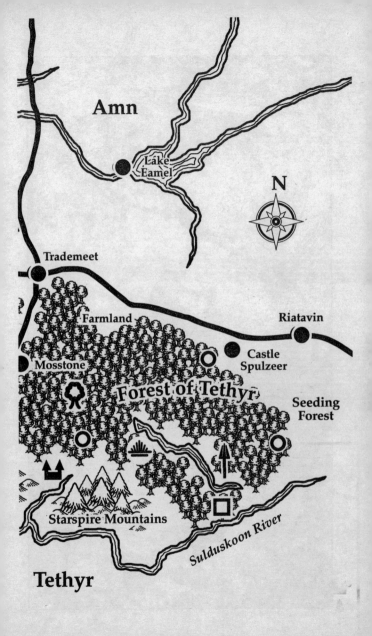

Prelude

Night fell quickly in the Forest of Tethir, and the caravan guards cast wary glances into the tall, dense foliage that walled either side of the trade route. The sounds of the forest seemed to grow louder, more ominous, as the darkness closed in around them. Overhead, the ancient trees met in a canopy too thick for the waning moon to penetrate, but the merchants pressed on, lighting torches and lanterns when their horses began to stumble.

The dim circle of firelight did little to push back the darkness or to assuage the merchants' unease. Their own torch-cast shadows seemed to taunt them, flickering capriciously and appearing as if they might at any moment break away and slip off into the trees.

There was an eeriness to this forest that made such things seem possible. All of the travelers had heard stories of the Watchers of Tethir, and there wasn't a man or woman in the caravan who did not feel the unseen eyes.

Chadson Herrick, a grizzled sell-sword who'd made

the road his home for more years than Elminster had
pipes, raised a hand to rub away the tingle at the back
of his neck. "My hackles are up. I feel like a cornered
wolf," he muttered to the man who rode beside him.

His companion responded with a terse nod. Chadson
noted that his friend—a too-thin, nervous youth who at
the best of times seemed as taut as a drawn bowstring—
was clutching a holy symbol of Tymora, goddess of luck,
in one white-knuckled hand. Chadson, for once, was not
inclined to tease the lad for his superstitions.

"Just a few more miles," the young man said in a soft,
singsong tone that suggested he'd been silently repeating those very words over and over, as if the phrase
were a charm that could ward off danger.

Their whispered conversation earned them dark
looks from several of the other guards, even though
there was no real need to keep silent. The Watchers
already knew of the caravan and had probably followed
it all the way from Mosstone, the last human settlement
on the trade route that cut through the forest. If anything, the travelers' tense silence seemed only to deepen
the impending cloud that hung over the caravan.

A sudden wild impulse came upon Chadson. He was
tempted to leap from his horse and dance upon the path,
all the while hooting and cursing and thumbing his nose
at their unseen escort. He imagined the reaction such an
act would elicit from the unnerved merchants, and the
mental image brought a wry grin to his face.

He was still smiling when the arrow took him
through the heart.

Chadson's body tilted slowly to one side and fell to the
path. For a moment the men nearest him merely stared,
their faces registering horrified recognition of the slender, ebony-hued staff protruding from the dead man's
chest. It was the dark-hued arrow of a wild elf, a bolt
aptly known as "black lightning" to the humans.

The silence exploded into frenzied action. Following
the shouted instructions of the guards, the merchants

scrambled down from their wagons and, heedless of their precious cargo, overturned several of the wagons to form a makeshift shield wall. There was no time to cut the traces, and some of the draft horses went over with the wagons, falling heavily into piles of writhing, kicking horseflesh. The animals' shrieks of terror and pain mingled with the screams of dying men as the black arrows descended upon them like stooping falcons.

From behind the scant cover of the wagons, archers returned fire, but they were shooting blind into the heavy foliage and had little hope of actually finding a mark. Some of the more intrepid—and less experienced—of the caravan guards drew swords and crashed into the forest to take the offensive. These were sent reeling back onto the path, unarmed, their eyes wide with shock and their hands clutching at mortal wounds.

The fighting was over in minutes. Many of the men on horseback had fled at the first sign of battle, and a few of the merchant wagons had escaped as well, careening wildly along the path in the wake of the panicked horses. From the north came the sound of fading hoofbeats, and a muffled crash as one wagon tilted over.

When all was silent, several shadowy figures broke free of the forest and crept onto the path. They fell upon the ruined wagons, cursing and bickering as they pawed through the spoils. One of them, taller and broader than most and clad in a dark, flowing cape, strode from the forest with a slight, limp figure slung over one shoulder. This he tossed onto the path to lie among the bodies of several of the slain merchants.

"A torch!" he commanded in a deep voice. "Get some light on this mess!"

One of the forest fighters hastened to obey, fumbling with flint and steel until a spark took hold. The sudden flare of torchlight fell upon the faces of the dead, one of which was an angular, elven face painted in elaborate patterns of greens and browns. A gaping wound slashed across the dead elf's throat and chest, tracing a deep,

diagonal line that started behind one ear and angled
down across his ribs. It had long since bled dry. The
dark-cloaked leader frowned and glanced at the fallen
men that surrounded the elf.

His eyes settled on a young man whose hand had
been pinned to his side by an arrow, apparently while
he was in the act of reaching for his sword. Tangled
among the ruined fingers was a leather thong from
which hung the symbol of Tymora. Oddly enough, the
arrow had struck the metal disk, skidding along its
length and leaving a deep score before sinking into
softer flesh. A silent sermon, the killer observed with a
bit of dark humor, on the capricious nature of Lady
Luck.

"That one," he said with a wolfish smile as he pointed
to the youth whose luck had run out. "Take his sword
and reopen the elf's wound—make it look as if he killed
the elf in hand-to-hand combat. If necessary, splash a
bit of the lad's blood around to make the kill look reasonably fresh. There's a caravan due to pass through
tomorrow."

But as his assistant reached for the sword, the
wounded fighter's eyes flickered open, and his good
hand closed around the grip of a wicked hunting knife.
Startled, the attacker fell back a step and reached for
the bow on his shoulder.

Smoothly, swiftly, he sent an arrow hurtling into the
young man's chest. This time no lucky medallion
deflected the arrow. The youth fell back, instantly dead.

The leader, however, did not look at all pleased by this
quick response. He tore the arrow free and brandished
it under the archer's nose.

"And what in the Nine bloody Hells do you call this?"

The man shrugged, his face apprehensive as he noted
the branded shaft and elaborate blue-and-white fletch-
ing that marked it as an arrow of his own making.
"Musta run out of elf arrows," he muttered.

"Damn you for a stinking ghast," the leader swore in

a low, ominous voice. "If you weren't the best archer this side of Zhentil Keep, I'd push this arrow into your left ear and pull it out your right! Search them," he ordered in louder tones, whirling toward the looters and holding the bloody arrow aloft so that all could see the error. "Make sure there are no more mistakes like this one. All of these men died at the hands of wild elves. See to it!"

One

To the casual observer, Blackstaff Tower appeared to be little more than an enormous, tapering cylinder of black granite, a tower some fifty feet tall and surrounded by a curtain wall nearly half that height. Stark and simple, the keep lacked the displays of magic—either fearsome or fanciful—that were so beloved by the wealthy and powerful citizens of Waterdeep. No watchful gargoyles peered down from the tower's flat roof; no animated statues stood guard; no cryptic runes marred the smooth black surface of wall or tower. Yet everyone who knew of the archmage Khelben "Blackstaff" Arunsun—and in Waterdeep, indeed, in all the Northlands, there were few who did not—regarded the simple keep with a mixture of pride and awe. Here, rumor suggested, lay the true power behind the City of Splendors. Here was a gateway to magical wonders beyond the imagination of most mortals.

It is a rare thing when bardic tales fail to exaggerate the measure of might, and when the speculations of

tavern gossips lag timidly behind the truth. Blackstaff
Tower was one such exception.

In a chamber in the uppermost level, Khelben's consort, the archmage Laeral Arunsun Silverhand, stood
before a mirror, a tall oval of silvered glass surrounded
by an elaborately carved and gilded frame. Fully six feet
tall and slender as a birch tree, Laeral possessed a
strange, fey beauty that hinted of faerie blood. Silvery
hair cascaded to her hips, and large green eyes—the
deep, silver-green hue peculiar to woodland ponds—
searched the mirror's frame with an intensity that
seemed oddly out of place on a face so exquisite. She ran
her fingers along the carved and gilded wood, seeking
the ever-shifting magic that few could perceive, and
fewer still could master. When satisfied that she had
found the elusive trigger, Laeral spoke a strange phrase
and then stepped *into* the mirror.

She emerged in a deep, forested glade. A few butterflies fed upon the flowers that dotted the meadow
grasses, and the ancient oaks that surrounded the glade
were robed in the lush green of early summer. It was
such a scene as might be found in the forests of many
lands, except for an aura of eldritch energy as pervasive
as sunlight. Laeral breathed in deeply, as if she could
take in the magic and the soul-deep joy that scented the
air of Evermeet, the island home of the elves.

In the center of the clearing stood an elven lady, as
tall as Laeral herself and clad in a silken gown of dove-
gray, the elven color of mourning. The elf's vividly blue
eyes had seen the birth and death of several centuries,
yet her face was youthful and the flaming luster of her
red-gold hair was undimmed by time. A silver circlet
rested on the elf woman's brow, but it was her regal
bearing and the aura of power surrounding her that
proclaimed her Lady of Evermeet, Queen of All Elves.

"Greetings, Laeral Elf-friend," said Queen Amlaruil
in a voice like music, like wind.

Laeral sank into a deep curtsey; the elven queen bid

her rise. Having dispensed with the formalities, the two women indulged in a burst of laughter, and then exchanged a sisterly embrace.

Holding hands like schoolgirls, they seated themselves on a fallen log and set to gossiping as if they were carefree maidens, rather than two of the most powerful beings on all of Toril.

But all too soon the conversation turned to matters that demanded their attention. "What news brings you to Evermeet this time, and with such urgency?" the queen asked.

"It's the Harpers again," Laeral said in a dry tone.

Amlaruil's sign came from a deep and ancient pain. "Yes. It often is. What is it this time?"

"It appears that some elves from the Forest of Tethir are attacking farms and caravans."

"Why?"

"How many reasons would you like me to name?" Laeral replied. "As you know, in a time not long past, all the elves who made their homes in the land of Tethyr, including those who dwell in the Forest of Tethir, suffered greatly at the hands of the human rulers. To all appearances, the destruction of Tethyr's royal family brought an end to this persecution. It is possible, however, that the elves are retaliating for past wrongs. Since the land of Tethyr remains lawless and chaotic, it is also likely that human settlements, trade routes, and trappers are encroaching upon elven lands. Perhaps the humans are pressing the elves, and the elves are fighting back."

"As is only natural. What interest do the Harpers have in this?"

"They want to promote some sort of settlement, a compromise that will end the turmoil and address—at least in part—the concerns of both sides."

"Ah, yes." Amlaruil paused for a grim smile. "We made such an arrangement in the forests of Cormanthor, many years ago. How well was that agreement kept, my friend, and for how long? Today, how many elves live among those trees?"

The question was not meant for answering. Laeral acknowledged the queen's assessment of the matter with a slight nod. "I have argued that very point with several of the Master Harpers, but the decline of the elven people is not an issue the Harpers have traditionally addressed."

"So much for their vaunted concern with maintaining the Balance," the queen murmured.

"What is Balance, to those whose lives are not as long as yours and mine?" Laeral pointed out. "The Harpers' concern is genuine, but the span of their vision is decidedly shorter. They are more worried about the disruption of trade and the possibility of increasing the civil unrest in Tethyr."

"Can't you make them understand what these compromises mean to the elven People?"

"Given a few centuries, yes," Laeral replied grimly. "Khelben understands, after a fashion, but his concern focuses upon the affairs of Waterdeep. And he truly believes that a compromise is the best solution, not only for his city's trade interests, but for the elves themselves. He sees it as their best chance of survival. The humans of Tethyr are not so tolerant of other races as they were even ten or twenty years ago. It would not take much provocation to turn them against the elves. There are far too many ambitious men in Tethyr, looking for a rallying cause to aid their rise to power. I can easily envision the destruction of the elves becoming such a cause. You know what happened under the royal family. Given the general lawlessness of the land, it could be far worse this time."

"Then there is only Retreat," murmured the elven queen. She sat silent for several moments, as if letting the decision take root; then she nodded decisively. "Yes, the *Sy-Tel'Quessir* must Retreat," she decreed, using the Elvish word for the forest folk. "I will send an ambassador at once to offer them a haven in Evermeet's ancient woods."

"And if they will not come?"

The queen had thought of that, as well. "Then they, like so many of the People, will fade from the land," she said with quiet resignation. "This is the twilight of the *Tel'Quessir*, my friend. You know that as well as I. We cannot hold back the darkness forever."

"But may that night be long in coming!" Laeral said fervently. "As for the Harpers, believe me when I say that sometimes the best way of controlling their enthusiasm is to work along with them," the mage added in a wry tone that suggested personal experience with this tactic. "Of one thing you can be certain: the Harpers will act with or without your blessing."

"What do you suggest?"

"Send a Harper agent to the elves' forest stronghold to bear your invitation—a Harper who will work toward a Balance that will favor the elven community. In this way, if the forest elves refuse to retreat to Evermeet, they will at least have an advocate. That is more than they might get otherwise."

Amlaruil studied her friend. The hesitancy in Laeral's silver-green eyes suggested that there was more to this matter, things of which the mage could not easily speak. Seldom was Laeral reticent about anything. Foreboding tightened Amlaruil's throat, but she waited with elven patience for the woman to find her own way and time.

"Let us say that I would agree to such a plan," the queen suggested calmly. "Have you an elven agent among the Harpers? A forest elf, one known to the community in question?"

"No," Laeral admitted.

"Then I do not see how your plan could succeed. Most *Sy-Tel'Quessir* are insular—suspicious of all elves from outside their tribe. The People of Tethir have not sworn allegiance to me, and so they might not receive an ambassador from the island. Pressed as they are, they would likely kill any non-elf who ventured too near their hidden strongholds. No, it seems to me your Harper would have little hope of survival and even less chance for success."

Laeral did not answer at once, nor did the queen press her. Their silence was filled by the sounds of the elven forest: the rustle of leaves, the soft hum of insects, the blithe call of carefree songbirds. This glade was a place of unparalleled beauty, surrounded and sustained by Evermeet's ancient magic. The island was the last haven of the elves, and its peace and security had seldom been breached. Knowing this, the mage considered her next words carefully. What she was about to suggest trod cruelly upon the elves' painful memories and touched the queen's deepest sorrow.

"There is a half-elven Harper," Laeral said slowly, "currently stationed in a city near the Forest of Tethir. She has passed successfully as an elf on other assignments. She is very convincing, very resourceful. I feel confident that she could find a way into the forest community."

The queen's face was suddenly wary. Her eyes darted toward the shimmering oval gate that had brought Laeral from the mainland to Evermeet. It was a magical bridge between the worlds of the elves and humans, and it had been born with a spark of life that had become a half-elven child—a child that Amlaruil would forever regret. That gate had cost Amlaruil the life of her beloved husband. Grief is seldom reasonable. In Amlaruil's mind, the child and the deadly portal were as one.

"Yes," Laeral said softly, confirming the queen's unspoken conclusion. She took Amlaruil's tightly clasped hands between both of her own. "You know of whom I speak. Half-elven by birth, but willing to do anything to serve the good of the People. She has proven this again and again. Perhaps that is her way of laying claim to a heritage that has otherwise been denied her."

The queen tugged her hands free, her expression implacable. "The half-elf bears Amnestria's sword," she said coldly. "A moonblade is a greater inheritance than most noble elves can claim and more honor than she deserves."

"It seems to me that steel is cold comfort," Laeral observed. "And as for honor, half-elven or not, she wields Amnestria's sword, a weapon so powerful that many an elven warrior could not touch it and live. Think on it, my friend: what better argument in the girl's favor?"

Amlaruil turned away abruptly to stare with undisguised hatred at the magical gate that had cost her so much. Duty and grief warred on her delicate face for long, agonized moments. Finally, she lifted her head to a regal angle and once again faced her friend.

"You truly believe that this . . . that she is the best person for the task? That through her efforts the lives of the forest People might be spared?"

Laeral nodded, her silvery eyes full of sympathy for the lonely elf woman and admiration for the proud queen.

"Then so shall it be." Queen Amlaruil rose, speaking the words in the manner of a royal pronouncement. "Evermeet's ambassador to the Forest of Tethir will be the Harper known as Arilyn Moonblade."

The elf queen turned away and began to walk toward the palace. "So shall it be," she repeated to herself in a whisper that seemed too fragile to bear the weight of her bitterness. "But I swear before all the gods of the Seldarine, the elves would have been better served if the sword she carries had turned against her!"

Two

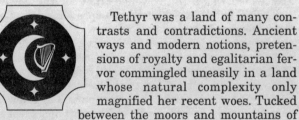 Tethyr was a land of many contrasts and contradictions. Ancient ways and modern notions, pretensions of royalty and egalitarian fervor commingled uneasily in a land whose natural complexity only magnified her recent woes. Tucked between the moors and mountains of Amn and the vast desert kingdoms of the far south, Tethyr possessed a mostly northern terrain and a temperate climate. The land was a hodgepodge of fertile farmland, deep forests, and sun-baked hills that were as dry and forbidding as any desert. The customs and interests of the peoples who settled each area were as diverse as the land itself.

But Zazesspur, the largest city of this troubled land, looked firmly to the south. A port city with an excellent deepwater harbor, it was set at the mouth of the Sulduskoon River and on the path of important overland routes. Zazesspur saw trade and travelers from many lands. Yet her current ruler, a southerner by the name of Balik, did his best to limit the influence of outsiders. The grandson of a Calishite trader, he styled himself as pasha and cultivated an oriental splendor—and a distrust of northerners—that recalled the attitudes of his forebears. Since Pasha Balik's rise to power some dozen or so years before, parts of the city had taken on a decidedly southern character. Both the best and the worst aspects of the great city of Calimport could be found in Zazesspur. Sleek palaces of white marble, formal gardens filled with exotic plants, wide boulevards, and open-air bazaars redolent with rare spices vied for space with sprawling shanty towns and narrow, crime-ridden streets.

Oddly enough, however, most of the illegal activities of Zazesspur were conducted from the better parts of town. The School of Stealth—a school of the fighting arts which was a thinly veiled front for the powerful assassins' guild—was housed in a sprawling complex at the edge of the city. Intrigue was always in fashion, and the going price for an assassin's services was high.

So, however, was the price on an assassin's life.

Arilyn Moonblade walked lightly down the narrow back-alley street that led to the women's guildhouse, making no more sound than the narrow shadow she cast. She was a broadsword's width short of six feet tall, with raven-dark hair that hung in careless waves about her shoulders and eyes of an unusual dark blue flecked with bits of gold—beautiful eyes that might have inspired bardic odes, had they not been so wary and forbidding. Pale as moonlight and alert as a stalking cat, Arilyn had about her a tense, watchful air and the too-thin, too-taut look of one who seldom paused for either food or sleep. For an assassin, the choices were few and straightforward: constant vigilance, or death.

The half-elf had been a member of the assassins' guild for several months, and she was no longer considered an easy mark. Zazesspur's professional killers were strictly ranked, and the sash of pale gray silk that belted Arilyn's waist proclaimed her to be a fighter of the highest skill. But there were still those who refused to believe that a woman—much less a half-elven woman from the barbarous Northlands—could defend the Shadow Sash she wore.

The system for advancement within the guild was simple: an ambitious assassin merely killed someone of higher rank and took his sash. Arilyn had defended her rank more times than she cared to admit. When forced to do so, she fought with an icy skill and an even colder fury that was becoming legendary among her associates. Not one of them, however, suspected that the half-elf wanted nothing more than to be rid of her dark—and largely undeserved—reputation. Nor would they ever know. Solitary and cautious by nature, with each grim challenge Arilyn became more intensely watchful and more fiercely alone.

Thanks to several months of hard-won survival, Arilyn's instincts were as keenly honed as a bladesinger's sword. She didn't need to hear footsteps or glimpse a shadow to know she was being followed. Nor did she expect such things. Silence was the first lesson taught to fledgling assassins, and the faint light coming from the high, narrow windows of the women's guildhouse up ahead cast all shadows behind her. Yet Arilyn knew she was being hunted. She could not have been more certain of this if the stalker had announced his intent with blaring horns and the yapping of hounds.

Even so, several heartbeats passed before she caught sight of him. Although half-elven, Arilyn had in full measure the keen sight of elvenkind: sharp detail, long range—and wide sweep. Behind her, at the outermost edge of her peripheral vision, she saw a tall, broad figure, cloaked and cowled into anonymity, rapidly closing the distance between them.

No one had reason to walk this particular path but Arilyn and her sole female colleague, for the tall, narrow tower that housed the women's guildhouse was the humblest and most remote building in the complex. It seemed likely, therefore, that the man behind her had career advancement in mind.

But Arilyn walked steadily on, giving no sign that she was aware of the assassin's presence. Just a few paces ahead was a walkway that branched off from the path, leading into the even narrower alley that ran between the high courtyard walls of the opulent men's guild-house and the council hall. The attack would surely come there.

When just one step remained between her and the alley, Arilyn exploded into action. In one fluid movement she whirled, seized the man's cloak with both hands, and threw herself back into a roll. The startled assassin went down with her. Before the man's weight could pin her to the ground, she twisted her body in a half-turn, brought her knees up to her chest, and kicked her feet out high and hard. The man somersaulted over her and landed heavily on the dirt.

Before his grunt of impact died away, Arilyn rolled up onto her knees beside him. She stiffened two fingers into a weapon, scanned his cloaked-and-cowled form for a target spot that would render him temporarily immobile, and drove down hard.

Her fingers plunged into the side of the man's neck—too deep, and far too easily! Arilyn grimaced as her hand disappeared into the dark-cloaked figure, winced as her fingertips drove into the hard-packed earth below.

Mouthing a silent curse, the half-elf snatched her hand out of the insubstantial body. She jerked back the cowl that obscured the apparition's face. The faint moonlight fell upon strong features, dark hair both silvering and receding, and a black beard distinctively streaked with silver.

"Khelben," she muttered with exasperation, settling back on her heels and staring with dismay at the figure who, with a dignity astonishing under the circumstances, coolly rose to his feet and brushed the dust from his cape.

At this moment Khelben "Blackstaff" Arunsun—the archmage of Waterdeep, a Master Harper, and her own superior—was hardly Arilyn's favorite person. The Harpers had sent the half-elf and her partner, Danilo Thann, to Zazesspur on a diplomatic mission, and although Khelben was not responsible for the grim role she had assumed as her cover, Arilyn found that she had little wish to face him—or, to be more precise, to face the *sending* that he had conjured and sent over the miles to speak in his stead. Arilyn assumed that Blackstaff's magical double would be as devoted to solemn discussion as the original model, and this she simply could not bear. She would do her duty by the Harpers, but she'd be damned if she'd sit around and chat about it!

"Nice sending," she said as she rose to face the archmage's double. "More solid than most."

There was a touch of regret in her voice. The implication—that she might have preferred to attack an even more solid target—did not escape the archmage. A sardonic smile lifted one corner of his dark mustache.

"Well met to you, Arilyn Moonblade," he said with a hint of sarcasm. "By Mystra, I swear that with each day that passes, you grow more like your father! I've seen that very expression on his face more times than I care to count!"

Arilyn stiffened. Her relationship with her human father was a tentative and fledgling thing, too new for comfort and too personal for casual talk. And if truth be told, although she found much to admire in the man, she did not care to be reminded of her mixed heritage.

"I doubt you conjured a sending merely to chat about your long-dead quarrels with Bran Skorlsun," she observed. "We're both here on Harper business. If it's all the same to you, let's get on with it."

The image of Khelben Arunsun nodded and asked for

her report. With a few terse words, Arilyn described the progress in her mission to help defuse an attempt by the guilds of Zazesspur to depose the ruling pasha and establish guild rule. Of her presence in the assassins' guild, and the ever-growing toll this subterfuge was taking on her, she said nothing. Fortunately, Khelben did not press her for details.

"You and Danilo have done well," the archmage said at last. "Pasha Balik is aware of the threat, and your friendship with Prince Hasheth has gained the Harpers a valuable contact in the palace. Now that the situation in Zazesspur is under control—at least for the moment—the time has come for us to speak of other matters. You are aware of the recent troubles in the Forest of Tethir?"

The Harper nodded, her face cautious.

"Then you've no doubt heard of the latest caravan attack. The elves have been blamed for this atrocity, as well as for many others. In your opinion, is there any truth to these reports?"

"There might be," she said candidly. "The green elves are a fierce, unpredictable folk, and they were ill-treated by the old royal family of Tethyr. They've ancient grudges aplenty, and who knows what might have provoked them recently?"

"This we must know," the archmage agreed. "Indeed, the Harpers have decided to send you to the forest to seek out such answers and to try to bring about a resolution to the conflict."

Arilyn's eyes went cold. "I'm being sent into Tethir? In what capacity?"

"Meaning?" the archmage inquired, his dark brows pulled down into a **V** of puzzlement.

"Am I being sent as an assassin?" she asked bluntly. Although the Harpers had never required of her anything remotely like this, it struck her that cutting down the leaders of the troublemaking elven band could certainly be considered one road to resolution!

"You know better than to ask such a question!" Khelben scolded her.

It did not escape Arilyn's notice that the archmage's words could be construed any number of ways. Not that she should have expected anything different. Khelben had an annoying habit of giving answers that were empty of information. Still, the wary half-elf would have been glad of an outright denial.

"So tell me," she requested evenly.

"Find out what's going on—what the issues and grievances on both sides are. Do what you can to promote some sort of compromise between the forest elves and the humans."

Arilyn received this information stoically, but her mind reeled under the weight of her assigned task. Get the elves to compromise? Compromise *what?* Surrender yet another section or two of the ever-dwindling forest lands to turnip farmers? Cut down a few hundred ancient trees to broaden the Trade Way? Agree to do no more than shrug helplessly when the fires of careless merchants or adventurers raged out of control? Set a quota of how many forest creatures could reasonably be taken in foot-hold traps or run down by hounds, both abominations by elven standards? Look the other way when the occasional Calishite or Amnite slaving band came to the forest to hunt elven youths and maidens to sell as "exotics"? Agree in principle to compromise one of the last strongholds of the forest elves, and thus to accelerate the demise of the elven People?

"Compromise?" With one word, Arilyn managed to portray all the force, if not the detail, of her unspoken objections.

Khelben's magical image faced down the wrathful half-elf. "What are the alternatives? What chance do the elves have if these conflicts continue and perhaps escalate into warfare? And what would such conflict do to the tenuous balance in Tethyr? No, you must make these elves see reason! Live among them; gain their trust."

In Arilyn's opinion, this suggestion was nearly as ludicrous as the first. No one, to her knowledge, had successfully infiltrated a settlement of forest elves. Most *Sy-Tel'Quessir* were reclusive, distrustful even of other elves. To be a moon elf was bad enough, but for Arilyn to reveal her half-elven nature would be to court instant death. The forest elves of Tethir had ample reason to hate and distrust humans, and among all of the elven subraces were many elves who regarded half-elves as unspeakable abominations. Of course, Arilyn had passed as an elf before, but never for the length of time such a thing would take.

At least Khelben was right about one thing: before a single word about her mission could be spoken, she would have to earn the elves' respect. Arilyn had learned years ago that the best route to respect for someone like her—a half-elven female who could not lay claim to family, lineage, or name—was to follow the point of her sword. As a fighter she was very good indeed, but elves were widely renowned for their fighting skills and thus were not easily impressed. Arilyn had taken on many difficult tasks for the Harpers, but this was the first that sounded truly impossible, the first she actually considered refusing.

"I will need time to think about this," she told the archmage's image.

"As I anticipated. The impossible always takes a little longer." Khelben responded with a wry smile as he quoted, of all people, his nephew and apprentice Danilo Thann.

Arilyn responded with a terse nod and then turned away. She did not want to think of Danilo just now, for her Harper partner would not be pleased to learn that she was being courted for a mission that would exclude him. Not, of course, that her departure—if indeed it occurred at all—would come any time soon. This mission would require the type of planning and attention to detail usually lavished on royal weddings or whole-scale invasions.

All thoughts of a night's sleep forgotten, the half-elf

left the School of Stealth complex and set out for a
waterfront tavern. Word had it that a certain Moonshae
captain, a former pirate who liked to keep a hand in his
original trade, had docked in Zazesspur the day before.
He had a special fondness for valuable documents—both
genuine and contrived—and he possessed a knowledge
of elven ways that far outstripped the understanding of
most humans. Rumor had it that one of his recent
female passengers, a green elven druid, had become his
friend, perhaps even his lover. Liaisons between wild
elves and humans were exceedingly rare, but Arilyn
knew this man well and saw how such might be possible.
Indeed, rumor had it that his ship, *Mist-Walker*, was one
of only a handful of human vessels ever permitted to
make port on the elven island of Evermeet. In short, he
was precisely what Arilyn needed.

If she was to pose as a visiting moon elf, she would
need some way to explain and legitimize her presence
in the Forest of Tethir. If anyone could provide her with
the needed forgeries—and perhaps suggest a strategy
that would gain her acceptance into the forest community—it would be this sea captain.

* * * * *

The night was warm for early summer, and the salty
tang of sweat and the sea hung heavy in the tavern. As
usual, the Breaching Whale was crowded with hard-
drinking sailors out for a bottomless mug and a bit of
fun, and the hard-eyed women who served up both for
the price of a few silver coins. It was fairly typical as
dockside taverns went, exceptional only for the dozen or
so bedchambers over the taproom, which boasted deep
feather beds and pristine linens, not to mention a
heavily armed guard at each door. Those who knew well
the ports of the Sword Coast came to the Breaching
Whale for a clean room and a safe night's sleep, luxuries
in any city and a rarity in Zazesspur.

Arilyn had no trouble picking Captain Carreigh Macumail out of the crowd. His mass of curly fair hair, his long and neatly braided whiskers, the bright blue-and-green weave of his trademark kilt, the extravagant lace-trimmed ruffles at the throat and cuffs of his white shirt—all these things set him apart from most of the Breaching Whale's rough-clad clientele. He was also by far the largest man in the room. More than three hundred pounds sat easily on a frame that stood just a handspan short of seven feet. Seated on a couple of chairs, one massive arm draped over the back of a third chair and his booted feet propped up on a fourth, Macumail sipped at a foam-crested mug as he happily exchanged war stories with a pair of Nelanther pirates.

As the half-elf made her way across the crowded tavern, she noted which heads huddled together over whispered plots, which fighters kept their hands close to their weapons. She declined an offer of entertainment proffered by one of the tavern's few male barhands, and met the measuring stare of a young tough with a cold gaze that sent him back to contemplating the contents of his mug. This was Zazesspur, and tonight all was business as usual.

By way of a greeting, Arilyn kicked the chair out from under Macumail's feet. The captain was standing, dirk held ready in guard position, with a speed that seemed incompatible with his vast size. When his dangerously narrowed gaze settled on Arilyn, his face registered first astonishment, then pleasure.

"Well met again, Lady of the Moonblade!" he said happily in a cultured voice made interesting by a lingering touch of northern Moonshae burr. "Word travels fast in this port. I hadn't thought to see you for another day or so!"

His words brought a puzzled frown to Arilyn's face. "You sent for me?"

"Aye, that I did." He paused and turned to the interested pirates. "It has truly been a pleasure, lads. Permit me to settle the evening's bill as a way of thanking you for the shared tales."

The two men took the hint. Picking up their half-finished drinks and balancing the large trencher of stewed mutton between them, they wandered off in search of an empty table.

Arilyn chose a vacated seat that enabled her to keep her back to the wall. As Captain Macumail summoned a barmaid and ordered wine, she turned the chair around and straddled it, her arms folded over the low-runged back. This posture was not only comfortable, but it provided her with a handy and nonlethal weapon to use in the event of a tavern brawl. No seasoned adventurer escaped her share of those, and Arilyn had learned to swing a chair as handily as she wielded a sword.

"So tell me," she said, to get matters rolling along.

Captain Macumail winked and reached for the flat leather pouch he wore strapped over one shoulder. "I've some fascinating reading for you," he said as he removed a sheaf of papers from the pouch. "Have a look at this, if you will."

The Harper glanced at the parchment that Carreigh Macumail thrust into her hands. The captain had provided her with bogus documents several times before, and each one had held up to the closest scrutiny. This sample was especially well done, from the delicate Elvish script to a reproduction of the seal of the Moon-flowers, Evermeet's royal family. It was a masterful forgery.

Arilyn let out a low whistle of appreciation. "Nice work."

"And don't I wish I could take credit for it." Macumail touched the creamy, luminous parchment with something approaching awe. "That, my dear lady, is the genuine article, and it's addressed to you."

The half-elf stared at him. "You can't be serious."

"Read it," he urged. "It looks serious enough to me."

"Retreat to the Island Home . . . find a welcome in the deep forests of Evermeet," Arilyn muttered, scanning the pronouncement and automatically translating from Elvish to the widely used trade tongue known as Common.

At length she lifted incredulous eyes to Macumail's face. "This is from Amlaruil of Evermeet. An official missive, and a commission naming me as her ambassador!"

"Aye, that it is," he agreed. "I took it from her hand myself. The Lady Laeral Silverhand was with the queen. There's a letter from her in that lot, as well."

Laeral Silverhand was one of the few magic-users whom Arilyn trusted and respected. Unlike most arcane scholars, who all too often seemed detached from the world around them and indifferent to the impact their spells might have on others, Laeral possessed a refreshing streak of practicality. A former adventurer and still a bit of a rogue, Lady Arunsun valued results over protocol. She and Arilyn got along just fine, and the half-elf was usually inclined to listen when Laeral spoke.

Still feeling stunned, Arilyn sorted through the pages until she found Laeral's letter. It urged her to act on Queen Amlaruil's behalf, to combine this mission with a task that would soon be offered to her by the Harpers.

The half-elf let the parchment sheets fall to the table. She leaned back and dug one hand into her hair as she considered this unexpected turn of events. In some ways, this was the answer she had been looking for. She didn't believe the forest elves would entertain the idea of compromise, but maybe—just maybe—they would consider retreating to Evermeet.

But the question remained: *Why send her?* Why had she been chosen as an emissary of Evermeet, she who had no claim to her elven heritage but the moonblade strapped to her side?

A small, cynical smile tightened the half-elf's lips. Perhaps that was it, Arilyn thought. Perhaps the royal family had finally contrived an honorable way to reclaim Amnestria's sword!

They'd wanted it some thirty years ago, when Arilyn's mother—the exiled princess Amnestria—had been murdered in distant Evereska, leaving her moonblade to her half-elven daughter. Amnestria's family had come to her funeral—from where, Arilyn had no idea—but she remembered with knife-edged clarity the elves' chagrin when they learned of this bequest, their impassioned claims that only a moon elf of pure blood and noble heart could carry such a sword. Although Amnestria's family had discussed the matter in Arilyn's presence, not one of them had a single word to spare for the grieving child—not one word of comfort or even of acknowledgment. The royal elves had worn mourning veils that obscured their identities. They had not given Arilyn so much as a glimpse of their faces. Now, all of a sudden, this aloof, faceless queen decided to grant Arilyn the honor of a royal mission? One that was most likely impossible and, Arilyn noted cynically, possibly suicidal?

In truth, the half-elf didn't believe the elven queen was deliberately contriving her death. But Arilyn could not fathom what the reasoning behind this commission might be, and not knowing—combined with her painful memories—made her deeply angry.

Arilyn reached for the royal commission. Slowly, deliberately, she crumpled up the parchment into a tight wad and dropped it into her half-empty wine goblet.

"I trust you will be so kind as to relay my answer to the queen," she said in a parody of a courtier's respectful tones.

"That's your final word?" Carreigh Macumail asked, dismay written across his bewhiskered countenance.

The half-elf leaned back and folded her arms over her chest. "Actually, I have a few more thoughts on the matter. Repeat them or not, as you choose." She then proceeded to describe what the elven queen could do with her offer, at length, in precise detail, and vividly enough to drain the color from the captain's ruddy face.

For a long moment the sea captain merely stared at Arilyn. His barrel chest rose and fell in a heavy sigh. "Well, it's been said there's no wind so strong but that it can't change direction," he observed. "*Mist-Walker* will be in port for a ten-day or two, should you decide you want to do business."

"I wouldn't lay odds on it," Arilyn advised him as she rose to her feet. She tossed a pair of coins onto the table to pay her portion of the tab and then stalked off.

Macumail watched the half-elf go. A tipsy female sailor rose to block Arilyn's path, her hand on her dagger's hilt and a leer of challenge twisting her lips. The half-elf did not even slow down. She backhanded the woman, who spun on one heel and fell face first onto a small gaming table. Dice and half-emptied mugs went flying, and the sharp crack of splintering wood mingled with the startled oaths of the interrupted gamblers. The woman lay groaning amid the wreckage of the table. Arilyn did not bother to look back.

The captain's gaze shifted from the downed sailor to the wine-soaked parchment. He regarded the ruined document with regret. Then he sighed again and took a duplicate copy from his bag.

Upon Laeral's advice, the elven queen had had five copies of Arilyn Moonblade's commission made. Laeral had warned both queen and captain that persistence would most likely be in order.

After witnessing the Harper's first rejection, Carreigh Macumail sincerely hoped five copies would be enough!

Three

 The baying of the hounds was louder now, and the dogs were so close that the fleeing elves could almost smell the fetid scent of their fur and feel their frenzy. They were like humans, these dogs, hunting not for food and survival, but for the sordid pleasure of the kill.

It was not the first time such animals had been brought into the forest. Great mastiffs, they were, so powerful that two or three of them might bring down a full-grown bear, yet fleet enough to run down a deer. They crashed through the underbrush on massive paws, slavering like moon-mad wolves as they closed in on their prey.

The elven leader, a young male known as Foxfire for his russet-colored hair, shot a grim look over his shoulder. All too soon, the hounds would have them in sight. The humans would not be far behind. It took little skill to follow the trail of crushed foliage the hunting dogs left behind like a thick and jagged scar on the forest.

Foxfire was not certain which of the intruders was the less natural—dog or master. He'd seen what the mastiffs could do to a captured elf. Gaylia, a young priestess of his tribe, had been herded by such dogs into the iron jaws of a foot-hold trap and then worried to death. The humans had left her torn and savaged body there for the elves to find. Left behind, too, were the tracks that told Foxfire the humans had stood by watching as their dogs killed the helpless priestess.

"To the trees," Foxfire ordered tersely. "Scatter, but do not let them follow you. Meet me at dusk in the ash grove."

The elves, seven of them, all armed with bows and quivers full of jet-black arrows, scrambled up the ancient trees as lightly as squirrels. There they would be invisible to the eyes of the humans and beyond the snapping jaws of the humans' four-legged counterparts. They disappeared into the thick canopy, making their separate ways from tree to tree.

Only Foxfire stayed behind, feeling uncomfortably like a treed raccoon as he waited for the human hunters to come to the call of their hounds. The mastiffs circled the giant cedar, baying and snarling and leaping against the massive trunk. Foxfire was fully aware of the danger of his position, and never would he have asked this of any elf under his command. There were answers, however, that he must have.

The elf waited patiently until the humans came into view. There were twenty of them, but Foxfire had eyes for only one. He knew this human by his massive size, by the dark gray cloak that flowed behind him like a storm cloud, and by the iron-toed boots he wore. The elf had found large, unusual boot prints very close to the place of Gaylia's death—bloodless prints upon blood-soaked earth, prints that indicated the man had stood by and watched the elf woman's horrible fate. And after a battle that had cost the lives of two elven fighters, Foxfire had glimpsed the swirl of that dark cape as the human shouldered the body of one of the elf warriors and bore him away—for what purpose, Foxfire could not begin to guess. He knew only that in this man the elves of Tethir had a formidable and evil enemy.

Carefully he committed the man's face to memory. It was a face easily remembered, a visage that matched the grim deeds of its owner: black-bearded, with a scimitar of a nose and eyes as cold and gray as the snow clouds that gathered around the peaks of the Starspire Mountains.

The man stalked toward the yapping hounds, his face a mask of fury. He kicked out hard, and his iron-clad boot caught one of the mastiffs in the ribs. The force of the blow lifted the large dog off its feet. It fell heavily on its side and lay there, kicking and yelping piteously. The others cringed away with their tails tucked tightly between their legs.

"Useless curs!" the man swore and kicked out again. This time the dogs mustered enough wit to dodge.

"Set the tree afire, Bunlap?" one of the men inquired. "That'd smoke the long-eared bastards out!"

The leader whirled on the fighter. "If you had the sense the gods gave a dung beetle," he said coldly, "you would know that the elves are long gone. They leap from tree to tree like Chultan monkeys."

"What, then?" another man demanded.

The man called Bunlap shrugged his massive shoulders. "We call the hunt a loss. Too bad. That farm south of Mosstone—the one that grows pipeweed—would've paid well for more wild-elf slaves! Best workers they've got, or so the man tells me."

"Seems to me those scrawny elves wouldn't be worth the trouble it takes to break 'em," observed another man, a thin, rangy fellow who carried the bow of a forest elf. Foxfire's eyes narrowed as he took note of that bow. He had little doubt how the man had obtained it, for no elf would part willingly with such a treasure.

Bunlap responded to the archer's comment with an

ugly smile. "Not if you've a taste for that sort of thing."

It was all Foxfire could do to keep from sending a storm of black arrows into the twisted and murderous humans. He could certainly do it; he was accounted the finest archer in the Elmanesse tribe. And surely, the world would be a better place without such foul creatures! Yet he could not, for he was a leader among his people and had more important things to consider than his own outrage. The humans were harrying the elves. This was nothing new, but there was a taunting quality to many of the attacks that puzzled Foxfire. It was as if these men were goading the forest folk, prodding them toward . . . Toward what, he could not say.

"Leash the dogs, and let's head out," Bunlap ordered.

Foxfire waited until the mastiffs had been secured and the men began to retrace their steps out of the forest. As he'd expected, the tall leader took his place in the rear, as was his custom. Foxfire noted that Bunlap was more alert and observant than most of his comrades. This made the man all the more dangerous.

High overhead, the elf followed, creeping along the branches and slowly, silently working his way down toward the humans. The heavy-footed tread and the constant, boasting chatter of the men made his task an easy one.

When the moment was right, Foxfire dropped lightly to the ground behind Bunlap. The man responded to the faint sound with a startled oath, but before he could turn around Foxfire seized a handful of the human's black hair and reached around to press a bone knife to his throat. Fire-forged weapons were rare in the forest, but this knife was long and boasted a keen, serrated edge. The man seemed to understand that the weapon was equal to the task, for he slowly lifted both hands into the air.

"You are far from home," Foxfire observed as calmly as if the two were sharing wild-mead and discussing the weather.

At the sound of his voice—a sound too musical to have come from a human throat—the other fighters whirled. Their eyes went wide with fear and wonder at the sight of the copper-skinned elf who had appeared in their midst. None of them had ever seen a wild elf up close—at least, not one that was alive and unharmed—and this creature possessed a deadly beauty that compelled both dread and awe.

"Hold fast the dogs and leave your weapons where they are," the elf advised them. "This is a matter between this man and me—a council of leaders, if you will."

"Do as he says," Bunlap said coolly. "You speak the Common tongue," he observed, his voice as steady as the elf's.

"I am Elmanesse. My tribe used to trade with your people until the risks became too high. But this is not a time for the telling of old tales. Why have you come to the forest?"

"Justice," the man said in a grim tone.

Foxfire blinked. On the lips of such a man, the lofty declaration seemed strangely out of place. "How so?" the elf demanded, giving his knife a little twitch to speed the man's reply.

"Come now," Bunlap chided him. "Do you claim to have no knowledge of the attacks your people have made upon human caravans and settlements? The looting, the helpless people they have slain?"

"This cannot be," the elf protested, although in truth he was not entirely certain it might not be so. The vast forest was home to several small groups, and there was little contact between them. It was entirely possible that some of the more reclusive and mysterious elven clans had decided to take up arms against the humans.

The human leader seemed to sense the doubt in Foxfire's voice. "I myself have done battle with wild elves," Bunlap asserted. "I stood beside the farm folk they tried to massacre. Some of the surviving marauders have

been put to work, to take the place of the men they felled
with their accursed black arrows!"

"Forest People, enslaved?" the elf demanded incredulously. Even among the lawless humans of Tethyr, there
were strictures against such things!

"A life for a life," Bunlap said coldly. "Justice comes in
many forms."

For a moment Foxfire stood silent as he tried to
assimilate the possibilities. But even if the man's claim
of elven attacks held some truth, they did not begin to
explain all the things this particular human had done.
Nor could Foxfire overlook the fact that these men had
come to the forest for the purpose of taking more elves
as slaves, perhaps to satisfy this bizarre and illogical
code of justice. Was it possible these humans actually
believed that the death or enslavement of one elf could
redress the grievances caused by another?

By the sky and spirits, he swore silently, if the forest
People thought that way, they would slay every human
who ventured within reach of their arrows! In truth,
some elves did think along these terms, and at the
moment Foxfire was less inclined to disagree with them
than usual.

"My tribe will not stand by to see the People enslaved.
If you come to the forest again, my warriors will be here
to meet you," Foxfire said softly. "I myself will be watching for *you*. I know your face, and I have seen your
mark. Know me by mine."

The bone knife slashed up, tracing a tightly curved
arch through Bunlap's thick beard and up onto his
cheek. With astonishing speed, the elf changed the
direction of the cut, curving the knife down and then
lifting it for another deft, curving slash. The man let out
a roar of pain and rage as he clapped one hand to his
bleeding face. Bringing his other arm up, he lashed back
hard with his elbow.

And met nothing but air. The elf was gone.

"Release the dogs!" Bunlap yelled, and the men

hastened to obey, although they suspected it would do
no good. The animals dutifully put their noses down
and circled and sniffed, but the wild elf had well and
truly disappeared.

The man with the elven bow pulled a wad of dirty
cloth from his pack and offered it to the leader. Bunlap
pressed the makeshift bandage to his cheek and glared
into the silent forest.

"Think he took the bait?" the archer ventured.

A slow, grim smile spread across the leader's face,
made ghastly by the smears of drying blood. "I would
wager on it. They will come, and we'll be ready to greet
them. But mark me: that elf is mine."

"I thought you wanted to stir up their war leaders,
not take 'em out!"

Bunlap turned his cold gaze upon the archer. "My
dear Vhenlar, this is no longer merely a business venture. This has become personal."

The archer blanched. He'd heard those words before,
many times, and each time as a prelude to serious
trouble. The first incident had been several years back,
when he and Bunlap were soldiers stationed in the
fortress of Darkhold. They'd been assigned to escort an
envoy from Zhentil Keep through Yellow Snake Pass.
One evening he, Bunlap, and one of their charges had
entered into a discussion of the dark gods, one that
quickly degenerated into a quarrel. Bunlap "took matters personally" and beat his opponent nearly to death.
When they learned that the injured man was a high-
ranking priest of Cyric, the new god of strife, they did
not stay around to see how the situation played out.
They'd headed south until Bunlap thought them beyond
the reach of the Dark Network, settled down in Tethyr,
and built a mercenary band of considerable strength.
But though Bunlap might have left the Zhentilar
behind, his goals and methods had not changed for the
better. In truth, there were times when Vhenlar dearly
wished he could be rid of the man. His own love of profit,

however, kept him at the side of the one person he
feared and despised above all others.

And profit there was! Vhenlar figured that in a few
years, he would have enough coin stashed away to
allow him to retire in splendor. If the cost of this was a
few elven lives, he, for one, would have no regrets.

Vhenlar fell into step beside his employer. As they
walked, he dreamed of the wondrous things his share of
the profit would buy him, and he stroked the smooth
wood of his stolen elven bow with a lover's touch.

* * * * *

Leaving Zazesspur behind, Arilyn followed the trade
route north into the sun-baked flatlands that lay
between the city and the Starspire Mountains. The
mountains themselves were deeply forested, watered by
numerous lakes and streams as well as an abundance
of rain and even snow. And this was well, Arilyn
thought with a touch of dark humor, considering the
number of magical conflagrations that had broken out
in the area in recent months!

The Harper veered off the path to follow the base of
the southernmost mountain. She reigned her mare in at
a thick stand of conifers and swung down from the saddle. After securing her horse, Arilyn pressed through
the trees to the steep, sheer rock wall they concealed. A
vertical crevice slashed through the moss-dappled rock.

Arilyn slipped into the cave's mouth and made her
way down the labyrinth of passages that led to a deep
and soaring cavern. Here, hidden from the eyes of the
skeptical—and the vengeful—labored the alchemist
known as Tinkersdam of Gond.

It was an odd-looking lair, vast and open, yet cluttered enough to give the impression of bustling activity despite the fact that it had but one occupant.
Several book-laden shelves were propped against the
cave walls, and half-finished mechanical wonders littered

a dozen or so long tables. Small cooking fires dotted the cave, and a muted symphony of hissing, crackling sounds rose from pots of bubbling, often luminous, substances.

Arilyn lifted her eyes to the ceiling vent, taking note of the new layers of viscous black substances staining the rocks around the overhead opening. Explosions were to be expected when dealing with Tinkersdam. Even the residents of Zazesspur no longer commented on the brief but spectacular displays of fireworks which lit the eastern skies from time to time, except to take the occasional snide jab at newly rich merchants who apparently possessed more money than taste. Arilyn had counted three such explosions since her last visit, and in truth was relieved to see that the alchemist was still hale and whole.

No one could mistake Tinkersdam for anything other than what he was. A native of Lantan, where Gond the Wondermaker, the god of inventors and artificers, was worshiped almost exclusively, Tinkersdam had the odd coloring typical for the Lantanna—only taken to extreme degrees. His sparse red hair approximated the color and texture of copper wire, his sallow skin captured the exact hue of yellowed ivory, and his large, rather bulbous eyes were a strange shade of light green that did not occur elsewhere in nature. Out of lifelong habit, Tinkersdam wore a short tunic of bright yellow— the traditional color of Lantan—and sandals on his bare feet. His plump, extremely bowed legs were hairless, as was his face—no doubt the result of the many explosions that his work occasioned.

A skilled inventor and a daring alchemist, Tinkersdam had a particular fondness for lethal gadgets that could kill or disable people in innovative ways. He had been exiled from Lantan years ago when one of his experiments blew up someone influential. He had since been invited to leave several other cities for similar reasons.

Arilyn would be the first to acknowledge that
Tinkersdam, although he was undoubtedly brilliant,
straddled the line between eccentricity and insanity.
Yet the odd little man had become one of her most valued allies. Theirs was a symbiotic relationship. Over
the years he'd provided her with any number of gadgets and alchemically derived substances. She devised
a practical use for them, in the process often finding
new and unanticipated applications that delighted the
alchemist.

Arilyn's gaze swept the workshop, searching for the
items she'd requested. There was never any guarantee
that Tinkersdam would complete a project by the
requested date. Time had little meaning to the man,
and he was likely to desert a given task to work on some
new and wondrously destructive toy that caught his
fancy.

At the moment Tinkersdam was standing before a
small stove, his attention wholly absorbed with the concoction he was stirring. Steam rose from the iron skillet,
and with it the rich, earthy scent of cooking mushrooms. It was a homey enough scene, except for the agonized screams that came from the pan, and for the large
brown mushrooms that lay on the table beside him,
twitching frantically and emitting shrieks of horror as
they awaited their fate.

Underdark mushrooms.

The realization sent a shiver up the Harper's spine.
She'd heard tales of the bizarre fungi that grew in those
deep tunnels. How Tinkersdam had managed to obtain
some—and what he planned to do with them—were
matters she did not care to contemplate.

"How is the eye mask coming?" she asked.

The sound of her voice did not seem to startle the
alchemist. Indeed, Tinkersdam did not so much as look
up. Arilyn was not certain whether he'd been aware of
her from the first, or whether her presence simply didn't
matter enough to register with him.

"Third table from my right," Tinkersdam muttered in a reedy voice as he picked up a small, moldering tome. "Sauté shriekers until silent; stir in powdered effreet lungs; add two drops of congealed manticore drool," he read aloud.

Arilyn shuddered again and went in search of the indicated item. She poked around in the clutter for several moments before she found it: a half mask of some pale, supple substance that looked remarkably like the skin of a moon elf, except for the incredibly tiny gearworks packed behind the mask's painted eyes.

A mirror hung on one wall of the cave. Despite his undeniable lack of physical beauty, Tinkersdam was quite particular about his grooming. Arilyn went to the mirror and pressed the half mask onto her face. The thin material clung to her skin, taking on color as it warmed until it matched exactly the pale hue of her face, even to the faint blue highlights on her cheekbones. Even more remarkable were the eyes. Not only were they an exact replica of her own—large, almond-shaped, a distinctive elven shade of deep blue flecked with gold—but they even blinked from time to time in a most realistic fashion. She could see through them, yet when she closed her own eyes and raised her hand to touch the mask, she was pleased to note that the false eyes remained open. Most extraordinary of all was that Tinkersdam had managed to imbue the mask with an expression of dreamy contemplation—perfect for its intended purpose.

"How is this done? Magic?"

Tinkersdam responded with a derisive sniff. This was an attitude Arilyn could appreciate. She herself had more faith in the alchemist's inventions than in the caprices of magic. Besides, the forest elves would sense a magical illusion more quickly than a mechanical one. Arilyn had not yet decided whether or not to attempt the mission into the forest, but of one thing she was certain: if she succeeded, it would be in no small part due to Tinkersdam's devices.

Posing as an elf was no problem for Arilyn—at least, not for short periods of time. In many ways she favored her mother's race, from her distinctively elven eyes to the preternatural speed of her sword play. Her pearly skin and raven-black hair were common to moon elves, and her slender form was that of an elf—although at three inches short of six feet she was far taller than most. The constant stress and struggle of her tenure in Zazesspur's assassins' guild had left her as finely drawn as any moon elf alive. While elven faces tended to be quite angular, hers was a smooth oval, but her ears were nearly as pointed as those of a full-blooded elf, and her features were delicate and sharp. There were little things, however, that could give her away. Not the least of these was the fact that she slept. Elves, as a rule, did not.

Most of Toril's elves found repose in a deep, meditative state known as reverie. Arilyn had never been able to enter reverie, and when passing as an elf she had to go to extreme lengths to get the necessary rest. This mask was such a ploy. Since no elf would approach another elf in reverie except in the direst of emergencies, she could put on the mask and sleep beneath it, undisturbed.

A sharp *pop* interrupted her thoughts. Arilyn spun to see a tendril of black smoke wafting toward the top of the cave. Tinkersdam was neither hurt nor perturbed by this development. He regarded the smoking contents of his skillet with satisfaction, then seized a funnel and carefully poured the liquid into a glass vial.

"That should do the trick," he said happily. At last raising his eyes to Arilyn, he inquired, "Do you sing?"

The Harper blinked. "I don't make a habit of it."

"A pity." Tinkersdam stroked his bald chin and mused. Suddenly he snapped his fingers. Reaching confidently into the general debris of the table behind him, he pulled from the pile the lid of a large pot. He poured a single drop of the still-steaming fluid onto the metal and then lifted the lid into a shield-guard position.

"Be so kind as to strike," he requested. When she hesitated, he pointed out, "The potion did no damage to a tin lid. It is unlikely to harm an elven sword!"

Seeing the logic in this, Arilyn drew her moonblade and obligingly smacked the flat of it against the makeshift shield. Immediately a deep, ringing sound rolled through the cavern, like the tolling of a giant bell might sound to someone who stood in the bell tower directly below it.

The Harper swore and clapped both hands to her sensitive ears. Tinkersdam, however, merely beamed, even though the vibrations from the "shield" ran up his arms and set his pair of chins aquiver.

"Oh, excellent! A fine result," he shouted happily.

Still smiling broadly, Tinkersdam tossed aside the lid, then stoppered the vial with a cork and handed it to Arilyn. "You might find a use for this in your travels. Don't drink it," he cautioned her loudly. "At least, not on an empty stomach. Rumblings, you know."

Since the rejoinder that came to Arilyn's mind paled before this latest absurdity, she merely took the vial and gingerly tucked it into her pack. "The other things?" she requested, shouting to be heard above the ringing in her ears.

"Most of them," the alchemist agreed in kind. He bustled over to the far side of the cavern and took a large, paper-wrapped bundle from a pile of similar packages. "This one is yours. I added a few new devices for you to test. Do tell me how they turn out."

Arilyn noted the insignia of Balik—the family name of Zazesspur's ruling pasha—adorning several of the packages. "Hasheth has been here, I see."

"Yes, indeed. Fine lad," the alchemist commented.

The Harper was not so sure she agreed with that assessment. Granted, the young Prince Hasheth had proven to be a valuable contact. Through him Danilo had gained access to the palace, and she herself had received much useful information about Zazesspur. It

was Hasheth who had helped her set up Tinkersdam in
a wondrous workshop hidden in the mountains overlooking the city, and who continued to supply the
alchemist with needed ingredients, often at his own
expense. Yet Arilyn could not forget the particulars of
their first meeting: Hasheth had been a student assassin, and she had been his assigned prey. Although the
young prince had opened a door for her into the closely
held assassins' guild and had since moved on to sample
several other professional endeavors, the half-elf did not
miss the predatory gleam in his black eyes whenever he
regarded her.

Or perhaps she was simply becoming too accustomed
to expecting the worst wherever she looked. "Soon I'll be
seeing ogres under every bed and drow in every
shadow," she muttered.

"That happened to me once," Tinkersdam commiser-
ated. Apparently, his hearing slipped back into the normal range with amazing speed. "Fumes, you know. I was
swatting at invisible stirges for days."

Arilyn sighed and shouldered her package. "I was
offered another assignment. I might be going away for a
while."

"Oh? We're moving again?"

It was not an unreasonable question. An explosion in
Suzail a few years back had destroyed a hefty portion of
a castle belonging to an influential nobleman and forced
Tinkersdam into hiding. Rather than hunt him down
whenever she needed him, Arilyn found it worth her
while to locate the alchemist near her current base of
operations. She paid most of his expenses through the
fees she earned adventuring for the Harpers and considered every copper well spent.

"You can stay here until I return. If you need anything, contact Hasheth."

"Fine lad," Tinkersdam repeated. "Although I do hope
he stays close to Zazesspur. I'm not precisely welcome in
Saradush, Ithmong, or Myratma," he confided, naming

the rest of Tethyr's major cities.

Arilyn sighed again. "Tell me, Tinkersdam, is there any city on Toril that you *haven't* blown up at least a portion of?"

"Zhentil Keep," the alchemist responded without a moment's hesitation. "But of course, that would take a far braver man than I."

The comment surprised a chuckle from the Harper. "Almost sorry to hear it," she said with a wry grin. "If any city needs a bit of forceful housecleaning, it's that one."

"Well, someone will get around to it sooner or later," Tinkersdam said absently, his large green eyes roving to the glowing substance popping and bubbling in a large caldron. "Now, if you will excuse me . . ."

Taking the hint, Arilyn left the cavern and began the ride back to the city. She pressed her mare hard, for she wished to be in the School of Stealth's council hall before moonrise. With the coming of night, new commissions were posted, and assassins came to bid on choice jobs. At no other time did Arilyn receive so much useful information on the underside of Zazesspurian politics.

She rode through the main gate of the complex at dusk. Tossing her reins to the stableboy who ran to greet her, she hurried to the council hall and scanned the bits of parchment nailed to the door. There was nothing of great interest: some baker wished to avenge an insult dealt to his pastry; a harem girl was willing to pay in trade for the death of a self-avowed and apparently spurious eunuch; a wealthy collector wanted a piece of stolen property retrieved from the treasure house of a rival.

"Scant pickings tonight," observed a whispery voice at Arilyn's elbow.

The Harper turned to regard the only other female in the assassins' guild—an exotic beauty who went by the name of Ferret. To Arilyn's way of thinking, the assassin resembled her namesake. The woman was whip-thin and sharp-featured, with black eyes that seemed not quite human, and a long slender nose that lacked only whiskers and a twitch. Remorseless, relentless, she was ferretlike in character as well.

To everyone in the guildhouse, the Ferret was a bit of a mystery. She was never seen without heavy makeup, a tightly wound turban, and gloves. Nor was she ever heard to speak above a whisper. Rumor had it that she'd been disfigured in some accident, but apart from these idiosyncracies there were no apparent flaws in her beauty, which she flaunted by dressing in scant silk garments so tight they appeared to have been painted onto her lithe form. Tonight she wore a gown patterned in jewel-like colors that echoed the resplendent plumage of a peacock. Earrings made from the eyes of a peacock's tail feathers dangled from her earlobes, the only part of her ears that were visible beneath her cobalt-blue turban.

The Ferret folded her arms and leaned indolently against the doorjamb. "So which job strikes your fancy? The baker, the whore, or the thief?"

"Not the baker," Arilyn said with a grim smile. "I've tasted his baking. No one should die for insulting it. I say long life to the critic, and may he do better elsewhere."

"Ah, yes," Ferret sneered. "The gods forbid you should take the life of an innocent man! By all means, take the second job—watching a harem girl at work could do you nothing but good."

The Harper shrugged off the insult. It was not the first time Ferret had mocked Arilyn's esthetics of solitude and chastity. In fact, the assassin's favorite taunt for her half-elven colleague was "half-*woman*," spoken with scathing innuendo.

Ferret, by all reports, had no such scruples. The woman was said to be omnivorous, with an appetite and skills that astonished even those wealthy and jaded Zazesspuran noblemen who sought to imitate the pasha by keeping extensive and exotic harems.

Ferret was also very, very good with a blade. Arilyn had wondered more than once why the Ferret had never challenged her. Of all the assassins in the guild, Arilyn thought Ferret the one most likely to successfully relieve her of her Shadow Sash. But the black-eyed woman seemed content with her rank, preferring to spend her time and energy on fee-paying assignments.

And speaking of fees, Arilyn noted that the collector was paying very well for the return of his stolen property. Her expenses had been high of late, so she ripped the third posting from the door. Ferret let out a gasp of mock astonishment. Removing a choice assignment before other assassins had a chance to bid for it was considered a severe breach of guild etiquette.

"The only people here are you and I," Arilyn pointed out, brandishing the paper under Ferret's long nose. "Do *you* want this?"

"It's a job for two, and the fee is certainly high enough to pay for both," the woman observed coldly, "but you're welcome to it all the same. I'd sooner take payment in the coin of the harem than partner myself to a half-elf!"

Arilyn blinked, surprised by the venom in the woman's voice. There were quite a few half-elves in Tethyr, and for the most part they were treated well. Animosity that burned this bright was unusual.

"Suit yourself," the Harper said as she turned to leave. She had little energy to spare the woman's prejudices, for there was much to be done: sending a messenger to the collector with a tentative acceptance and a request for more information, finding someone who knew the floor plan of the rival's palace and who would be willing to sell this information, planning methods of circumventing the guards and magical wards that would certainly protect the treasure. Fortunately, the requested item was small: a silver tiara studded with pale amethysts. It was not always so. Once Arilyn had been commissioned to steal back the stuffed and mounted head of a basilisk. That had not been her favorite assignment. On the whole, it would probably have been easier to hunt down and slay a fresh monster.

"I've no use for tiaras, but if you see some nice necklaces or pins, bring me back two or three," Ferret called after her in a penetrating whisper. "I'll pay you half the market cost of the gems and save you the trouble of finding a fence!"

Arilyn did not answer, for she had no intention of taking anything but the requested item, and she knew from Ferret's mocking tone that the woman suspected as much. This Arilyn found disturbing. The brief conversation with the exotic assassin had made it plain that, for whatever reason, Arilyn had yet another enemy within the School of Stealth, one who had taken the trouble to observe her closely.

Acting on impulse, the Harper turned and strode from the complex. She had intended to go straight to the women's guildhouse and make an early night of it. The tasks ahead of her were many and difficult, and she had slept far too little of late. Yet she doubted she'd get any rest this night if she stayed in the Ferret's den. There were enough coins in her pockets to buy her a room in a modest tavern, and a night's sleep would be worth every one of them.

"Soon I'll be seeing ogres under every bed and drow in every shadow," Arilyn observed as she walked, softly repeating the self-mocking phrase she'd used in Tinkersdam's lair. But she found little comfort in the exercise, for the once-jesting words now held the ring of presentiment and the resonance of a well-timed warning.

The wary Harper took her own advice to heart. As she walked through the lamplit streets of Zazesspur, she weighed every shadow and kept a sword's reach between herself and each passerby.

It was a lonely and exhausting way to live, perhaps, but Arilyn vastly preferred it to the alternative! Death was the constant companion of any adventurer. She had danced with it for nearly thirty years without surrendering the lead. Survival was a straightforward matter: one merely had to call the tune, know the floor, and never miss a step.

The analogy brought a faint smile to Arilyn's lips. She would have to remember that and pass it on to Danilo upon their next meeting. He would seize upon the inadvertent poetry and fashion it into one of his wistful ballads—a song that would never be heard by his frivolous peers. The young man was a prolific amateur composer with two distinct portfolios: a collection of humorous, often bawdy ballads that he performed in the salons and festhalls of Waterdeep, and the thoughtful songs and airs that were his gift to himself. And *of* himself. Arilyn was not unaware that she was the only person with whom he shared these deeply felt songs. They had spent many evenings beside wilderness campfires, Danilo singing to his lute while Arilyn contemplated the stars, receiving both starlight and music with silent, elven joy.

The measured tread behind her snatched Arilyn from her memories and returned her to the streets of Zazesspur. The cadence of it matched her own quick and long-legged stride, which was usually a sure sign that she was being stalked. Not an assassin this time—a cutpurse, probably, for the man was making no attempt at silence. The best thieves strove to blend with the crowd, depending upon cunning and quickness of hand for success.

Arilyn glanced to her left. Sure enough, a scruffy and ill-dressed man reeled along, holding a half-full bottle of rivengut and muttering thickly to himself. But for all this drunken meanderings, he managed to keep pace with her.

It was a common enough ploy: a pair of cutpurses chose a mark; then one jostled the victim to distract her while the actual theft occurred from behind. The counterstrategy was also simple. When the "drunk" reeled toward her, Arilyn seized his jerkin and spun him around, then hurled him into the outstretched hands of his cutpurse partner. Both went down heavily, the first man cursing with an articulate fervor that belied his inebriated state.

This "attack" earned Arilyn some dark looks from the other passersby, but no one bothered to challenge or berate her for it. She also noticed that no one made any effort to help the fallen men up, or to inquire after their well-being.

The half-elf continued on her way, and as she walked she tried without success to recapture the dream of the wilderness, the starlight, and the shared solitude. Such moments were becoming harder to grasp with each day she spent among these lawless humans. Soon, she feared, they would be gone past recall, and with them, the meager remnants of her elven soul.

Four

Days passed, and yet Arilyn was no closer to fulfilling her latest contract than she'd been the night she ripped the notice from the council hall door. As luck would have it, the man from whom she was hired to steal was one Abrum Assante, a member of her own alleged profession. Once a master assassin, he had retired from the School of Stealth a few years back to enjoy his hard-earned wealth.

So far the preparations had been far more difficult than Arilyn had anticipated. Not that looting palaces was ever easy—most rich men learned prudence somewhere along the line. A wealthy *assassin* could be expected to exercise even more caution. Assante had cocooned himself with enough layers of intrigue, might, and magic to discourage all but the most persistent. In her quest to infiltrate the man's stronghold, Arilyn found herself stretching her previous notions of perseverance beyond recognition.

Except for Assante's personal servants—all of whom were carefully sequestered—there was no man or woman alive who knew the palace's secrets. Arilyn went so far as to search for a few dead servants, for dead men *do* tell tales, provided one could afford the services of a cleric powerful enough to summon their spirits. The Harper had never before considered such tactics—elves were loath to disturb those who had passed from this life—but there was little information to be found among the living.

A few well-placed bribes gave Arilyn access to the records of various slave traders, which she checked for sales made to Assante over the last twenty years or so. She laboriously compared these names to the records listing those interred in the low-budget crypts reserved for slaves. But none of this paperwork—a task Arilyn despised nearly as much as she disliked the notion of disturbing the dead—yielded much insight. It seemed that none of Abrum Assante's servants had ever been buried in or around Zazesspur. Either they had somehow achieved immortality, or their bodies had been disposed of inside the palace grounds.

The latter explanation struck Arilyn as a distinct possibility. Assante's palace, a wonder of pink marble and clever illusions, was a testament to its owner's wealth and wariness, an enormous vault that held a thousand secrets. The extensive grounds were surrounded by a very high, thick wall that looked relatively easy to scale. This, however, was the first illusion. The wall, near the top, curved gently outward, then jutted straight up in a broad, steeply slanted lip. There was absolutely no handhold, no secure hold beyond for a grappling hook. Arilyn learned that would-be thieves often fell to their deaths on the stone walkways below.

Nor did matters improve inside the courtyard, which was all that most of Assante's guests ever saw of the complex. After seeking out and questioning many of these visitors—assuming a different disguise for each

interview—Arilyn pieced together the disheartening
details. Just inside the walls, lining all four sides of the
courtyard, were long, shallow reflecting pools. Rumor
had it that the placid-looking pools were filled not with
water, but a highly corrosive acid. Several visitors, however, reported seeing gliding swans and flowering water
plants in the supposedly deadly moat. After considering
all the available evidence, Arilyn was betting on the
acid.

On one thing all agreed. Four graceful bridges, one on
each side of the courtyard, spanned the pools, and
beyond each was a glowing azure cloud that dispelled
any magical illusions. No one could enter the courtyard
without either wading the pools or passing through the
mist. This alone was enough to convince the half-elf
that the pools were deadly. And after a few mugs of ale,
one of Assante's visitors had confided that he'd seen one
of the swans waddle into the mist and disappear. The
swan, apparently, was itself no more than an illusion.

Nor were the water plants and swans the courtyard's
only surprise. Most of the garden's statues and gargoyles came in matched pairs. It was rumored that one
of each was either an animated construct or a living
creature. No one was certain which was which. The
bridges, too, were each flanked by a pair of identical
Calishite guards. This was another small ploy, meant to
lull would-be challengers into believing there was but
one guard and a magical reflection. In reality, each pair
of guards consisted of twin-born brothers, carefully chosen and trained to mirror each other's movements with
uncanny precision—until the moment when it suited
them to strike individually and unexpectedly. Assante,
as Arilyn had come to know, possessed a very dark and
convoluted mind.

The palace itself was a massive, smooth oval: no corners to hide lurkers, no cover of decorative plants
around its base, no vines climbing upon its pink walls.
Several stories high, it was fashioned after an ancient

ziggurat—a stepped pyramid of successively receding, oval-shaped stories. Towers and crenelations there were in plenty, but only on the uppermost level. A high, central tower rose from the top floor. The sentries posted there had an unobstructed view of the grounds, the walls, and several blocks of the city that lay beyond. It was one of the strangest, yet one of the most defensible, fortresses Arilyn had ever encountered.

None of the usual assassin's tricks would work, for Assante knew them all and had no doubt taken every precaution. Magical disguises were useless, for all who crossed the bridges had to pass through the glowing mist that negated magical illusions. There was no way over, around, or through. That, Arilyn surmised, left *under*.

To her way of thinking, the palace had to have at least one escape tunnel. No assassin who'd lived to Assante's venerable age would have neglected such a basic precaution. The problem was finding its point of exit and then finding a way in. Most escape tunnels were contrived to be one-way passages.

The answer came to her slowly, in small pieces. One of the few visitors to enter the palace had spoken of a fountain that smelled of minerals—a sure sign that it was spring-fed. A watery escape route was unusual, but not impossible. But where was its source? Dozens of springs came down to Zazesspur from their origins in the Starspire Mountains. Public bathhouses built over warm, effervescent waters were commonplace in the city.

It was this thought that finally provided the connection. Although the wary Assante would never set foot in a bathhouse himself, he kept an establishment for the entertainment of his friends and business associates. This was hardly common knowledge. Arilyn spent the better part of two days tracking down the scattered trail of documents that confirmed Assante's ownership of the posh house of pleasure and healing. Along the way, she learned that the former assassin held an impressive amount of real estate in Zazesspur. She tucked away this information for future use and then got down to the business of finding the tunnel.

*   *   *   *   *

Mistress Penelope, the chatelaine and manager of the Foaming Sands, looked her new applicant up and down with a practiced eye. She had never employed a half-elven woman in the bathhouse, nor did any of her competitors. The sheer novelty of it might bring in new customers.

This one was a likely-looking wench. A bit too thin, perhaps, but such wonderful pearly skin! After a few hours in the steamy chambers, most of the girls looked as red and disheveled as fishwives on washing day. Still, the half-elf did look rather delicate. The job was not all beauty and pleasure; there was real work to be done.

The chatelaine looked down at the references the half-elf offered. They were impressive indeed. She had worked as a courtesan in the palace of Lord Piergeiron in decadent Waterdeep. That spoke well for her discretion and knowledge of courtly mores and manners. She had served as hostess in the Blushing Mermaid, a luxurious festhall and water spa in the rough-and-tumble Dock Ward of that same city. That indicated she knew the trade and could handle a wide range of patrons. And finally, she had been set up in a private household by a wealthy baron in the northern reaches of Amn. That proved that she was skilled enough to capture the attention of a man who could afford the best of everything. The half-elf was also an acquaintance of the young Prince Hasheth, and Penelope knew the wisdom of maintaining cordial ties with whatever ruling power currently prevailed.

One test remained, for Penelope was entrusted with

the safety of her patrons, as well as their pleasure. She opened a carved wooden box on her desk and took from it a pinch of yellow powder. This she sprinkled onto the palm of her hand and then blew into the air. Immediately the ivory pendant that hung over the half-elf's heart began to glow with azure light—a sure sign that the ornament held magic of some sort. The applicant did not look at all startled or chagrinned by this revelation. Penelope wondered how the half-elf might react if she knew that the simple spell also compelled truthful answers.

"What manner of device is that?" the chatelaine demanded.

A demure smile curved the half-elf's lips. "It is an amulet of water breathing. In my line of work, I have found that the ability to remain under water for a length of time can be very . . . useful."

Penelope gaped, then closed her mouth with a faint click. She nodded thoughtfully as she considered the possibilities. "Can you start tomorrow?"

* * * * *

Arilyn walked silently along the tunnel, counting her steps and concentrating intently upon distance and direction. She could find her way on the open moor or through the deepest forest as well as any ranger she knew, but her sense of direction was badly skewed in this deeply buried passage. Fortunately, the tunnel was short and relatively straight. There was little need for false turns and multiple passages, for the tunnel was well and truly hidden. And, if Arilyn's estimations were correct, the tunnel did indeed go under Abrum Assante's palace.

Suddenly the tunnel took a sharp downward slope. At the bottom of the incline, Arilyn could see the churning warmth of the mineral spring. This, she did not doubt, would lead her into Assante's palace. She was also quite certain that a surprise or two lurked in the water.

The Harper instinctively took a deep breath—although the amulet of water breathing made this unnecessary—and then slid down the hill into the water. She plunged down, then flipped and began to swim even deeper. The tunnel continued for what Arilyn estimated to be at least twenty feet. On the rocky wall near the tunnel's floor was a hole, not quite two feet across and as smoothly rounded as a ship's portal.

Arilyn peered through the opening into what appeared to be a large well. Several similar openings dotted the rock walls. All had been carved to similar size and shape. Arilyn took a small knife from her belt and wedged it into a crack near the opening. It would be exceedingly easy to wander from one portal to another before finding the way out. And even with an amulet of water breathing, her time in that larger well was best limited. On the well floor, some five feet below her, several enormous crustaceans milled about in a frantic search for food.

Arilyn had never seen such creatures, had no idea what they might be called. More than seven feet in length, not including their fanlike tails and long antennae, they scuttled along on several pairs of small, curved legs. Large, toothless mouths spanned the entire width of their heads, and their paired antennae groped about constantly—one sweeping the floor, the other flailing about in the water. The creatures were armored with a platelike, translucent shell. It took Arilyn a moment to realize what the things reminded her of. To all intents and purposes, they were gigantic shrimp.

One of the creatures swirled up into the water, legs churning. As it passed, close enough to touch, the Harper realized what had become of Assante's former servants. The giant crustacean's innards were clearly visible, from the single large vein pulsing along its curved back, to the partially digested halfling in its stomach.

Arilyn glanced down at the floor of the well. It was littered with large rocks, a few bits of rope, and nothing else. Obviously, anyone Assante wished to be rid of was weighted down and tossed into the well. The bottom-feeding shrimp devoured anything and everything that came their way.

But Arilyn felt safe enough where she was. The crustaceans were too wide to squeeze through the openings in the wall. She watched the creatures for a while, learning their patterns of movement and judging their speed. After a time she drew her moonblade and waited. When one of the creatures again ventured within reach, she lashed out and severed three of its legs. The limbs drifted down. The other crustaceans were upon them instantly, their antennae flailing each other like whips as they fought over the morsels. The wounded creature, unable to swim, spiraled down toward certain death.

Assured that the giant crustaceans would be occupied for some time, the Harper shot out of the tunnel and swam for the light. There was precious little of it, which indicated that she would probably emerge in some darkened—and hopefully deserted—chamber.

Even so, Arilyn eased her head out of the water slowly, silently, taking careful stock of her surroundings. The well was in a round, dark room with a low ceiling and a dozen arched portals leading off into long corridors. There was a deep, earthy smell and an intense moisture in the air—unusual for temperate Zazesspur—which suggested that this was a dungeon perhaps two floors below ground level. Yet the entire room—from ceiling to floor—was of the same exquisite pink marble that graced the outer palace. Nor was it without luxury. A tangle of pipes led from the spring to a low, curved bath, and a nearby table held the expected sybaritic accoutrements: a heap of towels, several candles in silver holders, a jeweled decanter, and a pair of goblets. Arilyn's keen eyes noted the faint sheen of dust on the table, and she suspected that the luxurious set-up was mostly intended to distract the eye from the well and its true purpose.

When she was certain she was alone, Arilyn climbed carefully onto the marble rim of the mineral spring. She unstrapped a tarpaulin bag from her back and took out a large linen square; with this she quickly dried herself off. She wanted to leave nothing—not even a damp footprint—that would enable Assante's minions to trace her back to the bathhouse. The thin silk garments she'd chosen to wear for her first day at the Foaming Sands were ideal for this. Not only did they dry quickly, but they were of a sandy pink hue, one especially woven and dyed to blend with the marble of Assante's palace.

The dungeon's silence was broken by distant footsteps that echoed though the marble corridors like large hailstones on a slate roof. Behind the labored tread was the scrape and clatter of some large, heavy object being dragged along. Soon the sound of a disgruntled male voice joined in the general racket. Arilyn got the gist of the situation from the muttered complaints and the occasional resonant clang that occurred whenever the servant stopped and kicked what she surmised to be a water-filled cleaning bucket.

The Harper crouched behind the fountain and waited. This was precisely the type of opportunity for which she had hoped.

Her optimism wavered for a moment when the servant entered the room, a mop over one shoulder and the bucket dragging behind him. He was a male dwarf, with a form that resembled nothing so much as a squat, two-legged mushroom and a face that brought to mind an image of storm clouds over a craggy mountain. The dwarf was young by the measure of his people—seventy or eighty, judging from the length of his dun-colored beard—and not more than four feet tall. Yet the Harper, for all her skill with the sword, was hesitant to tangle with the obviously ill-tempered little man.

On the other hand, what choice did she have?

Arilyn watched as the dwarf dipped and wrung the mop, then turned away and fell to scrubbing the marble floor, muttering imprecations all the while. She rose and silently came up behind him, her sword in hand. A well-placed kick overturned the bucket and sent a tide of soapy water racing toward the dwarf. He spun to face the sound, saw the battle-ready elf, and instinctively kicked into a running charge.

The dwarf's booted feet shot out from under him before he'd taken three steps. After a brief, airborne moment, he landed flat on his back. His shaggy head hit the marble with a thud so resonant that Arilyn could feel it in her bones and teeth. While the dwarf was still trying to uncross his eyes, she strode forward and plunged the tip of her sword through his beard until it pressed hard against his throat.

"Take me to the treasure room," she demanded.

"Rooms," the dwarf corrected her in a deep rumble. Arilyn noted that the gravel-filled voice had more in common with rain falling on a kettledrum than with human speech. "More'n one room, there be. Lots of 'em. But they're guarded by armed men the size of me mother-in-law's temper, and locked up tighter'n a gnome's navel. Don't have a key. Ain't none of the servants got keys."

"I don't need keys," Arilyn asserted, "and I've never met a man whose sword could match mine."

Since the sword in question was still pressed against his throat, the dwarf had opportunity to consider this claim and the fighter who made it. His gaze slid thoughtfully up the shining length of the blade and stopped at the Harper's resolute face.

"You got a lotta brass fer an elf woman," he admitted at last. "Might it be that you also got a way outta here?"

"Same way I got in."

A light kindled in the dwarf's eyes. "I'm a good hand at fighting, if you'd care t' pass over one of them knives you carry. Take me with you when you go, and I'll do fer you what I can. By Morodin's beard," he swore fervently, "fer the chance to get outta this place, I'd be tempted to help you loot me own ancestors' burial chambers!"

Arilyn hesitated only a moment; it was not in her to leave any intelligent creature in slavery. She slid her moonblade out of the thicket of light-brown beard and backed off a few steps. The dwarf scrambled to his feet. She tossed him a dagger, which he nimbly caught. He took off down one of the corridors, beckoning her to follow. Arilyn noted with relief that he could walk silently when he chose to do so.

True to his word, the dwarf led her to a massive locked door, before which stood three enormous men, all of whom were armed with wickedly curved scimitars. Also true to his word, fighting was something the dwarf could do well. In record time, the unlikely pair of conspirators stood over the downed guards.

The dwarf ran the back of one hand across his damp forehead and then regarded it, his bearded face twisted with disgust. "Sad state of affairs," he muttered. "Must be gittin' soft—shouldn't a broke a sweat on those three!"

Arilyn suppressed a smile. She and the dwarf dragged the guards to the well and tossed them in, then returned to the treasure rooms. With the dwarf looking on, the half-elf went to work. From her waterproof bag she took a small wooden box—unwittingly provided by her new "employer," Madame Penelope—and tossed a bit of the yellow powder at the door. There was no telltale blue light—no magic at work. Motioning the dwarf to stand back, she bent to examine the lock. It was trapped, of course, not once but thrice over, and it took her the better part of two hours' work to disable the lethal devices.

At last the door swung open on noiseless hinges. Arilyn edged into the first room, the dwarf following on her heels like a squat shadow.

The treasure rooms were utterly silent and darker than a moonless night, but both the dwarf and the half-elf possessed eyes that were keenly sensitive to heat and neither felt the need of torch or candle. As they passed from one room to another, the dwarf's eyes widened into avaricious circles, his mouth fixed in a permanent "ooh!" of wonder. His awe was not misplaced, for this was beyond doubt the most unusual collection Arilyn had ever seen. Many of the items were priceless; most were extremely valuable; some were merely odd.

There were rare musical instruments, including a six-foot harp with a soundboard that had been carved into the shape of a woman whose gilded fingers were poised over the strings. Magical, Arilyn surmised—awaiting a command to set it playing. Paintings, sculpture, and carvings from many lands filled several chambers. The art of taxidermy was also represented: rare beasts, some of which had not been seen alive for several generations, filled an entire room. There were piles of coins from every land Arilyn had ever heard named, and enough rare books to satisfy a dozen voracious scholars. There was an entire shelf of brilliantly colored vases, fashioned by fire salamanders from melted semiprecious gems. There were jewel-encrusted swords, crowns of long-dead monarchs, court gowns embroidered with silk thread and seed pearls, and a golden scepter inscribed with the runes of some far-eastern lands. Among these treasures of gems and gold Arilyn finally found the item she sought: a delicate, filigreed tiara set with a multitude of pale purple amethysts.

The Harper carefully wrapped the crown in a soft cloth and tucked it into her bag. "Time to go," she said, turning to her dwarven shadow.

"That's *it?* That's all we're taking outta here?" the dwarf demanded. When Arilyn nodded, he immediately began to snatch up small items and stuff them into his pockets. "Back wages," he said in a defensive tone. "Been working here for more'n ten years. I'm owed."

Arilyn didn't begrudge the dwarf his due, but gold

was heavy, and she worried about the weight he was adding to his already considerable bulk. "We're swimming out," she cautioned him.

The dwarf abruptly ceased his looting and stared at her, his face growing pale above his beard. "Not the well spring?"

When the Harper nodded, he groaned and then shrugged. "Ah, well. Always knowed I'd be a-goin' out that way sooner or later—suppose it's better to go it alive! But tell me this: what's waiting fer us in there?"

Arilyn told him. The dwarf pursed his lips and considered, then he emptied some of the booty from his pockets and selected a curved, jewel-encrusted dagger as his principal treasure.

They retraced their steps to the exit. The door to the first chamber was in sight when one of the treasures—a long case pushed up against the far wall—caught Arilyn's eye. The case was covered by a low, rounded dome of dusty glass, and through the film she glimpsed something that looked suspiciously like a woman's form. Curious, the Harper walked over and used the sleeve of her shirt to wipe clean a small circular window. She bent and peered in.

Within the case was the body of a beautiful elven female, not alive, but not exactly what Arilyn understood as *dead*, either. The elf looked—empty. There was no other word for it. The essence of the elf woman was gone, leaving her body behind in some form of deep stasis. How long she had stayed so Arilyn could not say, but the elf's ornaments were of ancient design, and the chain mail that draped her slender form was finer and older than any Arilyn had ever seen.

The elf was also disturbingly familiar. A single thick braid the color of spun sapphires lay over one shoulder. It was the rarest hair color among moon elves, a color Arilyn associated with her long-dead mother. The elf's face was also somehow familiar, although in truth she resembled no one whom Arilyn could name or remember.

The Harper's troubled gaze roved downward and
stopped abruptly. Resting on the elf's thighs was a
small shield emblazoned with a strange elven sigil: a
curving design made of mirror images reaching out to
each other, but not quite touching.

Arilyn's heart missed a beat. She *knew* that mark. An
icy fist seemed to clutch her gut as she slowly pulled her
sword from its sheath. Nine runes were cut into the
ancient blade; one of them matched exactly the mark on
the elf woman's shield.

"Well, I'll be a one-headed ettin," the dwarf murmured, his eyes round as he peered into the case. "A
sounder sleep than any I've ever had, and that's a fact!
I heard tell o' such a thing. Didn't believe the stories fer
a minute, though."

Arilyn didn't know which story he referred to, but it
hardly mattered. She herself had heard many such bed-
time tales—of sleeping princesses or heroes who lay
hidden in deathlike slumber until a time of crisis
brought them forth—and never had she given any of
them a speck of credence. There was something about
this slumbering elf, however, that made all the old legends seem possible. For once Arilyn rued her lack of
knowledge of elven ways, and her near-ignorance of the
sword she carried.

"You go ahead to the well," she urged the dwarf.
"There're several openings leading out. The dry tunnel
is due east and marked with a knife. I'll be along in a
bit."

The dwarf grinned, and a spark of battle lust set his
red eyes aflame. "Put the pot on t' boil and start chop-
ing up horseradish fer the relish—there'll be plenty o'
rimp fer dinner tonight!" he proclaimed gleefully as
ook off for the exit at a brisk clip. Arilyn heard his
intake of breath, then a mighty splash as he dove
water.

ne, the Harper turned back to the macabre
ing on impulse, she touched the moonblade to

the glass. A flare of magical power welled up within the sword, like lightning that could not find release. Because Arilyn and the sword were linked in ways she did not understand, she *felt* the moment of recognition as the almost-sentient sword acknowledged its former master. There was no doubt in the half-elf's mind: she was looking upon one of her ancestors, one of the elves who had once wielded the sword in her hand. But how could this be, and how had this elven warrior come to such a fate?

Arilyn knew little of her sword's history, beyond the names of the elves who'd wielded it and the powers with which they'd imbued it. Her mother had died before telling Arilyn of her heritage, and her mentor—the traitorous gold elf Kymil Nimesin—had been more interested in exploiting his young charge than educating her. As the half-elf pondered the sleeping elf woman, the vague dread she had always felt for her moonblade—but could never explain—enveloped her like a suffocating miasma.

She got a firm grip on her emotions and quickly reviewed what little she did know of the moonblade. Nine people, including herself, had wielded the moonblade since its forging in ancient Myth Drannor, and each had added a magical power to the sword. Although Arilyn knew what these powers were, she could not match each one to a rune, or each rune to the elf with whom it had originated. She did not know the name of the elf woman who slept here, but perhaps the answer to this could be found in the glass that entombed her.

Most humans did not realize that glass was not a solid object, but rather an extremely viscous liquid. It flow was too slow to be measured, much less noticed, a human's lifetime. After many years, a pane of gla thickened near the base as the slowly flowing s stance settled at the lowest point. Elves knew tha time, all windows would open—from the top. The lem was how to measure this flow without ac

breaking the glass. This Arilyn did not wish to do, for
fear of disturbing the elf woman's unnatural slumber.

But as she examined the coffin, she realized that this
was not a concern. The glass lid was not sealed, but
rather hinged on one side. And a long, meandering
crack had already begun working its way downward
from the top of the low-rising dome. Arilyn pulled a
knife from her sash and rapped the hilt sharply along
the crack, then again not far away. A second fissure rippled through the glass, and a curved shard fell onto the
sleeping elf. Arilyn carefully lifted the lid and picked up
the shard. She measured it with a bit of twine, then
broke off a piece from each end. These she wrapped
securely and tucked into her bag. Tinkersdam could
probably estimate the age of the glass with a quick
glance. That done, she turned one last searching gaze
upon her ancestor.

The elf was much smaller than Arilyn, with finer features and more delicate bones. Her long-fingered hands
lay at her sides, palms facing up. The Harper noted that
the elf had the deeply callused fingers and palm of a
swordmaster—but only on the left hand. This told her
the elf had likely been an early wielder, before the moonblade had acquired the speed- and power-enhanced
strike that demanded a two-handed grip.

Outrage, cold and deep, filled the Harper as she
slowly lowered the glass lid. It was not right for the
noble elf woman to be part of some rich man's "collection," displayed as if she were just one more curious and
beautiful object!

It would not always be so, Arilyn vowed as she
turned from the treasure rooms. She would return, and
she would take the moonblade's unknown wielder away
to a fitting rest. But this was not something she
could do now, or alone.

Her jaw in a grim line, the Harper made her
way to the well and dove in.

Someone, it seemed, had been busy. The split and

emptied shells of two giant crustaceans swirled through
the churning water, and the contents had been hacked
into bits the size of finger food. The surviving creatures
were in a feeding frenzy and, by the look of things,
would continue to eat well for days to come.

A glow of lingering heat drew Arilyn's eye toward the
bottom of the pool. There, its translucent carapace
bulging and heaving with some internal conflict, was
the largest-shelled monster Arilyn had yet seen, one
large enough—and stupid enough—to swallow a live
dwarf. The creature would have already died for its mistake had the dwarf not dropped his new dagger in the
struggle. The Harper caught a glimpse of the jeweled
weapon, which skittered about like a frantic squirrel as
the crustacean's many feet kicked it this way and that.

Arilyn pulled her knife from her sash and dove
deeper. The monster did not notice her approach, for it
was well and truly distracted by what was certainly the
worse case of indigestion it had ever suffered. The giant
crustacean whirled and twisted, occasionally toppling
over and then scrambling upright again. Although the
dwarf couldn't last much longer without air, he was still
putting up Nine Hells of a fight.

Arilyn drove the knife deep between two plates of the
monster's shell. Straddling the creature and gripping
its shell with her knees, she began hacking her way
through to the dwarf. As soon as she'd cut through the
surprisingly tough and elastic stomach lining, he
exploded upward.

Stubby legs and arms churning, the dwarf instinctively headed for air. Arilyn followed, quickly passing
the much-slower swimmer and darting into the marked
portal. She turned, seized a handful of beard and
dragged the dwarf into the opening.

They shot up through the water-filled tunnel and
bobbed to the surface. The dwarf grabbed a handhold on
the blessedly dry rocks that littered the tunnel floor,
and dragged in several long, ragged breaths. Arilyn

crawled past him and rolled onto the rocky ground. For
several moments she was content merely to lie there and
wait for her pounding heart to resume its usual pace.

At length she noticed that the dwarf, who was still
half submerged in the water, was regarding her with a
baleful stare. "You pulled me beard," he pointed out.
"You shouldn't ought to do that."

"You're welcome," Arilyn returned pleasantly.

"That too," he muttered. "Name's Jill, by the way.

It was more thanks than the half-elf had expected,
even without the introduction. Dwarves often declined
to give any name, even one as abbreviated and obviously spurious as this. Arilyn rose to her feet and
extended a hand to help drag her new friend out of the
water.

"Jill?" she repeated in an incredulous tone.

"That's right. Gotta problem with it?"

"Well, no. I was expecting something a bit . . . longer,
I suppose. More earthy. And possibly masculine."

" 'Twas me mother's name," the dwarf proclaimed in a
reverent tone that left very little room for discussion.

There was one more thing on Arilyn's mind, however.
"Now that you've seen the treasure, I suppose you'll be
back for it?" It was a logical question, considering that
dwarven people generally rivaled dragons in their love
for hoarding treasure. Arilyn wanted to return to the
treasure hold someday, and while the loss of a single
tiara and one dwarven servant might go unremarked,
the ravages caused by a band of dwarven looters would
almost certainly ensure that her hard-won entrance to
Assante's palace would be ascertained and secured
against future incursion.

But Jill merely huffed. "Been in that pink prison fer
ten years. Don't plan on going back, not ever. If'n there's
anything you want in there, elf, yer welcome to it. Just
don't git yerself caught. There ain't nothing in there
worth *that*."

As he spoke, his eyes roved toward the east—and to

the Starspire Mountains that were his home. Arilyn was inclined to believe him.

As they scrambled up the steep hill, she told him, briefly, what awaited them at the other side of the tunnel. The rapt expression on Jill's face as he contemplated these wonders far outshone his treasure-inspired greed.

"I thought you were eager to be back under the Starspires," Arilyn said. Even as she spoke, however, she slipped Jill a handful of silver coins. It would not do to have him pay Mistress Penelope's girls with coins taken from Assante's treasure trove.

The dwarf shrugged and pocketed his loot. "Been gone from those tunnels ten years, and I'm a-comin' back with pockets full o' treasure. Ain't no one gonna begrudge me a coupla hours more, or ask me how I spent yer silvers!"

* * * * *

Lord Hhune held the tiara in his plump hands, eying it with satisfaction as he turned it this way and that.

"The relic of a long-gone age," he breathed reverently. "This was the bridal crown of young Princess Lhayronna, who became queen to her cousin, King Alehandro III. A reminder that those who wear a crown must face the sword!" he said piously, quoting a common Tethyrian proverb.

A reminder that he himself was unlikely to heed, Arilyn noted in cynical silence. Lord Hhune was a powerful man in Zazesspur. Not only was he a wealthy merchant and head of the shipping guild, but he was also a member of the Lords' Council, which carried out the edicts of Pasha Balik. It was therefore likely that he'd been part of the recent attempt to organize a guild takeover of the city. Arilyn might not have persisted in her furtive assault upon Assante's stronghold, but for the prospect of meeting Lord Hhune face-to-face when the task was complete so that she might take his measure.

With each moment she spent in Hhune's presence, Arilyn's distrust of the man deepened. Rumor had it that this man had killed a red dragon. Arilyn was ready to accept that, provided that the dragon in question had still been in the egg at the time. Hhune was a large man, but he looked as if he spent more time downing pastries than wielding a sword. Even so, a less observant person might think him distinguished, even lordly. His dark, costly garments were carefully tailored to disguise his bulk, and his hair and thick black mustache were neatly groomed and just beginning to take on a bit of gray. His small black eyes were filmed over with a veneer of civility. Arilyn, however, had known many coldly avaricious men and was not fooled by this one. Hhune was not a man likely to be content with his current level of power. Nor, she suspected, was the tiara merely a treasure to be admired. Arilyn knew enough Tethyrian history to suspect what Hhune had in mind.

With the fall of the royal family of Tethyr, many of the royalists had fled to Zazesspur. For several years there had been a quiet underground movement to restore the monarchy, perhaps with a new royal family. Balik seemed well on the way to becoming just that, but Arilyn doubted the self-proclaimed pasha would enjoy the royalists' support for long. Pasha Balik's southern sympathies were becoming more and more apparent, and his inner circle was increasingly made up of men from Calimshan and even Halruaa. It would not be long, Arilyn suspected, before Pasha Balik was deposed and yet another powerful man or woman sought the crown. That was no doubt where the tiara came in. Possession of an item of such significance to the old royal family could help Hhune endear himself to nearly any faction or family that happened to rise to power. He might even use it as a prop in making his own bid for royalty.

And why not? Arilyn's mare possessed a more noble pedigree than the man seated before her, yet Hhune was accounted a lord for no better reason than the country estate he'd purchased a few years back. Nor was Hhune an exception. In Tethyr, land was valued above all other forms of wealth, and possession of enough of it granted instant nobility. In the years following the destruction of the royal family—as well as the decimation of many of the ancient noble houses that possessed royal blood ties—manorial lands, counties, and even duchies changed hands like trinkets at a country fair. Men and women who had enough money to purchase land—or sufficient might to seize it—earned themselves instant titles. Tethyr was peppered with ersatz barons and countesses.

This offended Arilyn's elven sensibilities, her deep respect for tradition, and her unspoken longing for family. But what disturbed her most about this trend was that even petty nobles were beginning to show signs of ambitions that reached far above their newly purchased stations. The threat of a guild takeover had been thoroughly, even ruthlessly, suppressed, but already Zazesspur buzzed with whispers of this baron or that lord gathering strength and supporters.

Ambition counted for a lot in Tethyr, and Hhune had it in abundance. Arilyn saw dreams of glory in his eyes as he regarded the amethyst tiara. She noted that it would be wise to watch this man and, if necessary, curb his ambitions.

At last Hhune placed the crown on his desk and turned his full attention upon the half-elf. "You have done well. I will pay you half again your original fee if you tell me how you got into Assante's palace!"

Arilyn had expected this. To refuse might earn her the same sort of fate that had befallen Assante's servants, so she had prepared a credible half-truth. She manufactured a smile that was both cold and seductive—a useful expression she'd copied from Ferret—and turned the full force of it upon Hhune.

"Assante has new women brought in from time to

time. It was a small matter to include myself among
them."

Hhune's black eyes gave her an appreciative sweep.
"Yes, I can see how that would be so," he said gallantly.
"But tell me of the treasure room!"

This, Arilyn had *not* been expecting. But she marked
the greed in Hhune's eyes and decided to exploit it. With
a little encouragement, perhaps he might offer to fund
her next expedition!

"What other items did you take?" Hhune continued
before she could speak. "I would be most grateful for the
opportunity to view them."

Arilyn spread her hands in a gesture of regret. "There
is nothing more. The clothes of the harem provide few
hiding places for plunder! But I destroyed some of the
things I could not take!" she said, suspecting that
Hhune would appreciate any blow dealt a rival.

The guildmaster chortled with delight. "Splendid,
splendid! But not *too* many, I trust!"

"I could not begin to describe the wonders that
remain," she said truthfully.

"Then, perhaps another expedition?"

"Not soon," Arilyn said softly. "When next I enter
Assante's palace, it will be to tend to a personal matter."

Hhune held her gaze for a long moment, then nodded.
"Such things require much planning," he said casually,
no doubt assuming—as Arilyn had intended him to
assume—that she planned to challenge and oust the
master assassin. "You will have expenses. Please send
all bills to me—discreetly, of course. In exchange, I ask
only that you give me first refusal on any treasures you
might acquire."

All but one, Arilyn agreed silently. All but one.

Five

The day was nearly spent. Foxfire knew this, even though in the deep forest no sun-cast shadows proclaimed the hour. Here the shade was cool and deep, the only sky a thousand layers of leafy boughs and velvety pines that filtered the sunlight until the very air he breathed seemed green and alive.

The elf was many miles from Talltrees, his tribe's hidden settlement, but he and his two companions walked easily through the thick foliage, as silent and invisible as a trio of deer. This forest—all of it—was the elves' home. Its rhythms coursed through their blood and sang in their souls.

Foxfire led the way steadily westward, to a grove perhaps a half-day's walk toward the east from the trading settlement known as Mosstone. In times past—in happier, safer times—the elves of the Elmanesse tribe had traded with the humans who lived in this forest-side town. Then came the brutal reign of the Tethyrs, the

family of human royals who seemed determined to
drive the elves from the land. The Elmanesse had with-
drawn into the forest shadows and proclaimed their
own government via the Elven Council. For many years,
all who ventured into the forests had lived and died by
the judgments handed down by this council. But in
these troubled times, even the wise, collective voice of
the council had faltered and fallen silent. The elven
alliance had splintered, and each clan had gone its own
way. In particular the Suldusk tribe, always chary of
alliance with their Elmanesse brothers and sisters, had
all but disappeared into the deep shadows of the south-
eastern forest. No one knew for certain how many elves
remained in the ancient wood.

Even so, a settlement of elves remained in the Council Glade, and the elders who lived there were still the
best source of news and information in the forest. Foxfire hoped to find answers that would make sense of
what was happening to his people.

Elves had lived in the Forest of Tethir from time
beyond memory—and elven memories were long,
indeed. But for the first time in his nine decades of life,
Foxfire feared that the days of his people in this land
might be numbered. Too many changes had come upon
the elves, too quickly for them to assimilate or adjust. It
was Foxfire's nature to find the good in every situation
and to expect that success would be his in all things. It
was his gift to inspire those around him with the same
confidence. Yet even he could not disregard the fears
that a new shadow had fallen upon Tethir. Recent events
suggested that the Time of Tyranny might soon return.

Nor were the elves helping themselves. Foxfire could
not dismiss from his mind the insinuations placed there
by the human, Bunlap. Was it possible that some clans
really were attacking farms and caravans? And if this
were so, what further trouble might this bring to the
tribes of Tethir?

"Not far now," commented Korrigash, a dark-haired

hunter-warrior who was Foxfire's closest friend. The taciturn elf seldom spoke, and the fact that he did so now was a sure measure of the gravity of their quest.

Though Korrigash was nearly as dour as a dwarf, there was no one under the stars whom Foxfire loved better or trusted more. The two were friendly rivals and had been since long ago when, as toddlers, they'd pelted each other with whatever weapons they could muster, whether pebbles found on the forest floor or the moss that lined their nappies. These days their rivalry took the form of contests of arms or archery, or the good-natured competition for an elf maid's smile. But when they were on patrol or doing battle, Korrigash fell naturally into place at Foxfire's back, instinctively deferring to the flame-haired warrior. Likewise, Foxfire had learned to hear the unspoken thoughts that lay beneath his friend's few words.

"Council Glade is beyond those cedars." Foxfire pointed with his bow to a thick stand of conifers. "The elders will know whether there is any truth to the human's tales."

Korrigash merely sniffed, but his brother, a stripling youth known as Tamsin, had no shortage of opinions on the matter.

"How can there be truth, where there is no honor?" he blurted out. "Humans have no knowledge of either! And if perchance the People have been pushing back the invaders, what of it? If I had my way, every human who stepped beneath the trees of Tethir would be greeted with a bolt through the heart, and may the silver shadows gnaw upon their bones!"

"Spoken with typical restraint," Foxfire told him lightly, but instinctively he lifted one hand and formed the traditional elven sign for peace. One never knew when the silver shadows might be watching. Only a very rash elf would speak lightly of these mysterious beings or risk incurring their rare but deadly ire.

The Elmanesse and the Suldusk were not the only

elves in the forest. There were, among these trees, People even more fey and secretive. The *lythari*, shapeshifting creatures who were more wolf than elf, had been living in Tethir when Foxfire's ancestors still walked beneath the trees of Cormanthor. Although it had been centuries since anyone in the Talltrees tribe had seen a lythari in elven form, from time to time they caught a glimpse of silvery fur or heard the lytharis' haunting songs soaring upward in search of the unseen moon.

"You are among friends, Tamsin, but I would take care before casting those seeds to the wind." continued Foxfire. "Think what might occur if such words took root, and the People came to regard all humans as enemies!"

The young elf shrugged and turned aside, but not before Foxfire noted the smoldering flame in his eyes. Suddenly he understood the true nature of his friend's brother. What Foxfire had taken to be yet one more outburst from the impulsive youth was something much more deadly: hatred, blind and unreasoning and implacable.

For a moment the elven leader was stunned by the sheer force of Tamsin's emotion. Foxfire did not like to think what might result should the hearts of too many of the People's young follow that narrow path.

"Less talk, more walking," Korrigash suggested grimly. "Night's not long to come."

The words were not meant as a distraction, but as a simple statement of fact. Although the three elves could see as well in darkness as in daylight, there was a certain practical need to reach Council Glade before nightfall. The forest was full of dangerous creatures: ogres, giant spiders, wolves, stirges, wyverns, and even a dragon or two. Many of these grew hungry with the coming of darkness, and there was every possibility that the elves, themselves hunters, might become prey.

"By the stars and the spirits," Tamsin swore in a choked voice. The young elf kicked into a run, dashing through the ferns and vines without regard for silence and without thought for the trail his passing left.

Foxfire's reprimand died unspoken. A dagger gleamed in Tamsin's hand. The youth often sensed dangers that older and wiser elves missed, and though he was impulsive, he did not enter battle lightly. Foxfire and Korrigash exchanged a quick, dismayed glance and drew their own weapons.

The elves ran lightly through the crushed foliage, pausing at the torn curtain of vines that had veiled Council Glade from their sight. Before them stood Tamsin, his copper-hued face strangely ashen, and beyond him lay a scene of utter devastation.

What had once been a lush forest glade now resembled the remnants of a careless merchant's campfire. A large circle of ground was black and barren, littered with piles of charred sticks. The swinging bridges—walkways that had linked the trees and the homes and chambers hidden among them—now hung against the blackened trees. The elven homes were gone, as were the inhabitants. Foxfire's throat tightened as he noted blackened bones lying among the remains of trees.

The home of the Elven Council had been utterly destroyed, and with it the best hope of unity among the beleaguered People.

A light touch on his shoulder tore Foxfire from his grim thoughts. He turned to face the hunter, who handed him a blackened arrow shaft.

"Took it from between two naked ribs. Look at the mark," Korrigash advised him.

The elf glanced at the shaft. The mark on it was familiar: three curved lines, combining to make a stylized foxfire, the bright flower from which he had taken his name. The arrow was unmistakably his, yet how had he lost it? He hadn't missed a chosen target since boyhood!

He lifted incredulous eyes to his friend's face. "But how?"

"The humans." Korrigash pointed to the shaft. "Note the length."

Foxfire nodded, understanding at once. The arrow shaft was shorter than it should have been by a width of perhaps two fingers. It had been broken off, the jagged edge trimmed smooth, and the arrowhead reaffixed. Since the forest elves retrieved and reused all arrows used in hunting, this one could only have been torn from the body of an enemy. It was possible that this arrow had been plucked from a wounded ogre or bugbear, but such creatures lacked the wit to plant it here for others to find. This was the work of the elves' human foe.

"Tribe against tribe," the hunter commented grimly.

Again Foxfire nodded in agreement. The marks of the best elven hunters and warriors were well known in the forest, and not every elf who stumbled upon the razed elven settlement would see the ploy for what it was. While it was possible that someone was attempting to turn the elven tribes against each other, the purpose behind this grim act was utterly beyond Foxfire's ken.

There was one human, however, who might well have the answers. Foxfire remembered his conversation with Bunlap, and suddenly he knew where he might find the human.

He walked up to Tamsin and put a hand on the young elf's shoulder. A surge of guilt filled Foxfire as he noted the haunted look on the fighter's face. Tamsin was fey, even for a green elf. It was likely the youth was seeing the carnage as clearly as if it was happening before him. Such gifts were as much torment as blessing, but Tamsin's was needed. The elf was twin-born, and he had a bond with his equally fey sister that enabled them to speak mind-to-mind.

"You must send word to Talltrees at once," Foxfire told him. "The tribe must send a war band with all possible speed to the border trees south of Mosstone. Thirty elves, armed with unmarked green arrows."

This last command was unprecedented, for the elf

arrows known as "black lightning" were crafted through a long and mystic process. Green arrows were raw and unfinished by elven standards, deadly enough when launched from elven bows, but lacking the rites that imbued the weapons with forest magic and linked the elven hunter-warriors to their home in ways that no human—and few elves—could fully understand. Yet Foxfire knew his request would be honored, and he understood that this was a measure of the high regard his tribe had for his leadership and judgment. He only hoped that with this decision he would not betray his people's trust.

"If there were no elven raids before, there will be soon," he added softly. "We will attack the farm where the elves are held as slaves."

At these words the haunted look faded from Tamsin's eyes, burned away like morning mist by the rising sun of his hatred. "In that case, I will send your words to Tamara with pleasure," he said grimly. "And I will tell her to urge the warriors to hurry!"

* * * * *

"So how's the farming going?" Arilyn inquired casually.

Her words seemed to irritate her young host, as they were intended to do. Prince Hasheth cast her a baleful look, then quickly composed his hawklike features into a lofty, lordly expression so studied that Arilyn was certain he'd practiced it before a mirror.

It seemed that Hasheth, a younger son of the ruling pasha, was having a great deal of difficulty finding a life-path suited to his ambitions and his exalted sense of self. Arilyn had met the young man several months before, during his attempt to gain fame and wealth as an assassin. He had been charged with killing another assassin, namely Arilyn. She and Danilo had managed, just barely, to convince the proud youth that this assignment was actually a death sentence handed down by guildmasters who wanted Balik's son out of the assassins' guild. Since then, Hasheth had become an ally, helping to insinuate Arilyn into the assassins' guild and sponsoring Danilo in the social life of the palace. And in doing so, he had finally found an activity that suited him. The role of Harper informant appealed to the young man, for intrigue was a skill highly valued in Tethyr. Yet his Harper activities did not bring him the overt wealth and status he craved. Since he'd left the assassins' guild, he had tasted of a dozen occupations. The latest, apparently, was no more to his liking than any of his previous choices.

"I have scraped the dung and the mud from my boots and left the manor house in the hands of a steward," Hasheth announced with disdain. "The life of a country lord is deadly dull. What need have I of lands or title, I who am the son of a pasha?"

Actually, Arilyn observed silently, lands and title would be a big improvement over Hasheth's current lot. As a younger, harem-born son, his status was roughly that of a skilled tradesman, and his prospects were considerably less promising. At last count Balik had seven sons from his legal wives; his harem had produced an additional thirteen or fourteen. Hasheth had at least a dozen older brothers. Even if he had perfected the assassin's art, it would have taken him many years to work his way up to the head of the line.

The half-elf nodded sympathetically. "Land is important, but Zazesspur's wealth comes largely from trade. Have you considered becoming a merchant?"

The prince sniffed. "A greengrocer? A camel salesman? I think not."

"How about apprentice to the head of the shipping guild, a man who also sits on the Lords' Council?" the Harper countered. "Trade and politics work together like a paired dagger and sword. In no place is this more true than in Zazesspur. You could learn much and gather the tools needed to carve out a place for yourself. Those who control trade will always have a powerful hold upon the rulers. And Inselm Hhune is an ambitious man. You might to do well to hitch your cart to his star."

Hasheth nodded, his black eyes regarding her thoughtfully. "And the Harpers—they endorse this Lord Hhune?"

His tone was casual, but Arilyn could almost hear the gears of Gond churning in his mind. Clearly, he understood that she had some purpose other than his career advancement in mind. The Harper suppressed a rueful smile. Hasheth was good and getting better.

"No, of course not," she said bluntly. "As I've said before, Hhune is ambitious. It would be wise for the Harpers to keep an eye on such a man. But there is no reason why you cannot do this for us and advance yourself at the same time."

This notion seemed to please the young man. Picking up a jewel-encrusted bottle, he leaned forward and added a bit more wine to Arilyn's goblet. She obligingly drank deeply, noting as she did so the glint that entered Hasheth's eyes. It was a common ploy, one he had used time and again in the hope that a quantity of potent Calishite wine would lower the half-elf's formidable reserve and deliver her to his bed. Arilyn knew without vanity that she was considered beautiful, and she was well accustomed to masculine attention. Hasheth's both amused and exasperated her, for the young man always expressed his admiration in a manner that suggested he was conferring upon her a great honor. Arilyn was an expert at saying no—her repertoire ranged from gracefully feigned regret to a disemboweling backstroke—but it was becoming increasingly difficult for her to turn down Hasheth's advances while keeping a straight face.

Fortunately for Arilyn, the young man seemed to be more interested in his future prospects than his immediate libidinous impulses. "I will ask my father to place me in Lord Hhune's service," he agreed.

"You do that, but first you should know that Hhune

was probably involved in the plot against your father," she cautioned him. "It is even possible that he had something to do with the guilds' attempt to have you killed. Even now, you'd do well to watch your back."

Hasheth shrugged as if these past offenses were unworthy of consideration. "If Lord Hhune is truly an ambitious man, he will take whatever path he must," he observed. His unspoken words, *And so will I,* rang sharply in Arilyn's ears.

The young man's attitude did nothing to reassure Arilyn. At best, Hasheth was overly pragmatic. He would do whatever needed to be done to advance his ambitions. As long as his interests lay along the same path as those of the Harpers, all would be well. Arilyn was not certain it would always be so. Yet honor demanded that she give the young man one more warning.

"I hope I am wrong, Hasheth, but from what I have seen and heard, it seems likely that the end of your father's rule draws near. It cannot be otherwise, when he slights so many ambitious Tethyrians in favor of southern courtiers."

The prince received this dire prediction with yet another shrug. "What is that to me? I stand too far from the throne to mourn its loss and have long known that I must seek my fortune elsewhere. But I thank you for your words. Now, on to other, more pleasant matters. More wine?"

Arilyn declined with a delicate wave of her hand and a small, hard-edged smile. Hhune and Hasheth were well matched, and she wished them the joy of each other's company! "I would, Hasheth," she purred in a courtesan's creamy tones, "but in company such as yours, I dare not drink too freely. I couldn't trust myself to behave!"

*　*　*　*　*

The shops of Zazesspur closed at twilight, but in the back room of Garvanell's Fine Ointments business

continued apace. Behind the lavish shop that offered
scented oils and spurious potions to the city's wealthy,
behind the counting room where the clerks labored to
tally the day's wealth, Garvanell kept a small private
room where he received payment of another, more personal sort.

Garvanell had been born to farmhands who labored
in the distant reaches of the Purple Hills. But from a
very early age it was apparent that he would not
remain in such remote and humble surroundings. The
gods had gifted him with a handsome face and a certain
smarmy charm. He had done well with these modest
attributes, trading them for the benefits that came
along with the favor of older, wealthy women. Step by
step, he worked his way up in society, until at last he
married a well-to-do widow of Zazesspur.

His wife was a good twenty years older than he, as
well as stout and exceedingly homely. Yet all things in
life had compensations. The woman possessed a thriving business and an ever-increasing passion for playing
at cards. Since she won more often than she lost, Garvanell was pleased she'd found something other than
him to occupy her time. He took over the perfume shop
and did a thriving business. Although less than half of
his earnings were paid in coin, he still managed to turn
enough of a profit to maintain appearances.

A soft tap at Garvanell's door, then a whispered pass-
word, announced that his latest payment had arrived.
His aging wife had her indulgences; he had his.

The perfume merchant opened the door and surveyed
the young woman his favorite client had sent him. He'd
often expressed a preference for novelty. This woman
was more exotic than most—her almond-shaped black
eyes and bright silk turban suggested a far-eastern heritage—but he doubted the client would have gone to
such trouble. Granted, Oil of Minotaur Musk was not
an easy commodity to come by, not even the imitations
fashioned by unscrupulous Lantanna alchemists.

Then the woman stepped into the room, and the
lamplight glistened upon pale skin, the rare color of
Shou porcelain. The merchant's pulse quickened. This
was the genuine article! For a moment, Garvanell
almost wished the same could be said for the Oil of
Minotaur Musk that had purchased her!

As Garvanell bolted the door, the bells of Ilmater's
temple began to ring out the midnight hour. The merchant grimaced. The temple was but a block away, and
at night the bells seemed deafening. He turned to the
woman, intending to pantomime an apology. He froze,
and his eyes widened with astonishment and fear.

The woman had removed her turban and gloves.
Slowly, deliberately, she raised a slender finger to her
cheek and wiped a bit of the ivory-colored ointment
from her skin, revealing the ruddy color beneath. Before
Garvanell could move, she pulled a dagger from the
folds of her gown and leaped at him.

Small and slender though she was, the speed and
fury of her attack sent the merchant tumbling backward. The woman straddled his chest, her knees pinning his arms to the floor. She buried one hand in his
hair and jerked back his head, then slid the edge of her
dagger against his throat. She leaned down to press her
lips directly to his ear.

"You should be flattered," she said. "I bought all my
ointments and cosmetics at your shop. They rub off on
the bed linens, I find, but so far no man has lived to
complain of it!"

At last the paralysing fear that gripped Garvanell
gave way, and he began to scream for help.

Ferret let him scream, for the bells of Ilmater's
temple more than drowned out his cries. Mockingly she
counted off the chimes of midnight into his ear. When
the final peal came, she rolled aside, dragging the dagger down and across as she went.

The assassin rose to her feet and stared down at the
dead merchant. She felt no elation and no regret.

Another tattling tongue had been silenced. It was a needed thing, as necessary as the hunt that provided food. This kill had been easy, but then, so were most. In this soft and decadent city, Ferret was like a hawk among doves.

Passions ran hot among her people, yet few who knew of Ferret's mission and methods approved. Regardless, she did what she could. Yet as time passed and matters grew increasingly troubled, she'd begun to realize the futility of her chosen path. Ferret's skills were considerable, but they were not equal to the layers of intrigue, nor was her mind fashioned to comprehend the complexity of plot and counterplot that was Tethyr. If she was ever to find and destroy the one she sought, she needed help.

"I need help," she murmured angrily, for the admission did not come easily to the proud and fierce female. The very idea was repugnant, but Ferret was committed to doing anything that might serve her people.

Unfortunately, finding help would be even harder than accepting it. Ferret had learned much about Tethyr and its people, but she had no idea where to turn, no knowledge of anyone in whom she might place a degree of trust.

Frustrated beyond words, the female picked up her gloves and turban from the floor and donned both. Next she smoothed the makeup on her cheek to hide her true skin color. When her disguise was once again firmly in place, she slipped from the shop and made her silent way to the nearest tavern. One of the things she had learned during her stay in Zazesspur was that useful information was more likely to be found in a festhouse than in a council hall. Perhaps tonight she would find the inspiration she needed to complete her chosen task.

* * * * *

Morning broke over the hills, casting long golden shadows over the lush and fertile landscape. With deep satisfaction, Lord Inselm Hhune gazed at the scene spread out before him. His country manor was set atop a high hill, and the view from the balcony outside his private study was vast and spectacular.

Hhune's estate was an oddly shaped little kingdom, a collection of small, well-tended farms that stretched along both sides of the Sulduskoon river for several miles—not coincidentally, giving him a certain degree of control over trade on that section of the river. To the north Hhune could see the narrow ribbon of hard-packed earth that was the Trade Way, and farther still, the rooftops of Zazesspur.

Though it was yet early summer, the fertile farmlands of these lands and the Purple Hills region to the south were lush and green. To the west lay the sea, and Hhune could just make out the glimmer of sunlight on the distant waves. He drew considerable wealth from the labors of the farming folk and more still from the sea. His labors as a merchant, and as guildmaster of Zazesspur's influential Shippers' Guild, had won Hhune power and wealth that far surpassed his early goals. But what had once been distant dreams were now merely milestones on Hhune's road to ever greater things.

"It is remarkable how ambition manages to keep apace of one's success," the Tethyrian mused aloud. "On such a day, all things seem possible."

A firm knock at his door pulled the lord from his comfortable thoughts. A frown dented Hhune's brow for a moment as he considered the possible source of this interruption. Then he remembered, and a slow smile lifted the corners of his vast mustache. His new apprentice was to report to him today, bearing gifts, as was the custom. Hhune was very interested to learn what gifts a son of Pasha Balik might deem worthy of his new master.

"Come," he commanded, and in response the door was flung open with a force that sent it thudding against the far wall.

Two armed men, clad in the purple tunics and leggings of the Balik house guard, strode into the room. They held between them a slender, golden-haired woman whose slightly pointed ears proclaimed her a half-elf. She was simply clad in a gown and kirtle, but the small silvery lyre she clutched to her chest was both old and valuable. It was clear she had not come of her own will. Her lovely face was frozen, her eyes so dilated with terror as to appear almost black.

Before Hhune could speak, young Prince Hasheth pushed past the trio and made his bow. There was a haughtiness about his manner that bordered on disdain; this insolence was not lost upon Hhune. With difficulty the lord swallowed his first, angry response. Hhune was low-born, and he bitterly resented anything that might be construed as a slight. But with him, profit ever came before pride.

"You see before you my gift," the young man began, gesturing toward the half-elven musician. He lifted a hand in a quick, peremptory gesture. "I do not offer you the woman. Those you no doubt have in plenty. My gift to you is something far more valuable: information."

"Go on," the lord said in an even voice. Despite the young man's lapse of judgment—it was never wise to anger or mistreat a bard of any sort—this struck Hhune as a promising beginning, for he dealt in many commodities, not the least of which was information.

"Just last night, I heard this woman singing a song recently brought down from the Northlands. It seemed important to me that you hear it," Hasheth proclaimed.

Hhune nodded to the men, who released their hold on the woman's arms. She stumbled a bit. The lord leaped forward, catching her before she could fall. With a solicitous air that would have done honor to a countess, he helped her into a nearby chair.

"My sincere apologies, my dear lady, for the ungracious manner in which you were brought to me. By all means, I would hear the song of which my too-eager apprentice speaks. But first, I pray you, rest and enjoy a bit of refreshment. The ride from Zazesspur can be very tiring, can it not?"

The lord chatted on as he reached for an embroidered bellpull, speaking lightly of inconsequential things. The balm of social amenities had the desired effect. The tension began to drain from the half-elf's face, slowly to be replaced by pleasure, even pride, as she came to understand that she was not a prisoner, but an honored guest.

In moments a servant appeared, bearing a tray laden with wine, fruit, and sweet breads. Lord Hhune waved the servant away and served the refreshments himself. He then offered brief and perfunctory prayers to Silvanus and Sune and Ilmater—the preferred deities of the land—and proposed a toast to the health of Pasha Balik. Hhune might not have been born into the nobility, but he had made a point to learn the proprieties and, like many newmade nobles, he adhered to them with a near-religious zeal. It would not be said of *him* that he was unmannered and common!

The half-elven bard warmed to Hhune's courteous treatment, even flirting a bit between sips of her spiced wine. Through it all, Hasheth bore himself with the patience of one well accustomed to courtly manners. But as soon as propriety allowed, the young prince turned to business.

"Might we now hear this song?" he asked.

Hhune bit back an impatient retort and turned to the woman. "If you feel ready to sing, we would be most honored to listen."

With a coy smile, the half-elf reached for her lyre and checked the tuning on the strings. She played a few silvery notes and then began to sing.

The song was a ballad, and as the story unfolded Hhune began to understand why his new apprentice was so eager for him to hear it. It was a story of betrayal and treachery, and of a heroic young bard who uncovered a plot to destroy the Harpers from within.

The Harpers. The very mention of this secret organization of meddling northerners was enough to set Hhune's teeth on edge. There had been rumors that the Harpers were courting Pasha Balik, but the city's ruler had spurned their advances, as he did those of any northern courtier.

Or had he?

Hhune often wondered how and why the guilds' plan to oust Pasha Balik had failed. It had been so carefully planned, so flawlessly executed. Yet the main conspirators had been found slain, and the pasha himself had sponsored laws that severely limited the powers of the guilds. Clearly, word of the plot had reached his ears, yet try as they might, no one could learn who might have turned traitor.

Hhune settled back in his chair and regarded the half-elven bard thoughtfully. Harpers, at work in *his* Zazesspur! He shuddered at the thought of adding this canny society to the ever-growing list of those who sought to seize power or influence events in Tethyr. Their agent must be removed at once, before more of Hhune's long-laid plans were discovered and brought down.

When the last silvery notes of the lyre shimmered into silence, the lord turned a smile upon the bard. "Thank you for this song, my dear lady. My steward will compensate you for your performance and for the troubles of your journey. But first, can you tell me where you heard this most interesting story?"

"In a tavern, my lord, just as did your young apprentice," the half-elf said. "It is widely sung. But it is said that the ballad was brought to Tethyr by the Harper bard who wrote it."

"And can you name this Harper?"

"I cannot, my lord. But they say that in his song, he has named himself."

Understanding jolted through Hhune like a dagger's thrust. Indeed, now that he considered the ballad, the

identity of this "bard" became achingly clear. Surely the
composer and the hero were one—the ballad was too
self-congratulatory for it to be otherwise! And the
description of the hero was very like someone Hhune
knew, not well, but far too well for his liking.

The lord carefully hid his response. Again he summoned his capable servant and placed the half-elf into
the man's care, instructing him to treat their guest with
all courtesy and have her escorted back to the city.

That settled, Hhune shut the door and took a chair
directly across from his watchful apprentice. The lord
knew, of course, who the Harper agent was. It was someone whose identity should have been apparent all along.
A newcomer, a northerner, a wealthy young man nobly
born into one of Waterdeep's powerful merchant clans—
all of these things were ample grounds for suspicion. But
with an audacious nerve worthy of master thieves, the
Harpers had hidden their agent in plain sight. Who would
have suspected that the frivolous young man who'd composed this ballad—to all appearances a fop and a fool—
was in reality a viper disguised by a jester's motley?

In short, who would have suspected Danilo Thann?

What Hhune wanted to know now was how this
knowledge had come to Hasheth.

"The pasha will be interested to learn that these
meddlesome northerners are at work in his kingdom,"
Hhune began, feeling his way a step at a time.

"He knows already," the young man stated coldly.
"This so-called bard sings his tales directly into my
father's ear. Word of it came to me. I do not approve."

"Yet it is a wise man who will take a valuable gift,
even from an enemy," the lord observed cautiously. He
could hardly voice his agreement with Hasheth's harsh
sentiments. For all he knew, this could be a trap, and it
would not do to have the young upstart run to his father
with word of Hhune's disapproval.

"The gift is given. We have no more use for this man,"
Hasheth continued.

"We?"

Hhune let the question hang in the air, observing his apprentice closely as the young man formulated a response. There was much in the youth's eyes that interested Hhune. Whatever Hasheth's talents might be, the prince had not yet learned to hide his emotions. There was a personal matter between him and this Harper, of that Hhune was certain.

"I am now in your service," Hasheth said, speaking with careful emphasis. "It seems to me that you would not be well served should a Harper remain within the guilds."

Well, that answered many questions, Hhune thought wryly. The palace was aware of the guilds' plot against Balik. It was even possible that young Hasheth had been placed here, in Hhune's service, to act as an informant, perhaps by the Harpers themselves. Well enough—information could flow both ways.

Hhune settled back in his chair. "I consider myself a fair judge of men. You know this Harper. You have something against him, something of a personal nature."

An image of Danilo Thann flashed into the lord's mind: a handsome blond youth, dancing at a recent party and charming the ladies of the court.

"A woman, perhaps?" Hhune concluded slyly, and was rewarded by a flash of sullen resentment in the prince's eyes. "A woman, then. And you want the rival for her affections removed."

"It is not so simple a matter. And even if it were, as your apprentice I would not act without your approval," Hasheth said stiffly.

"Ah. Let us say you have obtained it. What would you do?"

"I would hire every assassin in the guild to hunt him down with all possible haste," the young man said coldly. "This is more than a personal matter. Any amount of gold needed to buy the death of this particular traitor would be well spent!"

But Hhune shook his head. "Wait three days," he said. "The young fool has powerful friends in Waterdeep, and there would be grave repercussions should we in Tethyr move against him too quickly. Give the ballad time to do its work before we strike. The Harpers can hardly avenge an agent who betrayed himself with a song!"

"This ballad—"

"Will be sung in every tavern in Zazesspur," Hhune finished firmly. "You may believe me when I say this." With these words, he took a large gold coin from his pocket and flipped it to his apprentice.

The young man deftly fielded the coin and studied it. The proud, stiff posture of his shoulders melted, and the eyes he lifted to Hhune's face were wide with wonder— and the dawning of true respect.

"I see that you know the marks on that coin," the lord said dryly. "And it is well that you do, for the Knights of the Shield were largely responsible for your father's rise to power. If you are to enter my service, you should also understand my position with this powerful group, and your worth to me. That coin may mark me as an agent of the Knights, but *information* is the true currency. With this currency, an ambitious man can purchase power. Do you understand me?"

"Yes, my lord," Hasheth agreed eagerly.

"Good. You should also understand that very little happens in these southern lands that the Knights have not planned, and by which we do not profit. It is not so in the north. This could change, if we had agents who could infiltrate the ranks of the Harpers and bring us information gathered by those northern meddlers. Could such a thing be done, do you think?"

"It can, my lord."

Hhune noted the confidence in the prince's voice, the proud, determined tilt of his chin. So there was another Harper beside that Thann nuisance, Hhune mused, and one whom Hasheth knew. Perhaps the woman for whose affections Hasheth was willing to betray a former ally.

"She is very beautiful, this Harper?" Hhune asked casually.

"A goddess, my lord," the prince blurted out, and then bit his lip as he realized what he had revealed.

The lord chuckled. "I care not how you amuse yourself. Nor do I wish to know the name of this other Harper—not yet, at least. Do all that you can to gain her trust. Prove yourself a competent informant. In doing so, you will serve me well."

"As you wish, Lord Hhune," he agreed.

Hhune, who was in fact a rather astute judge of men, did not doubt that all would be done as agreed. He recognized the fires of ambition, and seldom had he seen them burn so brightly as they did in Hasheth's black eyes. This youth would do whatever he could to further his own cause.

The lord rose to his feet, signifying that the interview was at an end. "You will return to the city at once. My scribe, Achnib, has been instructed to teach you of my shipping affairs. Learn well. We will speak more when I return."

"Return, my lord?"

"Each summer I travel to Waterdeep to attend the midsummer fair and to receive the report of our agent there, a countrywoman, Lucia Thione, who is highly placed both in business and society."

The young man looked impressed, as Hhune had intended. The Thione family was related to the royal house of Tethyr. Few members had escaped the sword after the fall of the royal family. That one of these survivors was allied with the Knights of the Shield gave an additional luster to the secret society.

All things, including loyalty, had a price. As Hhune sent the young man on his way, there was no doubt in his mind that he was now the proud owner of a prince—a prince who also happened to be a trusted ally of the Harpers. It was, in his estimation, a bargain well made.

* * * * *

The night passed slowly for Arilyn, for try as she might, she could not banish from her mind the image of the elven warrior she had seen in Assante's treasure rooms. When at last she slept, her dreams were haunted by the face of her unknown ancestor and by a chorus of Elvish voices that demanded that the dishonor done to the swordmistress be redressed. Arilyn woke before dawn with the voices still ringing in her ears and the conviction that there was more to the night vision than the promptings of her own outrage. The dream had an eldritch intensity of a sort Arilyn had not experienced in over two years.

Instinctively her eyes went to her moonblade, which lay bared and ready on her night table, within easy reach. Arilyn reached out a tentative hand to touch the sword. As she expected, a surge of restless magic jolted through her.

The Harper snatched back her tingling hand. Then, with a sigh, she reached for the weapon and slid it back into its ancient sheath. She kicked off her covers and rose, buckling on her swordbelt with practiced fingers.

Barefoot and clad only in her leggings and under tunic—and, of course, the moonblade—Arilyn walked over to the window. The city below still lay sleeping, except for those who, like herself, were most likely to do business under the cover of night.

For a long time Arilyn stood at her tower window, staring at Zazesspur's rooftops with eyes that did not see, struggling to accept what she knew to be true. After a silence of more than two years, the elfshadow, the essence of the moonblade, was growing restless. Once again the spirit of the magic sword was demanding something of the half-elf who commanded it.

The last time this had happened, twenty and more Harpers lay dead before Arilyn finally recognized the voice of the sword. She knew the cost of ignoring the moonblade's warnings, yet the sunrise colors had faded from the sky before she was able to decide upon a course of action. The morning was nearly spent before she was ready to proceed.

The half-elf did not consider herself a coward. From an early age she had battled armed men, fought monsters of almost every description, met the Tuigan hoard in the lingering horror that was war. There was only one thing under the stars that Arilyn Moonblade truly feared: the unknown powers hidden in the ancient sword that was strapped to her side.

There were aspects of the moonblade's magic that Arilyn understood and wielded with skill. The moonblade warned her of danger, struck with preternatural speed and power, enabled her to take on a number of disguises, and gave her a resistance to fire that had spared her life more than once. It was the elfshadow, her own mirror image, that Arilyn dreaded. Yet what else could she do but summon the elfshadow and learn from it what she could?

The Harper placed her hand on the moonblade's hilt and drew a long, steadying breath. The elven sword hissed free of the scabbard and glittered in the bright morning light as Arilyn held it high in her two-handed grip.

"Come forth," she called softly.

In response, a faintly azure mist rose from the sword and swirled into the air, taking on a familiar, yet ghostly form. The Harper's arms lowered until the moonblade's point rested on the wooden floor. But Arilyn hardly noticed, so intent was she on the image taking shape before her.

For a moment she had the feeling she was looking at her own reflection in some moonlit pond. Then the elfshadow stepped out of the mist and stood before her, as apparently solid and mortal as Arilyn herself. Unlike the Harper, the elfshadow was dressed as if for the road, in the worn but comfortable boots and breeches that Arilyn favored when left solely to her own desires.

For a long moment the half-elf and the elfshadow regarded each other solemnly. A strange impulse—the urge to scratch her nose just to see if the elfshadow followed suit—flashed into Arilyn's mind. The absurdity of this brought a tiny smile to her lips.

"Well again, sister," the elfshadow said, speaking in an exact duplicate of Arilyn's contralto tones. "I had hoped you would call me forth long ere this."

The Harper folded her arms over her chest and glared. "I've been busy."

A sad smile crossed the elfshadow's face. "You still blame yourself for the death of those Harpers, though the hand that slew them was mine."

"There's a difference?" Arilyn asked bitterly.

"Oh, yes. For the time being, at least."

The half-elf's brow furrowed with puzzlement. She had many questions; this one seemed a logical place to start. "I don't suppose you want to explain that."

"No more than you want to *hear* the explanation," the elfshadow responded with an unexpected touch of dry humor.

Arilyn lifted an inquiring brow. "That's something I might have said," she observed. "What are you? Are you the moonblade, or are you me?"

"Both, and yet neither." The elfshadow fell silent, as if carefully measuring her next words. "You know that each wielder of a moonblade imbues the sword with a new power, but you do not understand the source of that power. Unlike any other moonfighter who came before you, you were not told of the moonblade's secrets before you claimed the sword."

"So tell me."

"It is not so simple," the elfshadow cautioned her. "The moonblades are ancient elven artifacts, and the mysteries that went into their crafting cannot be adequately described—no more than I could convey to you with mere words a melody you have never heard or a color you have never seen."

"Noted. Go on," Arilyn said tersely.

"First let me point out that the moonblade accepted you when you were but a child, not to mention the first half-elf ever to inherit such a sword! This decision was not lightly made, for it was foreseen that you would do a great service to the People."

"The elfgate," Arilyn murmured, naming the magical gateway to Evermeet that she had discovered and then fought to protect.

"That and more," the elfshadow agreed cryptically. "Once accepted, you slowly became attuned to the sword. That is how I came into being. For lack of a better description, I am the personification of your union with the sword."

"I see. Do all moonblades have people like you?"

"By the sea and stars! No, not at all. The ability to form and summon an elfshadow was one of the powers added to the moonblade you carry. By Zoastria," the shadow added in a lower voice.

Something in the elfshadow's tone convinced Arilyn that this was the name of the sleeping warrior. "So that's why I've been having these dreams. Not since the time of the Harper assassin have I had such visions! But why would finding Zoastria's body stir them, if you are the personification of *my* union with the sword?"

"Like the elves who have gone before you, you added a power to the moonblade," the elfshadow continued softly. "A power that reflects your character and your needs."

Arilyn shrugged, impatient for the elfshadow to move on to something she did not already know.

"Moonblades contain great magic, and they grow in power with each wielder. But as with all magic, the cost is high." The elfshadow paused and spread her hands, as if inviting Arilyn to observe in her what that cost might be. "My name is chosen well, *for I am the shadow of what you will become.*"

Arilyn stared at her image, not wanting to understand. Yet she suspected that she knew what the elfshadow meant. Suddenly, she realized that in some small way she had *always* known.

"Then when I die—" she began.

"You will not die, strictly speaking. Your life essence will enter the moonblade. This is the ultimate source of the sword's magic."

Arilyn turned abruptly away. For a long moment she stared at the wall, her face frozen as she struggled to control her roiling emotions. "So what you're saying is that this sword is full of dead elves," she said at last.

"No! That explanation is simplistic and crude, not to mention entirely inaccurate. Except in unusual cases, elves are immortal. We pass from this world on to the realms of Arvandor without tasting death as humans know it. But yes, each elf who accepts a moonblade understands that his or her passage to Arvandor will be delayed, perhaps for thousands of years, until the moonblade's purpose is fulfilled. When a sword falls dormant, the elves are released. It is an enormous sacrifice, but one that certain noble elves take on gladly for the greater good of the People."

"But what of me?" The words poured from Arilyn in an agonized rush. "I am *half*-elven! The gates of Arvandor are closed to such as I, and most of the elves I've known believe I *have* no soul! What will become of *me*? Of *us*?" she amended bitterly.

The elfshadow merely shook her head. "I do not know. None of us know. You are the first half-elf ever to wield such a blade. At the risk of sounding like a two-copper cleric discussing the afterlife, you will have to wait and find out."

"But your best guess would be eternal servitude, cooped up like some genie in a cheap bronze lamp?" Arilyn said with cold rage. "Thanks, but I'll pass."

"You cannot."

"The hell I can't. I didn't sign on for any of this!"

"Your fate was decided when you first drew the sword," the elfshadow insisted.

But Arilyn shook her head, her eyes blazing. "I'll accept *that* when I'm drinking tea and swapping stories with Zoastria's shade! There *has* to be a way out! Where would I find someone who knows it?"

"Arvandor," the shadow replied grimly. "And, possibly, Evermeet."

Arilyn threw up her hands. To her, one was about the same as the other. She would never be accepted on the elven island. And not even for the sake of her soul—if indeed she *had* one—would she take something unearned from the hands of her mother's people!

Unearned.

Suddenly the furious Harper remembered the missive from the Queen of Evermeet, and she knew what she must do. She would accept Amlaruil's impossible mission, and she would find a way to succeed beyond the elven monarch's highest expectations, *and* she would do it in her own way and on her own terms! And once that was accomplished, the queen would pay dearly for services rendered.

Arilyn lifted the sword and faced down her elfshadow. "In you go," she said grimly. "Where I'm headed, the patrons are already seeing double."

Six

 "It's been days, and no sign of them elves," Vhenlar fretted, and not for the first time. "How're we to know when they're coming? You'd sooner hear your own shadow coming up behind you than one of them unnatural things. Like ghosts, they are! For all we know, every man on patrol is lying under some bush right now with a second smile under his chin!"

Bunlap threw a quelling glance toward the nervous archer. "Maybe so, but we'll know," he said shortly. "*I'll* know."

As the mercenary spoke, his hand lifted to touch the livid scar on his cheek, three curving lines that combined in the simple but distinctive design of a woodland flower of some sort. Bunlap had seen that mark elsewhere, and since the day the red-haired elf had marked him, he had done his dead-level damndest to make sure other people saw it, too—people who wouldn't think kindly of the elf it identified. And by extension, the rest of Tethir's elves. Bunlap's hatreds were nothing if not inclusive.

They were a scrappy bunch, the wild elves of Tethir, even if they were short and scrawny. The half dozen that Bunlap's men had captured from the forest glade had put up a fight all out of proportion to their size and number. And these were but womenfolk, and half-grown elf-brats! The mercenaries kept these few around as bait for a trap, but there were many other elves in the forest who might well blame the red-haired elf whose arrows Bunlap had strewn judiciously around the ravaged elven settlement.

Bunlap liked the idea of angering some of the Elmanesse border tribes and turning them against the elven warrior who had maimed him, and who had eluded him for too long. Keep the long-eared bastards busy—that was what he was getting paid to do. But when it came time to kill the red-haired elf, Bunlap wanted the honor for himself.

The mercenary propped his boots up on a bale of dried and cured pipeweed. From his left boot he pulled a small knife, with which he began to carve some of the dirt from under his fingernails. From the small window across from him, he had a clear view of the field that stretched between the drying barn and the forest's edge. Sunset colors spilled into the small, winding creek that separated field from forest and provided water for the thirsty crops. In the dying light the shadows were deep and long. Even so, nothing, and no one, would be able sneak past him.

Most of the men in the barn's loft seemed to share Bunlap's confidence. A dozen men sprawled about throwing dice, whittling, or otherwise killing time. Several days had come and gone since their last foray into the deep shadows of Tethir, and as time passed their dread of elven retaliation had faded into nonchalance.

Vhenlar, however, was still as nervous as a mouse in a hawk's nest. The archer paced the barn's loft, watching the windows but keeping well out of the line of fire. In the field directly below them, six bedraggled elves were chained and staked amid the rows of aromatic plants. It was Bunlap's plan that the elves appear to be field slaves—a plan that was about as effective as hitching three wild deer to a plow and expecting a straight furrow to come of it. The strange little folk adamantly refused to cooperate with their captors. Even the smallest child would rather take a beating than harvest a single leaf. Weakened by lack of food and sleep and by the frequent lash of the whips, the elves nonetheless showed a fierce, stubborn resistance that Vhenlar almost admired.

The archer watched as one of the mercenaries on guard duty drew back his whip to punish a recalcitrant slave. His intended victim, an elven lass not yet old enough to bed, faced the man defiantly as the whip flashed up and forward.

Up came the girl's arm, moving with a speed that rivaled that of the flailing leather thong. Even as the whip curled around her wrist, the elf maid exploded into action. Moving faster than Vhenlar would have believed possible, the girl seized the whip with both hands and threw herself into a backward roll.

The sudden tug worked with the whip's momentum to pull the mercenary off-balance. He stumbled forward. Before he could recover, the elf was on her feet. With the speed of a striking hawk, she was upon him. A quick flash of her bleeding arm, and the now-slack whip was looped around the mercenary's neck.

Darting around him, the fierce elf child leaped up high and planted both bare feet on the small of the human's back. She kicked out hard, launching herself back and pulling at the whip with all her might. Vhenlar winced as the mercenary's head snapped back sharply. He fancied he could actually hear the distant cracking of bone.

"Another man down," he noted laconically, watching

as three of the guards rushed in and wrestled the girl to
the ground.

When Bunlap merely shrugged, the archer turned back
to the scene below. He felt oddly ill at ease in the barn's
loft. Trapped, almost. Yet Vhenlar was no stranger to the
task before him. During his years stationed in the fortress
known as Darkhold, he'd often hidden in the rocks above
some nearby mountain pass, picking off travelers. When
would-be invaders challenged the Zhentish stronghold,
Vhenlar was always called to the walls to help pin down
the attackers. His aim was almost legendary, and he had
over two hundred confirmed kills to his credit. But compared to the uncanny skill of the forest elves, Vhenlar felt
like a clumsy-handed novice. Not even the extra measure
of precision granted him by his elven bow evened the
score to his satisfaction.

Suddenly the mercenary captain leaped to his feet,
his gray eyes blazing in his elf-scarred face. "There it is,
men!" hissed Bunlap. "Take your places. Move!"

Although Bunlap's men exchanged uncertain glances,
all did as they were told. Kneeling beside the small windows that vented the loft, they gathered their weapons,
fixed their eyes upon the tree line, and waited.

"What d'you hear, Captain?" Vhenlar murmured as
he nocked an arrow—one of his own, this time, steel-
tipped and fletched with the blue-and-white striped
feathers of a bird that brightened the bleak landscape
of his native Cormyr. The arrow felt good in his hands,
not at all like the black-shafted arrows he had pillaged
from the quivers of slain elves or torn from the bodies of
his own comrades. There was something unnatural
about those elven bolts. Vhenlar couldn't pick up such
an arrow without the strange feeling that it might at
any moment turn against him.

"The call of a wood thrush," Bunlap returned with
grim satisfaction. "A sort of bird that never ventures
from the forest to the fields. It would appear that our
elven friend has less sense than the bird he imitates!"

Vhenlar squinted into the trees, but he could see nothing. He nodded toward the captured elves in the fields below. "If you recognize that birdsong, so do they," he pointed out.

This, Vhenlar thought, was the weakest point of Bunlap's plan. Surely the elven slaves realized they were bait for an ambush. If they had bothered to count, they would have to know there had been more humans in the raiding party that destroyed their homes than the few who now guarded them. But the elves also knew enough about their human captors to realize that they themselves would probably not survive a rescue attempt. Vhenlar had no idea whether the elves would try to warn away any would-be rescuers or whether they'd keep quiet and hope for the best.

Then a pale bolt arched up high over the field, followed by two more. The arrows descended upon the three guards who were busy subduing the elf girl with considerably more force than was needed. Startled oaths and shouts of pain floated up toward the barn as the guards leaped to their feet. The men whirled about, pawing at the arrows embedded between their shoulder blades.

"Just out of reach, just above the heart," murmured Vhenlar with admiration. It was an astonishing feat of skill. Even more remarkable was the range at which the shot had been made. Not even a crossbow-fired arrow could have taken the guards with a level shot. To reach the humans at all, the elves had had to shoot upward at a sharp angle, trusting that the arrows would fall in precisely the right place.

Before he had time to marvel at this feat of marksmanship, the unseen elves' purpose became apparent. The elf maid, suddenly freed, seized a hand-axe from the belt of one of the distracted men and with one fierce blow severed the chain that tethered her. At once a second barrage of arrows exploded from the forest and took all three of her tormentors through their throats. She

nimbly dodged their falling bodies and ran like a deer
for the trees.

Instinctively Vhenlar dropped the elf bow and
snapped his loaded crossbow up into place. Before he
could bring down the elf maid, Bunlap seized his wrist.

"Fool! You'll give away our position!"

"And she won't?" Vhenlar retorted.

For once Bunlap had no argument. He released the
archer's wrist and nodded grimly.

Vhenlar pulled the crossbow's trigger. The arrow
streaked toward the fleeing girl, and though she was at
the outermost edge of his range, he saw his aim would
be good.

But while the arrow was still hurtling downward
toward the elf maid's back, an answering flash came
from the forest's edge. There was a sudden bright spark,
clearly visible against the darkening forest, as Vhenlar's steel arrowhead met one of stone. Both arrows fell
to the ground, and the elf maid disappeared into the
trees.

"Bane's dark blood," the archer swore in an awed
tone. Had he not seen it with his own eyes, he wouldn't
have believed any mortal being could shoot accurately
enough to hit an arrow in flight, point-to-point.

Bunlap seemed to be having similar thoughts, for he
edged away from the open window. He cupped his hands
to his mouth and bellowed instructions to the men
below. The guards unchained the captured elves and,
holding them as shields, began to drag them back
behind the barn.

"Lot of good that will do," Vhenlar muttered. "Elves
are small; there's still too much human target exposed.
Those elven archers could put a bolt through a hum-
mingbird's eye!"

"So we might lose a few guards," the captain returned
coldly. "What of it? Enough men remain to bring the
captives out of range—and out of sight. The wild elves
won't stand and fight, but we'll give them something to

think about. Every now and again we'll cut one of their womenfolk. They can sit there and enjoy the music while we kill off their people, bit by bit, or they can leave the shelter of the trees."

The archer responded with a derisive sniff.

"An easy choice for them to make, is that what you think?" inquired Bunlap. "Mark me: that fox-haired elf will come. Hells' dungeons—*I'd* come, if for no other reason than to take up the gauntlets we've been leaving all over the forest!

"But more than that, he wants *me*," the mercenary captain continued with dark satisfaction. "I've looked into that elf's eyes. He's the sort who likes to think of himself as a noble leader, but deep down he's the same as I am. For both of us, this has become personal."

* * * * *

The elven maiden stumbled into the forest and into the waiting arms of Tamara Oakstaff, the only female in the war party. The young fighter steadied the child, then held her out at arm's length. Tamara's expert gaze slid over the girl, measuring her hurts.

These were many and considerable: welts and gashes dealt by the whip, skin rubbed into raw, angry wounds by rusted chains, a frail body weakened by lack of food and water and rest. There were unseen hurts, too, apparent only to Tamara's fey eyes. For a moment the elf woman flinched away from the terrors the child had endured. But any thought of pity died when Tamara's gaze reached the girl's fierce eyes. The older female nodded approval. This one would not only survive, but fight!

"Give the little hawk some water," she said with a smile, "and then give her a bow and quiver!"

But the elf maid waved away both and pointed to the retreating humans. "Too late for that," she said.

"They are beyond range," Foxfire agreed.

As the leader handed the girl a waterskin and indicated that she must drink, his eyes searched the windows placed high on the large wooden structure that
stood at the far side of the field.

There archers lay in wait for them. As he'd expected,
this was an ambush. What he hadn't bargained on was
that Bunlap would use elven children and females to
lure his opponents into the trap. Silently Foxfire
berated himself. He should have foreseen something
like this, given what he knew of the man.

"Tell us of our foe. How many humans do we face?" he
asked the elf maid, speaking as one warrior to another.

This show of respect brightened the child's eyes. She
bit her lip, concentrating, nodding off the count as she
silently tallied their foe. "More than a hundred men
attacked Council Glade; of that number, perhaps half
survived. We six managed to kill a few more since we
were brought here, but there were far too many for us!"

"A familiar story, when dealing with humans," muttered Tamsin, Tamara's twin-born brother.

"And in the barn?" Foxfire pressed.

"Ten, maybe more," she said. "There were twelve
guards in the field, and two patrols of ten each in the
forest."

"You needn't worry about them," Tamsin assured her
in a tone that left little doubt as to their fate.

"A score of humans. We outnumber them three to
two," exulted Tamara.

"And in the forest, that would be overwhelming odds,"
the leader said. "But the humans have turned this
battle around, forcing us into a stupid and suicidal
charge while they fight from cover as forest people do!"

"It is not our way, but if you say it must be done we
will follow you," one of the warriors said. The others,
thirty in all, nodded and raised their hands in a silent
gesture of assent, as the elves of Talltrees pledged their
lives to their war leader.

Foxfire thanked them with a nod, then turned back to

study the unfamiliar battleground. For a long moment the warriors at his back remained silent in the shadows, waiting with elven patience for his decision. As the darkness around them deepened, the only sounds were the night songs of birds and the quickening chirp of crickets.

Then the quiet twilight was rent by the sound of a female's scream, high and piercing and anguished. The elves tensed, their dark fingers curving around their bows and their muscles tensing as they prepared to sprint through the deadly field.

"Do not," Foxfire said softly, though his own face was twisted with distress. "They are baiting us, and their archers will pick us off long before we reach our people. Your deaths will only speed theirs!"

"What, then?" demanded Korrigash, coming up to his friend's side.

With a strange smile, the leader pulled his bone knife from his belt and cut the thong that bound his forehead and held back his fox-colored hair. From it hung a number of ornaments that helped his bright russet locks to blend in with the forest: feathers, cunningly woven reeds, a dried cattail he'd cut that spring from the Swanmay's glade.

Foxfire's hands moved deftly as he slid the cattail onto an arrow's shaft. Murmuring a quick prayer of explanation and apology, Foxfire slashed at the bark of a scrubby pine until it bled thick sap. He scraped up the pine pitch with his knife and pressed it into the cattail, then called for the loan of a fire-forged knife.

Wordlessly Korrigash handed one over. The horrified expression in his black eyes was echoed on the face of every elf in the company as Foxfire struck steel against stone. What the leader proposed to do was unthinkable to the forest elves, for in their world no force was as feared or as destructive as the one Foxfire prepared to unleash.

"The plants in that field are green and fresh," he said

softly as he struck a second spark. "And water runs between the barn and the trees. The barn will burn, but fire will not reach the forest. When the humans are forced from the building, we will attack. They force us into the open; we will do the same."

"But they will not let our people live that long!" protested Tamsin.

"They will," Foxfire said with absolute certainty. "They will keep them alive, and in torment, for as long as it takes to bring us to them. There is much about the humans I do not understand, but this thing I know: their leader will not rest easy until he has washed his pride with my blood."

Another scream pierced the night. Foxfire winced and bent over his fearful task. Again he struck steel to stone; this time the spark fell upon the pitch-coated cattail. The elf blew softly upon it, coaxing the makeshift torch into flame. When the arrow was ready, he quickly fitted it to his bow. With a strength far beyond that suggested by his slender frame, the elf pulled the arrow back to its flaming point. For a moment he held it, drawing up strength from the forest floor beneath him. Then he loosed both the arrow and a hawklike cry.

The fire-bearing arrow streaked through the night like a falling star, plummeting into the dried weeds, crushed and matted by the passage of many feet, that surrounded the wooden building. As smoke spiraled upward toward the stars, elven arrows kept at bay all those who tried to quench the gathering flames.

Vile oaths and shouts of anger and fear poured from the building like smoke, but at last the humans were forced to stagger from the burning barn into the night.

"Shoot while you can, fight hand-to-hand when you must," Foxfire said tersely. "Have ready a second weapon; as soon as possible we must arm any of the captives who are still able to fight. You, little sister, bide here and await our return."

But the rescued elf maid seized the steel knife from

his hands. "For my mother," she said before he could protest, and she showed him the bone dagger Tamara had already given her.

"You are a brave and blooded warrior, but you are hurt," he said gently.

"I can still fight," she insisted. Her eyes glowed with intense fervor as she seized his hand and pressed it to her lips. "And I will follow you to death and beyond!"

With these words, the elf maid darted out into the field, her thin, dark form silhouetted against the leaping flames. The other elves followed suit at once, fanning out as they went, running as silently as a pack of wolves.

Foxfire and Korrigash exchanged a wry glance and then kicked into a run. "I used to wonder why, of the two of us, you ended up as war leader," the dark-haired elf observed. "Especially seeing as how I can outrun, outshoot, and outfight you."

A fleeting grin softened Foxfire's grim face. "I'll remember that challenge, my friend, and disprove it another day! So what is this secret?"

"You know when to follow," Korrigash said.

The elven leader's black eyes settled upon the child warrior. She was the first to reach the humans. Her frail form was barely visible in the roiling smoke, crouched as she was astride a fallen man, but her arm rose again and again as the steel sank home.

Foxfire nodded, recognizing the truth of his friend's observation, though he himself had never thought long on the matter. Korrigash had a gift for saying much with few words.

"High-sun and two," Korrigash gritted out, naming a time of day and a direction.

Reflexively, his friend snapped up his bow and loosed an arrow ahead and to his right. The swirling smoke parted to reveal a human fighter, an elf-bolt buried in his gut and a look of surprise on his face. In his hand was a length of chain—still whirling—that he'd been preparing to launch at Foxfire. The impromptu weapon wrapped around the human's arm with a sickening thud and a crack of bone. When the human opened his mouth to scream, all that emerged was a sudden bright gush.

Foxfire turned away from the sight, for the death of his enemies gave him no pleasure. He touched the other elf's arm in silent thanks and pulled his dagger. Suddenly there was no more time for words. The battle closed around them with a hellish cacophony: a roaring of flames, the shrieks of rage and pain, and the deafening pounding of their own blood against their ears. The two elves spun and stood back to back to confront together a horror that both had long feared and neither understood:

A war against the humans.

* * * * *

The door of the Breaching Whale tavern slammed open, sending shudders through the many-paned windows that fronted the dock. An elf woman burst into the taproom as if she'd been thrust through the door by the winds of a freak summer storm. She was uncommonly tall for an elf, white-skinned and raven-haired—a startling coloring common to the moon people. Vivid blue eyes flamed like wizard fire as she stalked across the suddenly silent room.

Sandusk Truffledigger, the halfling barkeep, watched warily as the elf woman descended upon him with the force of a funnel cloud.

"Where is Carreigh Macumail?" she demanded, punctuating her question by slamming both hands upon the polished wooden counter.

The halfling was gratified to note that her voice, a melodic alto despite her anger, was definitely that of a half-elf—not as flat as a human's tones, but lacking the music and magic of an elven voice. Elves and humans both were trouble, but to Sandusk's way of thinking an elf-human hybrid was to be preferred over a pure-blooded version of either variety. Half-elves were treated well enough in Zazesspur, but they walked a thin rope and most of them knew it. The ever-increasing racial conflicts of Tethyr put half-elves in a tenuous position that prompted them to watch their manners and mind their own affairs.

This one, however, seemed determined to be the exception. When the barkeep did not answer fast enough to suit her, the half-elf seized his tunic with both hands and pulled him up over the bar until they were eye-to-eye.

"I know and appreciate the Breached Whale's reputation for protecting its patrons, and I assure you I have no intention of harming Captain Macumail," she said softly. "You, however, are another matter entirely. Now talk."

"He's gone!" the barkeep squeaked. "He left!"

Arilyn gave him a sharp shake. "I *know* that. I also know that he routinely informs you of his next destination. Tell me, or I'll skewer you like a roasting rabbit!"

"But I'm a halfling," Suldusk protested in a piercing whine that carried to every corner of the tavern. He had long ago learned that those larger than he could easily be shamed, and like most halflings he doled out guilt with a lavish hand. "I'm but half your size!"

The half-elf smiled coldly. "So I'll use a short sword."

Suldusk considered the grim practicality of this solution. "He's not gone far," he said in tones more modulated toward discretion. "*Mist-Walker* raised anchor just this morning. Captain Macumail said something about hooking up with some pirate-hunters. Might be that you could still catch him."

Arilyn stared at the halfling for a moment; then she gave a curt nod and lowered him to the floor. She turned and strode from the tavern. Without pause, she went to the edge of the dock and dove cleanly into the water.

One of the bemused patrons shook his head and snorted. "By the wounds of Ilmater! What's the fool elf wench thinking of? Swimming out to Macumail's ship?"

The halfling heard in these words the voice of opportunity. He smoothed his tunic back into place and then topped off his customer's mug from a foaming pitcher. "My dear sir, that wouldn't surprise me in the slightest. And if you're a wagering man, I'll happily lay odds that she'll have him back here by sunrise."

* * * * *

Arilyn dove deep and began swimming steadily toward the west. As she did, she blessed Black Pearl, an old friend and a half sea elf, for the enchanted amulet of water breathing that allowed Arilyn to enter her world. The Harper was not fond of magic or magical devices, but she'd kept the talisman for many years in honor of her friend. Of late, she'd had need of it so often she'd gotten into the habit of wearing it.

As she swam, she kept a keen watch for threats from the many dangers in Zazesspur's coastal waters. Colonies of sahuagin abounded; there were even rumors that the creatures had managed to capture several ships, which they used to engage in piracy. These rumors were unconfirmed. Lost ships were not uncommon, but survivors of pirate attacks were rare, and so far none could establish the truth of the strange buccaneers. But Arilyn knew what she knew. Where there were sahuagin, there were also sea elves, and she had long been on better terms with the People who dwelt below the sea than those who walked beneath the stars. She probably knew more about the sea folk's affairs than did the insular elves of Tethyr's forest.

The Forest of Tethir was vast and ancient, stretching from its easternmost point in the foothills of the Snowflake Mountains to the Starspire Peninsula, almost to the very edge of the sea. But few elves lived

on this swampy western arm of forest land, a part of
Tethyr that had long since been abandoned to the
humans and their clandestine activities. Poachers cut
down the ancient trees for mast poles; pirates docked in
fingerlike coves. Even the sahuagin had bases on the
Starspire. So, therefore, did the elves. And not just the
Sea People. Once the sea creatures had taken to ships,
the elven nation of Evermeet had sent in vessels of its
own to even the balance.

In a deep cove near the tip of the peninsula, shielded
from discovery by jagged rocks both real and illusion-
ary, was a small outpost of the elven navy, cloaked with
concealing magic and commanded by moon-elven
sailors from the royal fleet. Macumail had confided this
to Arilyn a couple years back, right after he'd first been
named elf-friend and allowed to make port on Evermeet. The captain had returned from the elven island
overbrimming with stories of elven wonders and glowing like a moon in the reflected glory of Queen
Amlaruil. Although Arilyn had little patience for his
stories about the elven queen, she'd listened and
learned what she could. Since Macumail could stay in
Zazesspur for only so long without raising suspicions
about his intentions, Arilyn guessed he was bound for
the elven port. She did not doubt that he would stay
close at hand until he had done Amlaruil's bidding.

From the corner of her left eye Arilyn glimpsed a
familiar shape in the dark water: an elven form, smaller
than that of land-dwelling People, and almost invisible
behind the writhing strands of seaweed he used as
cover. If not for her infravision, Arilyn would not have
seen him at all.

The elf was clearly part of a patrol. A tightly rolled
net was tied to his belt, and he wore several sharp
weapons and a wary expression. Arilyn had no doubt
that another elf, similarly armed, closed in on her from
the right.

She raised both hands high and to her sides to show

that they held no weapons. Then she slowly turned to face the first elf. Using the hand gestures she'd learned from Black Pearl, she laboriously spelled out her need to find Macumail. Grudgingly she added that she was on an errand for Amlaruil of Evermeet.

The sea elf's eyes brightened with adoration at the mention of the elven queen, an expression Arilyn had seen far too often on the face of Macumail, or for that matter anyone else who knew of Queen Amlaruil. Even Elaith Craulnober, a rogue moon elf of Arilyn's acquaintance who'd spent his many years away from Evermeet honing his reputation for battle prowess and cruelty, grew positively misty at the mention of the queen's name. The Harper gritted her teeth and focused her attention upon the sea elf's gesticulating, webbed fingers.

Macumail Elf-friend has spoken of you, Arilyn Moonflower. The People have been charged with watching for your approach, though we expected you to come by boat. He lifted one hand in the directional inflection that indicated humor.

Arilyn, however, was in no mood to be amused. "Moonflower" was the name of the royal family of Evermeet—her mother's name, and one that Arilyn had no thought of claiming for herself. A simple error, no doubt, but one that grated on her.

Moonblade, she corrected him, spelling out the word with emphatic deliberation, but the elf had already turned away and was gesturing excitedly to his partner, a female distinguished by her close-cropped green curls and the gleaming trident she carried. The two carried on a brief discussion, their fingers flashing with a speed Arilyn could not follow. Then the elves gestured that she should follow them.

The Harper sighed, sending a rift of bubbles floating upward, and then began to swim after the sea folk. Arilyn was a strong swimmer, but there was no possible way she could keep pace with these elves. Time and again her escort forgot her limitations and left her behind, only to circle back.

Fortunately, *Mist-Walker* had not gone far into the bay. By moonrise the trio had the ship in sight. The sea elves bid farewell to their charge and disappeared into the black waters, leaving Arilyn to approach the human vessel alone.

To Arilyn's surprise, the ship had dropped anchor. That was risky, for even so close to Zazesspur piracy was far from uncommon. She climbed the anchor's rope and quietly pulled herself over the side of the vessel. As she shook the water from her ears, she heard behind her the unmistakable hiss of steel sliding free of a scabbard.

Her own sword fairly leaped from its sheath. Moonblade held firmly in her two-handed grip, Arilyn whirled to face the challenger.

The swordsman was young—a son of one of the western Moonshae Isles, if his bright red hair and broad, blunt-nosed countenance spoke truth—and he was armed with a two-edged blade and matched dagger common to that area. Arilyn adjusted her grip slightly to prepare for the expected attack. Sure enough, the man feinted low, a common move that would no doubt be followed by a dagger feint and a sweeping overhead sword cut. There were many styles of swordplay among the humans of Faerûn; Arilyn was acquainted with them all.

She parried his sword feint with a hard downward swing that forced the point of his blade to the deck. Before he could bring his dagger into play, she swept the moonblade up and to her right with a force that sent the smaller weapon spinning. At the same time, she stomped down hard on the man's down-turned blade, wrenching the sword from his hand. The whole exercise took perhaps ten seconds.

For a moment the youth merely stood there, unarmed, too stunned by the pace of the battle to assimilate its results. Then understanding of his fate dawned in his eyes, and he drew breath to shout an alarm before he died.

Arilyn slammed the moonblade back into its sheath and plunged both of her hands into the young man's bright hair. She yanked him forward, drove her head hard into his forehead, then thrust him away as she pivoted hard to her left. Up came her right knee, slamming hard into his gut. As he folded with a soft "*oof!*" of surprise and pain, Arilyn changed directions and spun again, bringing her right forearm down hard on the back of his neck. Down he went—senseless, but with no lasting damage.

"A shame," observed a deep, faintly amused voice behind her. "And me having such high hopes for the lad. He hasn't his father's luck with the ladies, that's for sure and certain."

Arilyn spun and looked up into the bewhiskered face of the captain. "Oh, no. Not your son?"

"Maiden voyage," agreed Macumail with a wry grin, "and you should pardon the expression. Don't look so worried. The lad is well enough, though he'll have Umberlee's own tempest raging in his head come morning. Let him sleep it off, while we speak of other matters. My cabin?"

Arilyn nodded and allowed the captain to lead her into an usually large and luxurious cabin furnished with an enormous bed sufficient to Macumail's size and girth, a brass-bound chest, a small writing table, and a pair of chairs. As Arilyn took a seat, she was suddenly conscious of the puddle her dripping clothes left on Macumail's Turmish carpet.

"Drink this. It'll help stave off the chill," the captain said cheerfully as he handed her a goblet of wine.

She accepted it and sipped, then placed the goblet on the sea chest. "I've reconsidered your offer."

"I was hoping you might," he said with equal candor and then grinned. "You charmed word of my whereabouts from our little friend Suldusk, I take it?"

Arilyn shrugged away his teasing. Her methods had been abrupt, even by her standards, but the stakes in her quest were too high, and too personal, to allow room for regrets or time for diplomacy.

"Would you carry my answer—and my terms—to Amlaruil of Evermeet? And can you duplicate her commission? I'm in a hurry, but I'll need as good a forgery as you can manage."

"No need for that," Macumail said. He took a sheet of parchment from the pile on his writing table and handed it to her. Arilyn scanned the Elvish script; it seemed to be a duplicate of the document she had destroyed.

"The genuine article," the captain avowed. "Lady Laeral insisted that I carry a spare copy or two. And as for terms, the queen has authorized me to promise, on her behalf, any payment you might request."

"Such wisdom and foresight," Arilyn murmured dryly, still studying the parchment in her hands. "I'm seldom paid with blank promissory notes, though the benefits of time saved should be apparent to all."

When she was satisfied that the elven queen's offer was genuine and that all was in order, Arilyn put the parchment on the table and lifted her eyes to her host. "Can you take me back to Zazesspur? At once?"

In response, Macumail rose from his chair and tugged at the bellpull hanging against one polished wall. "My dear lady, I am entirely at your service. You know, of course, that the docks are chained off until dawn."

"Dawn's good," Arilyn agreed.

"There is a cabin next to mine. It is empty this voyage, and you are more than welcome to rest there. You might find some dry garments in the large sea chest that will do until morning. If you need anything else, you've only to ask."

Arilyn's face relaxed into a grateful smile, one that transformed her face and brought an answering—and familiar—spark to the captain's blue eyes.

The half-elf suppressed a sigh. Perhaps the captain was acting at the behest of the elven queen, but by all reports his fondness for elf women did not begin and end with Amlaruil. It did not surprise Arilyn to hear that the guest cabin boasted a feminine wardrobe, and she did not doubt that she would find a number of garments that would fit her elven frame. Rumors suggested that the green elf druid was not the only elf woman who had found a place in Macumail's heart. Furthermore, the glint in his eyes suggested he would not be averse to adding a half-elf to his collection of fondly held memories. Not wishing to pursue this path, Arilyn thanked her host and rose to follow the cabin boy who came promptly to the ring of Macumail's bell.

The captain watched her go and waited until he heard the bolt of her cabin door slide shut. Then he seated himself at his writing table and took up the parchment Arilyn had left there. Slowly, laboriously, he read the Elvish script to the place where the queen's ambassador was named.

Macumail opened a small drawer beneath his table and took from it a tiny bottle of ink. It was of elven make, a rare deep-purple hue fashioned from a mixture of berries and flowers that grew only on Evermeet. Carefully he unstoppered the bottle and dipped a quill into the precious fluid. With painstaking care, he added a few tiny curves and lines to the Elvish script.

It was fortunate, Macumail thought as he sprinkled the parchment with drying powder, that the Elvish words for Moonblade and Moonflower were so similar in appearance.

The captain had heard from Laeral the tale of the elf-gate and the deep sorrow it had brought to Queen Amlaruil. Having witnessed the sadness in the queen's eyes and mourned it for love of her, Macumail was loath to do anything that might bring additional pain to the wondrous elven monarch.

Yet Macumail also held the half-elven fighter in high

regard, and he understood the importance of the task
before her. And he knew, as well as any human alive, the
difficulty that would face Arilyn in the shadows of
Tethir.

He himself had loved a woman of the forest, a green
elf druid whose strange, fey ways had left him mystified
much of the time. But from his elven love he had
learned enough about the forest folk to suspect that the
People of Tethir would reject a half-elven ambassador
and perhaps even slay her. Passing as a full-blooded elf
was never easy for the half-elven, not even for one as
resourceful as Arilyn. Macumail had therefore devised
a strategy that might help her do just that.

Elven naming customs were endlessly complicated.
Although it was not unusual for an elf to take on a sur-
name that spoke of a particular skill or weapon— names
such as Snowrunner or Oakstaff or Ashenbow—these
descriptive titles were for common use: a name to use
during travels, or to give acquaintances or outsiders,
especially dwarves and humans. Among themselves,
however, elves considered the giving of a family name
and the recitation of lineage to be a vital step in formal
exchanges. For Arilyn to identify herself to an elven tribe
by only the sword she carried would be an egregious
breach of protocol. It would almost certainly shout that
her claim as Evermeet's ambassador was spurious. In her
case this was particularly true, for moonblades were
known to be hereditary swords, and a refusal to identify
herself by family would be regarded by the elves as a bla-
tant, arrogant admission that she was not what she
claimed to be. And that, Macumail noted wryly, would go
over in elven society about as well as an ogrish daughter-
in-law.

With this in mind, the captain had decided to *give*
Arilyn a family name and an ancient lineage—all with
a few small strokes of a quill pen. His opinion that these
honors were truly hers to claim eased his mind somewhat. Nor did he doubt that the borrowed glamour of

the royal family would drape a protective mantle over the half-elven woman and silence many questions before they were spoken. And after all, it was well known that of all the races of elves, moon people were most like humans!

The elves of Tethir's forest were insular, but they knew that no half-elves were allowed on Evermeet, and it would not occur to them that a half-elf would be permitted to carry the name of the royal family. A missive from Amlaruil's own hand, claiming Arilyn as her descendant, would settle the matter. It was not a ploy that would enter the proud half-elf's mind, nor would she agree to it if the captain explained his intentions.

To Macumail's way of thinking, they were much akin, the elven queen and the not-quite-elven swordmistress.

"Forgive me, my ladies," he murmured as he rolled the parchment and slipped it into a tube. "And may the gods grant that broad and stormy seas lie between me and either one of you when you learn what I've done!"

* * * * *

True to his word, Captain Macumail had Arilyn back in Zazesspur before sunrise. Her last day in the Tethyrian city flew by, for there was still much to do before she left for the forest. Arrangements long in the making had to be confirmed, messages sent, materials gathered.

There was one personal detail, however, that Arilyn left off attending for as long as she could. She could not leave Zazesspur without word to her Harper partner, nor would she inform him of her going by note or messenger. Yet she was reluctant to face the young nobleman. Danilo would understand at once the danger of her mission, and he would not accept lightly what might well be a final leave-taking between them. Worse, the stubborn fool might even devise a way to follow her!

But when the hour of evenfeast approached, Arilyn prepared herself to enter Danilo's world. She dressed

herself in her one fine gown, a simple shift of deep blue
silk with an embroidered overgown that was draped
and sashed in a manner that hid her weapon belt, yet
gave her quick access to her moonblade. Arilyn
arranged her hair so that it covered her pointed ears
and applied a bit of rosy ointment to add a more human
tint to her white skin. As a final touch, one that would
give her an aura of wealth and grant her instant admission to the posh festhouses and taverns that her partner frequented, Arilyn slipped gold-and-sapphire rings
onto several of her fingers and fastened a matching jeweled pin onto her bodice.

Danilo had a passion for fine gems and an apparent
desire to see her covered with them. After nearly three
years, Arilyn had amassed quite a collection. She had
declined his first few offerings, but he'd made it a point
to learn of elven festivals and special days so that he
could press his tokens upon her when it was hardest for
her to refuse. Among Danilo's annoying traits—and
these were numerous—was his ability to circumvent, if
not forestall, nearly any feminine objection. Nor did it
escape Arilyn's notice that she possessed a much
sterner resistance to his charms than many of the
women of Zazesspur did. Or the women of Waterdeep,
for that matter. Or Baldur's Gate, or . . .

With a sigh, Arilyn banished this unprofitable line of
thought. She climbed into her hired carriage and settled
down for a long evening. Danilo customarily took his
evening meal at one of several festhalls or taverns—at
her insistence, never in any predictable pattern. Thus it
might be some time before she would find him.

The first stop was the Hanging Garden, a tavern
fashioned to reflect the tastes and preferences of
Zazesspur's current ruler. Arilyn was not fond of the
place—it was too much like being in Calimport for her
liking—but Danilo came here frequently to enjoy the
quality of the wine and the music. Traveling bards, as
well as local musicians, performed nightly.

As a hostess dressed in filmy silk draperies ushered the disguised Harper to a table, the strains of a harp mingled with the sounds of soft conversation. As was the current fashion, the harpist played the melody of a ballad through once before joining the strings in song. There was something vaguely familiar about the tune. Arilyn was not one to give much heed to tavern performers, but she listened carefully when the singer—a young woman with the olive skin and dark hair common to natives of Tethyr—began the ballad.

The melody was catchy but common enough, the rippling chords of the harp pleasant but not especially clever, the singer's voice a clear but unremarkable soprano. In all, the music deserved to be no more than an agreeable backdrop to conversation. Yet by the time the ballad entered its third stanza, the Tethyrian woman sang into complete and utter silence.

Arilyn was no bard, but she understood full well the impact of the song. It told a story she knew all too well, even though the facts had been changed to conceal certain secrets and to glorify the alleged hero of the ballad, a nobleman and a bard who had done a great service to the Harpers by bringing to justice—single-handedly, if the ballad was to be believed—the gold elf assassin who caused the deaths of twenty and more of Those Who Harped. As Arilyn watched the listening patrons, she had no doubt that their sympathies fell firmly on the side of the gold elf killer!

Harpers were not welcome in troubled Zazesspur, and Harper heroes were hardly an acceptable subject for tavern tales. A visiting bard might possibly be forgiven for a social blunder of this magnitude, but Arilyn could think of only one reason why a Tethyrian-born singer would risk performing such a ballad: as a dramatic prelude to exposing a Harper in their midst.

Arilyn carefully painted an expression of disdain on her face and rose from her table. She slowly left the tavern, forcing herself to move with the languid stroll of a wealthy lady who had no more compelling purpose than to remove herself from a performance that did not suit her tastes and political inclinations.

She held her sedate pace until she'd reached the dimly lit side street where her hired carriage awaited her. Arilyn tossed a couple of coins to the driver and cut the traces that held her own mare to the carriage. She hiked up her skirts and leaped onto the horse's back. The mare seemed to sense her mistress's urgency, for she fairly flew over the streets that led to the assassins' guildhouse.

Normally Arilyn would have gone back to a safe room to change from her disguise and would have made several additional stops to distract any who might make a connection between the rarified world of high society and the guild of hired killers. She dared not take time for such precautions now. At dusk, the assassins of Zazesspur gathered to bid on the new assignments that were posted nightly. If this ballad had been widely sung, Danilo's name might well be among them.

Seven

Arilyn left the assassins' Council Hall with a large gold coin clamped in her fist and dread chilling her heart. The situation was worse than she had feared. The damning tavern song had spread through the city like lice, and a commission had been placed upon the life of the bard mentioned in the ballad.

Unlike most assignments, this one offered a fee to all and sundry who wished to take up the challenge. A half-dozen fighters had been hired to ensure that no single assassin removed the paper and hoarded the assignment for himself. Apparently speed was of more concern than money. There were many wealthy men and women in Tethyr who would pay dearly to swiftly eliminate even the possibility of Harper involvement in their multi-layered affairs.

Danilo's name had not been mentioned on the pronouncement, but Arilyn knew that the highly skilled assassins of the guild would not need much time to discover his identity. The fact that she had been the first to read the pronouncement did little to ease her mind.

She hurried to her room in the women's guildhouse, changed into her working clothes, and quickly packed her saddlebags with the things she needed for her mission. It was unlikely she would have an opportunity to return.

Without a backward glance at the complex that had been her home for several months, Arilyn rode as swiftly as she dared down the streets that led into the city's most fashionable quarter. Even so, she took a few twists and turns to make certain she was not being followed. Each one took her closer to the Purple Minotaur, the finest and most costly inn in all of Zazesspur.

The half-elf reined her mare to a stop several blocks away from her destination, for she could hardly ride up to the white marble walls that surrounded the garden courtyard and present herself at the arched gate. Assassins were heartily respected in this city, but that regard did not extend to social settings. Many of the Minotaur's guests were wealthy and powerful men—likely recipients of an assassin's blade. The guards posted at the inn's gate were about as likely to give Arilyn access to these guests as poultry farmers would be to invite a fox to dine at will among their hens.

And so Arilyn left her horse—and a handful of silver pieces—at a public stable in the care of an enterprising lad who had a talent for averting his eyes at precisely the right moment. While the boy tended to her mare, Arilyn climbed the ladder that led into the stable's hayloft. A large pile of straw leaned against one wall; this she climbed to the top. The half-elf studied the rough ceiling carefully, then she pulled her sword and used it to push open the nearly invisible trapdoor. She leaped up and grabbed the edge. Quickly she hauled herself up and crawled out onto the flat, tiled roof of the stable.

After replacing the trapdoor, Arilyn stood and surveyed the many levels of the city laid out before her. The

rooftops of Zazesspur offered a landscape of their own.
Here were paths well-worn by the feet of those who did
business in darkness. Although she had been in the city
but a few months, Arilyn knew these pathways as well
as most of Zazesspur's citizens knew the streets.

Between her and the soaring palace known as the
Purple Minotaur lay a festhall, two taverns, the homes
of several shopkeepers, the stables that served the posh
inn, and the humble dwellings used for the servants
and slaves who tended the pampered guests. With practiced ease, Arilyn made her way from rooftop to rooftop.

As she neared the Purple Minotaur, she glanced
toward the upper floors of the inn and noticed that
Danilo's window was flung open to admit the summer
night's breeze—and possibly in the hope of an unexpected visit. From the open window wafted the gentle
strains of a lute accompanying a well-trained tenor
voice.

Arilyn's first response was relief. Danilo was yet safe.
For a moment she paused to listen to the faint song and
the carefree singer who seemed far removed from the
sordid reality of the squalid streets.

For some reason, this solidified Arilyn's resolve. What
she intended to do this night would not be easy, but it
was a needed thing.

A sliver of new moon rose high into the sky as Arilyn
crept across the roof of the Purple Minotaur, but its feeble
light was veiled by the thick sea mist that settled in with
the coming of night. On the street far below, dim circles
of light clung to the street lanterns, and faint light spilled
from the windows of the festhalls and gambling parlors
on the lower floors of the building. But where she trod, all
was darkness. Danilo's chamber was only two floors
down from the roof, a location chosen to allow Arilyn to
make her infrequent visits with discretion.

Indeed, her slender figure was barely discernible
against the dark sky. The pale skin of her face had been
smudged with dark ointment, and she wore the garb of

an assassin: leggings and a loose shirt of an indistinct
dark hue that seemed to absorb shadow. In the mist-
laden air her black curls clung to her head in damp ten-
drils, and her only ornament was the sash of pale gray
silk at her waist.

Arilyn took a rope of spider silk from her pack and
affixed one end firmly to the nearest chimney. She crept
to the roof's edge and counted carefully down the rope's
knotted length. Holding the rope firmly, she backed up,
took a few running steps, and flung herself as far out
into the darkness as she could.

As she dropped, she braced herself, accepted the jolting tug that came when the rope snapped taut. Then
she swung like a pendulum toward the open window,
shifting her weight a bit to adjust her course. At the last
possible moment, she pulled up into a tight tuck.

The agile half-elf cleared the window. In one smooth
move she released the rope and pulled a dagger from
her boot, and then landed in a crouch. Her blue eyes
swept the room, checking for danger. Satisfied that all
was well, she stood and faced her Harper partner.

The young nobleman had apparently expected her,
for he stood facing the window, a smile of welcome lighting his gray eyes and a goblet of elverquisst in each
hand.

Arilyn had known Danilo Thann for almost three
years now, but she had yet to reconcile herself to the
disparity between his public persona and the man she
had come to know. Few saw him as anything more than
the youngest son of a Waterdhavian noble, a dandy and
a dilettante who dabbled in magic and music. It took a
keen ear to hear the artistry beneath the bawdy little
ballads he composed, a sharp eye to note the ease with
which he tossed off his "miscast" spells. But few people
were inclined to seek deeply, and as a handsome
charmer blessed with a noble's rank and a merchant's
heavy purse, Danilo was welcomed in circles that a half-
elven assassin could not hope to enter. Although Arilyn

recognized the worth of this disguise, the contrast between Danilo's appearance and his true nature did not, for one moment, cease to irritate her.

As was his recent custom, he was clad entirely in shades of purple—the traditional color of Tethyr—and bedecked with a small fortune in gold-and-amethyst jewelry. Arilyn had told him more than once that this affectation made him look like a walking grape, but in truth the opulent color suited him well.

Everything about the young man and his setting bespoke wealth, ease, and privilege. The room behind him was vast and luxurious, although a bit cluttered with the trappings of his public and personal endeavors. One long table was heavily laden with goblets and bottles of fine wine—a testament to his current role as a member of Tethyr's guild of wine merchants. Spellbooks were scattered across a reading table of Chultan teak, and the small crystal scrying globe on the table near the window was but one of many magic devices that protected the room and its occupant. The chamber's hand-knotted carpet—rendered in shades of purple, of course—was heaped with tapestry pillows. Lying among them was the lute Danilo had set aside, an exquisite instrument inlaid with darker woods and mother-of-pearl. Beside the lute was his swordbelt, which held not only his rapier, but an ancient sword in a bejeweled scabbard. A magic weapon, Arilyn guessed, noting the distinctive curved pommel that marked it as a sword of Halruaan make.

All this she took in with a single sweeping glance. Noted, too, was the sudden intense flash, quickly hidden, that came into the young man's eyes as his gaze swept over her. Arilyn knew her partner's perception and attention to detail at least equaled her own, and for a moment she wondered what he saw in a disheveled, too-thin, half-elven assassin that could kindle such a flame.

"Lovely night for second-story work," Danilo observed

in a casual tone as he handed her a goblet. "That jump
was most impressive. But tell me, have you ever mis-
calculated the rope's length?"

Arilyn shook her head, then absently tossed back the
contents of her goblet. "We're leaving Tethyr," she
stated, plunking her empty goblet down on Danilo's
table.

He placed his own goblet beside hers. "Oh?" he asked
warily.

"Someone has placed a bounty on your head," Arilyn
said in a grim tone as she handed him the heavy gold
coin. "These were given to any assassin willing to take
on the job. One hundred more to whoever makes the
kill."

Danilo hefted the coin in a practiced hand and then
let out a long, low whistle. The coin was about three
times the normal trade weight. The amount Arilyn had
named was a substantial sum, one likely to tempt even
high-ranking assassins to take on the assignment. But
the young Harper did not seem concerned by the danger. He examined the gold piece with the detachment of
a coin collector, running admiring fingers over the
embossed pattern of runes and symbols.

"It would seem I'm attracting a better class of enemies these days," he observed wryly.

"Listen to me!" Arilyn snapped, clasping both his fore-
arms and giving him a little shake. "I heard someone
singing your ballad about the Harper assassin."

"Merciful Milil," he swore softly, and Arilyn saw
understanding dawning in his eyes.

Danilo had written the ballad about their first adventure together. He hadn't performed it in over two years
and certainly had the sense not to sing it in Tethyr.
Although the song did not identify him as a Harper,
even a mention of those "meddling Northern barbar-
ians" could create a good deal of resentment and suspicion in this troubled land. Woven into the ballad were
hints concerning Danilo's identity, and the careful

listener could soon ascertain that the hero and the composer were one. He had written the song to convince Arilyn that he was a vain and vapid courtier, and it had effectively served its purpose. But the fact that it was being sung here in Tethyr would force a rapid end to their mission. The young Harper contemplated the loss of all this work with a rueful smile.

"The locals express their musical preferences rather forcefully, wouldn't you say?" he commented lightly.

Before Arilyn could draw breath for an exasperated rejoinder, Danilo silenced her with an apologetic smile and an uplifted hand. "I'm sorry, my dear. Force of habit. You're right, of course. We must ride north at once."

"No."

She reached out and touched one of Danilo's rings—a magical gift from his uncle, Khelben Arunsun, that could teleport up to three people back to the safety of Blackstaff Tower, or elsewhere if the wielder so chose.

Arilyn hated magical travel; in her mind, it was a choice of last resort. The knowledge of this was written clearly in Danilo's eyes. Understanding her urgency, he quickly donned his swordbelt and affixed to it the magic bag that held his wardrobe and travel supplies. He added three spellbooks to the bag and then absently dropped in the assassin's coin. With one hand he snatched up his lute; with the other he reached out to Arilyn.

She took a step backward and shook her head. "I'm not coming with you."

"Arilyn, this is no time to be squeamish!"

"It's not that." She took a deep breath, for the words were harder to say than she had imagined possible. "Word came from Waterdeep. I've been assigned another mission. I leave in the morning."

Danilo's eyes widened. For a moment, Arilyn glimpsed in them the poignant longing that he was so careful to hide from her. Then, deftly, his expression changed to portray the pique of a spoiled nobleman who

was unaccustomed to events that strayed from the path
of his preference. His eyes betrayed nothing but
incredulity that the Master Harpers would presume to
separate them. It was a fine performance. Arilyn, however, was not fooled.

But before she could speak, the alarm on Danilo's
magical scrying globe began to pulse again. The half-elf
snatched up the crystal and peered into it. The scene
within showed three shadowy figures moving toward
the edge of the roof, just two stories above them. Some
of Arilyn's colleagues were coming to collect their prize.

She tossed the alarm aside and cast a glace toward
the open window and the nearly invisible rope outside.
"There's no time to explain," she told him. "Go!"

But Danilo, who had also taken a good look into the
crystal, shook his head. "And leave you to face them
alone? Not bloody likely."

Arilyn attempted a smile and touched the gray silk
sash that proclaimed her rank among Tethyr's assassins. "I'm one of them, remember? I'll say that you were
gone. No one will challenge me."

"Of course they will," he snapped, for he well knew
how Tethyr's assassins rose through the ranks. Arilyn
was aware that her partner had paid out large sums to
keep apprised of her dark and solitary path. She'd been
able to keep news of many of her adventures from him,
but he knew she'd been forced more than once to defend
her reluctantly worn sash from ambitious fellow assassins. There were three of them now, and if she was
alone, they would almost certainly seize the opportunity
to attack her. Which of them would eventually possess
her Shadow Sash would be a matter they'd settle among
themselves at a later time.

The rope she'd left hanging outside Danilo's window
began to sway as someone inched down it toward his
room. "Go," Arilyn pleaded.

"Come with me," he demanded in an implacable tone.

The half-elf shook her head, cursing the streak of

steel that hid behind Danilo's foppish persona. She knew it well, and knew also that there was little chance of reasoning with him once his mind was set.

Predictably enough, the Harper tossed aside his priceless lute without thought or care, and pulled her into his arms.

"If you think I'd leave you, you're a bigger fool than I am," he said quickly, angrily, his words racing against the approaching danger. "This is hardly the moment I'd have chosen to mention this, but damn it, woman, I love you."

"I know," Arilyn replied softly, clinging to him in turn. For a single, intense second, she let her eyes speak her heart. Then she eased out of his arms and lifted one hand to stroke his cheek. It was the first such acknowledgment, the first caressing gesture, she had ever offered him. His eyes darkened as he cupped her hand in both of his and pressed her fingers to his lips in a fervent kiss.

Leaving his midsection conveniently unguarded.

Arilyn doubled her free hand into a fist and drove it hard into a point slightly below his rib cage. Danilo folded and went down like a felled oak.

As the winded nobleman struggled to draw breath, the half-elf stooped and twisted the ring of teleportation on his hand that would send him back to Waterdeep and safety.

He lunged for her wrist, obviously intending to drag her along, but Arilyn was already on her feet. The moonblade, glowing the intense blue that warned of approaching battle, hissed free from her scabbard as Danilo faded from view, one hand outstretched for her and naked anguish written on his face.

Although she'd seen no other way to save her would-be lover, Arilyn's necessary act of treachery left her feeling shaken and strangely empty. She took a long, ragged breath and turned to face the trio of Tethyrian assassins, feeling a certain grim comfort at the thought of impending battle.

That, at least, was something she understood.

Eight

The spider-silk rope swayed as Ferret worked her way down toward the Harper's open window, cursing silently as she went.

The female assassin had encountered many frustrations during her sojourn in Zazesspur, not the least of which was the odd fact that under Pasha Balik's rule, men enjoyed social dominance. It was, in her opinion, a folly beyond comprehension. Ferret only hoped this bit of stupidity didn't cause her to lose her quarry! Had she gone first, she'd be down already, and her task would be done. But no—the two men had to proceed her.

For a moment Ferret entertained the idea of stomping on the head of the man below her and knocking him off the rope. She would have done so gladly, but for the fact that he was unlikely to oblige her by falling to his death in silence!

Indeed, only the need for stealth had kept her from battling the two other assassins who had converged on the rooftop with such inconvenient speed. All three had realized the folly of such action, and they'd agreed to cooperate for a quick kill and a share of the reward. But once they were all within Danilo Thann's chamber, Ferret would gladly turn her blade against them to defend the man she had been hired to kill. Perhaps doing so would pique the Harper's interest and convince him to listen to her tale and perhaps to help her.

Seeking aid from humans and Harpers! Ferret could think of no surer sign of her desperation than this.

But what else was she to do? Her skills were many and considerable, but there were things at work in Zazesspur that she simply could not comprehend. A chance-heard tavern song had sparked an idea: who better to solve this puzzle than a Harper, a member of that legendary tribe of spies, informants, and meddlers? It was unfortunate that a contract had been placed upon this particular Harper, for if Danilo Thann bred true to type, he would surely be able to find his way to the source of the problem. That was all Ferret needed. She knew what had to be done, but she needed to know who to do it *to!*

At last the first of the male assassins ducked in through the Harper's window. Ferret heard his startled oath and then the first bright clash of steel on steel. She prodded the man below her with her boot.

"Hurry, or Samir will make the kill by himself and claim the full reward," she demanded, speaking the words most likely to coax haste from the assassin.

Her reasoning was sound; the avaricious man slid the rest of the way down the rope and virtually dove into the room.

With her way now clear, Ferret let go of the rope and fell the last several feet. As she passed the open window, she grabbed the sill and pulled herself up to it with all her might. She tumbled through, tucked her head down, rolled into the room, and came up on her feet, a long dagger already in her hand. Ready—or so she thought— for anything.

The sight before her stole her breath and froze her feet to the lush carpet.

An eldritch blue light filled the room, tossing the dancing shadows of three fighters against every wall of the chamber. The source of the light was a living moonblade, and it was held in the two hands of a half-elven assassin.

Like a hero from some ancient elven legend, Arilyn stood firm against her two attackers, beating back every thrust and slash of their wickedly curved scimitars. Her magical sword flashed and spun, leaving dizzy ribbons of blue light to mark its path.

A moonblade, Ferret thought dazedly. A true, living moonblade!

She knew the half-elf carried such a sword and even presumed to take her name from it, but Ferret had assumed the weapon had been dormant for centuries, and that Arilyn had purchased it from some ignorant peddler, or plundered it from some ancient elven tomb. Moonblades were hereditary swords of fearsome magic, and according to legend, none but moon elves of true blood and noble spirit could wield them. To see such a weapon in the hands of a half-elf—and a hired killer—raised implications that staggered Ferret's imagination.

Just then Arilyn's blazing eyes settled on the new intruder. Instinctively Ferret lifted her dagger into a defensive position.

Just in time. With the speed of a striking snake, the half-elf whirled on the nearest man and feinted high. As he lifted his blade, she spun away in a quick, tight circle and then ducked in under her opponent's defensive parry. She lunged past him toward the female assassin, her glowing sword leading with deadly intent.

The elven sword struck Ferret's parrying dagger with a force that sent bright sparks of pain dancing up her arm to explode in her head like festival fireworks. The half-elf's intent was apparent: in a battle against greater odds, it was wise to eliminate the most dangerous opponent first, and quickly. In some corner of her mind, Ferret reminded herself that a moonblade could not shed innocent blood. She was not, however, convinced of her safety. The path she had taken was a needed thing, but it may have tarnished her in the sentient sword's perception.

Fortunately for her, the two men recovered from their surprise and closed in on the half-elf. They charged at her, scimitars aloft, fueling their attack with yells of bloodlust. Without turning, Arilyn lifted her moonblade high overhead and met the first downward strike. At the same time she kicked forward; her booted foot caught Ferret in the gut with a force that folded the smaller female over and sent her staggering back into a table. In the next heartbeat the half-elf pivoted, using the momentum of her turn to press the joined blades toward the second attacker. The three swords met with a ringing clash. Arilyn pulled hers free of the tangle and danced back. Her gaze again settled upon the female.

Ferret saw her own death in the half-elf's eyes and knew that her next action would either be brilliant, or it would be her last.

The ache in the assassin's lower ribs gave her inspiration: she bit down hard on the inside of her cheek, hard enough to draw blood.

Pressing one hand against her rib cage, Ferret let out a groan. As she did, bloody foam spilled onto her lips. She wiped it off, regarded her hand with dawning horror, and then fixed a venomous glare upon the half-elf. Slowly, she slid down, the table's edge scraping her back, until she lay crumpled on the floor, clutching her ribs and moaning softly. Seeing that the female was down for good, Arilyn turned away to face the other assassins.

Ferret was not surprised that the half-elf accepted her performance as genuine. In her time as an assassin, Ferret had seen enough men die, in enough ways, to know exactly what the process looked like. A kick like that could have broken a rib, which in turn could have pierced a lung. Death by drowning was the inevitable, albeit slow, result of such an injury. But what *did* surprise Ferret was the flash of compassion that came into Arilyn Moonblade's eyes as she realized the manner of death she had dealt. It was just as well for Ferret that the half-elf was otherwise engaged, or she might well have granted her fallen adversary a quick and merciful end.

Better die quickly, Ferret admonished herself with a touch of grim humor.

Lying as still as she could, the assassin closed her eyes to mere slits and watched the battle from beneath the thick curtain of her lashes.

Ferret had to admit that her half-elven enemy was brilliant in battle. She had never seen anyone who possessed a surer knowledge of the sword. Yet much of what Arilyn did seemed to be pure instinct. She seemed to sense when and how the next strike would come, and she was quick enough to keep a step ahead of both her opponents.

In fact, the speed and force of her strike seemed all out of proportion with her size. Granted, the half-elf was tall, and her slender form had an elf's surprising resilience and strength, but those things could not account for the power of her fighting. Ferret wondered what secrets lay behind the glowing aura of the half-elf's moonblade.

Just then Arilyn's sword dove in past Samir's guard and buried itself in his throat. She pulled the moonblade down hard, thrusting deeper as she went, sweeping through bone and sinew with terrifying ease. Ferret suppressed a wince as the elven blade cleaved the man from gizzard to groin.

Seeing an opportunity in his comrade's death, the other man grinned wolfishly and raised his scimitar high overhead for the killing strike. To add force to the blow—and perhaps in unconscious imitation of his half-elven foe—he gripped the blade with both hands and began the downward slash.

But his intended victim had other plans. Arilyn tore the blade free of the assassin's body and continued its downward cut. The sword gained momentum as she traced a sweeping circle back and around. As the elven sword reached the zenith of its swing, Arilyn spun to face the surviving assassin and stepped hard into the attack.

The two blades met with a shriek of metal. Arilyn ducked aside instinctively as jagged shards flew from the man's ruined scimitar.

With a hiss of rage, the assassin lunged at her with the ragged stub of blade that remained to him, apparently hoping to catch her while she was still off-balance.

The half-elf nimbly side-stepped the attack. She pivoted in a quick circle and brought the flat of her sword down hard on the man's outstretched arm, striking him just below the elbow. Immediately she dropped to one knee, using the moonblade as a lever and forcing the man's elbow to bend down. The jagged end of his blade turned upward; the momentum of his charge did the rest. The assassin stumbled forward as the broken scimitar plunged through his own throat.

Arilyn rose, sliding the bloody moonblade from the crook of the dead man's arm. The sword's magical blue fire slowly faded away, apparently quenched by the blood it had shed. The half-elf stooped and wiped the blade clean on the fallen assassin's shirt, then slid the sword firmly into its ancient scabbard.

Without a backward glance, she turned and strode to the open window. She climbed up the rope, hand over hand, and disappeared into the night sky.

For several silent moments Ferret lay where she had fallen, busily sorting through all she had seen. Very little of it made sense to her.

Arilyn was half-elven, yet she possessed a moonblade. She had taken an assassin's path, yet the sword continued to do her bidding. Was it possible the sword's magic had somehow been perverted to evil? Or was Arilyn, like Ferret herself, something very different from what she appeared to be?

And what of Danilo Thann? According to the intelligence Ferret had gathered, the nobleman was in the Purple Minotaur. Minutes before, she herself had heard his voice lifted in song. Where, then, had he gone? And what part did Arilyn play in this mystery?

Of one thing Ferret was certain: she needed the Harper, and if he was still within her reach she would find him. It grated on the proud female that the key to her success seemed to be in the hands of the half-breed fighter.

When she judged the time to be right, Ferret rose and crept silently to the window. The rope was gone, of course, and so was the half-elf.

No matter. Ferret was no stranger to climbing, and her slender, nimble fingers could find a hold in nearly any surface. She was also a hunter who could track a hare through the densest thicket or follow a squirrel's path through the forest canopy. No mere half-elf could elude her, not even in the relatively unfamiliar terrain of this crowded human city.

Setting her jaw in a determined angle, the female slipped from the window and followed Arilyn out into the night.

*   *   *   *   *

"A dream," muttered Prince Hasheth, trying to dismiss the faint, insistent thumping that roused him from slumber. He rolled over and buried deeper into his pillows, imperiously willing sleep to return and the annoying dream to vanish.

But no, there was that sound again, and it was coming from the secret door that led into his chamber. Hasheth listened and recognized the rhythm of an agreed-upon signal.

Grumbling and still drowsy, he batted aside the filmy

curtains surrounding his bed. He stumbled over to the hearth and pressed the latch hidden among the stones. As he expected, the half-elven Harper burst into the room as the heavy door swung open. Judging from the look in her eyes and the grim set of her face, Hasheth doubted that she had come to take him up on his offer of an evening's entertainment.

"It's time," Arilyn said. "I leave Zazesspur now."

"First thing in the morning," Hasheth agreed, responding to the urgency in her voice.

"No. *Now.*"

The prince threw both hands into the air and cast an exasperated glare skyward, but he knew better than to argue with Arilyn Moonblade. Young though he might be, he was quickly learning how to measure the men— and the women—around him. Hasheth would no sooner try to reason with this headstrong woman than he would attempt to discuss philosophy with a camel.

And he *had* agreed to help her—he'd even seen to most of the preparations. Honoring his word was important. Hasheth knew that the measure of a man was not necessarily the sharpness of his blade or his wit, not the sum of the wealth he possessed or the rank he could claim. The true measure of a man was the weight his word carried. Someday, Hasheth planned to wield enough power to send men into frenzied compliance to his every command. For the present, and with this woman, he wished to be known as a man of honor, a trusted and important part of her interesting, clandestine plans. And besides, Lord Hhune had bid him to gain the trust of the Harpers.

Hasheth reached for a bellpull and gave it an imperious tug. A young servant appeared promptly at the door, rubbing sleep from his eyes. The prince handed the lad a sealed note. Explanations were not needed; the servant had been schooled at great length and knew precisely what must be done. The note would go to another contact, who would set in motion a well-planned chain of events. Hasheth had been a willing apprentice to the Harper, and he had learned much.

"The boat?" she demanded.

"All is in readiness," the prince assured her. "I will slip from the palace, get one of the horses I've boarded at the public stable, and ride for the southern gate. When it opens at dawn, we will both join a certain trade caravan and ride south to the Sulduskoon River, I as a representative of Hhune's shipping interests, you dressed as a courtesan employed to sweeten my journey. When we reach the river you will slip away. After the caravan's alleged business is completed, I will see your mare safely to the tinker's hidden lair while you travel upriver to a destination that you have not seen fit to share with your trusted ally."

Arilyn responded to this recitation only with a curt nod of approval. To Hasheth's pointed attempt to pry information from her, she responded not at all.

"At dawn, then," she said and ducked through the low doorway.

Hasheth listened to the faint sound of her boots on the narrow stairs and marveled anew that she did not stumble and fall in the darkness. The door was hidden in the stone of the hearth that warmed his room on chill nights, and the tunnel itself was chiseled into the thick walls of the palace. He wondered what his father, the pasha, would say if he knew that an assassin of Arilyn's rank could enter the palace almost at will.

Nothing good, Hasheth concluded with a tight smile. He closed the door and began his hasty preparations for the journey ahead. Of late, the pasha had not had many good words to spare the restless young man and had not been pleased with Hasheth's request to enter the service of Lord Hhune, yet in time he agreed to arrange it simply to silence his troublesome younger son.

It amazed Hasheth that his father could not see the importance of such men as Hhune, or the potential threat that their ambitions posed. He remembered the warning Arilyn had given him, and he nodded his head in grim agreement. Pasha Balik's short but spectacular reign would soon come to an end.

And that was as it should be. From his first encounter with Arilyn he had learned an important lesson: know your enemies. If Balik could not recognize his, then he deserved to fall from power.

And he, Hasheth, would find a way to benefit from this eventuality. Perhaps, he concluded as he slipped beyond the palace gates, he would even help to bring the inevitable to pass.

*   *   *   *   *

In the lush gardens that surrounded the palace grounds, nearly invisible among the branches of some exotic flowering tree, Ferret watched as the half-elf crept along in the shadow of the palace wall.

Arilyn lifted the vines that sheltered a section of wall and ran her fingers over the smooth stone. A door opened where none had been a moment before, sliding noiselessly to one side. It closed after her, and the vines fell back into place. Even to Ferret's keen eyes, there was no apparent outline, no sign that the hidden door was there.

Perched in her tree, Ferret waited patiently until the half-elf had finished her meeting and slipped away into the night. And then she waited a bit longer. The mystery that was Arilyn Moonblade could not be solved in direct confrontation. Ferret would have to piece it together as best she could. She wanted to see who else emerged from the palace.

To her surprise, the half-elf's contact was not a palace guard or a half-elven maidservant, but one of the lesser sons of the ruling pasha. Ferret remembered the lad from his ill-fated attempt to learn the assassin's trade. Now that she thought of it, she remembered that Arilyn had entered the guildhouse shortly after Hasheth had left. She had not made a connection between the two; apparently, she should have.

Ferret crept along after the young prince. Following him was easy, for in this part of town lavish gardens were the norm, and the exotic flowering trees that lined the broad streets were so closely planted that their branches entwined. She was able to follow him for several blocks without her feet once touching the ground.

At length he turned into a stable, emerging in moments on the back of a fine Amnish stallion. Ferret grimaced. She herself did not like the idea of riding upon horses, but if the boy had far to go, following him on foot might prove to be difficult.

The assassin climbed down to the street and crept into the stable. She silenced the stablehands, then quickly selected a likely-looking mare. She wrapped the animal's hooves to muffle the sound, and then, as quietly as she could, she led the horse from the stable. She climbed onto its bare back. She would ride if she had to, but no power beneath the stars could compel her to shackle an intelligent creature with saddle and bridle!

Ferret seized the horse's mane and leaned forward, whispering a few words to her in the centaur language. Apparently the mare understood the gist of it, for her ears went back and she set off at a brisk pace in pursuit of Hasheth's stallion.

*   *   *   *   *

As the long night slipped away, the deep shadows of the forest began to fade to green, heralding the coming of dawn. The elven warriors who had survived the raid picked up their pace, for the death that pursued them would travel more swiftly with the coming of light.

Exhausted, heartsick, bearing the marks of battle as well as their dead and wounded comrades, the elves retreated into their forest home. Their progress was slow, for they would not abandon their wounded and take to the trees, and they feared what use might be made of the slain elven folk. Word had reached them that Sparrow's body had been placed among the slaughtered humans of a northbound caravan and that his arrows had been used against the merchants.

The distant yapping of hunting hounds lifted into a triumphant, baying howl. "They have found a blood trail," Korrigash noted grimly. He shifted the limp body of an elven male that he carried across his shoulders, as a hunter might carry a slain deer.

Foxfire nodded, and his eyes fell upon the face of the girl he carried in his arms. Hawkwing, her name was, a new name Tamara had bestowed upon the girl to mark her acceptance into a new tribe. It suited her well; she had fought like a cornered falcon and brought down several of the humans before a coward's dagger took her through the back—from the back.

She would survive, Foxfire repeated silently, staring into her pain-bright black eyes and *willing* her to live. The tribe had need of courage and spirit such as this child possessed. Tamara had claimed Hawkwing into the Oakstaff clan. She would raise the girl, but Foxfire would train her. He knew a war leader when he saw one.

Hawkwing stirred in his arms and met his intense gaze. "Put me down," she said in a barely audible whisper. "Flee! We are too few to fight, and the People cannot bear to lose more this night than have already fallen."

"She is right," Korrigash said softly.

But Foxfire shook his head. Quickly he took stock of the forces remaining. The prospects were not good. Twenty-and-four of the elves from Talltrees could still run or fight, but only two of the rescued elves could walk without assistance. The elves carried three dead and several who were gravely wounded. There was not one among them who had escaped injury entirely. They could not stand and fight. Not as they were.

He turned to Tamara. "You are the fastest among us. Take word to Talltrees. We need as many warriors as can be spared to meet us in the fen lands south of here."

The female nodded, seeing at once the wisdom of this

plan. The elves needed to rest and treat their wounded, and no nearby haven was better for this than the low-lying fens. Always dark and cool, in this valley the forest lay under a thick mantle of mist. The massive trunks of several ancient cedars—trees that no longer lived and grew, but whose roots still held firm—had been hollowed out to make emergency shelters. Healing plants grew in abundance. And if the humans followed them so far, they would find a battleground not at all to their liking. The soil was soft, in some places dangerously boggy, and the ground was densely covered with large, fernlike plants large enough to reach an elf's shoulder.

"We must do what we can to hold back pursuit," Foxfire added. "You, Eldrin, Sontar, Wyndelleu—take to the trees and circle back. Hunt down the dogs. Stop them, and you have stopped the humans. Harry the men and herd them toward the north. Green arrows only," he admonished them.

"And you, Tamsin," he said, turning to the young fighter whose leathers were dark with blood, none of which was his own. Foxfire dared not send this one after the humans—after this night's battle, Tamsin was as blood-ravenous as a troll. "Go straight north, into the caves that lie beyond the ashenwood. Awaken the young white dragon who slumbers there and lure her out after you. Lead her to the humans; see that she is fully engaged with them. Then take to the trees and return to us."

A savage grin spread across the younger elf's face as he visualized the results of his leader's plan. "And I will leave bundles of wintermint in the dragon's lair, that she may later cleanse the foul taste of the humans from her tongue!"

The elven warriors melted into the forest to do their leader's bidding. Korrigash turned to his friend. "Good plan. But is this enough to stop them?"

"For now? Perhaps," Foxfire said in a low tone. "But not for long."

Nine

 Each morning at dawn the massive gates of Zazesspur swung open to admit the flow of commerce that was the city's lifeblood. The city's coffers benefited from tariffs placed on exotic goods that passed through on their way north from Calimshan and points east. But the markets of Zazesspur were much more than a stopping place for merchant caravans. The people of Tethyr took great pride in their craftsmanship, and their goods were in great demand in lands to the north and south.

Into the city poured the raw materials that ships and overland caravans brought from all over the known world. Chultan teak and Maztican rosewood were fashioned into the carved wooden boxes for which Tethyr was famed, and delicate contraptions of gears and tiny chimes came from Lantan to transform some of these boxes into wondrous musical toys. Fine metals from the icy Northlands were brought into the city to be worked into vessels and armor and jewelry, gems to be set into sword hilts or

ladies' rings. Tethyrian furniture was prized for its durability and elegant lines. For sheer practicality, Myratman
fabrics were considered second to none. A cloak woven
from the wool of the sheep that grazed the Purple Hills
often lasted long enough to be handed down from father
to son, and few were the weavers outside Tethyr who
could spin thread so fine that the results were nearly
waterproof.

Another form of commerce, also important to the city's
well-being if somewhat less glamorous, was the trading
for foodstuffs grown in the fertile Purple Hills south of
the city. Daily caravans traveled between Zazesspur and
Marakir, the farmers' market located at the intersection
of the Trade Way with the Sulduskoon River, to purchase
fruit and grain and mutton. It was an important task,
but a routine one, and therefore one that seldom fell
under close scrutiny.

And so it was that Quentin Llorish, the captain of one
such caravan, was none too happy to be awakened from
his slumber and informed that Lord Hhune's new
apprentice would be riding along on the day's trip.

Not that Quentin had anything against Hhune—far
from it! The lord and guildmaster paid well, and he
treated the men and women in his employ with a
degree of fairness unusual in Tethyr, which made him
quite popular among the people and purchased loyalty
more surely than would coin. At least, fair treatment
worked that way with *most* men; Quentin, frankly, preferred hard silver.

Quentin was not a man overly constrained by the
bounds of loyalty or by a compulsion for honest dealing.
He was not above skimming a thicker layer of cream
from the caravan's daily profits than that to which he
was strictly entitled. The thought of a young and eager
apprentice looking over his shoulder and thumbing
through his books made Quentin's stomach burn with
the pain that was becoming his constant companion.

And so, as he watched over the caravan's predawn

preparations and waited for the city's gates to open, Quentin sipped at a large flask of goat's milk mixed with some chalky mineral that he could not identity. It was a vile concoction, but according to the local alchemist it would in time soothe his sour stomach. If it did not, vowed Quentin grimly as he downed the last of the swill, he would gladly spend every copper of this day's profit to have the wretched alchemist slain, preferably death by drowning in goat's milk.

"Captain Quentin?" inquired an imperious voice to his left. "I am Hasheth, here on behalf of Lord Hhune."

The man let out a mighty, chalk-scented belch and turned to regard his dreaded passenger. Hhune's apprentice was a young man, probably not yet twenty years of age. Maybe a by-blow of the lord himself, judging from that dark hair, though the lad's curved nose and sun-browned skin suggested a bit of Calishite blood. Well, that was common enough in Zazesspur these days, what with the pasha and all. It was fashionable among society folk to keep a southern woman as mistress, or so Quentin had heard tell. He himself had to make due with a wife—his own, unfortunately.

"Welcome aboard, lad!" he said with a heartiness he certainly did not feel. "We'll be on our way with the dawn. Pick any horse that catches your fancy, then I'll show you what's what."

"That will hardly be necessary," Hasheth said, his lip curled with disdain. He gestured to a covered carriage pulled by paired chestnuts, beautiful, fine-boned animals whose glossy red-brown coats had been groomed to the sheen of fine sable. The carriage horses were all the more striking for the fact that they were nearly identical, even to the white stars on their foreheads. To add excess to opulence, a magnificent black stallion and a long-legged gray mare were tied behind the carriage.

"As you can see, I have brought my own conveyance as well as additional horses, should I choose to ride. As for your business, you do it well enough to suit my lord

Hhune, and that is good enough for me," the lad continued coolly. "I am required to be here as part of my education, so let us strike a deal. If you are asked, you will
report that I observed you closely. If I am asked, I will say
that all I observed was in order."

There was a slight edge to Hasheth's voice, a shrewd,
almost smug nuance that hinted the young man
already knew far too much about the caravan's affairs.
Quentin darted a look at the lad, hoping he'd heard
wrong. In response, Hasheth lifted a single eyebrow in
unmistakable challenge.

The banked flame in Quentin's gut flared up hot and
high, sending a surge of acid up into his throat.
"Agreed," the captain muttered, wishing mightily that
he could spit without offending the lordly young man.

Hasheth nodded again to the carriage and to the
veiled woman who peeked out from behind one curtain.
"You need not bother yourself with me. As you can see,
I have brought a diversion to sweeten the journey.
Which brings us to another matter. The lady has a delicate skin and a desire to see the marketplace before the
heat of highsun. I understand this requires an unusually brisk place, but my own desires would be well
served by indulging hers. May I tell her that you will
accommodate us?"

Quentin merely nodded, for this throat was feeling
too raw for speech. He watched as the imperious youth
climbed into the carriage and pulled the curtain firmly
shut; then he shook his head and strode away to tend to
the caravan. He was not at all certain what to make of
this strange encounter or of the young apprentice who
saw far too much.

When at last the morning sun broke over the distant
peaks of the Starspires, the mighty gate swung slowly
inward. By the time the caravan started off on its
journey—at an extremely brisk pace, as requested—
Quentin was feeling much better. Quite chipper, in fact!

He'd often worried about discovery, but now that it

had come he found it to be a relief. Although Quentin took his orders from Hhune's people, he had no window into the lord's affairs and no way of knowing how his own actions might be perceived—or which of them might have come before Hhune's eyes. This Hasheth was bright enough to uncover Quentin's embezzlement. Surely he could also manage to keep it from prying eyes. And better still, the lad was ready to deal. Quentin felt certain that he could persuade Hasheth to provide him a bit of protection, plus maybe pass along a bit of information from time to time that would help the caravan captain gild the inside of his pockets.

Yes, he concluded happily, Hhune's newest apprentice was someone with whom he could do business, to the profit of both!

* * * * *

"Did I chose my man well?" Hasheth inquired in a smug tone.

Arilyn nodded, perfectly willing to give the young man his due. From all that she had seen and heard, Quentin Llorish was a perfect choice, one who would no doubt continue to serve Hasheth in a dependable, if dishonorable, fashion.

In fact, her departure from Zazesspur had gone more smoothly than Arilyn would have thought possible. Every step of the agreed-upon plan had been flawlessly executed. Hasheth was good and getting better by the day.

Why, then, did she feel so ill at ease?

With a sigh, Arilyn leaned back into the cushions and steeled herself for a long morning's ride. She was none too happy about spending several hours in inactivity, with nothing to absorb her but her own troubled thoughts. Too much had happened of late, too many revelations had been thrust upon her—more than she could possibly sort **through between Zazesspur and the Sulduskoon.**

Arilyn liked to deal with problems as they arose: quickly, cleanly, decisively, with diplomacy if possible and with swift violence when necessary. Yet she had been forced to ignore her nature, her accustomed methods, and her own better judgment to tend to the elven queen's commission.

So here she was, bound for the elven forest and burdened with someone else's problems, while her own life was in utter disarray. Her ancestor slept in some rich man's vault, and Arilyn had done nothing to redress this dishonor. Danilo had declared his love for her, and she had decked him and sent him packing without so much as taking time to consider what her own eventual response should be. Then there was the matter of the elfshadow, and the bleak future that it foretold.

Arilyn could not forget for a moment the destiny inherent in the moonblade she carried and the unwitting vow she had made so many years ago when first she drew the elven sword. The half-elf had never before feared death, but she could not help but feel her mortality. She was headed toward an extremely dangerous mission, bearing a sword that would, in all likelihood, claim her in eternal servitude. To say that this added a note of urgency to her quest, Arilyn concluded dryly, was something of an understatement.

All told, the half-elf was in no mood to parry Hasheth's inevitable advances with anything approaching diplomacy. Indeed, it would take every shred of self-control that she possessed to keep from tossing the young man out onto the roadside with his first manipulative compliment, his first double entendre.

But either the gods took pity upon her, or Hasheth was beginning to learn in this matter, as well. The morning passed without incident. Indeed, Hasheth kept Arilyn so busy with his questions that she had no time to contemplate the troubling path before her.

The young prince was full to overbrimming with questions about Harper ways and the foes that the

Harpers faced. He was also eager to learn everything of Tethyrian history and politics that Arilyn had to share, and was curious about the affairs of other lands, as well. Apparently the palace saw no need to include matters of state in the education of a thirteenth-born son.

Arilyn gave each question a terse but complete answer, and she noted that Hasheth listened well—an important skill for a Harper informant. It was plain that the young man enjoyed taking part in the activities of this clandestine group, and that he reveled in intrigue and secrecy. He was also justly proud of his growing skill in devising and putting into place complex plans. But Arilyn was also aware that Hasheth's main tie with the Harpers was not personal conviction or even a respect for the Harpers and their ideals, but a sense of obligation to her and to Danilo. Now that they had both left the city behind, she was not so certain that Hasheth would continue in this role.

"And what will you do with all this knowledge?" she asked him at last.

Hasheth shrugged, taking her question at face value. "Knowledge is a tool; I will use it for whatever task comes to hand."

A good answer, Arilyn admitted, but hardly a reassuring one. In all, she was not sorry when the distant clamor of voices and carts announced that they were nearing Marakir.

Slipping away from the caravan was an easy matter. In her skirts and veil, with her well-draped travel packs adding a matronly bulk to her frame, Arilyn blended in with the matriarchs and chatelaines who came to purchase supplies for their families or their business establishments. For a while she wandered among the busy stalls, tapping melons and pinching cherries with the best of them.

Finally she found the place she sought: Theresa's Fine Woolens, a large wooden stall that offered ready-made clothes. The establishment had a prosperous air, as well as a prime location right next to the river, but Theresa's reputation for high prices kept away all but the most affluent buyers.

Inside the shop, Arilyn found an assortment of serviceable but quite unremarkable garments: woolen cloaks, trews, gowns, and shawls, as well as shirts of linen or linsey-woolsey. The cost of the garments, Theresa insisted, reflected the quality and the service. The casual patron might assume that by "services" she meant the helpful shop clerks who offered advice and refreshments, or the curtained booths, each walled with silvered glass, that enabled the patrons to dress with privacy. What was not commonly known was that the mirrors were actually hidden doors that allowed well-informed patrons to slip out the back.

Leaving her cumbersome skirts—as well as a small bag of silver coins—in the changing booth, Arilyn left Theresa's and slid down the steep incline of the riverbank. A small skiff awaited her there, further evidence of the discreet services Theresa offered.

The Harper settled into the boat and nodded to the two burly servants who manned the oars. One of them flicked loose the rope that secured the craft to a post driven into the shoreline. Then the men leaned into the oars in well-practiced unison, and the little boat lurched out into the river.

Arilyn noted with approval that the oarsmen displayed an admirable lack of curiosity. They spared her hardly a glance, so intent were they on maneuvering through the heavy river traffic. It took all their considerable skill to dodge the many skiffs and flatboats and small, single-sailed boats that thronged the busy waterway. Once they were beyond the crush and turmoil of the marketplace, the men settled in and set a straight, hard-pulling course upriver.

The Sulduskoon was Tethyr's largest river, stretching nearly the entire breadth of the country. From its origins in the foothills of the Snowflake Mountains, the river traveled over five hundred miles until finally it spilled into the sea. Not all of the Sulduskoon was easily navigated. There were stretches of shallow, rapid waters, deep pools inhabited by nixies and other troublesome creatures, and treacherous, rock-strewn passages that claimed a toll of nearly three boats out of ten.

But here the river was deep and broad, the water relatively calm, and the current not strong enough to impede their progress. Arilyn guessed they would reach the fork in the river—where a second boat awaited her—by nightfall. From there, she would travel up a large tributary that branched northward past the Starspires, close to the part of Tethir that she sought. In the southern parts of the forest lived an old friend. Arilyn's plan rested heavily on his friendship and on his ability to convince his people to come to her assistance.

From what she knew of the legendary silver shadows, Arilyn realized this would not be an easy task.

* * * * *

Eileenalana bat K'theelee stirred and grimaced in her sleep as the first arrow struck her. It was a fearsome expression, appearing as it did on the face of a young white dragon, yet the dreams that enveloped her were not entirely unpleasant.

The slumbering dragon dreamed of a hail shower and the pleasures of flying high into the churning summer clouds. Hail storms were a rare treat in this land, which was far too hot for a white dragon's comfort, and in her dream Eileen was enjoying the swirling, icy winds and the tingle of formulating hail against her scales.

Suddenly a particularly sharp hailstone struck her neck. Eileen's head reared up, and through her still-sleepy haze two simultaneous and contradictory conclusions occurred to her: the storm was nothing but a pleasant slumber-fantasy, and the sting of the hail stones seemed all too real.

In an effort to rouse herself, the better to contemplate
this puzzle, the young dragon rolled over onto her belly
and unwound her tail from her pile of treasure. It was a
small pile, to be sure, but how much could a dragon
hoard in a mere century of life? And how many opportunities did she have, she who was reduced to a few
short bursts of activity? The Forest of Tethir was cool,
but hardly cold enough to provide comfort to a dragon of
her kind. Eileen spent much of her time in her cave, in
a stuporous lethargy.

She dared not venture out too often. Though she was
nearly thirty feet long and almost full-grown, there
were still creatures in the forest who could give her a
good fight. These enemies could find her far too easily;
with her enormous size and glistening white scales,
Eileen didn't exactly blend into the landscape. Unless
forced by hunger into hunting, she stayed in the cave,
for she felt dangerously conspicuous except on those few
days when a dusting of snow touched the forest, or
when storm clouds turned the sky to a pale and pearly
gray.

All things considered, Eileen longed for the frozen
Northlands of which her parents had spoken—and to
which they had returned when she was barely more
than a hatchling.

Eileen had been too small to keep pace with the
larger dragons, but she had managed to fly from her
birthplace on the icy peaks of the Snowflake Mountains
as far as Tethir. Someday, she would fly to the far north
along with the forest's other white dragons who shared
her plight. A flight of dragons, and she its leader! How
glorious! All she needed was an extended cold snap and
favorable winds. . . .

Another sharp, stinging blow brought Eileen back to
the matter at hand. The dragon yawned widely, then settled back on her haunches to consider the situation. The
air was moist and fairly warm, even down here in the
cavern. Yes, it was early summer, the most reasonable

time for a hail storm, yet she was in her cave, which meant that actual hail was highly unlikely.

The dragon came to this conclusion, not so much with words, but with the instinctual awareness that even the slowest-witted creature must have of its surroundings in order to survive. Of all Faerûn's evil dragons, whites were the smallest and the least intelligent. And even by the modest measure of her kind, Eileen was hardly the sharpest sword in the armory.

Swinging her crested white head this way and that, the dragon looked about for the source of the disturbance. Another stinging slap to the neck—this one dangerously close to the base of one of her leathery wings—came from the direction of the eastern passage.

Eileen squinted into the tunnel's darkness. A shadowy form lurked there. She could make out a two-legged shape and the loaded bow in its hands. But whether the bowman was human, or elven, or something more or less similar, she could not say, for the tantalizing aroma of wintermint masked his scent.

The annoying creature let loose yet another arrow. It struck the dragon squarely on the snout and bounced off without penetrating the plate armor of her face. Even so, it *stung!*

For a moment, the dazed and cross-eyed dragon stared at the pair of humanoid archers that had invaded her lair. She gave her head a violent shake, and the two melded back into one. Still, that was one too many.

Eileen let out a roar of pain and anger and exploded to her feet. The archer turned on his heel and ran down the tunnel, with the dragon in hot pursuit.

Well, maybe *warm* pursuit; Eileen's last nap had lasted several weeks, and since she had a habit of sleeping on her side—plate-armored cheek pillowed on scaly paw—one foreleg was numb and uncooperative. Therefore what she had *intended* to be a fearsome charge was in fact reduced to an uneven, loping, three-legged hop.

Eileen skidded to a stop and plunked herself down on her haunches. She lifted both forelegs and regarded them. After a moment's thought, a solution presented itself, one she thought quite ingenious. The dragon sucked in a long breath of air, held her *good* leg up close to her fanged jaws, and blew upon it a long, icy blast. This, Eileen's breath weapon, could put out a raging fire or freeze a full-grown centaur to solid ice in midstride. It could even slightly benumb her own flesh, despite her natural armor and her uncanny resistance to cold.

Eileen dropped back onto all fours and tested her front legs. Yes, they were both equally numb now. With her equilibrium restored, the dragon resumed her charge, slowly, to be sure, but with a more even and dignified gait.

Her two-legged tormenter was well out of sight now, but Eileen easily followed the scent of mint. Although her wit was about as sharp as a spoon, she possessed a keen sense of smell—not to mention a particular fondness for wintermint.

As the dragon trotted through the cavern's tunnels and out into the forest, two things happened. First, both of her front legs gradually returned to normal and her pace accelerated into a dizzying, plant-crushing charge. Second, it began to occur to her that she was very, very hungry and that perhaps this interruption was not such a bad thing after all.

*   *   *   *   *

Night was falling upon the Forest of Tethir, and Vhenlar eyed the deepening shadows with an intense and growing dread. In the days that followed the battle at the pipeweed farm, the mercenaries had pursued the elven raiders deep into the forest—far deeper than ever they had ventured before, and much too deep for Vhenlar's peace of mind.

The ancient woodland was uncanny. The trees had a

watchful, listening mien; the birds carried tales; the very shadows seemed alive. There was magic here— primal, elemental magic—of a sort that put even the hired mages on edge, even the high-ticket Halruaan wizard in whom Bunlap put such store.

Other, more tangible dangers abounded. Since daybreak, unseen elves had been clipping arrows at the humans' heads and heels, nipping at them like sheep dogs gathering a flock for spring shearing. Beyond doubt, the mercenaries were being herded—toward what, Vhenlar could not say.

But he had little choice other than to move the band as swiftly northward as they could go. He'd tried to keep on the trail of the southbound elves, and lost five good men for his troubles. And so they headed northward, as their unseen tormenters intended. They would pick up the trail later, after . . . whatever.

Nor were the wild elves the mercenaries' only unseen foe, or their unknown destination their only worry. There was trouble enough to be found along the way. Not even the best woodsmen among them—and these included foresters, hired swords who'd knocked about in a dozen lands, and a couple of rangers gone bad—could identify all the strange cries, roars, and birdcalls that resounded through the forest. But all of the men had seen and heard enough to know there were creatures here that were best avoided. They'd stumbled upon a particularly unsubtle piece of evidence shortly before highsun. It was an image that stuck in Vhenlar's mind: a pile of dried scat in which was embedded the entire skull of an ogre. Whatever had killed that ogre—which had been an eight-footer, by the look of the skull, a creature probably as strong as any three men—was big enough to bite off the monster's head and swallow it whole. Ogres were bad enough, in Vhenlar's opinion, and he didn't even want to contemplate a creature big enough—and hungry enough—to eat such grim fare.

Monsters had always lived in the forest, but if tavern

tales and lost adventuring parties were any fair measure of truth, the sheer variety and number of such
creatures was spiraling into nightmarish proportions.
To Vhenlar's way of thinking, this was partly the result
of the troubles the elves were currently facing. Their
attention had been diverted from forest husbandry to
the more pressing matter of survival. This was, of
course, precisely what Bunlap and the mercenary captain's mysterious employer had intended.

"Bunlap just had to order us to follow them elves,"
muttered Vhenlar. "Don't matter to him, what with his
being snug behind fortress walls with nary a tree in
sight, and no damn wild elves planting arrows in his
backside!"

"Speaking of which," put in Mandrake, a mercenary
who also doubled as the company surgeon, "how's yours?"

It was not an unreasonable question, considering
that the surgeon had plucked two arrows from the back
of Vhenlar's lap since sunrise. The unseen elves who
harried them had slain the hounds, but they apparently
had a more lingering, humiliating fate in mind for the
mercenaries.

"It's in a Beshaba-blasted sling, that's how it is!"
Vhenlar said vehemently. "Along with yours, and his,
and his, and his, and every damned one of us in this
thrice bedamned forest!"

"Big sling," agreed Mandrake, thinking it best to
humor Bunlap's second-in-command.

The archer heard the condescending note in Mandrake's voice but did not respond to it. He grimaced as
a new wave of pain assaulted him. Walking was exceedingly painful, what with his new and humiliating
wounds. The elven arrows had dealt him shallow and
glancing blows, but somehow Vhenlar couldn't find it in
his heart to be grateful for small mercies. Nor could he
continue walking much longer. The damp chill that her-
alded the coming night was making his legs stiffen and
wasn't doing his aching butt one bit of good.

"Send Tacher and Justin to scout for a campsite again," Vhenlar said.

"And let those wild elves pick us off while we sleep?" the surgeon protested. "Better to keep moving!"

Vhenlar snorted. If the man was such a fool as to think those deadly archers would be challenged by a moving target, there was no sense in wasting breath telling him otherwise. "A campsite? Now?" he prodded.

The mercenary saluted and quickened his pace so he could catch up to the men Vhenlar had named.

He might have disobeyed, Vhenlar noted resignedly, but for the fact that Bunlap had made it plain they were all to follow Vhenlar's orders. People tended to do what Bunlap said, and not merely for fear of reprisal—although such was usually harsh and swift in coming—but because there was something about the man to which people responded. After years in Bunlap's company, Vhenlar thought he had this elusive quality figured out. The mercenary captain knew precisely what he wanted, and he went about getting it with grim, focused determination. Men who lacked a direction of their own—and Tethyr was full of these—were attracted to Bunlap like metal filings to a magnet. So when Bunlap told them to pursue the elves into the forest, they went. And they were still going, and they would likely *die* going, Vhenlar concluded bitterly.

Their task was important, Bunlap had insisted, though he himself had taken off for the fortress to gather and train men for the next assault. The captain had left right after the failed ambush, for he realized they were unlikely to catch up to the elven raiders, much less engage them in pitched battle. Vhenlar's task was to follow the elves, kill a few if he could, and collect as many bows and bolts of black lighting as he could get. His men were also supposed to retrieve the bodies of the elves slain in battle, as well as any who might die of their wounds and be discarded along the way, for such would be useful in turning still more people against the forest elves.

The elves, however, seemed determined that Vhenlar would get none of these things. They apparently carried their dead and wounded, and they used green arrows that, although finely crafted, were of little use in Bunlap's plans. If the mercenaries did not have hounds to sniff out the nearly invisible trail of blood, the elves would have eluded them altogether. It was a stroke of genius for the fleeing elves to send a party of archers to circle back and slay the hounds. Even Vhenlar had to admit that. But what else the elves had in mind, he could not begin to say.

A distant roar sent a spasm of cold terror shimmering down the Zhentish archer's spine. The two scouts hesitated, looking back at Vhenlar as if to protest their assignment. In response, he placed a hand on his elven bow and narrowed his eyes in his best menacing glare.

"I'm for lighting torches," Justin said defiantly. "Can't see where we're going, otherwise."

Vhenlar shrugged. Tales were told of the fearsome reprisals the forest folk took against any who dared to bring fire into the forest, but he doubted their elven shadows would kill the scouts—leastwise, not until they'd herded them to their unknown destination! And Justin had a point: it was *dark*, for in the deep forest not even the faint light of moon and stars could penetrate the thick canopy.

So he watched as the scout took a torch from his pack and struck flint to steel. A few sparks scattered into the night like startled fireflies, and then the flame rose high. Vhenlar blinked at the sudden bright flare of light. His eyes focused, and then widened. There were not two, but *three* figures standing in the circle of torchlight!

A wild elf, a young male with black braids and fierce black eyes, hauled back a waterskin and prepared to douse the flame. Or so Vhenlar assumed. He watched, as transfixed as the two dumbfounded scouts, as the elf hurled the contents of the skin. Not at the torch-wielding Justin, but at *Tacher*.

And then he was gone, before any of the mercenaries could unsheathe a blade or nock an arrow.

Justin sniffed, and his face screwed up into an expression of extreme disgust as he regarded the other scout. "You smell like something my mother drinks outta painted teacups!" he scoffed.

The analogy was apt. Tacher had been doused with a strong infusion of mint. Vhenlar, who could see no reason for this action, turned to one of their rangers—a tall, skinny fellow from the Dalelands. Once a noble ranger—whatever the Nine Hells that meant—he'd fought the Tuigan horde and seen his illusions about humankind burn to ash in the inferno that was war. Since then, he'd taken to looking out for himself and had developed a real talent for it.

"You know more about the forest than most of us," Vhenlar said. "Why'd the elf do that? He coulda killed Tacher and Justin both, easy."

The ranger shook his head impatiently and held up a hand, indicating a need for silence. The others fell quiet and listened, but their ears were not as sharp as those of the Dalesman. To Vhenlar's ears, there was only the constant hum and chirp of insects, the occasional shriek of a hunting raptor, and the whispering of the night winds through the thick forest canopy. A whispering, Vhenlar noted, that seemed to be growing louder.

Suddenly the ranger's eyes went wide. "Wintermint!" he muttered and then took off at a frantic run.

The others watched, bemused, as the ranger crashed off heedlessly toward the south. Before they could follow suit, a roar rolled through the forest—a fearsome sound that was both shriek and rumble, a cry of rage such as few of them had ever heard before. Yet there was not a man among them who did not know instinctively what it meant:

Dragon.

Vhenlar had heard men speak of dragonfear, the paralyzing terror that comes from looking into the eyes of

a great wyrm. He now knew that the very sound of a
dragon's cry could root a man's boots to the soil and
turn his legs to stone.

The dragonfear lasted but a moment, but that was
long enough. With the speed of a wizard's transformation, the dragon's passage through the forest changed
from a rustling murmur into a deafening crash. Like a
tidal wave, the dragon came on. Vhenlar would never
had guessed that something so large could move with
such speed!

Then he caught a glimpse of it through the trees, still
a couple hundred feet away but closing fast. It was a
white, and it glittered like some enormous, reptilian
ghost against the darkness of the forest. The creature
stopped, fell back on its haunches, and inhaled deeply.

The trees parted, the leaves cringing away and falling
in brittle shards as an icy winter wind tore through the
forest. Widening as it came, a cone of devastation
blasted everything in its path and reached icy, grasping
hands toward the mercenaries.

With the clarity of absolute terror, with a heart-
stopping fear that made everything around him seem
to slow down to a speed of a drifting snowflake, Vhenlar watched it come.

The dragon's breath reached the scouts, so quickly
that it froze Justin's face in its derisive sneer, so suddenly that it caught Tacher in the act of turning toward
the onrushing sound. It leached all color from their skin,
coating their hair and clothes in a thick layer of frost. To
all appearances, the men were as completely frozen as if
they'd been turned to ice statues by a vengeful sorceress.

Then the cold hit Vhenlar, bitter, searing, but not quite
enough to immobilize him. Quite the contrary, like a slap
to the face, it tore him from his momentary terror. He
realized the dragon's breath weapon had reached its
outer limits with the unfortunate scouts. Even so, he did
not intend to stay around in case the monster could
repeat its trick.

"Run!" he shrieked, and he kicked into the fastest gait his benumbed limbs could manage.

Bunlap's secondhand authority was not needed this time. The men followed Vhenlar without pause or question. As they fled wildly into the forest, their steps were spurred by the sound of cracking ice, a horrid crunching, and the faint and deadly scent of wintermint.

Ten

From the palisades of his fortress, Bunlap had a splendid view of Tethyr and its varied landscapes. To his east lay the Starspire Mountains, their jagged and lofty peaks snow-tipped even now in early summer. On the western side of his land were the rolling foothills, and just north of him the sudden, dense tree line that marked the southern edge of the Forest of Tethir.

A brisk wind ruffled his black beard and sent his cloak swirling up behind him. Bunlap caught the flying folds and wrapped them around himself, folding his arms to keep the garment firmly in place. Mornings were chill, even this time of year, for the western winds came straight off the Starspires, as did the icy waters that spilled into the river below—the northern branch, most called it, but Bunlap liked to think of it as "his" river.

Located as he was, on a cliff overlooking the plain where a dozen or more small waterways converged into a single flow, he could exact a tariff from every small-time farmer or trapper who floated down the tributaries to paddle his goods downriver to the Sulduskoon, and thence to Zazesspur.

It amused Bunlap that his demands were never challenged. The people of Tethyr were too accustomed to paying tariffs and tributes and out-and-out bribes at every turn, for petty noblemen bred like rabbits in this land. Not a single traveler questioned Bunlap's right to tax their cargo. He held this remote territory with a fortress and men-at-arms. In the mind of the Tethyrians, that made him nobility.

"Baron Bunlap," he said aloud, and a wry smile twisted his lips at the irony of it. Not a man alive was more lowly born than he, but what did that matter in Tethyr? In the few short years since he'd left his post at Darkhold, the former Zhentish soldier had amassed more land, wealth, and power than was possessed by most Cormyran lords. Bane's blood, how he loved this country!

"Two-sailed approaching!" called a man from the southern lookout.

Bunlap's mood darkened instantly. He'd received word of this ship's approach the night before, for he kept runners and horsemen stationed along the river to bring him news of water traffic. It was an organization nearly as swift and efficient as the town criers of any city a man could name, and as a result Bunlap knew the business of nearly everyone who traveled Tethyr's main waterway.

Which is why this particular ship disturbed him. Shallow-keeled as a Northman's raiding ship, single-masted but flying a jib as well as a mainsail, the ship was built for speed and stealth. She was small enough to escape the notice of everyone but the most observant and suspicious of men, small enough so that two or three might sail her, yet large enough to hold a dozen men or stow a considerable amount of contraband. In short, it was the sort of ship that carried trouble and a prime example of what his informants had been trained and paid to notice.

Yet his man at Port Starhaven, one of the few towns that lay along the northern branch, had been the first to note its approach. Bunlap had checked the fortress's log the night before. Recent entries indicated that there were no reported sightings of such a ship on the Sulduskoon, not on either side of the place where the northern branch met the main river. It was as if the ship had fallen from the clouds.

Or, a more likely possibility, and even more disturbing, it had been carted overland to a point on the northern branch and kept hidden in dry dock until it was needed. But why, and by whom?

Bunlap well knew the difficulty and expense of overland shipping. Whoever had gone to such trouble must have deep pockets and a compelling motivation. Well enough; he would empty those pockets and demand to know the reasons.

"Raise the chain behind her, bring it up fast and pull it as tight as it'll go," he bellowed, raising an eyeglass and peering down at the swiftly sailing craft. "On my mark. . . *now!*"

Several men hurried to a massive crank and began to turn with frantic haste. A huge chain, nearly as thick as a dwarf's waist, began to wind around a gathering spool. The other end of the chain was tethered to the far shore, bolted and welded to a platform that was itself pile-driven into the rocky bank. Once the chain was raised, no ship—not even this shallow-keeled phantom—could escape downriver.

As Bunlap anticipated, the sailboat tacked sharply, heading straight toward the eastern shore. This was the response most ships made, and it was the most logical. Put some distance between the ship and the apparently hostile fortress—a reasonable dodge. But what most travelers did not realize until too late was that the raising of the chain alerted men who were stationed on the

eastern shore and along each of the tributaries. These
men poured from their hidden barracks, those on the
east shore seizing arms and those along the north
putting small, swift craft into the water and rushing
toward the pinned-down ship. They would surround it,
capture it, and escort the ship and crew to Bunlap's
fortress. It was a well-planned maneuver, put into practice often enough to have become almost routine.

But to Bunlap's surprise, the sailboat continued
straight for the eastern shore and the forces that
awaited her there. Several sets of long oars flung out
over the side, and unseen oarsmen pulled hard as they
rowed with breakneck haste for the beach.

The mercenaries assembled at water's edge scattered
as the shallow boat thrust up out of the water. A dozen
or more fighters leaped from the boat onto dry land and
hurled themselves at Bunlap's men. One of them, a
minor mage of some sort, sent a tiny ball of light
hurtling toward the sails. The canvas had been treated
with some kind of oil, for immediately flames leaped
outward in all directions to engulf the entire ship.

Dark billows of smoke forced the battle back from the
shore. Bunlap squinted into his eyeglass, peering
through the gathering cloud of smoke and trying to find
some clue that would help him make sense of this ship
and these tactics. What he saw thrust him even deeper
into puzzlement.

Most of the crew of the strange sailing craft were clad
in tunics and leggings of a distinctive dark purple
which marked them as hired swords of the palace, mercenaries who reported to the lesser members of the
Balik family. This was an oddity, for Pasha Balik and
his pleasure-loving kin were not known to venture
beyond the walls of Zazesspur. Odder still was the sole
exception among these purple-clad fighters: a female,
and an elf!

She was not one of the forest people, of that Bunlap
was certain. The elves of Tethir were copper-hued and

tended to be small in build and stature. This one was raven-haired and tall as most men. Bunlap caught a glimpse of her face—it was as pale as a pearl, a shade that was peculiar to moon elves. These were common enough in Tethyr, but most were fairly recent arrivals who had settled in the trade cities and farmlands. Bunlap hadn't a clue as to what might bring palace guards and a moon elf wench to this part of the country.

Whatever her purpose, the elf woman was a swordmaster of rare ability. The mercenary captain watched in helpless rage as she cut through his hired men with dizzying speed and terrifying ease. Not a man among them could stand before her sword. Bunlap was not certain that he himself could match her. Then the smoke grew too thick for him to see more, and there was nothing to do but wait.

The clang of battle and the cries of the wounded drifted up to him across the expanse of water. Bunlap noticed that the chorus of steel on steel was rapidly thinning out. The battle was winding down faster than he would have thought possible. At this rate, it would be over before any of his other boats could reach the eastern shore!

At least he had the satisfaction of knowing that the elf woman and the purple mercenaries would soon be in his power. With their ship destroyed, they could hardly escape. They had nowhere to go—except to Bunlap's fortress!

Even as this thought formed, Bunlap noted a flurry of movement several hundred yards south of the battle. Two small boats, bottoms up, emerged from the thick smoke and scuttled toward the river like bugs—large bugs that boasted three pairs of purple-clad legs each.

Several more Balik guards hurried along behind these boats, some carrying pilfered oars, others brandishing their curved swords and watching their backs for pursuit. There was none. Bunlap's men were lost in the smoke, battling a deadly elf woman who, unlike them, could see in darkness better than any cat. For all he knew, by now she had them fighting each other!

A surge of rage swept through the mercenary captain as the escape strategy became clear to him. Using the smoke as a cover, the guards were stealing Bunlap's boats, walking portage around the chain, and making their escape downriver!

There was nothing he could do to stop them, not even if he had the chain lowered so his other boats were able to give pursuit. He had no way of getting new orders to the men. Nor would they take such action on their own, for the strong westerly wind was blowing the dark, oily smoke across the river in a thick and effective screen. It was unlikely that any of the men who fought on the eastern shore or who were still on the river could even *see* the escaping boats!

As he waited for the battle to end, Bunlap's rage and frustration deepened. He could not vent his spleen upon the men, for he would need every one of them for the coming battles. And he was fairly certain he would get no satisfaction from the elf wench. Bunlap was ready to bet big money that when the smoke cleared, there would be no trace of her.

He was also fairly certain of her destination. It would not be the mountains, which were catacombed with dwarven tribes, but the elven forest.

This was not a heartening thought. A moon-elven warrior, smart enough to elude him, powerful enough to claim assistance from Zazesspur's ruling family? As if he hadn't problems enough in that thrice-blasted forest!

Bunlap spun away and stalked down the steps that led from the palisades to the courtyard. For several moments he stood, watching as his lieutenants took the new recruits through their morning weapons training. They were good, this batch, and as he watched Bunlap felt his rage cool—but not dissipate, never that. Bunlap's anger was like a forge-heated sword: it only got harder and sharper as the heat slipped away.

He'd counted on the reclusive nature of the forest
elves for his plan's success, and so far it had served him
well. If this moon elf had a notion to join forces with the
wild folk, she'd likely find they had ideas of their own!
And even if she did, what of it? One more sword would
not turn the balance in favor of the elves of Tethir. And
when the time was right, he, Bunlap, would take great
pleasure in ending the career of this elf woman. She
would have to wait her turn, of course, but she'd be just
as dead for the delay. There was enough elf-hatred in
Bunlap's heart to sink Evermeet into the sea.

The captain's hand instinctively lifted to his cheek
and to the still-fiery brand the wild elf had left there.
With each day that passed, his latest assignment was
becoming more and more a personal crusade.

* * * * *

Ferret pressed her stolen horse as hard as she dared.
It was no easy task, keeping pace with a swift-sailing
boat and yet staying out of sight. To make matters still
more difficult, this terrain was unfamiliar to her. The
mountains were dwarven territory.

But the female assassin had earned her reputation as
a tracker. She made her way to the river's mouth in
time to witness the battle between the half-elf's hired
men and the locals—she might even have joined in, had
the river not lain between her and the fight.

Ferret watched with keen interest as Arilyn engaged
the mercenaries, sent her own men southward, and then
slipped away in the confusion. Despite her personal
opinion of the half-elf, Ferret could not help but admire
the smoothly executed plan. She needed to know more
about this half breed's talents—and her motivations.

When the fight was over, the female urged her tired
mount into the hills, for she had to give wide berth to the
fortress. Although she had not known of the stronghold's
existence and knew nothing of its lord, she'd had ample

experience with petty noblemen and knew what to expect
from them, even if she hadn't seen the attempted ambush
of Arilyn's ship.

Throughout that day and most of the following night
and the day after that, Ferret pursued her half-elven
quarry. By late afternoon she caught her first glimpse of
Arilyn—just as she was slipping into the edge of Tethir.

The assassin shook her head in disbelief. To cover
such a distance, the half-elf must have run the entire
way, with very little pause for rest. Elves could do this,
when pressed, but Ferret never would have credited
that a half-elf could manage such a feat. She herself
had traveled even farther, but she had done so on four
legs.

Ferret swung down from the horse and grasped the
animal's tangled mane in both hands. She drew down
the horse's head and spoke for several minutes in the
centaur tongue: an apology, as well as instructions for
the journey ahead.

The mare seemed to grasp the gist of it, for she
turned southward and set off at a jog in the direction of
the fortress. There, Ferret reasoned, the horse would be
fed and cared for. However ill the local lord treated
passing travelers, he would be unlikely to disdain such
a valuable gift. And the horse could not survive otherwise. It had become an unnatural creature, stripped of
its instincts and made dependent upon humans.

The female set off for the forest with an easy, running
stride, confident she could pick up the half-elf's trail
and have the wench in her sights by nightfall. And then,
she would learn what had brought a half-elven assassin
into the shadows of Tethir.

The waxing moon rose high over the forest's canopy,
but only a few stubborn shafts of moonlight worked
their way through the thick layers of leaves. Ferret
found that Arilyn's trail was harder to follow than she
had anticipated. Somewhere along the line, the assassin
who walked the streets of Zazesspur with such grim

assurance had also learned a considerable amount of
woods craft!

At last Ferret caught sight of the half-elf, down on one
knee examining what appeared to be wolf sign. She
placed her palm down on the soil as if measuring the
print, then nodded in satisfaction. With a quick, fluid
movement she was back on her feet. She set a brisk, silent
pace toward the north, stopping from time to time to
examine the soil, or to pick a tuft of fur from a bramble.

To all appearances, she was tracking a wolf.

Why, Ferret could not say, but she could easily guess
Arilyn's destination. There was a small glade not too far
away, a place with lush grasses and a spring pool that
did not dry up until late summer. Deer and other animals came there to drink. If the half-elf was indeed
tracking a wolf, this is where she would likely find one.

Ferret hesitated, and then nimbly climbed an ash
tree. From this perch she could follow the half-elf,
unseen, and yet remain beyond the reach of any wolf
Arilyn might encounter.

Not that forest wolves posed a serious threat. They
were shy, intelligent creatures who kept to themselves
and killed only what they needed for survival. Only in
the borderlands, where human poaching had stripped
the forest of the wolves' natural prey, had they become
a nuisance. From time to time, hungry wolves ventured
out into the fields and farmlands. Most of these contented themselves with the mice and voles that were
plentiful in cultivated lands—wolves could live solely
on such prey—but a few developed a taste for mutton.

If cornered by an indignant shepherd, a poaching
wolf would defend itself. It was possible that just such
a wolf had wounded or even killed someone who had relatives wealthy enough to purchase the half-elf's services.
There were other possibilities, however, that dictated a
certain amount of caution on Ferret's part. Extremely
rare, although more common in these troubled times, was
a rogue wolf, one that either through sickness or despair

had left its nature behind to become a ravening beast.
Most often the atrocities attributed to them were not
committed by wolves at all, but by lycanthropes—
humans who'd been cursed with a wolf's form and an
unnatural lust for blood. Although Tethir's ancient magic
acted as a barrier to many such abominations, it was
possible—*possible*—that the half-elf had been hired to
track and slay such a monster. Best to keep a distance
from that battle!

From her leafy perch, Ferret followed Arilyn toward
the glade. At the half-elf's approach, a pair of deer lifted
dripping muzzles from the pool and bounded off into the
trees. There was no sign of any wolf, however, nor did
the half-elf seem concerned by this lack. She shouldered
off her pack and began to remove several items from it,
including a small, shimmering mound of what appeared
to be liquid silver.

The half-elf removed her green cape and stripped off
her clothing—the dark, nondescript garments of a
Zazesspurian assassin—all the while wearing an
expression of extreme distaste. She stuffed them into
the hollow of a tree and then waded into the pool,
splashing and scrubbing herself repeatedly as if to
wash off some invisible taint.

Arilyn's pale skin appeared almost luminous in the
tree-filtered moonlight. Even to Ferret's critical eyes,
she was as pale and slender as any moon elf—an apparent sister to the white-limbed birch trees that ringed
the forest glade.

At length the half-elf waded back and began to dress
herself in the garments she'd taken from her pack: leggings, under tunic, shirt—all of which were dyed in
practical shades of deep forest green. Then she picked
up the fluid silver. It fell like a waterfall into the shape
of a fine hauberk, a long tunic of elven chain mail finer
than any Ferret had ever seen. This the half-elf slipped
over her head; it molded immediately to her form and
moved with her like water. Arilyn belted on her ancient

sword so that the moonstone-hilted blade was prominently displayed. She raked both hands through her still-wet curls, tucking her hair behind her pointed ears and then tying an elaborate green-and-silver band around her forehead to hold it in place. In moments, the half-breed assassin was gone; in her place stood a noble warrior, a proud daughter of the Moon People.

Ferret shook her head in silent disbelief. Had she not seen the transformation herself, she would not have believed it possible. Oh, she knew that Arilyn had a knack for disguises, but this went far beyond an assassin's tricks.

Before Ferret could assimilate this, the half-elf took a small wooden object from her pack and lifted it to her lips. An eery, wavering cry floated out into the forest and froze the watchful Ferret to her perch. She had heard that sound before, but never from a mortal throat!

There was a moment's silence, and then an answering call came from the trees beyond. Arilyn blew again, a long high call followed by several short, irregular bursts—some sort of signal, no doubt—and then she waited calmly.

The vines on the far side of the glade parted, and an enormous silver wolf padded into the clearing. It was twice as large, perhaps even three times as large, as any wolf Ferret had ever seen. In truth, it could be said to resemble a forest wolf only insofar as a unicorn could be likened to a horse, or an elf to a human. The creature's blue eyes were large and intelligent, almond-shaped like those of an elf, and its ears were long and pointed above its sharply triangular face. There was a fey grace to its step, and lingering about it was an eldritch aura that seemed to capture and embody the essence of the forest's magic.

Lythari.

Ferret formed the word with silent, awed lips. All her life she had heard tales of the lythari, an ancient race of shapechanging elves, the most elusive and most magical of all the forest People. Few knew of their existence beyond those who dwelt in the forest. Those who spoke of the Silver Shadows did so with reverence—and dread.

The lythari were usually as reclusive as the wolves they resembled, but from time to time they moved with incredible ferocity against some enemy of the forest. Even the wild elves, who—next to dryads and treants— were the most attuned to the ways of the woodlands, did not understand the ways of the lythari and occasionally fell under their swift wrath. Few forest dwellers had caught a glimpse of a lythari, and never in elven form.

As if to mock Ferret's unspoken thoughts, the lythari's wolflike form shimmered and disappeared. In its place stood a young elven male, beautiful and fey even by the measures of elvenkind. Ferret bit her lip, hard, to keep from crying out in wonder. The lythari was taller than the half-elf and just as pale, and his hair retained the shimmering silver color of his wolflike form. He called Arilyn by name, speaking the common Elvish tongue, and embraced her warmly. But try though she might, Ferret could make out nothing of the low, earnest conversation that followed.

She watched in wonder as the lythari slipped back into his wolf form and stood patiently, allowing the half-elf to climb onto his back. Thus mounted, Arilyn Moonblade slipped beyond the forest glade—and beyond Ferret's reach. No one, not even a tracker as skilled as she, could follow a lythari who did not wish to be found.

To Ferret, this could mean only one thing: the lythari intended to take Arilyn to his den and wished to remove all possibility that someone could trace her to this hidden place.

As Ferret slipped down from the tree, she pondered the mystery that was Arilyn Moonblade, a half-woman who bore the sword of an elven warrior and had earned the friendship of a lythari. Yet Ferret knew of several times that Arilyn had killed for no other apparent purpose than the coins the deed would place in her pockets. The other assassins applauded her cold-blooded skill and accepted her as one of their own. But having seen both sides of Arilyn, Ferret simply could not reconcile the two halves.

The lythari male apparently knew the better part of Arilyn Moonblade, the noble elven warrior, the identity that Ferret had just now glimpsed. Unfortunately—and herein lay a danger beyond reckoning—the lythari also knew all the secrets of the forest.

Did this young male know that he was about to betray them to a half-elven assassin?

Eleven

There was nothing, Hasheth was coming to learn, that could lift the heart and enflame the pride like a good plot successfully executed. Not even the grinding, mind-numbing chore of copying piles of receipts into Hhune's ledgers could dim the young man's inner glow of excitement. He had done well—even Arilyn Moonblade, Harper and Shadow Sash, had admitted as much.

And in truth, Hasheth did not mind his apprenticeship so very much. In a way, these bits of parchment and paper were like pieces of a puzzle, and there was little that he enjoyed more than a good puzzle. The Harpers, what a life they had—traveling the world, tracing convoluted plots to their source. The only thing that could possibly be more interesting would be *devising* such a plot, one so tangled that not even the best among the Harpers might unravel it!

Despite his pride, the young prince possessed enough self-knowledge to know that he himself was not capable

of such a thing. But in time—why not? And what better
training could he have than learning at the foot of the
complicated and ambitious Hhune?

As guildmaster, merchant, land owner and member of
the Council of Lords, Hhune possessed considerable
power. Yet already Hasheth's sharp eye had found hints
of other, clandestine affiliations and shadowy outlines
of plots that were as ambitious as they were intriguing.
A busy man, was Lord Hhune!

"Not finished yet?" demanded a nasal, querulous
voice. "The other clerks have already entered their allot-
ments and gone out to take their midday meal."

Hasheth set his teeth and lifted his gaze to Achnib,
Lord Hhune's scribe. "I am not a clerk, but an apprentice," he reminded the man, and not for the first time.

"It is much the same," the scribe said in a tone meant
to dismiss the younger man. He turned away and strut-
ted off in search of someone else to intimidate.

Hasheth watched him go, marveling that a man as
astute and ambitious as Hhune would suffer such a
fool. Achnib carried out his lord's instructions well
enough, but if a single original thought should ever
enter his head, it would surely die of loneliness!

Yet Achnib was a born sycophant, and such men often
enjoyed a degree of success. The scribe curried favor
with his master in the most shamelessly obvious ways,
even to imitating Lord Hhune's appearance. He sported
a thick mustache and smoothed back his black hair
with oils as did Hhune. He patronized the same tailor
and went so far as to mimic the lord's manner of speaking, his gait, and his meticulous attention to social
niceties. What Achnib lacked, however, was Hhune's
apparent love of intrigue and his understanding of the
nuances of power. Unlike Hhune, the scribe made no
attempt whatsoever to ensure the loyalties of those in
lesser positions, instead seeking only to bask in the
reflected light of greater men.

A fool, Hasheth surmised. He was but half the scribe's

age, and already he sensed that power flowed in all directions—upward as well as down, for even the greatest lord was in some small part dependent upon the efficiency and the goodwill of his lowliest servants. Those who wished to lead must know how to control and manage that flow.

As soon as Achnib was well beyond sight, Hasheth slipped a large gold coin from beneath a stack of papers. It was identical to the one Lord Hhune had shown him, and Hasheth had gone to no little trouble to procure it so that he might study its markings. Some of them he knew. Hidden among the designs was Hhune's guild mark, a secret symbol known only to ranking members of the various guilds. Hasheth had purchased this information during his brief sojourn in the assassins' guild, not realizing at the time how important it might become.

The other Harper, the northerner Danilo Thann, had been keenly interested in these symbols and had committed them all to memory. Hasheth had followed suit, and now he blessed the northerner for his foresight. Young Lord Thann was not such a bad sort, and for a moment Hasheth was almost glad the bard had escaped Hhune's hired assassins. For without such knowledge as Lord Thann had insisted Hasheth acquire, the prince would not have been able to make the connection between his new master and the other members of the mysterious group known as the Knights of the Shield. And if he was to take his place among these men, he must know their names.

Hasheth ran one fingertip over the circular pattern of runes around the edge of the coin and the shield in its center. He knew that mark well, for his own mother had worn this symbol upon a pendant until the day she died. It marked her, she said, as one under the protection of the Knights. She had brought it with her from Calimshan and had worn it always until the night she died birthing yet another son to the pasha.

Hasheth had been weaned on stories of this secret

society, which was apparently as active in the southern lands as the Harpers were in the Dalelands far to the north. Their power was rumored to come from a combination of great wealth and the ability to gather and hoard valuable information. What the ultimate aims and goals of the Knights were, no one could say, but it was known that they had no love for northerners and bore a special dislike for Waterdeep and her Lords. Hasheth had long suspected that his father had some involvement with these shadowy folk. Lord Hhune's words to him had removed all doubt. Of one thing Hasheth was certain: affiliation with the Knights would almost certainly be a step toward the sort of power he intended to wield.

"Where did you get that?"

Hasheth jolted. He had not heard Achnib's approach, so intent was he upon his study of the coin. The scribe pounced on him like a hunting cat and tore the coin from his hand.

"This bears Lord Hhune's mark. Where did you get this?" the man demanded in an accusing voice.

"At the Purple Minotaur," Hasheth said, honestly enough. The mere mention of Zazesspur's most luxurious inn set the scribe back on his heels and stole some of the indignation from his face. In fact, Achnib looked so nonplused that Hasheth could not resist the urge to continue.

"As you no doubt know, Lord Hhune engaged the services of assassins to rid the city of a suspected Harper agent. Two of these assassins were slain at the inn where their mark resided; one of them carried this coin. Since the hired man failed at his assigned task, I took the liberty of removing the coin from his body so that I might return to it Lord Hhune. If you wish to check out the particulars," Hasheth continued in a casual voice, "the chatelaine of the Minotaur will happily vouchsafe my tale. You might also wander by the assassins' guildhouse, if you like."

The scribe's eyes narrowed, for Hasheth's seemingly innocent words held a triple insult. First, Achnib did *not* know of this matter, and the fact that Hasheth *did* placed him subtly higher in the hierarchy surrounding Lord Hhune. Secondly, since Achnib was neither wealthy nor well-born, he would not find a welcome, much less the offer of information, from the lofty chatelaine of the exclusive Purple Minotaur. And finally, an invitation to stop by the assassins' guildhouse was tantamount to wishing a person dead. Yet since Hasheth himself had briefly tasted the assassin's path and had lived to speak of this adventure, he could mask this curse in the garb of a casual, if boastful, suggestion. Even so, it was beyond bearing!

"Hhune will hear of this," the scribe warned.

Hasheth inclined his head in a parody of gratitude. "You are kind, to offer to speak of me to my Lord Hhune. I had planned to give him the coin myself, not wishing to trouble you with matters outside of your duties, but of course it is better so. It is unbecoming of a man to put himself forward in such a manner."

Achnib's face turned deep red. "You meant to do no such thing! You would have kept it for yourself!"

In response, the young man reached for the cash ledger and thumbed to the day's page. He held up the book so the scribe could see that the entry had already been made.

"I will let your insult pass, for it is beneath me," he said in a soft, dangerous voice. "As a son of the pasha, I have little need for gold. But now that the coin is in *your* hands, perhaps you should sign for it as well?"

The scribe sputtered angrily, but no suitable response came to his mind. Nor could he refuse the proper procedure that Hasheth had suggested. At length he shut his mouth, snatched the quill from the apprentice's inkwell, and scrawled his mark next to the neat entry. He spun on his heel and stalked from the room.

Only then did Hasheth permit himself a sneer. The

fool had no idea what he held in his hand! Achnib saw
a piece of gold, no more.

Very well. He would come to know in time, to his sorrow.

In the young prince's mind, the lines of battle had
been clearly drawn.

*　*　*　*　*

Foxfire stood in respectful silence as the body of yet
another elf was lowered into the bog—the last of their
number who had sustained mortal injuries in the farmlands to the east—and he listened as the songs were
sung that marked the return of yet another forest spirit
into the great caldron of life. The others stood with
him—the survivors of the raid, the reinforcements from
Talltrees, even the volatile Tamsin—all taking solace
and direction from their leader's dignified mourning.

But Foxfire was far from feeling as calm as he
appeared. Nor did he accept the deaths of his people
with anything approaching resignation.

He was young, by the measure of elvenkind, not long
into his second century of life. Yet he had seen much
death—too much death, and too much change. Life in
the world beyond their forest's boundaries swirled past
them at a dizzying pace; events came and went too
swiftly for the elves to absorb, much less assimilate.
During the short span of Foxfire's years, kingdoms had
risen and tumbled, forests had given way to farmland,
whole human settlements had sprung up like mushrooms after a spring rain.

It often seemed to Foxfire that humans were rather
like hummingbirds: they whizzed past and were gone in
a moment's time. Suddenly, unaccountably, the elves of
Tethyr had been caught up in this pace, dragged along
in the wake of this headlong flight. He did not know
how to stop it. He did not know if it *could* be stopped.

Tamsin, however, was not beset with such doubts. The

young fighter, along with the three archers who had been sent northward, had found his way back to the fen lands moments before his kinsman's body was to be returned to the forest. After the songs had been chanted and the rituals complete, the elf sought out Foxfire and asked to give his report.

"I did as you said," he stated bluntly. "We all did— Eldrin, Sontar, Wyndelleu. They pushed the humans northward with their arrows, making sure along the way that the hounds would not live to betray us to their masters. I awoke the white dragon and led her to the humans. By now she is probably back in her lair, sleeping, with a belly full enough to keep her through the rest of the summer. Of the warriors who pursued us, perhaps ten are dead."

"You did well," Foxfire told him. "But for your efforts, the People would not have reached the safety of the fen lands."

"Yet we could have done more!" Tamsin burst out. "Why let *any* of them escape? Our lives would be better if we killed every human that ventures into the forest!"

Foxfire was silent for a long moment. "Not all," he ventured at last, "for there are humanfolk in the forest who actually do good—the druids, rangers, even the swanmays."

Tamsin's eyes flashed with excitement as he regarded his leader, measured the meaning of his hesitation. "But the men who pursued us—"

"Will not stop," Foxfire concluded grimly. "It is time to turn hunter."

The young elf nodded eagerly. "As before? Small parties of archers?"

"No. We are rested now, and all those who yet live are ready to fight. We have also six fresh warriors from Talltrees. I say we strike hard and have done with them."

"I will scout," Tamsin offered immediately.

For once Foxfire did not try to temper the young elf's impetuous nature. "You know the way; you will lead the first group. Find the humans, take to the trees, and pass over them, then attack from the north. Korrigash will lead from the east, Eldrin will take his archers to the west, and Wyndelleu to the south."

"And you?"

Foxfire placed a hand on the younger elf's shoulder. "I will fight beside you, or elsewhere as I am needed, but the command of the northern band will be yours. Now go, and gather your fighters."

His eyes sparkling at the thought of his first command, the younger elf spun and raced back toward the main camp. The news came as no surprise to the others. In moments the camp was gone as if it had never been there, and the elven fighters were ready to move northward from their fen-land refuge.

They followed Tamsin's confident lead, traveling throughout the day and well into the night. Shortly before dawn they came upon the humans' camp, not far from the place where the white dragon had fallen upon them. By all appearances, the humans did not realize this. Their panicked trails had taken them in wide circles, and they had wandered still farther in an attempt to gather their scattered members. Yet it seemed they had made a good recovery. The camp was neat and orderly, and three alert sentries circled the site.

Tamsin pointed to the sentries, then to himself, to Sontar, and young Hawkwing. All were good choices, Foxfire acknowledged silently as the three elves slipped up into the trees and moved into position, though it pained him to see a maid as young as Hawkwing in battle. But war had chosen her, and she did not flinch from the burden that had fallen her way.

At a signal from Tamsin, the three elves dropped silently to the ground, directly in front of their chosen marks. Before the humans could move or cry out, three bone knives slashed forward and dealt swift and silent death. The elves caught the falling humans and eased them silently to the ground—a difficult feat for the tiny

Hawkwing, who used her own body to muffle the sound of the falling human. Foxfire winced, but the elf girl crawled out from under the dead sentry and signaled that all was well.

Foxfire nodded to the group leaders, and the elves scattered into the forest. He followed Tamsin into the trees. As they crept through the canopy over the campsite, he took careful note of the men who slept below. There were a total of three-and-forty humans—a large band, far more than Foxfire had anticipated. More, in fact, than had pursued them into the forest. Somehow they, like the elves, had managed to send for reinforcements. The implications of this did not bode well for the elves.

Although he knew little of humans, Foxfire understood that they did not possess the elven gift of rapport, that mystical closeness that enabled elves to share thoughts and feelings, even across long distances. Rapport was strongest among the twin-born—Tamsin and Tamara shared such a bond with each other and a strong empathy with other elves—but most often rapport occurred between elven lovers who forged a bond strong and bright enough to weld their spirits together for all time. It was the deepest commitment known to elves, rarely undertaken and never done so lightly. Foxfire knew that humans could not send messages through rapport; they *could* do so through use of magic.

Suddenly a sharp *crack* split the silence of the night—the heart-chilling sound of a metal trap springing shut. There came another, and a third, and then a quick brutal crackle that came too quickly to count. The sounds roused the humans, who leaped from their bedrolls and seized their weapons: wooden shields, small crossbows, swords, and daggers.

Tamsin's body contorted in a spasm of agony as the backlash of the trapped elves' pain swept through him. Foxfire reached out to steady him, then captured the younger elf's anguished eyes with his own. It was clear

that Tamsin not only felt the elves' suffering, but
blamed himself for it. Had he not been so focused on the
hunt, he might have sensed the coming danger.

"Shield yourself," Foxfire said sternly. "What's done
cannot be undone; you will not help them by sharing
their deaths."

"How could this happen?" demanded Hawkwing, her
black eyes wide with horror. "Why could they not see the
traps?"

"The humans have a wizard," Foxfire replied as he
nocked an arrow. He elbowed Tamsin, for the young elf's
gifts were needed. Of all of them, Tamsin had the best
chance of discerning the deadly foe.

The young fighter shook himself, scattering his borrowed emotions like an otter casting off droplets of water.
He put aside his grief and his guilt and took a deep,
steadying breath. Swiftly, surely, he focused on the unseen
threads that tied him to the forest and to the web of magic
that was its essence.

Tamsin knew the pattern—they all did—but more
than most elves, he felt it in his blood, traveled its gossamer paths whenever he rested in reverie. And thus he
sensed quickly and surely the ugly, gaping tear in the
fabric of life that indicated that a human wizard was at
work.

"There," he said, pointing to one of the men crouched
below—an easy target, for he was one of the few
humans who did not hold a shield.

Foxfire swung his bow into place and loosed his ready
arrow. The bolt tore through the layers of leaves,
straight toward its mark . . .

. . . and burst into flame.

Blue fire flashed down the length of the shaft, and a
thin line of black ash drifted to the ground at the wizard's feet.

The other humans were not quite so lucky. The
archers under Wyndelleu's command bombarded them
with a small storm of arrows; most clattered harmlessly

off the wooden shields, but a few got through. No humans sustained mortal wounds, but at least a few of them would be slowed during the battle to come.

Undeterred by the cries of his comrades and the arrows that flamed and fizzled around him, the wizard began to move his fingers rapidly in some sort of silent, arcane language. He concluded by banging both hands together. The result was like a summer storm, like lighting and thunder combined into one killing stroke.

A thunderclap rolled outward from his hands and through the forest; every arrow that was in flight at that moment flared with brilliant white light. A bolt of energy sizzled *back* from each glowing arrow, following an invisible path through the air and back to the archer who had sent it forth.

Foxfire watched in horror as five of his people were blasted into ash.

He drew in a breath to call for retreat, but the sound died in a strangled gasp as all the world seemed to burst into flame. There was no heat, just a sudden, searing light that was nearly as painful.

The elf dug both fists into his eyes, trying to rub away the painful sparkles that danced and whirled behind his eyelids. When at last his eyes adjusted to the unnatural brightness, the possibility of retreat vanished from his thoughts.

The humans had dragged the captured elves into the clearing. There were seven of them, and all were alive, though the foot-hold traps—clearly visible now that they had been sprung—had inflicted terrible wounds upon them. A few men guarded them, loaded crossbows leveled at their hearts. And surrounding them was a circle of human mercenaries, swords drawn.

One of these men waved his weapon at the trees overhead and shouted something. Foxfire and Tamsin exchanged helpless shrugs—neither of them spoke the language of Tethyr's humans. Before Foxfire could call down a request for parley in the Common trade tongue,

the human found another, more visual way to get his
meaning across.

He spun and lunged in a single, quick movement, sinking his sword deep into one of the helpless elves. Then he
turned to the forest and brandished his crimson blade.
The challenge was clear, as was the price of refusal.

The first to respond was Hawkwing; she dropped to
the ground with the speed of her namesake, her dagger
gleaming talon-bright in her hand. Without hesitation,
all the elves who could still fight followed the fierce elf
maid into the circle of wizard-light and death.

*   *   *   *   *

In another part of Tethir, far from the clash of
weapons and the scent of death, Arilyn clung to her
friend's silver fur as he carried her swiftly toward the
hidden den of the lythari.

She had known Ganamede from childhood, but nothing in their shared experience could have prepared her
to enter the hidden world of the lythari. The den of the
shapeshifting elves was not in an underground cave, as
Arilyn had anticipated, but in some middle realm, an
unseen world.

There was no visible passage, no magical gate; one
moment they were in Tethir, the next, they were not.

Although the journey might have felt seamless, there
was no mistaking that a momentous change had taken
place. She and Ganamede were still in a forest, but one
quite different from the dense, cool shade of Tethir. The
trees were taller, more majestic, and like nothing that
Arilyn had ever seen before. The air was warmer, more
alive. But the most compellingly apparent change was
that the waning night had been replaced by the long
golden shadows of late afternoon. This was the time of
day Arilyn loved most, the moment near the end of a
perfect spring day that was almost heartbreaking in its
beauty, a time that was almost, but not quite, twilight.

Almost twilight.

Suddenly Arilyn understood why Ganamede had insisted she cling to his back: no mortal could make the passage to these fabled realms unassisted. She slid from the lythari and rose slowly to her feet.

"Faerie," she whispered, naming the land which legend claimed to be the elves' first home, a land left behind in a time far beyond memory. According to elven myth, Faerie was a place of incredible beauty that would last for a single day, albeit one nearly immeasurable in its length. Some of the elves, knowing that their day here would eventually end, had ventured beyond Faerie into other worlds in hope that they might find a way to escape the coming night. Or so legend claimed. Arilyn had always assumed that Faerie was an allegory and not a literal place. She seized Ganamede's face between her hands and repeated the word, this time as a question.

The lythari's wolflike form shimmered and gave way to that of the otherworldly elf. Ganamede smiled at his awestruck friend, his blue eyes gently indulgent.

"Faerie? Well, not quite. This is a place between the worlds—quite fitting for people such as you and I who are neither wholly one thing nor another. But come—you wanted to meet the others."

Too stunned to give voice to the thousand questions that whirled through her mind, Arilyn followed as Ganamede set off toward the sound of falling water. There, by a waterfall in a glade the color of an emerald's heart, the lythari made their home.

After one glance, Arilyn understood that her quest was futile. She could think of nothing that could entice the lythari into the conflict of war. The peace and beauty of this place made the very thought of it an unspeakable obscenity, as was the notion of disturbing the serenity and joy of these magical beings.

Several adults in elven form danced to the haunting music of a bone pipe, played by a lythari woman so

delicate she seemed carved of moonlight. Two more
elves bathed in the splashing waters of the falls, laughing as they watched the antics of a trio of wolflike young
that tumbled and played at the edge of the pool.

An involuntary smile curved Arilyn's lips. This was
how Ganamede had looked when she first met him—
although not nearly so carefree and joyful.

The young lythari had ventured into the outer world
too soon, only to be caught in a snare. Arilyn had been a
child herself at the time, willful enough to ignore the
warnings about venturing alone into the wild Greycloak
Hills that surrounded Evereska, young enough to be
charmed with the idea of keeping a pet wolf. Her mother,
Z'beryl, had had other ideas. She sent word to the
lythari's tribe—exactly how, Arilyn had never learned—
and a stern, pale-haired male elf came the next day to
whisk away the errant cub. But it seemed that the young
lythari had a contrary streak to match Arilyn's own.
Many times over the next several years he slipped away
to seek out his half-elven playmate. When Arilyn left
Evereska after her mother's death, Ganamede had given
her a summoning pipe and a knowledge of the "doors to
the gate" where she might find him. Only now did Arilyn
understand what that meant. Although there was but
one gate to the lythari's lair, they could probably emerge
at will in Tethir or Evermeet or Cormanthor. But why
would they choose to do so, other than to hunt?

"The lythari will not come," Arilyn said softly.

"No," agreed Ganamede, "but I had to show you, else
you would not have understood why."

He took her arm and drew her away from the peace-
ful glade. "But I myself will take you to the nearest
settlement of the green elves, a place known as Talltrees. It lies a day's walk to the north, but I can get you
there in a matter of hours. I wish there were more I
could do for you."

Despite her disappointment, Arilyn couldn't help but
smile as she pictured the impact Ganamede's appear-

ance would make. "That's more helpful than you know," she said in a wry tone. "If an entrance like *that* doesn't impress the forest people, I'll know enough to turn around and go home!"

*   *   *   *   *

The palace of Pasha Balik was without doubt the largest and most impressive building in all of Zazesspur. At its core was a summer palace built by Alehandro III. Amazingly, it had escaped the destruction of the royal family—followed by the demolition of most of the royal properties—virtually unscathed. When Balik came to power he'd taken it over, bought up the surrounding land, and expanded the original buildings into an enormous marble complex ringed by even more spectacular gardens.

One of the newer additions was a large chamber suitable for meetings of state. Here met the Council of Lords—a dozen men and women of noble rank—to hear important cases, debate policy, and make decisions that would address the good of all the people of Zazesspur. At least, that was the Council's original and stated intent. The Council, inspired by the lords who ruled Waterdeep, had been created shortly after the downfall of the royal house. Though it was intended to be the ruling body, most of its members came to view their seats as stepping stones toward greater power. In recent years, however, the Council had done little more than carry out the will of the pasha.

Balik was a vain man who allowed himself to be seduced by the notion of his own importance. He had grown increasingly deaf to the voices of the coalition of southerners, royalists, and merchants who had brought him to power. Seldom these days did he hear anything but his own inclinations.

Today, however, Pasha Balik seemed unusually willing to listen to counsel. "You are all aware of the growing threat from the elven people," he began. "Caravans ransacked, trade lost, farms and trading posts attacked. We will set all other business aside and consider how best to deal with this problem."

Lord Faunce, one of the few noblemen present who had actually inherited his title, rose to speak. "What do the elves have to say about this matter?"

"That is something none but the gods can tell you. The Elven Council has been destroyed, the settlement burned to ash," supplied Zongular, a priest of Ilmater, speaking this dire news with lugubrious relish.

Lord Hhune, guildmaster, rose to his feet. "My lords, must I remind you that in less enlightened times an effort was made to push the elves from this country? Their lands were seized, many were slain, some were pushed deep into the forest. I speak for patience and urge forbearance," he said passionately. "At the very least, let us take time to examine the reports against the elves and see if perhaps the tales have grown somewhat in the telling. To move too quickly would certainly result in a waste of fighting men and most likely in the deaths of many innocent elven folk!"

A few of the other lords exchanged arch looks. Hhune had been quite young during the "less enlightened times" he spoke of, yet few present doubted that he would not have been among the most zealous in carrying out his king's desire to exterminate the elves of Tethyr. But ever changeful were the winds of fortune, and few among them could match Hhune's skill as a social weather vane. For the most part, they admired him for it.

Even so, the Marquessa D'Morreto couldn't resist putting in a dig. "The memories of the elves are long. It may well be that they act in retaliation for the wrongs done them," she suggested piously.

"We do not even know that the elves are truly responsible!" thundered Hhune.

"But if not, then who? And why would so much be laid falsely on the elven folk of Tethir?" asked Lord Faunce.

"That is precisely what I intend to find out," Lord Hhune said grimly. "I will learn what there is to know of this matter, and I will pass this knowledge on to you." He paused to give weight to his next words. "There are those in this land who can find answers to any question. I ask your indulgence only in the matter of time."

The Council considered this in silence. All knew that Hhune referred to the secret and dreaded Knights of the Shield; more than a few suspected he had ties to this shadowy group. Whatever the case, they were content to leave the troublesome elves in his hands. As the Marquess had pointed out, there was no one among them who had as much at stake in this matter as did Hhune.

Fortunately for Lord Hhune, there was not one among them who understood exactly what it was that he planned to do, or what he held at risk.

None, that was, but the lord's bodyguard—a tall, heavy-chested man with a black beard, cold gray eyes, and a flower-shaped scar on one cheek. As this man listened to Hhune's impassioned speech, he passed a hand over his bearded lips to hide a grimace—or perhaps a smile.

Twelve

It was difficult to surprise an elf at any time, and almost impossible to creep up on a green elf in his own forest stronghold. Yet the lythari were called "silver shadows" for good reason. In his lupine form, Ganamede moved more swiftly and silently than the wind—not even the leaves rustled when he passed. And Arilyn, who rode upon his back with her arms flung tightly around his massive silver neck, thought she knew why this was so. The lythari walked between worlds, even when their feet trod upon the solid face of Toril.

They reached the outer boundaries of the Talltrees settlement late that day, slipping easily past the layers of secrecy that enfolded the elven village. The forest had strange magical properties, Ganamede had told her, that distorted the senses of outsiders. Arilyn could hold her direction as well as most rangers, but even she felt oddly disoriented as they neared the hidden village.

Nor were these the only magical barriers. Twin dryads—

beautiful sylvan creatures who were not quite either
human or elven—peeked out at them from behind a stand
of beech trees. Any male who wandered near this lair would
have the image of wondrously beautiful dryads giggling
behind their white hands as his last memory of this part of
Tethir forest. A male who fell under a dryad's charm usually awoke, dazed and utterly lost, under some unfamiliar
tree. When at last he found his way back to settled lands,
he invariably learned that as much as a year had passed
without leaving a single footprint upon his memory. It was
a gossamer web that the dryads wove, but a powerful one.

Beyond the dryads' grove, not even silent Ganamede
could escape detection. Sharp-eyed elven warriors
walked the surrounding forest. Other sentries, the birds
and squirrels that chattered and scolded in the trees,
carried warnings that were heard and heeded by the
elven folk. Arilyn noted the subtle changes in the song
of forest birds that no doubt announced their coming.

"They know we're here. You might as well let me
down," she said quietly. The lythari came to a stop; Arilyn slid down and rose to her full height. She smoothed
down the vest of elven chain mail, adjusted her swordbelt, and then squared her shoulders for the trial ahead.

Lifting her chin to an angle that approximated that
of a proud elven courtier, Arilyn placed one hand on the
lythari's pale silver shoulder. "Here we go," she murmured. "We should be fine, but if things start getting
hostile I want you out of here like a flea off a fire newt."

Ganamede cast an exasperated look up at her, his
blue eyes stating beyond doubt what he thought of her
chosen figure of speech.

A wry grin brightened Arilyn's face—and dissipated a
bit of her tension. "How indelicate of me, bringing up
fleas," she said with mock gravity. "Nearly as thought-
less as mentioning heartburn to a red dragon!"

"Are you quite through?" the lythari inquired patiently.
"Or would you like to compound the insult by scratching
behind my ears?"

Arilyn's shoulders shook in a brief, silent chuckle. "I meant what I said," she repeated, suddenly serious. "Get out at the first sign of trouble."

"And what of you?"

What indeed? she repeated silently.

"If I fall, try to reclaim my sword at some later time. I know this is asking a great deal of you, but if you were to ask anything of the forest elves, they would surely give it. I would not ask, but mine is a hereditary blade, and its magic will continue as long as there is a need for it and a worthy descendant to wield it. When its purpose has been fulfilled, it will go dormant."

And until that distant day—and perhaps far longer than that, Arilyn added silently—her spirit would be imprisoned within!

"A hereditary sword. Then you have children?" Ganamede inquired.

It was a logical question, but it struck Arilyn like a kick to the gut. She had never considered that particular aspect of the moonblade's demands, for she had never given a moment's thought to the possibility that she might bear children of her own. Arilyn knew all too well the ambiguity that defined a half-elf's existence, and she would not wish this upon another. Nor would any child of hers be a likely candidate for the moonblade. As far as Arilyn knew, she was the only moonblade wielder in the entire history of these ancient swords who was not of pure moon-elf heritage. Not even a full-blooded elf of another noble race—the gold elves, or the green, or the sea folk—had every held such a sword and lived. What chance would a child of hers have against the moonblade's silent test? And knowing what she did about the nature of the elfshadow, how could she pass such a sentence along? Immediate death, or eternal servitude. It was not much of a legacy.

Even if her offspring should claim the sword and fail, that death would not purchase her freedom. The moonblade she carried was of the Moonflower clan, and the line would not die with Arilyn. The gods only knew how many unknown royal aunts and uncles and cousins she had running blithely about on distant Evermeet!

Which brought her to a second disturbing realization: since she had no children of her own, she would have to name a blade heir from among her mother's kin. It occurred to her, for the first time, that the ties between her and her mother's people were far more complex than their common bloodlines.

"Lamruil," she blurted out, remembering a name from her mother's long-ago tales. "Prince Lamruil of Evermeet, youngest son of Amlaruil and mother's brother to me. I name him blade heir. There are 'doors to the gate' on Evermeet. If I fall, see that he gets the moonblade."

Ganamede gazed up at her, purely elven wonder shining through his wolflike features. "You are of Amlaruil's blood? Why have you never spoken of this?"

Even the lythari were not immune to the power of the queen, Arilyn thought bitterly. What was it about Amlaruil that inspired such reverence?

"Maybe I don't like to brag," she said shortly. "But come on—they know we're here, and they're probably wondering what's keeping us."

Together they walked for several hundred paces. Ganamede stopped suddenly and for no reason that Arilyn could ascertain.

"Look up," he advised her softly.

Arilyn did so and found that she stood in the center of what appeared to be a thriving settlement. The elven village itself was a wonder. Small dwellings had been fashioned high in the trees, connected by swinging walkways. So cleverly did the settlement blend in with the forest that no one could see it unless he stood in its midst and looked straight up—which, unless one had the benefit of a lythari escort, was about as likely to occur in the natural course of things as a salad-eating troll.

This, then, was Talltrees. But there was still no sign of the elven inhabitants.

"Where are they?" she said softly.

"All around. Read them the queen's proclamation," he urged her.

But the half-elf shook her head. That was Amlaruil's plan, and by Arilyn's estimation it had little chance of success. The offer of Retreat was a last resort. She would earn her freedom fairly, and she would do it in her own fashion.

"People of Talltrees," she called in a clear, ringing alto, speaking in the Elvish common tongue. "I am come to you from Amlaruil, Lady of Evermeet, Queen of the Elven Island. Will you hear an ambassador of the queen?"

There was no sound to herald their coming, but suddenly the forest around her was alive with watchful, copper-skinned elves. Where they had been a moment before, Arilyn couldn't say. She herself was considered skilled in matters of stealth, but these folk were of the forest, and one with it.

Their garb was simple and scant, fashioned almost without exception from the forest's bounty: tanned hides, rough linen beaten and woven from wild flax, ornaments of feather and bone. But there was nothing primitive or crude about these green elves. They were an ancient people with ancient ways. Arilyn they regarded with detached, wary curiosity, but most gazed at Ganamede with an awe that approached reverence. It was likely the first time most of them had ever laid eyes upon one of the elusive silver shadows. This meeting, Arilyn suspected, would be a tale they would pass down to their children's children.

A tall male, whose features struck Arilyn as oddly familiar, stepped forward with the dignity of a stag. Like most of the green elves, he was lightly clad. His ruddy skin was painted with swirling designs of greens and brown, and his dark brown hair was worn long and plaited back.

"I am Rhothomir, Speaker of the Talltrees tribe. For the sake of the noble lythari who has seen fit to lead you here, we will consider the words of Amlaruil of Evermeet."

Consider. For the sake of the lythari.

That was not exactly welcoming, but in truth Arilyn took a certain perverse satisfaction in the rare lack of enthusiasm this male showed for the elven queen.

But now came the tricky part. Propriety demanded that she give her name, her house, and her credentials. Since she was woefully short on all three, she would simply use what she had, follow the elf's lead, and hope for the best.

Arilyn pulled her moonblade, lifted it high in a sweeping, formal elven salute, and then went down on one knee before the Speaker. "I am Arilyn Moonblade, daughter of Z'Beryl of the Moonflower clan," she said, using the name her mother had taken in exile. "As sworn swordmaiden, I have forsaken clan ties to take the name of the ancient and magical sword I carry. Word of your troubles has reached Evermeet. In the name of Queen Amlaruil, I offer my sword and my life in defense of your tribe."

With these words she laid the moonblade at the green elf's feet.

For a long moment Rhothomir regarded her in silence. "Evermeet's queen sends us a single warrior?"

"What would your response be if she had sent a thousand?" Arilyn retorted. "What benefit would there be if so many feet were to trample a path through the woodlands, a path so broad your enemies could walk in comfort to your very door? With the help of my friend, Ganamede of the Greycloak tribe, I have left a path that none can follow."

A moment's silence. "You walk silently, for a *n'tel-que'tethira*," he admittedly grudgingly, using an Elvish word that roughly translated as "city-dweller." He considered the matter for another span of several moments, then turned away.

"Take up your sword and leave this place as silently as you came. We have no use for it, or you."

"No."

A silent ripple of astonishment ran through the elven assembly. Apparently, such a direct challenge to the Speaker's authority was an uncommon event.

An elven female walked to Rhothomir's side, her black eyes fixed upon Arilyn and the watchful lythari.

"Do not send them away. Think, Brother. If the silver shadows would fight for us, how quickly we could deal with those humans who defile our forest!"

Arilyn's eyes widened. She had never heard that voice, but somehow she knew it. It belonged to a female assassin who spoke only in whispers, one who used cosmetics to dim the luster of her skin and to transform her elven features into the exotic almond-eyed beauty of a woman of the far eastern lands. The silk turban had concealed ears as pointed as those of a fox, as well as gleaming chestnut hair that was now pulled back into a single braid. If there had been any doubt in Arilyn's mind about the elf woman's dual identity, it would have been removed by the sight of the tatoo on her bare shoulder: the stylized, graceful form of a hunting ferret.

The Harper also heard the dual meaning in the elf woman's words: people of human blood defiled the elven forest, but for the sake of an alliance with the lythari, Ferret would consider accepting Arilyn's presence and her secret. But if the elf woman were to reveal Arilyn's true nature, Prince Lamruil would fall heir to the moonblade at once! The sanctity of Talltrees, though honored by the presence of a lythari, would be deemed profaned and put at extreme risk by a half-elf's presence. They might even attack the lythari who had brought her here, thinking him a traitor to elvenkind. No matter what else came of this meeting, Arilyn vowed, she would see that Ganamede escaped safely.

Since Arilyn was still on one knee, she was roughly at eye level with the wolflike being. She turned to gaze into Ganamede's eyes. "Speaker Rhothomir, listen to your sister's counsel. I have asked the lythari of the Greycloak tribe to come to your assistance," she said, her eyes pleading with her friend to play along. "The noble Ganamede will leave now to hold council with his people as to what might best be done."

The lythari gave her a searching look. She responded with a faint smile and nod that suggested all would be well.

After a moment, Ganamede inclined his head. "I will ask them," he said softly, but his eyes were deeply puzzled. He turned and loped silently off into the forest.

Arilyn released her breath on a long, silent sigh of relief. She hated deceiving her friend. Fortunately, Ganamede seemed to have taken her request at face value. He was disappointed in her, that she apparently did not understand the nature of the lythari folk. Even so, he would do as she asked, though he knew what his people's response would be. Better that than letting him know how tenuous her own position was.

As soon as Ganamede was beyond reach, Arilyn reached for her sword and stood. She met Ferret's steady gaze. If there was yet any hope of forging a link with the green elves, it would be here.

"I can offer more than a possible alliance with the lythari. Most of you have not fought humans. I have. I know their ways, their world, their tactics."

"There is something in what you say," Rhothomir admitted. He turned to his sister. "You are the lore-keeper; you have more knowledge of the humans than any of us, as well as the elves who live beyond the forest. What do you say?"

"I would speak with this one alone," Ferret said. "There are things we should know about her and about the sword she carries. We all have heard tales of such swords. It may be that this moonblade was forged for just such a task."

"There is great risk in accepting outsiders," the Speaker said.

"And we will weigh the risks along with the benefits. Let me speak with this . . . moon elf, and judge whether what she offers is worthwhile."

After a moment's deliberation, Rhothomir agreed. Ferret strode over to a stout oak and tugged one of the vines that entwined its trunk. A long ladder unrolled, spilling down from one of the dwellings overhead. The elf woman indicated with a deft, impatient gesture that Arilyn should ascend the ladder.

With Ferret close behind her, the half-elf made the dizzying climb into trees. The dwelling was small and sparsely furnished: a bearskin served as a bed; some large clay pots held personal effects; a few garments hung from pegs on the wall. The elf motioned for Arilyn to take a seat on the bearskin and then seated herself on the floor, as far away as the small room permitted.

"How is it that you know a silver shadow?" Ferret demanded.

"We are friends from childhood. I freed him from a snare."

"In Tethir?"

"No. In the Greycloak Hills, a place many days' travel to the north of here. Ganamede's tribe takes its name from those hills—or perhaps it is the other way around. Lythari can travel far distances in ways that seem magical, even to an elf," Arilyn added, anticipating the elf woman's next question.

Ferret's gaze slipped to the sword at Arilyn's side. "How is it that you carry one of these swords? It is alive—I saw it glow with magic when we fought in the Harper's room!"

"Yes. That was a very convincing death scene," Arilyn added dryly. "As for the sword, it came to me as such a blade comes to any who wields it. It was passed down to me from my mother, Z'beryl."

"But how is that so? No moonblade has ever before been turned to evil!"

"Nor has this one," Arilyn said softly. "It cannot shed

innocent blood. If you would like to test this in combat, I would be happy to oblige you."

The challenge hung heavy in the silence that followed. "What are you?" Ferret said at last. "Half-elf assassin, or noble elven warrior?"

"What are *you?*" Arilyn countered. "When last I saw you, you were three against one, fully prepared to kill a good man for the sake of a few gold coins."

Ferret leaned forward. "You know the Harper? Where is he?"

"Far beyond your reach," Arilyn said coldly.

The elf woman gazed thoughtfully at Arilyn for several moments; then a slow, taunting smile spread across her face. "Well, well. The half-*woman* is not so cold a fish as she appears! This Harper, this human, what is he to you?"

"I don't see how that could possibly interest you."

"Oh, but it does. As it happens, the People have a use for just such a hound as a Harper. Even if we could push the human invaders from the forest, what is to stop them from returning? No, there is something more at work here. The tribe needs someone who can sniff out the trail to its source."

"And that's what you hoped to do in Zazesspur? By murdering the business rivals and faithless mistresses of any man who could afford your services?"

Ferret's gaze did not falter. "Those, and others of my own choosing," she said candidly. "I worked for myself and on behalf of my People. Those whom I thought to be enemies, I killed."

The two females regarded each other in silence for a long moment. "There is something in what you say," Arilyn admitted. "There are things at work here that must be understood. Had Danilo not been forced from Zazesspur, he and I could have worked together—he among the humans, I among the People. I will find my way to the source of Tethir's troubles, but part of that answer must be found in the forest."

"So you also are a Harper," Ferret said thoughtfully. "That would explain much. Do you think what is said of the People is true?" she demanded in an abrupt change of mood.

"I must know," Arilyn said simply. "It may well be that your people have provocation for all and anything they have done, but you must understand that these attacks—whether true or contrived—can bring only more trouble to the forest elves."

She held up a hand to silence the angry tirade that Ferret clearly had ready. "You spoke of pushing the human invaders from the forest. I must know of this, too. This would be the first step: stop them, and then follow their trail back wherever it might go. If there is a plot against the elves, the conspirators will be dealt with."

Ferret considered this. "If you are a Harper, why do you claim to be Evermeet's ambassador?"

Arilyn took the copy of the queen's pronouncement from her pack and placed it on the floor in front of the green elf. Ferret picked up the parchment and read it slowly.

"Evermeet's queen thinks we would Retreat?" she said scornfully.

"And the Harpers think you should compromise with the humans of Tethyr," Arilyn added with equal feeling. "I know that neither path will serve the forest folk; yet I'm obligated to act on behalf of both Amlaruil and the Harpers. If you give me a chance, I believe I can do better. I have already said how."

Ferret tossed the royal pronouncement aside and asked casually, "Tell me one thing more: do you have any idea how the others would respond, if I should ever speak of your true nature?"

"I have named my blade heir," Arilyn said simply.

This answer brought a small, tight smile to the green elf's face. "Very well. I will keep your secrets for now. Do what you can, Harper and half-elf, and know that if the

People are well served I will fight at your back."

Arilyn nodded, accepting Ferret's words—and the threat implicit in them. At any time, the elven assassin could betray her or, more likely, kill her.

A light tap at the open portal forestalled any answer Arilyn might have given. Both females turned toward the sound. A young green elf female with glossy black hair and frantic black eyes peered into the room.

"You are needed, Ferret," she said quickly. "I bring word of battle; it is dire. The humans have brought magic to the forest. They have captured some of our people, and our warriors fight them hand to hand. They are sorely pressed."

Ferret leaped to her feet and snatched a quiver of black arrows from a peg on the wall. She took a thick handful of arrows from one of the clay pots and handed them to Arilyn, who had also risen from the floor.

"You have a chance to prove your worth to the People, sooner than you might have anticipated. Know that one human more or less is of no consequence to me," she said coldly.

"Understood," Arilyn agreed. She took the arrows and followed the nimble elves down to the forest floor.

Perhaps forty elves were gathered there; the rest of the village, the young ones and the aged, had vanished into the trees. Arilyn's gaze swept over the warriors, taking note of their weapons and the totem animals tattooed onto their shoulders. These totems and spirit guides said much of an elf's skill and character.

"I have several fire-forged short swords and daggers in my packs. You are a strong hunter, and you, and those two females standing together," she said as she removed the weapons and tossed them to the ground.

The elves she'd indicated eyed the fine weapons with interest, but all cast inquiring glances at Rhothomir.

"What do you know of human magic?" he asked Arilyn.

"Nothing good."

The answer came from her before she could consider its impact, but it brought a grimly amused smile to the face of the elven leader. "But you *have* faced it in battle?"

"Many times."

Rhothomir turned to the assembled warriors. "Ferret has made her decision. I add to it my own: the moon elf will lead this battle. Pick up your swords."

Arilyn accepted command with a curt nod, then turned to the raven-haired elf woman who had brought word of the battle. "How far?"

"Two hours' run, maybe less"

And then she was off, running like a rabbit through the thick foliage. The others fell in behind without sparing so much as a glance at their new war leader. Nor did Arilyn expect otherwise. She worked alone most of the time, but she had learned much from observing some of the best leaders the northern lands had known. There were times when the best thing to do was shut up and follow.

And so she did, running as lightly as any green elf, toward what she suspected would be the first of many such battles.

Thirteen

 The clash and the cries of warfare rang through the forest, speeding the footsteps of the green elves who ran toward battle. True to her word, Ferret stayed at Arilyn's back, running as softly as a shadow. The Harper did her best to ignore the threat the elf woman posed, so that she might concentrate on the battle before her. The sounds coming from the vale ahead—the clanging of swords, the grunts and screams of pain, the horrible, hate-filled oaths hurled by the human fighters—promised that the battle would be difficult and ugly.

Arilyn pulled to a stop some hundred yards from the battlefield, just as the first of the Talltrees warriors nocked an arrow and sent it hurtling into the midst of the wild melee. Before the first arrow found its mark, the elven archer followed with a second. Both arrows disappeared in a burst of white light, just short of their target.

"Hold!" shouted Arilyn, flinging out a hand toward the other ready archers, for at least six other elves had bowstrings drawn and arrows ready for flight. Something in her tone and her face stopped them.

Before the elves' horrified gaze, twin bolts of arcane lighting sizzled back toward the first archer. The white lines of fire engulfed the elf. A brilliant areola flared around him, briefly, and then it was gone, leaving nothing of him but a flurry of black ash.

"They've got a Halruaan wizard," she told Rhothomir—and the watchful Ferret—in a grim tone. "That's bad."

The Harper quickly took stock of the battlefield. There was a small open area, thickly shaded by the giant trees that ringed it and crowded with men and elves in fierce hand-to-hand combat. More than two hours had passed since Talltrees had received word of the battle, and by all appearances it had raged without pause since that time. The ground was trampled and blood-soaked; few of the combatants had escaped wounds. In the center of the battlefield, five or six elves had been manacled with foot-hold traps and were crowded together. This, Arilyn reasoned, was the bait that had lured the green elves into open combat. Five men, three of them swordsmen and one an archer, stood over these prisoners. The other, the only unarmed person on the field, had to be their wizard. The armor he wore was more affectation than protection. The odd ensemble—metal-studded leather augmented with metal shoulder plates, chest guard, and cod piece—could only have come from the imagination of a Halruaan artificer. Around this inner group, standing in a circle with their backs to the captives, was a ring of well-trained swordsmen. These engaged the elves, all of whom fiercely tried to break through to their kindred. The lone human archer in the center of the circle was able to easily pick off any elf who managed to get past the outer perimeter.

Arilyn glanced at the ground in the battlefield's center; no spent elven arrows lay there. Nor did any of the humans bear arrow wounds. Clearly, the elven archer who had just perished by magic fire was not the first to

meet this fate. There were limits to the number of times
a wizard could cast such a powerful spell; this one probably had some sort of device that stored a number of fire-
arrow spells, or that put a sphere of protection around
him. Such things were not common, not even in magic-
rich Halruaa, but neither were they particularly rare.

Arilyn thought fast, then turned to the elves clus-
tered behind her. "Who's the best archer among you?"
she demanded of Rhothomir.

The Speaker pointed with his bow to one of the fighters—a male, taller than most of the green elves and
marked by his autumn-colored hair. "Foxfire, our war
leader. None can match his bow."

"Call him," she said tersely.

Rhothomir lifted one hand to his mouth and let out a
high, sharp call, like that of a hunting eagle. The red-
haired elf tensed, hesitated, then backed away from the
fighting. He turned and ran toward the waiting elves.
His black eyes widened in astonishment when they settled upon the moon-elf woman.

"How many shots can you get off in one breath?" she
asked. "Three? Four?"

"Six," he answered reflexively.

Arilyn grimaced. "That's pushing it. Four's about my
limit. Here's what I want you to do: shoot four bolts
straight at the wizard, then get the hell out of my way.
The returned fire will keep him busy and take out some
of the men guarding your people."

"How—"

Before the elf could give voice to the question, Arilyn
answered it. Her moonblade flashed from its sheath,
slicing up toward the male's face. He flinched away
instinctively and raised his dagger to parry the blow. Not
fast enough. Arilyn completed the stoke, reversed her
sword's direction, and slapped his dagger out wide with
a one-handed backstroke. As she completed the counter-
move, she stepped in close and held a small object
directly in front of the elf's eyes. It was a feather, one

that had been hanging from his headband just a moment before.

"Fast sword," she said by way of explanation.

"Four bolts," Foxfire agreed, his black eyes bright with astonished admiration—and the beginning of new hope.

"Here's the plan," Arilyn said quickly, turning to the other elves. "Foxfire and I will give the wizard something to think about. The Halruaan will be distracted, but just for a moment. I'm going to charge him. As soon I as begin to move, you need to do two things: cut me a path through that circle, and take out the archer in the middle as well any guards who still stand. Got it?"

Foxfire pointed out four of the warriors. "Bows ready. Aim for the humans who are fighting Xanotter and Hawkwing, then shoot for the guards. Name your man, first and second."

The elves quickly called off descriptions of their chosen targets, then turned intently to the moon elf. Their war leader's excitement seemed contagious; apparently if Foxfire was willing to follow the moon elf's instructions, they would do likewise.

"Several fighters need to follow me into the breach," Arilyn continued. "Turn the battle inside out; engage them from inside the circle."

"You would have us surrounded?" demanded Ferret suspiciously.

"She would present our archers with the humans' broad backsides as targets," Foxfire corrected her with a grin. Still smiling, he turned to Arilyn and held up four black arrows. "I am ready to begin."

The Harper nodded and lifted her moonblade into guard position. Foxfire went down on one knee before her and pulled back his drawstring for the first shot.

Black lightning streaked toward the Halruaan wizard, followed by a second bolt and then two more, faster than Arilyn would have believed possible. The arrows burst into flame just short of the wizard. As Foxfire

dove to one side, Arilyn gritted her teeth and prepared
to meet the first sizzling line of force. Black lighting to
white—the transformation happened almost too
quickly for the eye to absorb.

The moonblade flared with eldritch blue light as the
first magical attack seared toward its wielder. Deftly
Arilyn parried the bolts, one after another, moving her
sword just slightly to meet each one and to send them
shimmering back toward the astonished wizard.

Immediately Arilyn kicked into a run. She heard the
ping and whine of the elven arrows that flashed past
her—almost close enough to touch—as she ran toward
the humans Foxfire had pointed out. One of them, a
large man with a badly cut face and bloodstained beard,
dropped his sword to clutch at the pair of arrows that
suddenly sprouted from his throat. He fell forward. Arilyn leaped over his prone form and hurled herself,
sword leading, at the Halruaan.

The wizard was surrounded with a blaze of his own
magical fire, but the same amulet that protected him
from arrows kept the lightning from blasting him. It
merely set fire to his magic shield. Within his glowing
sphere, the wizard began the casting of yet another spell.

Arilyn did not fear the fire—one of the moonblade's
ancient powers was a resistance to flame. Her moonblade plunged into the arcane fire, and white lightning
licked up her sword to stop at the glowing moonstone in
its hilt. Arilyn felt no pain, but a twinge of worry began
to gnaw at the corner of her mind. Her sword did not
pierce the glowing bubble.

She flung the moonblade out wide and at least managed
to thrust the wizard's hands apart, to interrupt whatever
dire casting he planned to unleash upon the elves.

Glowering, the wizard conjured a sword of his own
and lunged at her. His blade did not pierce the glowing
sphere, either. Apparently the wizard's field of protection kept everything but magic from passing through.
Unfortunately, Arilyn had none to hurl.

But she noted how his sword thrust pressed the fire line, causing it to bulge out toward her. A plan came to her—a variation on the most basic and dirty trick in a gutter fighter's repertoire. It was well, she thought wryly, that no one would expect such an attack from the noble moon elf she appeared to be.

She darted in, sword held high. The wizard parried; sparks flew, even though their blades were far from touching. Again Arilyn lashed out, and again, measuring each time the distance between his sword and the point where hers clashed against the protective shield. It seemed to be lessening with each stroke, and the fire dimming. That meant the final attack she had planned would not be a killing stroke. Even so, Arilyn was willing to bet that it would put the wizard out of action for some time to come.

Holding her moonblade firmly in both hands, Arilyn swung upward, catching the wizard's fire-enshrouded blade and throwing his arm up high. She continued the swing in a tight, abrupt downward arc, pivoting her body to one side to follow through. The moonblade's point drove into the ground; Arilyn leaped, kicking out hard to the side and pushing herself off the embedded sword.

She aimed directly for the wizard's metal cod piece, and her aim was true. Though the fiery shield kept her boots from connecting directly with the armor, the wizard's shrill bellow announced that the fire had done its work well enough.

Arilyn scrambled to her feet and yanked her sword from the ground, blinking in the sudden darkness that followed the dissipation of the wizard's shield. Apparently the surge of pain had sufficiently disrupted his concentration to dispel the protection. The wizard danced and howled, torn between removing the hot armor—and in the process searing his magic-wielding fingers—or leaving the cod piece where it was and suffering a somewhat more personal injury. Ultimately, his devotion to his Art took second place.

"Figures," Arilyn muttered as she turned to survey the battle. The wizard frantically cast aside the steaming metal and fled stumbling into the forest, and she let him go. He wouldn't be casting any more spells today, and the elves faced a more immediate threat.

One of them, a female who was little more than a child, had faced off against a swordsman who was easily four times her weight. The girl had the advantage of speed and stamina—large dark circles stained the sides and front of the man's tunic, and his breath came in loud, snorting gasps—but still she was at a disadvantage in terms of strength, experience and—most importantly at this crucial moment—reach.

Even as Arilyn turned toward the duel, the swordsman lunged at the elf maid's throat at the same time as the girl thrust toward his belly. She had a dagger; he held a hand-and-a-half sword that could run her through before she even came close.

Arilyn darted in and thrust her moonblade between the two combatants, catching the longer blade and forcing it up. The elf child ducked reflexively, but she did not turn aside her thrust. Her dagger plunged deep; she wrenched it free and whirled to face the nearest human, leaving Arilyn to finish the man or let him die in his own time.

The green elves, Arilyn noted, did not intend to take prisoners.

Even as this thought formed in her mind, a few humans broke ranks and fled into the forest. One of them stopped suddenly, his head jolting back and his arms outflung. Several arrows bristled from his back.

"Foxfire, no! Let them go!" Arilyn shouted as she turned toward two more combatants. There was a moment's hesitation; then she heard the shrill, birdlike command that called off the vengeful elves.

Arilyn prodded the swordsman with the tip of her blade, drawing him away from the wounded and exhausted elf woman he was battling. The man whirled, lunged, and lunged again. A ranger, Arilyn noted with disgust, catching a glimpse of the unicorn pendant he wore at his neck—the symbol of the goddess Mielikki. There were few humans she held in higher regard than rangers, and none that she despised more than those handful of noble woodsmen-warriors who had forsaken their path.

This one fought in the style of the Dalelands—a single sword, a quick and aggressive attack. Arilyn fell back a step, drawing his next attack. Rather than parry it when it came, she leaped back. The sudden and unexpected lack of resistance threw the swordsman off-balance for a moment. That was enough. Arilyn spun away from his attack, pivoting on her outer foot and swinging her sword up and around as she circled behind him. She brought it down, hard, on the back of the man's neck. The moonblade cut through bone and flesh in a single strike, beheading the faithless ranger.

"Give my regards to Mielikki," Arilyn muttered darkly and then turned to look for another fight.

There was none. All around her the elves were tending to their wounded, cleaning their weapons, collecting their spent arrows. Ferret, however, still had the light of battle in her black eyes; she came at Arilyn like a stooping falcon.

"Why did you let them go? What base treachery is this? They will be back; they are too near Talltrees!"

"They *had* to go," Arilyn said calmly, stooping to clean the former ranger's blood from her sword. "Else, how would we follow them and find out to whom they report?"

Again the elves looked to Foxfire. He nodded, not once taking his eyes from the moon elf. "That is good counsel. Faunalyn, Wistari—you follow them and report what you learn."

The two scouts left at once to do his bidding. Foxfire came over to Arilyn and offered her his hand. She took it and allowed him to help her to her feet.

"I have prayed to the Seldarine for guidance, and this is how they have rewarded me," he said with a smile. "Only one god, the patron of the forest, would answer me so well; Rillifane Rallithil himself must have sent you!"

"Actually, that would be Amlaruil Moonflower. Not that there's all that much difference between the two," Arilyn said dryly as she tugged her fingers free.

To her surprise, this irreverent comment brought a grin to the green elf's bronzed face. She liked that. He had a steady nerve in battle but also possessed a warmth unusual among the aloof and insular People.

As Arilyn watched Foxfire move about the battlefield, she understood why this elf was a leader among his people. There was a natural charisma about him, an aura of confidence and energy that was contagious. They respected him, that was plain, but there was more than that. Arilyn noted that Foxfire had the gift of making each individual his eyes fell upon feel as if he or she were the most valued person beneath the stars. He greeted the adolescent elf maid with a warrior's handclasp, which Arilyn suspected would please the fierce child more than any praise. And he let each elf tend the task to which he or she was best suited, giving no commands where none were needed. The young female—the one who had brought word of the battle to Arilyn and Ferret—was obviously some sort of healer. She moved from one wounded elf to another, judging the severity of their wounds and giving orders regarding their care. Foxfire had little need, it seemed, to stake out territory of his own for the sake of pride or status. What needed to be done was done as best it might; that was enough.

Enough? It was a damn sight more than most leaders accomplished, Arilyn noted with ever-growing admiration.

Later, after the wounded had been tended and litters fashioned from skins and poles to carry those who could not walk, the elves set out for Talltrees. Despite the success of her battle strategy, the elves seemed wary of Arilyn. She heard the whispers that explained her presence among them to those who had not witnessed her arrival—and noted wryly how frequently the word "lythari" came into these explanations.

After a while Foxfire made his way to Arilyn's side. Although he did not seem to share his people's reservations, it was obvious that he was aware of them. "Your ways are strange to us, and the forest folk are slow to accept that which is new," he said softly. "But in time, they will accept you as a leader."

"Not a leader. An advisor. The People follow you."

The elf considered this, then accepted with a nod, apparently seeing the wisdom of the arrangement she suggested. "How did you know what to do in battle?"

"I know these men. Not these very ones," she amended, "but I have a knowledge of the breed."

"You are a warrior of Evermeet. How is it that you know the ways of humankind?" he asked.

Arilyn was not one for talking, but she found she did not mind his questions. Unlike Ferret's, these bore no note of accusation, but a genuine interest. "My clan is from Evermeet, but I have lived all my life upon the mainland."

"Yet you do the bidding of Evermeet's sovereign. Your devotion to Queen Amlaruil must be great indeed," he said solemnly.

Arilyn did not miss the faint twinkle in his eyes, however, that marked his words as teasing. Nor did she miss the subtle question that lay under his words.

She did not answer at once, for nothing that came to mind would ring true. From the corner of her eye she glimpsed Ferret, who followed her like a shadow—far enough away to eschew suspicion, but close enough to come to the aid of her tribe's war leader if Arilyn should lift a treacherous blade against him. She remembered something Ferret had said earlier that day, when she had unexpectedly spoken up in Arilyn's behalf.

"I have a duty to the elven people, and all my life I have done what I could. This task, however, was laid upon me by the sword I carry. It is a matter of destiny," she said quietly.

The words were true; the fact that she was trying to *avoid* her likely destiny was one of those small details best left unexamined. Foxfire accepted her explanation without further questions. He pointed to the trees ahead, and to the thin wisps of smoke curling up toward the stars.

"Talltrees," he said with quiet satisfaction.

Contained in that word was more than Arilyn could explain—more than she had ever experienced. Never had she called a place home, not in the sense that Foxfire expressed with a single word: a yearning satisfied, a journey ended, a place to which a person belonged.

And a wondrous homecoming it was. The elves who had stayed behind came to greet their warriors with an outpouring of emotion that would amaze anyone who ever had thought of elves as cold and aloof. Among their own, in the security of Talltrees, the green elves showed a warmth that amazed Arilyn.

The wounded were tended first and the warriors fed; then all the tribe erupted into celebration. Those who could dance did so, to the pulsing of resonant skin-covered drum and the haunting music of reed pipes. Skin of berry wine, potent and deceptively sweet, were passed from elf to elf.

At last the revelry subsided into a contented calm. Rhothomir called for the lore-talker to tell the story of the day's battle.

To Arilyn's surprise, Ferret stepped forward. It still seemed odd to Arilyn, who was accustomed to hearing the female speak in whispers, to hear that low and resonant voice. But the elf woman's love of story, and her duty to her role, was soon apparent. Ferret told the story of the battle, sparing none of the painful details—although Arilyn thought it odd that she did not give the names of the elves who were slain. Nor did she omit the contribution that Arilyn had made. It was a fair and evenhanded account, told with a flair any bard might envy.

Seeing Arilyn's puzzlement, Foxfire leaned in close to whisper, "The time for mourning will come with the dawn, or perhaps the day after—or perhaps not at all. The spirits of the green elves are slow to leave their forest home; we do not name them as lost who are still among us."

Arilyn merely nodded, hoping her silence would signify respect rather than extreme lack of interest. The afterlife was not a matter she cared to discuss. Fortunately, Ferret had bowed to the request for another tale.

"In a time beyond the years of any here, our people walked beneath a forest far different from the one we now call home," she began. "Cormanthor, it was called, and in its shadows thrived an elven kingdom of such might and wonder as this world has never known. But even there the elves glimpsed the coming twilight. The world changed, and Cormanthor fell.

"The People who survived were forced to flee. Many retreated to Evermeet, but there were tribes of green elves who would not forsake the land named Faerûn, in honor and in memory of the first elven home. These faithful scattered over the land, carrying with them seedlings from the sacred forest, the children of the maple, the oak, and the elm. We walk beneath these trees today, the children's children of Cormanthor.

"Nor were these green folk the only ones who wished to keep alive that which was Cormanthor. There were many People, some of the moon and the gold races, who continued to walk upon Faerûn. One of these is remembered with honor by all the People of Tethir: the moon fighter Soora Thea, who carried a sword of Myth Drannor.

"There was in times past an evil race of beings, neither human nor ogrish, that made war upon the forest folk. Their power came from a vast image of stone, the hideous image of a creature from the dark planes. Long ago these people fell, but at certain times their restless undead ventured from the gorge in which they once had lived to make war upon the goodly folk. With them were fearsome creatures from the dark planes. From all sides these creatures pressed the elves, and for a time it seemed as if the fall of Cormanthor would be a nightmare relived. But Soora Thea was a mighty war leader, and it is said she had the power to command the silver shadows. In the final great battle, the undead creatures and their Abyssal allies were utterly destroyed.

"What became of Soora Thea, we do not know. Unlike the green folk, she was a traveler, and her home was all of the land. But before she left Tethir, she promised that in times of greatest need, and for as long as the fires of Myth Drannor burned within her sword, a hero would return to the People."

Ferret turned her burning black eyes directly upon Arilyn. There was nothing to be added, but the half-elf understood at last why Ferret had accepted her presence here. Even more than most elves, these folk revered the silver shadows. The very possibility that Arilyn might command the lythari gave them hope and awoke in them the strength that could be found only in ancient tales and traditions. She could see it in their eyes—the bright hope that spilled over into a uniquely elven display of joy.

The drums and reed flutes took up the refrain again, and every elf who could stand whirled into the dance. Foxfire pulled Arilyn to her feet and into his arms. She rewarded his hospitality by treading squarely on his toes.

"I move better with a sword in my hand," she said ruefully.

Foxfire tossed back his head and laughed. "If you dance half so well as you fight, you will have grace enough to charm the entire Seldarine."

Arilyn smiled. Speaking of charm, this one had it by the bucketful. "A silver tongue is rare among the forest folk. I was given to think that you preferred plain words," she teased him.

"Then I shall speak plainly. I am glad you have come."

The intricate pattern of the dance changed, and Arilyn was whirled away into the circle. The elves spun and dipped, drawing down the starlight, weaving it into threads of magic with their music and dance.

Like the stardust spoken of in a lullaby, the mystic dance settled upon the elves and lulled them to repose. The wounded who could not dance rested comfortably, many smiling softly as their unseeing eyes gazed upon pleasant and healing memories. Most of the children had slipped deep into reverie, and their parents bore them quietly away to their rest. The celebration ended, not in a drunken stupor as did so many human revels, but on a note of quiet exultation.

Arilyn treasured the moment of peace as a rare gift. Along with the elves, she quietly made her way to her resting place.

A small dwelling had been given her, and as she climbed the ladder it began to occur to her just how tired she truly was. She stripped off her clothes and washed from the basin of mint-scented water that had been left there for her. Before sleeping, she pulled on fresh leggings and a tunic—clothes better suited for fighting than sleeping. But not even the peace of Talltrees could erase the habits of a lifetime, or the memories of the many times she had leaped from bed to battle.

One final preparation remained. Arilyn took from her pack the mask Tinkersdam had made for her, and she pressed it carefully to her upper face. Should anyone happen to look upon her, they would see not a slumbering half-elf, but a moon elven warrior in well-deserved reverie.

Despite all that had happened, despite the success in battle, and despite Ferret's tales, Arilyn knew what would become of her if the green elves realized that a human's daughter slept among them.

The dance was long finished and most of the elves had retired, but for some reason Foxfire did not share their calm. He felt unaccountably restless—excited, perhaps, by the first real hope he had felt for many days. He had managed to hide his growing despair, but not until now did he realize how heavy the burden of it had been.

He noticed that Korrigash, too, seemed immune to the magic of the star-web woven by the dance. The dark-haired hunter sat alone by the embers of the cookfire, staring at the few pinpricks of light left among the coals.

Korrigash was one of the elves who had been caught in the traps, and his pride was no doubt more sorely wounded than this leg. Tamara insisted that Korrigash would soon walk and run and hunt as well as ever he had, but Foxfire knew how unwelcome the prospect of even a brief period of inactivity must be to the hunter.

Foxfire walked over to sit at his friend's side. Immediately Korrigash fixed a concerned gaze upon him.

"She is an outsider," he said without preamble. "Nothing good can come of it."

The war leader frowned, realizing that Korrigash spoke of Arilyn but not understanding the apparent depth of his friend's concern. "How can you say that, after what you saw? She turned the battle."

"True enough. But I was not speaking of battle."

"Ah." Foxfire turned aside to stare into the fire. His friend's concerns were of a more personal nature, had more to do with Foxfire's fascination with the moon elf. It was well that not everyone in the tribe had eyes so sharp, else his own position as war leader would swiftly be brought into question. Accepting a moon elf as battle leader was one thing; a more personal alliance was simply out of the question.

Foxfire reached over and patted Korrigash's shoulder, accepting his counsel without responding to it.

In truth, he did not know what his response should be. Yes, the moon elf was very different. But so were arrow and bow, and yet they worked together to become more than what either might be alone. His duty was to his people: could he turn away from anything—or anyone— who might aid them?

Foxfire rose and bid goodnight to his friend. But the calm of reverie eluded him, and he walked through Tall-trees until the song of the night insects had dimmed to a murmur. Shortly before dawn, his restless path brought him to the base of Arilyn's tree.

After a moment's hesitation, he began to climb the ladder to her dwelling. There were plans that must be made. He had much to learn of her, and she of him.

But he saw at once that Arilyn still rested. A surge of disappointment flowed through him, but no elf would disturb the reverie of another except in the direst of emergencies. For several moments, however, Foxfire gazed upon his new advisor.

How strange were the moon folk, with their cloud-colored skin and eyes the shade of a summer sky! Perhaps their colors were a sign of how far the city-dwelling elves had removed themselves from the earth. No longer did the tints of earth's browns and coppers and greens linger about them. It was said that of all the races of elves, the moon folk were most like humans. He could see that in Arilyn. In many ways she resembled a human woman, albeit one far more delicate and beautiful than any Foxfire had seen in the marketplaces during those years when the Elmanesse still traded with the humans.

She stirred, as if somehow the intensity of his gaze had pierced her dreams. Yet if that were so, why did she seem distressed? He wished her nothing but good. She tossed her head back and forth as if in denial and spoke a strange name with such pain and confusion that Fox-fire could not help but flinch. After a few moments, the painful reverie subsided, and her breathing returned to its odd rhythm: deep, slow and soft.

Foxfire froze, easing his thoughts away slowly so as not to disturb her. Quietly, thoughtfully, he made his way down to the forest floor, to await the coming of the dawn.

Fourteen

Lord Hhune paced angrily about his chamber, keenly aware that the amused gaze of the mercenary captain followed him. This only made him more wrathful—not only had the man overstepped his bounds, but his insolence was beyond bearing!

"You understand what you have done, do you not? The logging operation cannot continue! The money I have lost, the wealth I have yet to lose, is beyond reckoning!"

Bunlap seemed singularly unconcerned by this outburst. "You have your private navy. The risk of acquiring more ships is far greater than the benefits."

This was true, but Hhune did not care to hear it from a hireling. "Your task was not to start a war, but to protect the foresters from the elves!"

"Which is precisely what I have done," the captain said coolly. "Do you think there is but one band of elves in all of the Forest of Tethir? We subdued the Suldusk tribe, but did not wish to risk word of your activities reaching the stronger and more warlike tribes to the north and west. What better way to keep these elves out of your business than to busy them with other matters?"

"The plan is all well and good, but its execution is utterly out of control," Hhune said. "You raised too much trouble with the elves, and now it has become a matter that demands resolution. What if there is all-out war and the pasha of Zazesspur sends armed men into the forest? What if my logging activities come to light?"

"There are still trees enough in the forest. It's not likely an invading army would notice that a few have gone missing," the mercenary retorted. "And if so, what of it? You've covered your backside with so many layers of paper that you couldn't feel the lash of a whip through them all! Even if the logging operation were discovered, no one could trace it past those holding companies of yours."

"We take no more chances. Close up the logging camp at once."

"And the elves?" Bunlap said.

Hhune shrugged. "The elves always have been and always will be. Let them melt back into their shadows. I have bought a bit of time with the Council of Lords. before that time is up, the troubles will stop and the attention of the people will be drawn to other matters. Are we clear on this?"

"Ah, but there we have a problem," Bunlap said in a smug tone. "Certain things, once set in motion, are difficult to stop. The farming folk north of Port Kir live in mortal dread of elven attack. Business in Mosstone has fallen off, except for the hiring of mercenary guards. I can't seem to get enough of my men up there to satisfy demand. And I notice that you yourself are preparing to travel northward with far more than your usual guard," Bunlap added.

"It is my custom to attend the summer fairs in Waterdeep," Hhune said stiffly. "I have my responsibilities to **the shipping guild to tend.**"

"Ah, yes. Commerce. And how does overland trade fare these days?"

The guildmaster glared at the man. "Not well," he admitted.

Bunlap tsk-tsked. "A shame. I would hate to see you lose your position in the shipping guild. Not to mention the negative impact upon your future prospects when word spreads that these elven attacks are actually in retaliation against atrocities committed against them, atrocities in which you played no small part."

"Do not presume to blackmail me," Hhune said coldly. "You are as deeply involved in this as I am. You cannot fling stable-sweepings without the scent clinging to you!"

"Then I see no reason why we should not both continue to profit," the mercenary returned. "I will close down the logging camp, send the hired foresters back to the Vilhon Reach, and man the camp as a second base of operations. My men will take on the elves, and take *out* the elves. Once this is done, your problem is solved. Your precious trades routes will be hampered only by the usual bandits and brigands, and the villages and farms will have only the petty noblemen to torment them. In short, life in Tethyr will return to normal. I gain a second stronghold and settle a few personal scores. And you, my friend, can take whatever credit for sudden calm that suits your purposes—and give whatever explanation for it that you like."

"If you think to defeat the elves in their own forest, you are utterly mad," Hhune scoffed. "That was attempted; the best the army could do was to drive them deeper into the trees."

"Granted, the total destruction of the elves is little more than a pleasant fantasy. Yet I shall do my small part. And frankly, who will know the difference, but for you, me, and the few elves that survive?"

Hhune thought this over. It was not an ideal situation, but it was a workable compromise. It would not be

the first time he had been pressed into shady alliances
or forced to work outside the bounds of law, nor would it
be the last.

After Tethyr's civil war, laws were passed in
Zazesspur, as well as in several other cities, that strictly
limited the arms and forces that any citizen, guild, or
private group could maintain. It was quite illegal for
Hhune to own the type of fast, maneuverable, and well-
armed vessels that could protect his merchant ships
from piracy. Hhune considered these laws unreasonable, so he'd found ways to circumvent them. Yet within
the very guild he strove to protect were those who
would gladly betray his activities in the hope of climbing to his position. Guild monies were carefully moni-
tored, and embezzlement was out of the question. And
although he was a wealthy man, it was not within his
means to finance the sort of fleet he needed. It had
occurred to him that the resources he needed were close
at hand: the ancient trees of the elven forest.

Logging in the Forest of Tethir had been forbidden for
as long as human memory stretched back. Perhaps
because the strictures against this were so deeply
ingrained, Hhune found setting up an operation to be
far easier than he expected. First came the chain of
merchants and messengers and companies that stood
between him and the hiring of foresters from distant
reaches of the Vilhon to the east. This had gone well,
until attacks by the eastern tribes of elves had brought
logging to a standstill.

That was when Hhune had hired Bunlap, and the
man had proven his worth ten times over. The mercenary captain had at his disposal a veritable army, as
well as an information network as efficient as any affil-
iated with the Knights of the Shield. The captain's
knowledge of river traffic was such that loggers could
find brief windows of time to float the cut lumber downriver. At a point just south of the Starspire Mountains,
below the river's fork on the southern shore, the logs

were netted, loaded onto wagons, and brought in overland until they met up with the trade route west of Ithmong and east of the ruins of Castle Tethyr. False
papers claimed that the logs come from the forested
south. Hhune "paid" for the logs and made a nice profit
selling the lumber to a shipyard in Port Kir. He then
used the funds—under the guise of several blind companies—to pay for his fleet of illegal ships.

It was a good plan, and so far all had gone well. But
keeping this information from his guild, from the
Knights of the Shield, and from the officials of Zazesspur
was becoming an increasingly delicate balancing act.
One, Hhune feared, that Bunlap might well upset. It was
best to give the man his way in this matter.

"Do what you will with the forest elves," Hhune said
coldly. "As you have pointed out, I do not care what
becomes of them. Do whatever is needed to see that the
trouble dies down soon, but do it quickly and quietly."

"Agreed," Bunlap said and rose to leave. It struck the
mercenary captain that this was a promise easily made.
Indeed, the task would be far easier than the foolish
merchant thought. In the tumultuous climate of Tethyr,
a few rumors served remarkably well to create panic.
Let some new and different sort of disturbance arise,
and the "elven threat" would fade soon enough. Especially considering that Bunlap and his men were the
source of most of it!

It was also ridiculously easy to draw the elves into
conflict. They were protective of their own and their forest. Threaten either one, and the long-eared idiots came
at a run.

Bunlap looked forward to hearing Vhenlar's report. If
all went as he, Bunlap, had planned, he would have satisfaction enough to justify the gold the Halruaan wizard
was costing him.

As he strode toward his waiting horse, Bunlap
absently traced the scar on his face, a gesture that was
fast becoming a habit. No amount of gold would settle

that particular account. There were some matters that could be paid only in blood.

That, he would have in plenty. When he was done with the Suldusk tribe, every elf in Tethir would flood to his new stronghold to take their vengeance.

And he would be more than ready for them.

* * * * *

The days passed quickly in the forest, for there was much to be done. Arilyn found that though the elves were superlative archers, they had little knowledge of the various human styles of swordplay. They were quick, agile, and utterly fierce in battle, yet these things were no replacement for knowledge.

She spent much time drilling those who possessed blades, and encouraged the production of other weapons. The forest people looked with horror upon the crossbow, but she stubbornly insisted that the artisans of the village fashion as many copies of hers as possible. As days slipped by, Talltrees began to acquire a considerable arsenal: spears, javelins, bone daggers and throwing knives—anything and everything that could be used as a weapon.

This worried Rhothomir, who saw, as the inevitable end of all this, a huge war that his people could not win.

"It is not our way, attacking the humans in large numbers. And why should we? It is utterly foolish to go against so many."

"We do not yet know how many we must fight," Foxfire reasoned. "You speak as if the humans were of one mind and purpose! It may be that our foe can be overcome. If not, at least we are better prepared to keep them from the forest."

And so it went, at great length. Arilyn kept away from the arguments, letting the elven war leader speak for her. She had enough to occupy her time without dealing with the tradition-bound Speaker.

Chief among her problems, oddly enough, were her most avid supporters. There were among the younger elves many who applauded her vision; Hawkwing and Tamsin were leaders among them. This worried Arilyn more than it reassured her. The sheer power of the hatred these elves held for all things human did not bode well—not only for her own safety, but for theirs. The Forest of Tethir was vast and deep, but the simple fact of life was that its boundaries, now defined by human farms and roads and towns, were shrinking. This was to be a battle, not a crusade. The best that Arilyn could hope for was to buy more time for the forest folk, time for them to enjoy the peace and beauty of their ancient ways, time in which they could learn new ways, perhaps come to terms somewhat with their human neighbors. In this Khelben Arunsun and the Harpers had been correct: there was no way to push back the humans except to move back the hands of time itself.

So she was more than a bit concerned to see Tamsin and his crowd gathered together, talking with an excitement that fell just short of a fever pitch. She strode into their midst and drew a long, relieved, breath. The scouts had returned.

"Go get Foxfire and the Speaker," Arilyn bid one of the younglings. He hurried off, to return in moments with the older elves.

Faunalyn, a young female well named for her doelike eyes and tawny skin, spoke with great excitement. "We followed the humans, as you said. They traveled south, past the spring pool and out of the forest. We followed them still," she added in a voice still rounded with the remembered wonders of the outside world. "There is a vast dwelling of wood and stone. They went within."

"A fortress?" Arilyn asked sharply. "Was it on a low cliff, overlooking the river?"

The elf woman nodded, then recoiled with surprise when the moon elf let out a sharp and earthy curse.

"Do you know this place?" Foxfire asked her, taking her arm and drawing her aside.

"I've been past it. Just barely. The local lord is a mercenary by the name of Bunlap. Nasty piece of work."

Foxfire stared at her. "You are certain of this?"

"Oh, yes," Arilyn said dryly. "I spent a small fortune making certain of the fortress and its defenses. Of course, at the time I was just planning how to get *past* it, not how best to attack."

"Attack," he repeated softly, shaking his head as he tried to absorb this. "Can we do such a thing?"

The Harper sighed and dug one hand into her hair. "Give me a few minutes to think about it, would you? I don't happen to have a plan in mind just yet."

"If you are to consider this matter, there are things you should know," Foxfire said in a somber tone. "I have met this Bunlap. He claims to seek justice for elven wrongs, yet from all I know it seems he is bent upon blackening the name of the People. Why this is so, I cannot guess. But he has reason to hate me—he bears my mark on his face."

He took a black arrow from his quiver and showed Arilyn the mark upon it—the stylized design of the flower from which he took his name. "I carved this onto his cheek."

She looked sharply at the elf. "You couldn't have told me this sooner?"

Foxfire shrugged, but he looked a bit sheepish. "Once the humans leave the forest, they are all but lost to us. It did not occur to me that you might be able to trace this man to his lair."

"Hmm. Do you know anything else that might be of interest?"

He hesitated for several moments before answering. "You may wish to speak with Ferret. She has lived among the humans, trying to find just such answers as we now seek. It is not widely known where she went, or how she passed the months away. Please trust me when

I say that it is best left this way. There are those among us who do not approve of her methods, and yet others who would be too quick to imitate them."

Arilyn nodded, for she understood this matter far better than he knew. "I'll do that. What else?"

"The tribe has been willing to undergo your training. They have made your weapons and would use them in defense of their home. But I do not know whether they would leave the forest and follow you—or me, for that matter—into battle. It is not our way."

"And yet your people have done just that in the past," Arilyn mused. Something from Ferret's tale clicked into place in her mind—an incredible possibility that might just galvanize the forest folk. "I need time alone to think about these things," she said abruptly. "Where can I go where I will not be disturbed? It is important."

"If you like, I myself will stand guard below your dwelling. None will pass," Foxfire said, looking a bit puzzled by her vehemence.

Arilyn noted this, but did not take time to respond to his unspoken questions. She strode over to her tree and climbed the ladder to her small dwelling. Although it seemed rude to do so, she pulled up the ladder after her and laced shut the deerhide flaps that covered the small windows.

When all was secured, Arilyn pulled her moonblade from its sheath and held it up before her face.

"Come forth," she said softly, steeling herself for the appearance of her magical double. The ghostly mist swirled up from the elven sword, quickly taking the form of its half-elven mistress.

"What is it that you seek to do, and to undo?" the elfshadow asked, but there was a note of reproach in her voice.

"I need to call you out in battle," Arilyn said, ignoring the elfshadow's rhetorical question. Of course the thing knew what she planned—it *was* her, albeit a straightlaced and rather too noble version of herself. "Actually,

I might need to call *all* of you—all the elves who ever have wielded the sword. Can this be done?"

The elfshadow clearly had not expected this response. "Only once before, but yes, this is possible."

"Good," she said briskly. "I need to infiltrate a fortress. There are nine of you, and one of me. That's enough to start a pretty good fight and to get the doors open."

"You must realize that there are risks," the shadow cautioned her. "Calling forth all the elfshadows takes a tremendous toll upon the sword's wielder. Not even Zoastria, who endowed the moonblade with the elf-shadow entity, called forth her own double more than a few times."

"Which brings me to my next question," Arilyn said. "Zoastria and Soora Thea. Is it possible that these are one and the same?"

"I do not know. Would you like to speak with her?"

Arilyn took a long, deep breath. This was the moment she had longed for—and dreaded—since she had first learned the secret of her moonblade's magic. It was mind-boggling enough to regard her own image as the entity of the sword. The possibility of conversing with the essence of an ancestor was utterly beyond her imagination. And not just some unknown ancestor—the essence of her own mother lived within the sword!

Yet as much as she longed to see Z'beryl again, Arilyn was not entirely sure how her mother would react to Arilyn's quest to avoid the destiny the moonblade had chosen for her. Arilyn was well accustomed to being considered less than adequate, for she had grown up a half-elf in an elven settlement. But never once had she seen disappointment in her mother's eyes. She was not certain she could bear to witness it now.

Yet Zoastria she could—and must—confront.

"How is it done?" Arilyn asked.

"The same way you called me forth. But the power of the sword is diminished when you call forth the others. You will be at risk in ways to which you are not accustomed."

Arilyn accepted this with a nod, and then once again lifted the sword. "Come forth, you who were once Zoastria," she said in a firm voice.

Again mist rose from the ancient blade, and as the elven form took shape Arilyn's heart seemed to turn to stone in her chest. This was the very form she had seen in the treasure chamber—the slumbering ancestor who haunted her dreams.

But oddly enough, the shadow of Zoastria did not appear to be nearly as solid as Arilyn's double. She was ghostly, insubstantial—not at all the heroic figure needed to lead the elves to victory.

"What do you want of me, half-elf, and how is it that you command the sword of Zoastria?" the elfshadow demanded in a tone of voice that Arilyn knew all too well. She had not expected to confront such scorn from her own ancestor, nor would she yield to it.

Arilyn squared her shoulders and faced down the misty image. "You are Zoastria, who bore the sword before me. Are you also the moon fighter known as Soora Thea?"

"Once. Thus did the forest folk say my name, for the language of Evermeet was beyond their grasp."

"You are needed again," Arilyn said softly. "Their descendants need the return of their hero."

But the image of Zoastria shook her head. "You know so little of the sword you carry. I cannot; I can only appear as you see me. Of all the sword's powers, the ability to call forth the elfshadow essence is the weakest. You should know that, to your sorrow," she added sharply.

Arilyn's cheeks burned, but she did not respond. For as long as she drew breath, she would grieve for the evil use made of her elfshadow by her former mentor and friend. The gold elf Kymil Nimesin had wrested control of the elfshadow from the sword and turned it—and therefore, Arilyn—onto an assassin's path.

"Why not? Why are you different from the others?"
the half-elf demanded.

"Because unlike most of the moon fighters, I did not
die," Zoastria said. "It is possible to pass on the sword to
a blade heir without tasting death. This is not a choice
lightly made, but I made a pledge to return and this is
how it is honored. There are others who have done this.
Doubtless, you have heard legends."

The half-elf nodded. Stories of a sleeping hero who
would return in a time of great need were told from the
Moonshaes to Rashemen. And now she understood why
all these stories had in common an ancient, mystic sword.

"But there *is* a way for me to honor my pledge," Zoastria continued. "Elfshadow and mistress must again
become one. This cannot be while that which I once was
sleeps in a rich man's vault. Unite the two, and I will be
as alive as ever I was."

The half-elf nodded slowly. "Is this your wish?"

"What question is this? Better to ask, is this my duty?
If there is no other way, then call me forth. I will come."

And with that, the ghostly image dissipated and
flowed into the sword. Arilyn's own shadow disappeared
with it.

Arilyn slid the moonblade back into its sheath and
considered what she had learned. To retrieve the slumbering Zoastria would be no easy task and was not one
she could attempt anytime soon. As her ancestor
advised, she must try to find another way.

* * * * *

Hasheth left his horse at the public stables and set off
down the docks of Port Kir on foot. The dock area was
not the safest place to be, not even during daylight, but
Hasheth walked alone with his confidence utterly intact.
Had he not spent time among the assassins of
Zazesspur? Though his apprenticeship might have been
brief and ill-fated, he had learned enough to be awarded

his sand-hue sash. He might not have notches on his
blade to mark successful kills, but he could throw the
unblooded knife hard and straight.

He had another weapon as well, one keener still,
which he was honing with each day that passed.
Hasheth had little doubt that his wits were equal to
anything the docks of Port Kir might serve up.

His surroundings grew increasingly rougher as he
made his way toward the sea. Small shops offering oddi-
ties of every description gave way to rough-and-tumble
taverns. Before long the wooden walkways grew narrow,
and between the boards he could see the dark water of
Firedrake Bay lapping at the shore. As he neared his destination, the stench of fish became overwhelming. In open
warehouses on either side of the dock, men and women
went about processing the day's catch, seemingly oblivi-
ous to the piles of discarded shells and shrimp heads and
fish innards that were heaped around their boots.

Hasheth lifted one hand to his nose and picked up his
pace. At the end of this dock was the Berringer Shipyard. It was here that all his work had led him. For days
he had examined Lord Hhune's many books and
ledgers, carefully piecing together bits of information
and innuendo—even finding and deciphering some outright code. It had been a wondrous puzzle that led him
at last to this place. All that remained for Hasheth to
accomplish was to discern the purpose of Hhune's
scheme, and then to find some way to turn it to his own
benefit!

Berringer Shipyard was a bustling, noisy, smelly
place, not at all what the young man had expected. He
bought his way in at the gate by using a copy of the credentials that Hhune had supplied to one of the many
merchant companies that purchased ships for him.

Hasheth wandered about, taking note of all. Dockhands
by the dozen grunted and sweated as they rolled immense
logs from flat-bottomed barges onto a large dock. These
logs were then handhewn, the outer wood fashioned into

planks and beams and the heart of each shaped and
smoothed into a strong, tall mast. Some planks, previ-
ously cut, soaked in an enormous vat of seawater mixed
with some unspeakably vile-smelling concoction. Well-
softened planks had been clamped onto curved frames so
that they might take on the needed shape as they hardened and dried. A half-built ship rested on enormous tres-
tles, looking for all the world like a well-picked skeleton.
Three finished ships stood in dry dock.

The quality of work at all stages was well within the
high standards expected of Tethyrian craftsmen. The
ships were trim and sleek and showed every promise of
remarkable speed. But it was the ironworks that
impressed and enlightened Hasheth.

He stood and gazed at the trio of ships, to which several
smiths were adding fittings and weaponry. These were to
sail with an impressive arsenal: ballistae and catapults
provided a considerable amount of firepower. Rows of
iron-tipped bolts stood ready by each ballista, and piles of
grapeshot—spiked iron balls linked with chain—would
prove deadly when hurled from the catapult.

This, then, was it—the answer Hasheth had been
seeking. These three ships were surely destined to
become part of a private fleet of fast, heavily armed
ships that could escort merchant vessels safely through
pirate-infested waters or blockade a harbor.

Hasheth would have applauded either use. As head of
the shipping guild, Lord Hhune had responsibilities and,
perhaps, higher ambitions. And so did he. It was a shame
that one of these ships must be sacrificed, but a man
must be prepared to pay for his ambitions. The fact that
he was using another man's coin would make it considerably easier.

His questions answered, the young man hurried back
to the inn where he had rented a room. From his pack
he took a new suit of clothing. The finely made dark garments of a prosperous merchant had been fashioned by
the tailor who made all of Lord Hhune's clothing, as

well as that of his boot-licking scribe, Achnib.

Hasheth pasted a thick mustache onto his lip and slicked back his hair with scented oil. He even swathed his middle with rolls of cloth to help approximate the scribe's spreading midsection and stuffed a bit of resinous gum between teeth and cheeks to pad his face a bit. When all was in readiness, he slipped from the inn and made his way back to the docks—and to a dark and dangerous tavern at the very edge of the black water.

This drinking hole suited his purpose perfectly. The crudely lettered sign outside labeled it "The Race," a name taken from the channel of swift winds and dangerous waters that led into Firedrake Bay. Those ships that entered Port Kir ran a gauntlet of Nelanther pirates, a few of whom were bold enough to come ashore. Rumor had it that they drank here.

Hasheth found a corner table near some likely-looking toughs, one who sported a beard divided into twin prongs, the other of whom was more or less cleanshaven. A barmaid with an ale-soaked bodice and worldweary eyes came over to take his order.

"Wine, if you please," he demanded in an imitation of Achnib's pinched, querulous tones. He dropped his voice a notch or two. "I also need passage to Lantan, if such can be arranged."

The men at the next table exchanged glances. One of them propped his boots up on the empty chair at Hasheth's table.

"Couldn't help overhearing you. Might be that we could do the arranging you were speaking of."

Hasheth darted wary glances left and right, then leaned forward. "From Zazesspur? I would be grateful to you if this could be arranged, and swiftly."

"Oh, well, from Zazesspur," the other man said with more than a bit of sarcasm. "That's too easy by half. Sure you don't want to set sail from Evermeet, while you're at it?"

"I've business to attend in my home city," Hasheth

said stiffly. "It should be concluded in ten days or so, and I need to leave quickly upon its conclusion. Can this be done?"

"Maybe, but it'll cost you. What were you thinking of paying?"

"I will pay you with information," he said in a low, furtive voice. "Tell me what cargo you prefer, and I can name you a likely ship, tell you her route and the strength of her crew. The merchant vessel will be guarded, but I can find out the name of the armed ship and help you place your own men upon it. Take over the escort ship, and the caravel and her cargo will be yours as well."

The first pirate picked at his teeth with a dirty fingernail as he considered this outrageous scenario. "And how would you be knowing so much? What's to say that this information you're eager to pay with is worth more than clay coins?"

Hasheth took a scrap of parchment and a bit of charcoal pencil from the bag tied to his augmented waistline. He scrawled a name and title on the sheet, then passed it to the men. They looked at him and burst into raucous laughter.

"What do you take us for, a coupla priests? Who learns to read but sandal-footed priests and wide-ass clerks?" hooted the bearded pirate. Nonetheless, he picked up the bit of paper and pocketed it, as Hasheth had hoped he might.

"My name is Achnib," Hasheth said with as much dignity as he thought the man he imitated could muster, "and I am chief scribe to Lord Hhune of Zazesspur."

"Hmm." This information seemed to impress the pirate. "But why the ten days, especially?"

"My lord is away on business. It behooves me to remove myself from the city before his return."

The men chuckled. "Been skimming, have you? Well, Lantan's a good place to be taking your coins. There's money to be made in some of them new weapons coming out off the island. Get in on the business early, and you'll likely do well."

"I require passage, not advice on my investments," Hasheth said in a haughty tone as he began to rise from his chair. "Do you wish to do business, or shall I look elsewhere?"

"Haul in your sails a might, lad," the bearded pirate said dryly. "You want to go to Lantan. Tell us what you know, and if it holds water then maybe we can see about getting you there."

This was precisely what Hasheth had hoped to hear. Let them ask questions about Achnib—the more the better.

When the arrangements were completed, an elated Hasheth made his way back toward the inn to rid himself of his borrowed persona. He was not so enamored of his success, however, that he did not notice the two men lounging against the alley-side wall of a shop. They fell into step behind him, obviously considering the well-dressed and portly young man to be a ripe, easy mark.

Hasheth's lip curled with disdain. These clods did not even know how to tread silently—the first lesson given to fledgling assassins. He did not slow his pace, did not react at all until their sudden, board-thumping rush began. Then he whirled, tossing his assassin's knife with a quick, underhand snap. The blade spun once and then sank into one thug's gut with a wet, meaty thud.

The other man lacked the presence of mind or the rapid reflexes needed to halt his charge. Hasheth let him come, stepping aside at the last moment and extending one rigid forearm, elbow braced against his waist. He caught the second thug slightly below his center. The man's heavier top half flipped forward over Hasheth's arm. The thug crashed heavily into the wooden dock, leading with his teeth.

Before the stunned man could move, Hasheth stooped beside him and pulled a rusty, pitted knife from his belt. He snatched a handful of the thug's greasy hair, yanked

back his head, pressed the edge of the knife to his throat
and then—hesitated.

The young man was pleased that the skills he had
learned in his training served him so well on the street.
But he was young, and he had yet to kill a man. He
glanced at his first victim, noted the red bubbles forming at the corners of the man's gaping mouth, and knew
this would hold true only for a few moments more. But
this second man—he was already down and dazed. Was
there truly a need to kill twice?

Hasheth needed only a moment to think. He was
dressed as Achnib, a man too soft and slow to have done
what he himself had just accomplished. If word of his
feat should spread, it might jeopardize the plans he had
laid this night. The possibility was slight, but it was
there. That was enough.

The young man pulled the dagger hard and fast,
curving his hand back and around as he had been
taught to do. Blood spurted forth in a pulsating geyser,
but not so much as a drop of it stained Hasheth's hands.

Hasheth stood and regarded his handiwork. His time
in the assassins' guild had served him well—not even
an assassin of the Shadow Sash rank could have handled this matter more smoothly. It was just as his royal
tutors always claimed—no knowledge is truly wasted.

The young man walked the few paces over to the first
dead thug and ripped his dagger free. He wiped the
blade clean on the corpse's tunic—or as clean as it was
likely to get on the filthy garment—and slipped it back
into his belt.

Later, when he reached the solitude of his hired room,
he would carve two marks upon it, the first of what
Hasheth expected would be many.

* * * * *

Throughout that night and into the next day, Arilyn
could think of little but her strange conversation with

the magical entity of her moonblade. If the elves must fight, and if they would not follow the leaders they had, then would she not have to find them a leader they would follow? Try as she might, she could think of no other solution to the problem.

There was something about Talltrees, however, that acted as a balm to her troubled thoughts. Each day was longer than the one before, and the time of midsummer was fast approaching. The summer solstice was a time of celebration for all elves, but Arilyn had never seen such joyous anticipation as that which gripped the elven settlement.

Twilight of midsummer eve came late and softly, with a deepening of golden green light. With it came those woodland creatures who would celebrate with the elven tribe. There were fauns, small feral folk with wild thatches of hair, furred hindquarters and legs that ended in dainty cloven hooves. Satyrs—larger, more ribald relatives of the fauns—came as well, already full of mead and high spirits. Several centaurs, grave and dignified even in this most joyous season, brought gifts of fruit and flowers to their elven hosts. There were pixies and sprites and other fey creatures for which Arilyn knew no names. And there were others who seemed to be there one moment, and not the next. At midsummer, she reasoned, the walls between the worlds were so thin that even a half-elf might catch glimpses through the veil.

All joined in the feasting and the sharing of summer mead, a wondrous honey wine distilled from flowers and fruit. No green elves kept bees, but they carefully harvested a part of that stored nectar that they found in hollowed trees, adding to it the essence of wild raspberries and elven magic. The result was far from primitive. Arilyn would easily place the mead alongside the best elven wines she had tasted.

At a certain, very prescribed point in the celebration—when the elves were growing merry and before the satyrs were entirely given over to impulse—the midsummer

prayers were chanted and sung. The elves venerated the
Seldarine, particularly the god of the forest, but homage
was also paid to the gods of their visitors.

At last the music began. A lilting tune played on pan-
pipes was the traditional invitation to dance. As the
merrymakers joined in, so did other instruments: pipes,
shaken bells, and pulsing drums.

For a while Arilyn only watched. There had been midsummer festivals in Evereska in the days before her
mother's death, but she had been deemed too young to
take part. Nor would she have been welcomed to many
of the celebrations. Among the elves there were subtle,
sacred overtones to such times that none other could
share. Yet there was that about the music that drew her
steadily closer to the dancers.

Arilyn had never quite understood the mystic fascination the elven people had with dance, nor was she
particularly skilled. Yet at the urging of Hawkwing, her
protege turned mentor, she had dressed in a filmy green
gown made for dancing away a warm summer's night. It
was by far the loveliest thing Arilyn had ever worn.
Gossamer-soft, light enough to float around her as she
moved, it captured the clear, fresh green of a perfect
summer day. It was also the scantiest costume she had
ever put on; the skirts were short, and her arms and
legs were bared for dancing. At Hawkwing's insistence,
Arilyn wore a wreath of tiny white flowers in her hair
and had left her feet bare. Oddly enough, all the elves
were dressed in similar fashion. There was no deerskin
tonight, no ornaments of bones or feathers. It seemed as
if the folk of Tethir had stepped back for one night into
a still more ancient time.

Hawkwing had already joined the dancing, wearing
proudly the emerald that had been Arilyn's midsummer
gift to her. Most of the gifts exchanged were simple:
fruit or flowers for the most part, but the memory of the
purely feminine joy this gift had ignited in the girl-
child's eyes warmed Arilyn still. She worried for the

child; Hawkwing was too young to hate so passionately and to kill with such ease. It was good to see the girl whirling in Tamsin's arms, laughing as gaily as if she truly were the carefree maiden she should have been. The sight was well worth the cost of the emerald—yet another of Danilo's costly tokens. As she enjoyed Hawkwing's happiness, Arilyn doubted Danilo would disapprove of the use she'd made of his gift.

The child caught Arilyn's eye, and her thin face lighted in a smile. Hands outstretched, she ran to the moon elf and pulled her into the dance. The circle began, the final dance that would celebrate the solstice. Arilyn moved along with the others, not caring that her steps were not nearly so light or intricate as those of the fey folk. There was something about the festivities that made such matters unimportant.

Arilyn allowed herself to be swept away in the peace and joy that the circle dance wove around them all, knowing that this would be the last part of the festivities in which she would join.

Among the elves, midsummer was a time when marriages were celebrated and lovers rejoiced. Children born of this night were considered a special blessing of the gods. Even those elves who had no special partner often sought out a friend with whom to share the magic that was midsummer.

It was almost impossible not to. As the cycles of the moon pulled on the tides, the inexorable wheel of the year drew them all into the celebration. Fauns slipped away into the shadows, two by two. Pixies and sprites flitted off like paired fireflies, at this sacred time, each to his own.

Arilyn pulled away from the circle slowly, for she was loath to end the rare and wondrous communion she had known this night. A light touch—startling against her bared shoulder—had her spinning about, hand at the hilt of the sword she was pledged to wear even on such a night. She turned into the circle of Foxfire's arms. He did not speak, but his eyes were dark with unmistakable invitation.

Instinct and habit took over; Arilyn went rigid and began to pull away.

Foxfire placed a gentle hand at the small of her back, stopping her retreat. "The night is short," he said quietly, the traditional phrase exchanged between the lovers or comrades who shared the gift of midsummer.

Arilyn's breath caught in her throat as the full impact of the elf's invitation swept her. In Foxfire's eyes, she was worthy of this most elven of celebrations, which was not only merrymaking, but also a sacred union with the land. She had never dreamed of such acceptance into the elven world—had never considered such a thing to be possible. The temptation to be what he thought she was was too great for the lonely half-elf to bear.

For the first time in her life, Arilyn did not draw away.

"The night is short," she agreed.

* * * * *

Korrigash and Ferret watched as their war leaders slipped away into the forest together. "It is not right," the male said, his face deeply troubled. "Are not you and Foxfire promised?"

"For many years," Ferret agreed, her black eyes unreadable. "But what of it? As long as those two win battles, I care not what else they do."

"But Foxfire is my friend, and in this he does danger to himself."

"How so?" Ferret said sharply. For many days she had kept a gimlet eye on the half-elf. To all appearances, Arilyn's actions ran the course her claims had laid out. But Ferret could not rid herself entirely of the fear that Arilyn would fall back into the role she had played with such skill among the humans. It seemed possible to her that once the two were alone, an assassin's blade would find Foxfire's heart.

But such was not Korrigash's concern. "For good or ill, a bond is formed between a male and maid. Never is this more true than at midsummer. The People follow Foxfire now; they might not if he aligns himself too closely with the moon elf."

"And if they do not follow Foxfire, then you will lead," Ferret said calmly, reassured by the hunter's words. "Let this thing fall as it will. But come," she said in an abrupt change of mood, "the night is short."

"But you are promised to Foxfire," Korrigash protested. Clearly, he was both troubled and intrigued by her suggestion.

"He is otherwise engaged," the female pointed out. "Consider it practice, in case you are required to take his place elsewhere."

The hunter began to protest, but his words wandered off uncertainly and then ceased altogether. The magic of midsummer was already upon them.

* * * * *

Foxfire gazed up through the thick canopy of the forest, watching as the solstice moon sank low in the sky. Her pale light seemed to linger on the long, white limbs still entwined with his. He dropped a kiss—soft as a butterfly's wing—on the closed eyelid of the sleeping half-elf and wondered what he should do next.

He had suspected before, but now he knew beyond doubt: whatever she might be in her heart and in her soul, Arilyn's blood was half human. No elf slept as she did.

As war leader, Foxfire was pledged to follow Rhothomir. He might argue with the Speaker—and he did so far more than did any other elf in the tribe—but he respected the older male. He owed him this knowledge. By every tradition of the elven people, he was bound to tell him what he knew of the newcomer in their midst. But how could he, knowing Rhothomir as he did? To the Speaker, all humans were enemies, and half-elves were an obscenity, an abomination. He would probably order Arilyn slain even if there were no threat to the tribe. And now, during this troubled time, neither Foxfire's influence nor arguments would save her.

And what of Arilyn herself? How would she react if she knew her secret was out? Here, also, Foxfire had little doubt of the outcome. She would flee the forest, and that he could not bear. She must not know he had caught her in slumber.

But how could she not? Foxfire did not know how it was with sleep—perhaps it was like reverie, a state that was entered slowly and in deepening stages. She had just drifted off moments before. Perhaps he could ease her awake, using her own astonishing innocence as an ally. She was unfamiliar with her own responses—Foxfire marveled that this could be so—but perhaps she would confuse a moment's sleep with the wondrous, languid haze that followed their private celebration.

Gently, deftly, he began to coax her back toward awareness. Her sky-colored eyes opened and grew wary.

Foxfire smiled. "I accept that the ways of the Seldarine are a mystery, but never did I understand why the goddess of love and beauty is of the moon people. Now I understand, for in you I have seen her face."

There was nothing disingenuous about his words—he meant them exactly as he said them—but there was a second layer of meaning hidden beneath. He saw it catch flame in Arilyn's eyes. The goddess Hanali Celanil was the epitome and the essence of an elven female. No words could have expressed more strongly his regard for Arilyn as a lover, or his acceptance of her as an elf. He hoped fervently that she heard the tribute in his words, and not the lie.

And so it was. Her white arms came up around his neck, and the magic of midsummer began for them again.

Fifteen

Kendel Leafbower slipped into the dockside tavern known as the Dusty Throat and made his way through the throng of sweaty, hard-drinking patrons toward an empty seat at the far corner of the bar. Not to his liking was the rough crowd, or the bitter ale, but he was tired and thirsty after a long day's work on the docks of Port Kir.

The Dusty Throat was renowned for the ribald wit of its barmaids and the vigorous brawls that broke out almost nightly. Indeed, the tavern had been closed for nearly a tenday following a particularly spectacular fight and was just this night resuming business. Despite the obvious dangers, this particular tavern was favored by many of Kendel's fellow workers, so he felt a bit safer here than he might have otherwise.

The recent brawl had left a number of new marks on the battle-scarred tavern. Two of the supporting beams had been gouged deeply and repeatedly at a height of about three feet off the floor. To Kendel's eyes, the beams

resembled partially felled trees. The damage suggested
the work of either a very tall beaver or a very short
woodsman. There was a splinter-edged hole in one
wooden wall at about the same height and about a foot
across, which afforded the patrons a glimpse of the wine
cellar and gave the resident rats a convenient window
from which to peek out at the patrons. A large section of
the bar had been replaced, and the light wood was a
marked contrast to the old, ale-stained counter. Several
of the chairs were obviously new, and the splintered
rungs on perhaps a dozen more had been bound with
string in a make-do attempt at repair. Even the stone
hearth, a massive thing that spanned the entire west
wall of the tavern, had not gone unscathed. There were
several deep chips in the stones, all of which were starkly
obvious against the smoke-blackened hearth.

Nor had the tavern's employees escaped injury. The
burly cook stood at the hearth, haranguing the halfling
helper who struggled to turn the spit and basting a
roasting lamb with one hand. His other arm was thickly
bandaged and supported by a food-stained sling. The
appearance of the hideous half-orc who did odd jobs and
heavy lifting was rendered even more disreputable than
usual. His snoutlike nose had been splattered flat across
his face, and his badly swollen jaw was mottled with
shades of purple and the ugly yellow-green of a fading
bruise. He labored noisily to draw air through his
swollen mouth, and the jagged shards of broken teeth
were clearly visible with each rasping breath. One of his
lower canine tusks was missing entirely, making his
appearance oddly lopsided. Even some of the barmaids
bore the lingering marks of battle, including blackened
eyes, torn knuckles—and triumphant smirks.

This was by far the most extensive damage done by any
tavern brawl in Kendel's memory, which was long indeed.
He noticed all of these things in a glance. Port Kir was a
dangerous place, and those who wished to survive learned
to sharpen their senses and keep alert for signs of danger.

Kendel was also keenly aware of the fact that he was conspicuous even in this crowded taproom. Most native Tethyrians had olive skin, dark eyes, and hair that ranged from chestnut to black. Most of the sailors and dockhands who packed the tavern were heavily muscled from their labors. In stark contrast to his fellows, Kendel had red-gold hair, sky-colored eyes, and a pale skin that no amount of southern sun could darken. He was strong, yet he remained slightly built and stood no more than a hand-span or two over five feet. He was, in short, an elf.

"Wuddle y'have?" demanded an exceedingly deep, gruff voice from somewhere beyond the counter.

Puzzled, the elf leaned forward and peered down over the bar. Glaring at him was the upturned face of a young dwarf with a short, dun-colored beard and a face as glum as a rainy morning.

"An elf! Well then, no need to be telling me," the dwarf continued sourly. "The ale here's too rough fer the likes of you, so yer wanting a goblet of bubbly water. Or mebbe some nice warm milk."

"Or perhaps elverquisst," Kendel suggested coldly. The delicate appearance of the elven folk often led other races to make such assumptions, while in reality, elven wines and liquors were among the most potent in all Faerûn.

"Oh, elverquisst, is it? Sure, this place's got barrels of fine elven wines," the dwarf rejoined with heavy sarcasm. "And the privies out back is full to overflowing with jools, too, if'n you get my meaning."

An involuntary smile tugged at the corner of Kendel's lips. He shared the new barkeep's dubious opinion of the Dusty Throat's wine cellar. And although he himself might not have phrased his criticism in quite the same manner, he had to agree the dwarf's comparison was apt.

"Truth be told, wouldn't be minding a big mug of that elverquisst stuff meself right about now," the dwarf

continued in a wistful tone. "Now there's a drink that
can strip paint an' melt scrap metal!"

"I've never heard elverquisst described in quite those
terms," Kendel replied mildly. "You have troubles that
require drowning, I take it?"

"Aye."

Belatedly, the dwarven barkeep seemed to recall both
his duties and the dour reputation of his people. He
closed his mouth with an audible click and snatched up
the bar rag draped on a small, squat keg behind him.
With this he began to wipe the counter, hopping up
repeatedly as he took one swipe at a time.

The elf suppressed a smile. "You might pull the keg
closer to the bar," he suggested. "That might make your
duties easier, as well as enable you to see the patrons."

"Ain't nobody here worth seeing," grumbled the
dwarf, but he promptly did as Kendel suggested. After a
moment, he climbed onto the keg and thunked a frothy
tankard down before the elf. "Ale. It ain't good, but it's
the best this place has got. Me, I find ale tastes better
without the seawater what they add to stretch it out!"

Kendel accepted the drink with a nod and took a sip.
It was indeed better than any he'd ever tasted in the
tavern. In return, he slipped a small silver coin from his
pocket and slid it toward the barkeep. The dwarf fielded
it with a quick, insouciant sweep of the bar rag.

"Can't be letting them see it, or they'd have it from
me faster'n a drunken halfling with a willing maid. The
folk what run this place is mighty quick to take coins
what ain't theirs."

"You've been robbed?" Kendel asked cautiously. It was
not wise to inquire too closely into the troubles of
others, yet he felt inexplicably drawn by the barkeep
and charmed by his grumpy overtures. Such friendli-
ness was rare in Tethyr, especially to an elf.

"Robbed? You might say that," the dwarf retorted. "I
come in here, same as you, to wet my throat after a long
day." A fleeting grin lit his face with an unexpected

touch of nostalgia. "Though truth be told, the day weren't no hardship on me. The Foaming Sands—ever heared tell of that place?"

The elf nodded, for the reputation of that exclusive bath and pleasure house stood tall in the city. He did not credit the dwarf's claim as entire truth, however, for the Foaming Sands was well beyond the means of dock workers and barkeeps.

"Had me a pocketful of gold and a fistful of silver," the dwarf continued wistfully. "Earned the gold, mind you, with ten years of hard labor, and the silver were a gift and rightfully mine. Spent every one of them silver coins at the Sands, and counted it a bargain. Then I come here. Afore I even finished one mug the fight started. Good thing I was feeling uncommon mellow, or I mighta done considerable damage."

"To all appearances, you did well enough," Kendel murmured. "Your gold, I take it, went toward repairs?"

The dwarf snorted. "What they took from me was enough to build a new place from cellar to chimney, with enough left over to hire half the girls who work the Foaming Sands to tend tables! Then they say it weren't enough, and the local law of course backs 'em up. So here I am, working off the rest. Been here fer days, and seems like I can't get ahead nohow. Seems like I traded one kinda slavery fer another," he concluded glumly.

Kendel received this pronouncement in silence, for it would hardly be wise to voice his outrage. Slavery was not uncommon in Tethyr, but the thought of this oddly charming dwarf's being held in servitude was particularly galling to the elf. Times were difficult in Tethyr, especially for those folk not of human blood.

If there was any benefit to a long life, Kendel mused, it was the ability to see the wheel of events turn full circle, again and again. This was also, in many ways, a curse. In Tethyr, this was perhaps doubly true.

Kendel had come to Tethyr before the grandsire of any human in the room had wailed his way into the world. He had built a home and raised a family, only to have his property seized when the humans in power decided that no elf could own land. By his sword and his strength he had rebuilt another life, his fortunes rising along with those of the royal faction for which he fought. Then the mood of the Tethyrian kings shifted, and vicious pogroms decimated even the most loyal elven folk. Kendel had survived; the royal family had not. For years an egalitarian fervor had gripped the land, extending even to members of other races. Once again Kendel had thrived, only to see the cycle of public sentiment whirl back toward low ebb. Three years ago, he had been a merchant. Now the best work he could find was as a dockhand.

The elf sipped at his ale, but though he was deep in his memories, he did not neglect to watch for possible dangers. From the corner of his eye, Kendel noted the group of men that pushed their way into the room. Five of them, all mercenaries. He knew the breed well enough to recognize them at a glance; they were marked by a swaggering gait that bespoke bravado, but which also suggested a certain lack of purpose or direction. Masterless men, for the most part, looking for a reason to fight and therefore to live.

But these men seemed to be an exception; they had purpose enough. All four of them pushed their way through the crowd, coming straight toward the place where Kendel sat.

The elf surreptitiously loosened the dagger he kept strapped to one thigh. It had been many years since he'd had to use it, but elven memories were long. If he were required to fight, he felt confident he could make a good accounting of himself.

"I know you," one of the mercenaries proclaimed in a loud voice, pointing a beefy finger in Kendel's direction. "You're one of them wild elves what attacked the pipeweed farm south of Mosstone. Burned the barns to the ground, they did, and slaughtered the whole family and most of the farmhands."

In the suddenly silent room, Kendel swiveled to face his accuser. "Not so, sir," he said evenly. "If there is any quarrel to be had with the elven people, you would do better to seek it among the Forest Folk. Surely you can see by my hair and my skin that I am not one of them."

"Well now, I don't know about that," another of the mercenaries put in. "I seen a red-headed elf among the raiders. Word has it he cut his mark onto our captain's face. For all we know, you might even be him."

"That is not possible. I have not left Port Kir for many months," the elf protested. "I've worked the docks since early spring. There are men here who can vouch for me!" Kendel looked around the room, seeking confirmation.

There was none. Even some of the men who lifted alongside him day after day sat in stolid silence, their eyes averted.

But the elf's words elicited a burst of raucous laughter from the mercenaries. "Hear that, boys?" one of them hooted. "He works the docks, if you please! If any of you ever laid eyes on a more unlikely dockhand, I'd surely like to hear tell of it!"

By now it was clear to Kendel what path this confrontation would take. He had played this scene before, albeit upon different stages. A farm, a palace, a counting-house, a tavern—it was all much the same in the end.

The elf's gaze remained calm and even, but his fingers closed around the grip of his dagger. If he struck first, and struck fast and hard, there was a good chance he could to work his way to the door.

A good chance—that was more than he usually had. He would escape, and then he would rebuild, as he had so many times before.

"I heared tell there was elven slaves working that farm, against what passes fer law in this land," observed a gruff voice from behind the counter. "If you boys was smart, you might not be so quick to claim fighting to keep 'em there."

The mercenaries exchanged startled glances. There

came the screech of wood dragging across wood, and a
dwarf with a dun-colored beard popped into view and
affixed the men with an accusing glare. The mercenaries exploded into laughter.

"A dwarf! And here was me, thinking we was hearing
the voice of the gods!" hooted one of the men.

"He's a bit short for a god," noted another man, grinning widely when his dubious witticism inspired a new
burst of mirth.

"Mind your affairs, dwarf, and let us tend ours,"
growled the largest man among them. The dwarf
shrugged and lifted both hands in a careless gesture of
agreement; then he hopped down off the keg and disappeared. The mercenary lashed out with one foot, kicking
the stool out from under the elf.

Agile Kendel was on his feet at once, his dagger
bright and ready in his hand. His attacker reached over
his shoulder, drew a broadsword from his shoulder
sheath, and closed in.

Fortunately for the elf, the crowds put his attackers at
a disadvantage. There was little room for the swordsman to maneuver, and Kendel was able to parry the first
of several thrusts. But only the first few. With the ease
of frequent practice, the patrons pushed the tables and
chairs against the walls to clear an impromptu arena.
Many of the others, especially those who still bore the
scars of the last brawl, made hastily for the exit.

Kendel soon found himself faced with five men and
an open field. The bar was to his back, and the mercenaries surrounded him in a semicircle. Swords drawn
and confident leers twisting their faces, they began to
close in.

A tremendous crash ripped through the ominous
silence of the tavern. The dwarven barkeep exploded
through the wooden wall under the bar counter, head
leading and held down like that of a ramming goat. It
occurred to Kendel suddenly how the large hole in the
wall of the wine cellar had come to be.

Bellowing a cry to his god of battle, the dwarf barreled straight toward the largest mercenary. His head connected hard, significantly below the man's swordbelt.

The mercenary's eyes glazed, and his sword clattered from his hand. His lips fluttered soundlessly, and his hands lowered to grasp at his flattened crotch. After a moment's silence, he tilted and toppled like a felled tree. A small, high-pitched whimper wafted up from the floor where he lay.

But the dwarf suffered no ill effect from the impact. Few substances on all Toril could rival a dwarven skull for sheer durability. He staggered back a few paces, rebounded off the bar, and sprinted across the room in search of a weapon. The patrons parted before him like cockroaches scattering from a suddenly lit torch, and the hearth came into full view. Before it stood the bemused cook, who balanced on one arm and hip a large platter holding a leg of freshly roasted lamb.

The dwarf headed for the hearth at a run. On the way, he grabbed a cloth that had been left on a table and wrapped it twice about his hand. Then he seized the leg by the joint and whirled back toward the battle. Using the roast meat as a club, he aimed a hard upswing at the nearest mercenary.

The man got his sword down to meet the unusual weapon, but the blade sank to the hilt in the tender meat and did not seem to slow the dwarf's blow in the slightest. Up swung the leg of lamb, driving the hilt of the sword into the man's face. There was a crunch of bone as the hilt struck and shattered his nose, then a splat as the sizzling meat slapped into the man and splattered him with hot juices. Howling, pawing at his ruined nose and blinded eyes, the mercenary reeled off.

"Waste o' good food," muttered the dwarf. Nonetheless, he tossed the leg of lamb to the floor so he could tug free the sword. The weapon was too long for him to use, but judging from how well the elf was holding forth with just a dagger, he figured his new friend would know the use of it well enough.

Between parried blows, Kendel glanced toward the hearth as another dwarven battle cry ripped through the tavern. His new ally held a sword before him like a lance, hilt braced against his belly, and was already well into another charge. The dwarf's chosen mark turned toward the low-pitched shout and neatly sidestepped. The dwarf could not change course in time to hit his original target, but his sword plunged deep into the protruding belly of yet another mercenary.

"Oops," murmured the dwarf, but he quickly made the best of his mistake. He leaned into the sword and began to run in a circle around the impaled man, looking for all the world like a farmhand pushing one of the handles that turns a millstone. The sword tore through the man's flesh with sickening ease. His insides spilled forth, and he slumped, lifeless, into the spreading pile of gore.

The elf, meanwhile, leaped forward to parry a blow from the first man, a vicious downward sweep that would have felled the dwarf. He caught the man's sword on the crossguard of his dagger, but the force of the blow forced him to his knees.

Before the mercenary could disengage his sword for another strike, the dwarf closed in. Reaching high over the joined blades, he delivered a punch to a point just below the man's rib cage. The man's breath wheezed out in a single gusty rush, and he bent double over the kneeling elf.

The dwarf seized the man by the hair and forced his head up. "Seems like we finally see eye to eye," he quipped, and then he smashed his fist into the mercenary's face. Once would have been enough, but the dwarf hit him again just for the practice. Casually he shoved the insensible man aside and picked up his fallen sword.

"Use this one, elf," he advised Kendel. "The other's a finer weapon, but you'll find the grip a mite slippery."

The elf seized the offered sword and leaped to his feet, whirling to meet the final challenger and slapping his dagger into the dwarf's hand. But the last standing mercenary did not like his chances against these two. He slid his own sword hastily into its scabbard and bolted for the door.

"After 'im," bellowed the dwarf, kicking into a run.

Kendel hesitated and then followed suit. He had drawn steel against human soldiers; the penalties would be stern. Wherever this dwarf might be going would certainly be safer for him than Port Kir. And it occurred to Kendel that the journey might well be worthwhile in itself.

He found the dwarf in the courtyard, bouncing wildly as he sat atop the struggling mercenary. Kendel strode over and placed a blade at the man's throat.

" 'Bout time you got here," grumbled the dwarf as he rolled aside. "This one's jumpier than a bee-stung horse. On yer feet," he instructed the man. "Start a'walking east down the street. I'm behind you, and if you run a step or sing out fer help, I'll dig this fine dagger into yer backside."

"What do you plan to do with him?" Kendel asked as he fell in beside the dwarf.

The dwarf pursed his lips and considered. "Truth be told, I'm a'getting mighty tired of all that's been going on in these parts. I'm for going back to the Earthfast Mountains and my kin, but first I'm thinking we should take this scum back to whatever pond he's used to floating on. I'd like to meet the man who hired him," he said in a voice full of grim promise.

"Why?" Kendel asked, surprised.

"I been a slave fer ten years. More, if'n you add the days I was forced to work in that sow's bowels of a tavern. Didn't much like it. Don't much like the idea of anybody, not even them pixie-licking wild elves, being forced into slavery. I wanna know the who and why of it. Hired swords don't come cheap, and taking elves as

slaves can only bring a keg of trouble. There's cheaper
and easier ways of picking pipeweed leaves. Something
else is going on."

Kendel eyed the dwarf with new respect. Seldom did
the insular dwarven people consider the well-being of
other races. He was also a bit shamed by the dwarf's
concern. He had long heard tales of the forest elves'
troubles, but had been unwilling to get involved. To
many humans, an elf was an elf, and incidents such as
the one in the tavern were far too common. Yet here was
a dwarf, ready to go to the aid of the forest folk.

"Is that why you fought in the tavern that first
night?" he asked softly. "In defense of a beleaguered
elf?"

The dwarf snorted and prodded at the mercenary
with the tip of the dagger. "They spoke ill of me mother,"
he said. "They shouldn't ought to do that."

"Indeed they shouldn't," Kendel agreed. "You did well
to defend her honor."

"And her name," the dwarf added. "Seems like I do
more'n my share of that. See, me mother passed her
name along to me. I wear it right proud, but not everyone sees things the same."

"Ah. My name is Kendel Leafbower," the elf said, curious as to what the dwarf's name might be and hoping to
speed the introductions.

"And I be called Jill," responded his new friend, shooting a cautious, sidelong look up at the elf. His expression dared Kendel to comment.

"That explains much," murmured Kendel solemnly.
"In Elvish, the word 'Jill' means 'fearsome warrior,' " he
lied hastily, for storm clouds were already gathering on
the dwarf's brow.

"Aye, that she was," Jill said happily, his ire forgotten.
"The name come down through the clan to male and
female alike. And odd enough, it seems like every male
dwarf who bears it fights better 'n most."

"Probably because you have more practice," the elf

observed; then he winced as it occurred to him how the proud dwarf might take these words.

But to his surprise, a deep rumble of laughter shook the dwarf's belly and rolled upward in waves. "Aye, there's something to that," Jill admitted.

The new friends shared a companionable grin and set off with their hostage at a brisk pace toward the east, and whatever answers might await them there.

Sixteen

 After his meeting with Lord Hhune, Bunlap set off for his fortress with a new contingent of hired men and a dark heart full to overbrimming with plans for the destruction of the elves who had taunted and eluded him for far too long. One of his new employees, a priest of Loviatar whose fascination with the concept of suffering lay well beyond the bounds of orthodoxy, had agreed to accompany him eastward and interrogate the slain elves that Vhenlar and his men had retrieved. In time, they would strike the elves in their most secret places.

But the mercenary captain was none too happy with the news that greeted him upon his arrival. Most of the members of his last war band had died in the forest, and his best archer had been stuck more times than a seamstress's pincushion. The expensive Halruaan wizard still lay abed, suffering from low spirits and unspecified injuries. Worse, Vhenlar had not managed to retrieve a single long-eared corpse for the priest to interrogate.

"Leave 'em or join 'em. That was the choice we had," Vhenlar informed his captain. "I say we leave 'em altogether—and forever—and let well enough alone."

"In due time," Bunlap informed him, staring moodily at the forest.

"What's to be gained from going on?" pressed Vhenlar. "The logging operation is over. You got your money out of it and came away clean. What more do you want?"

"It's a personal matter—" the captain began.

But Vhenlar wasn't having any of that. "Not again! I've seen you plunge headfirst and neck-deep into trouble one time too many. I didn't spend four years dodging the Zhents just so I could live the rest of my years looking over my shoulder for vengeful elves. I've had a bellyful. Give me my pay, and I'm gone."

The captain shook his head, not even bothering to look at the angry archer. "Three more battles. That's all it should take. The first will be a minor skirmish. Then it's on to the logging camp. Old Hhune put a fair amount of money into it. That site is strategic and it's ours. We can even pick up the lumbering trade, once things cool down a bit, only there will be no need to split the proceeds with anyone else. You could retire a very, very rich man."

"I'm not going back into that forest," Vhenlar began.

"You won't have to. You can fight this one in your preferred fashion—from behind the parapets, shooting down at the attackers. For this you need not leave the safety of the fortress."

The archer considered this. "How are you going to arrange that?"

"We wait," Bunlap said simply. "The elves will come to us, of that I am confident."

"Don't suppose you'd care to tell me why."

The mercenary captain fixed an icy glare on his longtime associate. "You do remember the Harpers, do you not?"

Vhenlar groaned. The secret society known as the

Harpers was devoted to thwarting the plans of the
Zhentarim, curbing the ambitions of ruthless and powerful men, and just generally being a boil on the backside of any man out for a bit more than what the
meddlers considered to be his fair share. "*They're* snoop-
ing into this mess?"

"Indeed. It is well that I returned to Zazesspur. Word
is that a Harper agent bungled his cover and managed
to slip out of the city just ahead of the local assassins. I
asked around and learned there was yet another
Harper in the city, at least until just recently. The elf
woman who slipped right past our fortress with that
clever little smoke screen is one of their more troublesome agents. You might even recall the name: Arilyn
Moonblade?"

"Not the one they say snuck into Darkhold and killed
old Cherbil Nimmt?"

"The same. She knows who I am and, if she meets up
with the forest elves in time, they'll figure out between
them that the source of their troubles lies behind these
fortress walls."

"Oh, she's met up with them," Vhenlar retorted.
"She's a gray elf, right? With a magic sword? Well, she
was right there with the wild elves, telling 'em what to
do. And they were listening, though never would I have
believed it. But for her, they would have killed us all!"

"All the better. You can be certain that elven scouts
followed you here. I expect they'll come calling in force
anytime now. And that is where your skills with the bow
come into play. Kill me a certain moon elf, and you're
free to go where you want," Bunlap concluded grimly.

The archer nodded, but in truth he had little faith in
the other man's assurances. Nor could he muster a
shred of enthusiasm for the coming battle. Having faced
those elves and that Harper wench, he had no desire to
do so again anytime soon. Not one night passed by but
he didn't relive the elf woman's blue-fire charge, or
awake sitting bolt upright and drenched in sweat,

dreaming of enemies he could never see or touch, but who constantly surrounded him.

Yet what choice did he have? Vhenlar would be forced to fight the wild elves until he was either slain or went mad. Bunlap would not let him go until his desire for vengeance was slaked. And from all that Vhenlar had seen of his captain, that was not likely to happen easily . . . or soon.

* * * * *

Several days after the midsummer celebration, Arilyn walked off alone into the forest. The key to the lythari's den, the wooden pipe that approximated the call of a lythari, was gripped in one fist. What she intended to do was not easy, but she saw little choice.

The half-elf went as far out into the forest as she dared. Even now, she easily got turned around in the magic-laden area surrounding Talltrees. She raised the wooden summoner to her lips and sent a long, mournful call wavering through the trees. Choosing a fallen log as a likely seat, she sat down to wait.

Arilyn was not certain Ganamede would even answer the summons. The young lythari had been puzzled, perhaps even hurt, by her apparent inability to understand the gift he had given her in taking her to the lythari den. Nor could she explain to him that she'd had no real intention of asking him to recruit his peace-loving people to join the green elves' battles. In suggesting this to Rhothomir, she had been buying time, purchasing Ganamede's safety. But how could she explain this when it was precisely what she now intended to do?

"Arilyn."

The half-elf spun toward the soft voice and found herself nearly nose to muzzle with the silver-furred lythari.

"I heard a strange story in Talltrees," she began without preamble. "The green elves tell of warrior who saved their tribe a few centuries back. It turns out that this warrior was one of my ancestors, Zoastria. Soora Thea, they called her. Word has it that she commanded the silver shadows. Is it true your people once allied in battle with the forest folk?"

"Once, long ago," Ganamede agreed reluctantly. "But the evil that came to the forest in those long-ago times was great, one that threatened its very fabric. Undead abominations, creatures from the dark plane, and an orcish tribe that fought for them, battled for no purpose other than the pleasure to be found in the death of elves. These creatures were an ulcerous growth upon the land, and so the lythari fought until the enemy was no more."

"The humans we're dealing with now are none too pleasant either," Arilyn pointed out.

"Even so, humans are intelligent folk, and there is much good among them. From time to time the lythari strike against an evil individual—a rogue human, if you will, and sometimes even against an elf. But to do battle with many humans? How can we be certain the good are not slain along with the evil?"

"Sometimes you can't," she admitted. "At times I've resented my sword for judging those who face me, but it's a comfort to know that because of its magic, I can't accidentally kill an innocent. Most warriors don't have that advantage.

"If you will not fight," she added with a sudden surge of inspiration, "perhaps you'd consent to scout? Surely there are many 'doors to the gate' in the forest. You could slip in and out and give us a better idea of what we face."

The lythari considered her suggestion. "It is as you say. Yes, I will do this, and bring word to you of threats against the green folk. It is not much, but it may help."

Arilyn smiled and placed a hand on her friend's furred shoulder. "It's quite a bit, and more than I like to ask of you."

"I know this," Ganamede replied softly. "For a time I

doubted your purpose. But like us, you also walk
between two worlds. It is not an easy thing to do, and
sometimes others, who see through only one pair of
eyes, do not understand."

"Sometimes I don't understand, myself," Arilyn
admitted.

The wolflike elf placed his muzzle on her shoulder in
a rare caress. "In time, you will. And when you do, I will
take you where you need to go."

And then he was gone, bounding off through the trees
with eerie silence.

Arilyn puzzled briefly over his words, then set them
aside for more practical and immediate concerns.
Despite her words to her friend, what Ganamede
offered wouldn't be nearly enough. Scouting would be
helpful, certainly, but without the silver shadows beside
them, it was unlikely the wild elves would venture
beyond the boundaries of their forest.

And unless they did, and unless they won, Bunlap
and his men would continue to press and harass the
elves.

It was clear to Arilyn that the Harpers' original goal
of compromise with the humans was out of the question. Briefly, she wondered what Khelben Arunsun
would think if he knew he'd urged her to make a deal
with a former Zhentilar soldier. This much she had
learned of Bunlap when she'd researched his fortress's
defenses. The Zhentarim were devoted to evil gods and
their own personal profits, but they often showed a special enmity against the elven people. Arilyn knew
enough of Bunlap and his ilk to know that his war
against the elves was not due to a misunderstanding,
nor was it solely for profit. It was a vendetta.

And it was taking a grim toll. Before her arrival in
the forest, Talltrees had been a thriving settlement.
Now, fewer than a hundred elves remained to the tribe.

Perhaps it was time to present Queen Amlaruil's invitation to Retreat to Evermeet. Arilyn doubted the elves

of Tethir would accept, and after midsummer, she understood this better. They were bonded to the land, as firmly rooted in their forest as any of the ancient trees. Even so, they should be given the option. There was nothing else for them to do. They were too few to fight alone.

Or were they? Talltrees was one settlement, its inhabitants one clan of one tribe. Surely there must be others! The Forest of Tethir was a vast place, and the elves of the Elmanesse tribe were relative newcomers. There were other elves who had been living in the forest from time beyond memory. Surely now they would come together to fight a common enemy! As Arilyn considered this notion, she became more and more convinced that this was the path to take.

Excited, she returned to Talltrees and sought out Foxfire. To her surprise, the war leader was not encouraging.

"Yes, there are other tribes, and many clans among each tribe," he said cautiously. "Many of the Elmanesse clans were slaughtered during the reign of the royal Tethyr family. There are small groups here and there, but they are too few and too far removed from us to be of much assistance. There is a small community of Elmanesse on Tethyr Peninsula, and other clans that live in the forest to the southeast of Trademeet. These elves are unlikely to aid us. In many ways their interests are tied more tightly to those of the humans. They trade with the farming folk who live to their east, and they carry goods north on the same path used by the caravans of humans and halflings. When the troubles started, we sent scouts northward to see if these folk were the source of the problem." Foxfire paused for a wry smile. "Oddly enough, our scouts met with a delegation they had sent to inquire the same of us!"

"But how many are there?" Arilyn pressed.

"There are perhaps two hundred elves in the northern forests, the border lands, and the towns," Foxfire said. "Some are moon folk or gold elves who mostly dwell in towns. There are a number of half-elves as well, but these seldom come to Tethir. Then there are a few solitary elves scattered about the forest: druids, skin-walkers, possibly even some outlaws."

The Harper considered this. "But what about the Suldusk tribe?"

"You know more of Tethyrian history than most," he commented. "The river that waters half of Tethyr bears the name of the Suldusk people, yet few people know of their existence. They are more remote than most of the Elmanesse, in inclination as well as in distance.

"Do you find the folk of Talltrees more insular than the moon people?" he asked abruptly, not waiting for or expecting an answer. "So likewise do we find the Suldusk. In times past the clans of these two tribes raided back and forth. In recent centuries we have agreed to abide by the peace and keep our distance. No one even knows how many of the Suldusk remain. Even if we were to seek help from them, we would find none."

Arilyn threw up her hands in exasperation. "Fine. So we just sit here and let Bunlap's men whittle us down, a few each battle?"

"There is something else to consider," the elf said with obviously reluctance. "Perhaps the humans should settle with this Bunlap. They have laws, do they not?"

"Lots of them, but not the means to enforce them," Arilyn said glumly. "No, our best chance is for me to take out Bunlap and scatter his men. At the very least, I can keep them busy and out of your hair until I think of something better to do." She nodded decisively, then turned and began to stride away.

Foxfire stared after her, bemused by her quicksilver decision. At moments like this, the half-elf seemed utterly foreign to him, utterly human: impetuous, impatient.

He decided it did not matter.

The green elf jogged to Arilyn's side. "Tell me what you need, and I'll see that you get it."

She smiled thinly. "Several nice pelts would be a good start. I could also use some dried trail food—I'll be traveling fast and the less time I spend hunting, the sooner I'll get there."

"You will not go alone," he told her. "I will go, and Ferret as well."

Arilyn hesitated for moment, then nodded. She still didn't like or trust the elf woman, but Ferret had proven to be an effective assassin. The wild elf female possessed deadly skills that might prove valuable, as well as no discernible scruples. Both would be useful qualities for the mission ahead.

As it turned out, there were four who set out on the three-day journey to the southern parts of Tethir. Hawkwing demanded to come along and, though Arilyn had reservations, she had to admit the young elf held up her end of the load. Hawkwing was among Arilyn's finest students and had proven herself in battle more than once, but the Harper was not entirely certain the elf maid would perform as well once they were outside of the forest. The girl was too impetuous, utterly without fear or forethought. But as Arilyn had begun to realize, she had to accept whatever allies in this battle she could find.

The southward journey passed quickly, and shortly after highsun of the third day the four stood beneath the open sky. A stream ran southward from the forest. Arilyn set a path along this waterway, which quickly broadened and deepened as it neared the place where it would join the northern branch of the Sulduskoon. They walked along this tributary for several hours more before the Harper indicated a halt.

"See that hillock up ahead?" she asked, pointing. "It has been hollowed out to make a dwelling. See the stumplike chimney and those doors along the side?"

The green elves squinted, then nodded uncertainly. All the fey folk had in some measure the gift of perceiving hidden doors, but this skill was seldom used by the

forest-dwelling folk. In the forest, they could find a trail
that would be invisible to the best human ranger, but
out here, Arilyn's eyes were sharper than theirs.

"This is an outpost for the fortress. The men stationed
here control trade coming and going along this branch
of the river. There are too many of them for us to fight,
and even if we could attack in larger numbers than we
have, they'd still have the advantage of position and
arms. So this is what we'll do. First, gather some poles
and lash together a raft. I'll need those pelts," she said,
nodding to the bundle Foxfire carried on his back.

The elf shouldered off the skins and watched with
interest as Arilyn took two small vials from her pack.
The Harper carefully sprinkled some brownish powder
on one pelt, then doused it with liquid from the second
bottle. That done, she pressed the two pelts together.
This she repeated with each skin until they formed a
small stack. She tied the bundle securely with a length
of rope from her pack. By then Ferret and Hawkwing
had finished their raft and come over to watch.

"I'm going to put this bundle on the raft and ride,
alone, past that encampment. As a moon elf, I'm the
most human-looking among us," Arilyn said, fore-
stalling Hawkwing's ready protest. "They'll think me a
trapper, floating goods downriver to the nearest trading
post."

She ran a hand lightly over the glossy pelt of a river
otter. "I doubt they'll let me pass by without demanding
a few of these beauties as tax. More than likely, they'll
shoot me out of the water and take the whole pile.

"But no matter how bad it looks, stay out of sight,"
she cautioned the elves. "I'll hit the water as soon as I
can and swim away. When the mercenaries take their
plunder in to examine, they'll have a nasty surprise.
Any one of those pelts, pulled away from other others,
will trigger an explosion that should blow the top off
that hillock."

"Explosion?" queried Hawkwing.

"A sudden blast, like lightning," Ferret explained tersely. "Like that human wizard threw at us in the forest. I didn't know you could cast such spells!" she demanded, turning accusingly on Arilyn.

"I don't," Arilyn retorted. "This isn't even magic—although it's much the same in many ways. I just happen to have an associate who enjoys finding new ways to blow things up."

"Like tossing a torch into rising swamp gas?" Foxfire asked.

"Exactly," she agreed, relieved to have an explanation of alchemy the others could understand. "After the explosion, we'll revive a few of the survivors. We piece together uniforms, boats, passwords—anything that will help Ferret and me get closer to the fortress."

The half-elf slipped off her chain mail, cloak, and boots and stashed them in the bushes near the stream. Not only would it be difficult to swim wearing such garments, but glittering armor and boots of elvenkind were not exactly the type of gear a poacher might wear!

Arilyn hesitated a moment before adding the rest of her disguise. She'd grown comfortable in her elven role, and she was none too eager to take on another. But she'd fought the men of Bunlap's fortress before. It was likely that few moon elven females passed by, and any one might leave an imprint on their memories—especially one who had handed them a rather embarrassing defeat.

So she took a tiny pot of dark unguent from her pack and spread the cream over her face. She smoothed her hair down over her ears and tied it back at the nape of her neck with a bit of leather thong. Her pack yielded a rough cap, tightly rolled, which she shook out and placed low over her eyes. She loosened her shirt and let it hang over her swordbelt, then rolled up her leggings to her knees. That finished, she placed one hand on her moonblade and brought to mind a gangly, sun-browned human lad. The trio of gasps from the elves told her the blade had done its task.

One of Arilyn's predecessors had endowed the sword with the ability to cast minor glamours over the wielder. It was a slight effect, a small shifting of perception. Arilyn had learned to work with the moonblade's magic to create a number of personas. Part of the transformation was done with small changes of costume, and she had learned to mimic the stance and movements of each character type she portrayed: a human lad, a courtesan, a gold-elf priestess, and perhaps a half-dozen more. But to the wild elves, her transformation from moon elf warrior to adolescent Tethyrian poacher must have been as startling—and as foreign—as anything a human wizard might accomplish!

But there was no time to soothe their surprise or explain the sword's power. She ordered them to take cover in the bushes and to follow along out of sight. As soon as her companions were away, Arilyn tossed the furs onto the raft and waded into the stream. She knelt on the raft and began to guide it downriver with a long pole.

She was almost abreast of the hillock when the first arrow came at her. It went wide, but the visibility from the narrow strips of window carved into the barracks was such that she doubted the archer would know the difference. With a cry of feigned agony, she toppled off the raft and into the water.

Sound traveled well under the water, and as Arilyn clung to the rocks at the bottom of the river, she heard the puzzled oaths of the mercenaries who'd come out to finish off the poacher, only to find no trace of him. Arilyn watched as they caught the raft and pulled it ashore, and she blessed Black Pearl, her half-sea-elf friend, for the gift of the amulet that enabled her to stay underwater.

But it occurred to her, belatedly, that she should have explained this bit of stored magic to her companions. Apparently the admonition to stay hidden and quiet

regardless of how things appeared to be going had not
been sufficient for the loyal Hawkwing. Arilyn's blood
chilled as a long, shrill cry filtered down to her through
the water. She'd heard the elf maid's battle yell often
enough to know what it was.

Arilyn braced her bare feet against the stones and
pushed up with all her might. She broke the surface of
the water and swam for shore so that she could join her
friends in battle. Where Hawkwing went, the others
would surely follow.

The half-elf splashed ashore, drawing her sword as
she came. The scene before her was not encouraging. At
least thirty men poured from the barracks—far too
many for the four of them to handle. Arilyn kicked into
a running charge. Even so, she could do nothing but
watch as the fierce elf child went down, clutching at the
bright ribbon that a mercenary's sword had opened
along the length of her fighting arm.

But Hawkwing was nothing if not resilient. She
rolled aside, slapping her dagger into her other hand as
she went. The elven girl came up with a fire in her eyes
that no amount of blood could quench—not hers, and
certainly not that of her enemies.

Arilyn reached the nearest of the mercenaries and
delivered a vicious backhanded slash. The man got his
sword up in time to parry, but the speed and force of her
blow knocked the weapon from his hand. The half-elf
stepped back, then lunged in, her sword driving precisely between the man's third and forth ribs and into
his heart. She pivoted slightly, putting the soldier's body
between herself and the charging attack of a second
man. She planted her foot in the dead mercenary's
middle and kicked him off her blade—and into the second man's path.

The charging mercenary couldn't pull up in time, and
the sword he held before him in a lancelike attack
thrust deep into his comrade's body. Arilyn circled
around behind the confused human with three quick

steps. With a mighty, chopping blow she severed his spine before he could withdraw his blade.

She whirled, moonblade held before her in guard position, to face the approach of a third man. This one moved with a light, measured tread and wore an expression of supreme self-confidence. He smirked as he raised his sword in a parody of the salute that would begin a gentleman's duel.

A nobleman's son turned soldier-of-fortune, Arilyn reasoned, one who was prepared to amuse himself at the expense of the commonborn lad before him. In short, an idiot.

Arilyn let out a brief, disgusted hiss. She parried the rogue nobleman's first lunge, countered with a quick underhand sweep—which was also deftly parried—and followed up with a flurry of ringing exchanges. He met each of the thrusts and returned as often as he parried. The man was good, but not nearly as skilled as he seemed to think he was.

The half-elf spun, faked a stumble, and went down on one knee with her back toward him. To all appearances, it would be a fatal fumble. She could almost feel his supercilious smile as he raised his sword for the killing blow.

Arilyn listened to the whistling sweep of the descending blade; then, at precisely the right moment, she lifted her moonblade up high overhead to meet it. She leaped to her feet and turned hard to confront him, pushing their joined blades around and down as she came. The speed of the unexpected attack threw the swordsman off-balance. Arilyn, however, lashed up high and hard, severing one of the man's ears as the moonblade flashed up over his head. Her opponent howled with pain, but only briefly, for Arilyn pivoted to the left and swept the moonblade across in a hard, level stroke. The man's head rolled from his shoulders.

Arilyn continued the swing, pulling her right elbow back until her two-fisted grip was tightly pressed

against her right shoulder. She face off against the
nearest man and stepped toward him, her left foot leading and sword thrusting out straight and hard toward
his throat. He could not even lift a blade in time to
parry.

Pulling her sword from the dead man's throat, she
spun about to see how her companions were faring.

Not well. Hawkwing was down, and Ferret was
pressed on all sides. The elven war leader was doing his
best to work his way through to any one of the beleaguered females, but he was badly outnumbered. Even if
he'd been fighting one-on-one, Foxfire's bone dagger was
not designed for battle against tempered steel.

As if in response to her thoughts, the elf's dagger
shattered under the attack of a mercenary's sword. The
elf leaped aside, agile and quick, but several men closed
in, and Arilyn knew he could not long avoid them.

Her next response was pure instinct. She held her
bloodstained blade high and shouted a command to the
magic imprisoned within: "Come forth! *All* of you!"

At Arilyn's summons, magic exploded from the moonblade—a white, swirling mist that rose into the air with
a force and fury rivaling that of a waterspout at sea.

Every combatant on the field froze and stared at the
brief, spectacular manifestation. Then it was gone, and
in its place stood several battle-ready elven warriors,
each armed with a sword identical to the moonblade
that had called them forth. These advanced on the
befuddled humans, and the battle began anew.

For a moment Arilyn could do nothing but gaze in
awe at her ancestors, all the elves who had wielded her
moonblade since the days of its forging in long-ago
Myth Drannor.

There was Zoastria, tiny and wraithlike—the most
insubstantial of the elfshadow warriors. The elf
woman's angular face was a mask of frustration as she
slashed at the human mercenaries with her sword, a
sword that drew no more blood than would a breath of

wind. Yet Zoastria's efforts were not without effect. The mercenaries shrank away in terror from the ghostly elven warrior—and onto the blades of the others.

A tall, ancient elven wizard, his long white hair a mass of tiny braids, held his shadow-moonblade out at arm's length, point-down, as if it were a mage's staff. The sword blazed with blue fire, as did his eyes and the fingertips of his outstretched hand. Pinpricks of blazing eldritch light darted toward the mercenaries like vengeful fireflies.

A small, slight male elf held his sword with two hands, yet he wielded the single blade with a dizzying speed that brought to mind the dual swords of a bladesinger's dance. The crest on his tabard, a bright-plummaged bird rising from flames, proclaimed him to be Phoenix Moonflower, the elf who, centuries before, had imbued the sword with its rapid strike.

Another male elf, this one with flame-colored hair, wielded a shadow-sword that flickered and seared with arcane fire. Heat rose from the blade, which glowed a red so intense that it brought to mind a dwarven forge. Arilyn recognized him as Xenophor, the elf who had lent the power of fire resistance to the blade, and she watched in awe as he fought, for his shadow moonblade leaped and darted and licked like wildfire in a capricious wind.

There was a tall, rangy elf woman who seemed oddly devoid of color. Her skin was starkly white, her eyes and hair the color of jet, her leathers and boots a dusty black. There was nothing colorless about her fighting, though. Never had Arilyn seen anyone fight with such bloody fury. And there were others as well—Arilyn's own elfshadow and two males, one small and fierce and the other taller than the rest and golden-haired.

All this Arilyn noted in an instant, for the churning battle did not allow for leisurely study of her elfshadow allies. But as her well-trained mind took note of the shadow warriors and the general course of battle, her

eyes instinctively swept the fierce group for a glimpse of
a face she had last seen when she was only a child—
that of her mother, Z'beryl.

A tall, thick-bodied man reeled toward the Harper, his
hands clutching at his torn and bloody jerkin. Arilyn
shoved him aside and looked up into the face of his killer.

An icy fist clutched at Arilyn's chest as she gazed
upon her mother. She was as beautiful as Arilyn
remembered—as tall as her daughter, with the same
milky skin and gold-flecked blue eyes, but her small,
fine-featured face was crowned with a cloud of thick,
wavy hair the color of spun sapphires. Beautiful, yes,
but grim and terrible. This was not Z'beryl of Evereska,
the loving mother and patient instructor of swordcraft.
This was the elf Z'beryl had once been: Amnestria,
daughter of Zaor and Amlaruil of Evermeet, crown
princess of the elves, battle wizard, and warrior. And
this was the face Amnestria showed to her enemies.

The regal elf woman raised her blood-drenched sword
and pointed it at Arilyn. To the stunned half-elf, the gesture seemed ominous, accusing. Amnestria spoke, but
only a word: "Beware!"

Arilyn heard the ringing clash of steel on steel, so
close and so loud that it seemed to echo through her
bones and teeth. Instinctively, she raised her moonblade
and whirled toward the sound.

Her own elfshadow stood behind her, shadow-sword
uplifted in a defensive parry against the broadsword
that would have cleaved Arilyn's head from her shoulders. The man who held the sword was easily the size of
Arilyn and her elfshadow combined. Grinning with
sadistic delight, he forced the joined swords downward,
pressing Arilyn's shadow slowly to her knees.

The half-elf recovered her wits and lunged forward.
Her moonblade dug between his ribs; she wrenched it
out and plunged it in again. Arilyn's elfshadow threw
aside the dying man's sword arm and wheeled away to
find another fight.

Arilyn took a deep steadying breath and made a quick survey of the battle. Although she now understood that her mother's elfshadow had meant to warn her of the danger behind her, she could not rid herself of the feeling that Z'beryl—no, from now on she would forever be Amnestria—was ashamed of the course her daughter and blade heir had taken. Arilyn's mother had willingly embraced the service and the sacrifice required of those who wielded a moonblade, as had all the elves who now fought. Was Arilyn, a mere half-elf, incapable of such nobility?

Instinctively, the Harper knew this was not so. She would do what she must for the elven People, as she always had. If that meant giving up her dream of freedom from the demands of the moonblade, then so be it. She would serve the sword, throughout eternity if need be.

With new resolve, Arilyn waded through the fighting toward the place where young Hawkwing had faltered and fallen. But her own arms seemed numb and heavy, and the moonblade refused to move at quite its usual speed. Too late she remembered the warning her own elfshadow had given her: she could not expect both to call forth the magic and wield it.

She managed to block a chest-high thrust and then flung the attacking blade aside. But a second mercenary got through her guard—not with a sword, but with a mailed fist. The blow struck Arilyn's jaw hard and sent her reeling to her knees. It was then she saw the wound that had at last brought Hawkwing to ground.

The elven girl lay on one side, staring forward with a single fierce black eye. From the other protruded the hilt of a dagger.

For just a moment, grief clenched Arilyn like a giant fist, squeezing the breath from her body and stealing her will to fight. It was just for a second, but even that was too much. A shadow fell over Hawkwing's body; Arilyn looked up into the point of a nocked and ready

arrow. This man had seen her fight; apparently he was
not going to chance facing her sword.

Before he could release the arrow, a large missile hur-
tled over Arilyn's head and toward the archer. The man
staggered back, and the arrow soared upward in a limp
and harmless arc. Arilyn stared at the horrid, sticky
mess that had taken the place of the archer's head.

"I say, that was a good one," announced a satisfied
male voice behind her. "Custard and cream, I should
think, and a vast improvement in matters of size and
aim. Though to be quite frank with you, my dear, the
spell for Snilloc's Cream Pie was rather a benign missile for this blighter. Not his just desserts at all, you
should pardon the expression."

The tone was familiar—a cultured and lazy-sounding
tenor—but oddly enough, the words were spoken in the
Elvish tongue. Arilyn whirled, staring up in horrified
silence into the handsome, smiling, *human* face of her
Harper partner.

She knew at once how he'd come to be here, though
never for a moment had the possibility occurred to her
that such a thing might come to pass.

Each wielder of a moonblade added a power to the
sword. Two years past, Arilyn had done the same,
removing certain restrictions so she might share the
moonblade and its magic with her partner. Never once
had she suspected that in doing so, she had created an
elfshadow entity that linked Danilo to the magic
sword—and condemned him to her own fate.

"Oh, my goddess," she said in a despairing whisper.
"No, Danilo. Oh, not you too."

Seventeen

 After several hours, the darkness that had cocooned Arilyn's mind since the battle began to dim around the edges, and bright, blinding colors seeped in to whirl and dance madly behind her closed eyelids.

The half-elf groaned and tried to sit up. Strong and gentle hands pressed her back down. "Not yet," Foxfire told her. "You drained your moonblade's magic for Hawkwing's sake, and for us all. Much strength was taken from you, as well."

Hawkwing. Memory returned in a vivid, horrible rush. Arilyn turned her head away, unwilling to let her elven friend witness the grief and guilt the elf maid's death brought her. Perhaps, if she had not drained her own strength to call forth the elfshadow entities, she could have made her way to Hawkwing's side in time to save her.

"You missed the best part of the fight," announced Ferret's voice, wild and exultant still from the excitement of battle. "Never have I seen such warriors! Nine

champions on a field at once! Who could stand against
such a force, and who beneath the stars would not follow them? It was a marvel I will long remember."

"The shadow warriors returned to the sword at
battle's end," Foxfire added. "All but one—the tall gold-
elf wizard who carried you here. He would not return
unless he had your direct command, or, at least, reasonable assurance that you were safe. Although in the case
of that one, I do not know what might be considered reasonable," he added in a wry tone.

Arilyn's lips twitched in an involuntary smile. She
knew at once the true identity of the wizard of whom
Foxfire spoke. In a few terse words, the wild elf had
sketched a remarkably accurate picture of the Danilo
she knew: a stubborn, exasperating soul who would
have his way no matter what and who usually took center stage while doing so. On the other hand, he was also
perhaps the most caring, intuitive, and gifted human
she'd ever met. Of course his shadow-spirit could recognize the problems inherent in showing these elves his
true face, and certainly he was skilled enough in the
magical arts to cast such an illusion over himself.
Despite all, Arilyn could not help but be amused by the
image of Danilo as a gold-elf wizard. That was a role he
would certainly play to the balcony seats! The gold elves
were widely considered to be the most beautiful and
regal of the People. Knowing Dan as she did, Arilyn
could guess that his shadow took on this guise with typical flamboyant élan.

The warmth these thoughts brought her was rapidly
chased away by the chilling memory of what Dan's
shadow meant, and the realities of the battle they had
fought. Danilo's spirit had been condemned to serve the
moonblade. And Hawkwing was dead.

"The gold wizard left you a message," Ferret said, cutting into Arilyn's grim thoughts. "He bid you remember
the legend lore spell, which you heard when first you
and he sought the answers to your moonblade's magic."

The elf woman began to recite words that Arilyn only dimly remembered, words that the archmage Khelben Arunsun himself had coaxed from the moonblade more than two years before:

"Call forth through stone,
Call forth from steel.
Command the mirror of myself,
But ware the spirit housed within
The shadow of the elf."

"He said to tell you that you cannot call the shadow warriors again without great risk to yourself," Ferret continued. "It is a shame. With them to lead, the Talltrees clan could face nearly any foe!"

"Never heared tell afore that elven folk feared to go into battle," taunted a gruff, vaguely familiar voice. "You couldn't be gittin' soft. Yer too ding-blasted scrawny fer that!"

After a moment's shock, Arilyn placed the deep tones with a face—that of a young dwarf with a short, dun-colored beard and an unusual zest for both rowdiness and romance. Yet how could this be? When last she'd seen him, the dwarf was reveling in the luxuries afforded by the Foaming Sands, and was washing away the memories of ten years of servitude with as much warm, bubbling water and half-clad women as his coins would buy him.

"Not Jill?" Arilyn whispered. She struggled to sit, to open her eyes, but could not yet do either.

"The same," the dwarf said gruffly. "Hold still, now. Yer wrigglin' around like a worm on a hook, and with no fish to show fer yer efforts. Rest. That were some fight, though sorry to say ol' Kendel and I missed the best of it."

"Kendel Leafbower," supplied a soft, melodious elven voice. "At your service, Lady of the Moonblade."

Arilyn recognized the moon-elven clan name. The Leafbowers were renowned as travelers and fighters.

Such an elf was an unlikely companion for the dwarf. "How did you come to be here, Jill?" she murmured.

"Well now, that's a story," the dwarf admitted in a conversational tone. "Leave it to say that Kendel 'n me borrowed somebody's hired sword and persuaded him to head fer home. This is where he brung us—a bit too late for the fight, like I said, but soon enough fer him to die with people he knew. More'n he had comin' to him, by my way of thinkin'."

"Kendel and you," she repeated, somewhat bemused by the idea of a dwarf and a moon-elf warrior on such friendly terms.

"Yep. You might say him and me is tighter'n ticks," Jill agreed happily, "though no one what heared us talkin' on the way east mighta guessed it. Argued like brothers, we did, about which of us would git to kill the hired sword and when he'd git to do it. Never meant a word of it. But fun it were!" he concluded gleefully.

"I see the gold-elf wizard spoke truth," Ferret broke in coldly. "He said you knew this dwarf. You've strange allies, Arilyn Moonblade."

"You're not fer knowing the half of it, elf woman," the dwarf retorted. "I been in more fights than you've had tumbles, an' I thought I seen it all. But never once have I seen an elf ghost come to the aid of the living! Are you thinking that the ghost of that liddle blue-haired elf woman follered you from the treasure room?" he asked Arilyn. "Morodin's Beard, if'n you could put some starch in that one, she'd be worth fighting!"

Yes, Arilyn admitted silently. That was precisely what she must do. Perhaps she could not call forth the elfshadow warriors again, but she could restore to the forest elves a hero they knew, one they would willingly follow. She would have to, as Jill so aptly phrased it, "put some starch" back into the elven battle leader Zoastria. It was time to reunite the elfshadow with the slumbering form of her ancestor.

But first, she had to regain her own "starch."

Arilyn willed her swirling thoughts to find focus. She noted that her cheek was pillowed on something deep and fragrant, like moist velvet. Moss. The air was cool here and heavy with magic she had not been able to sense a fortnight ago. These things could mean only that they were back in the forest.

"Did you bring her home?" she whispered, thinking of the fallen Hawkwing. In her time in Tethir, Arilyn had come to realize that the ties between the elves and their forest went too deep for death to sever. The green elves returned to the forest in ways that could not be understood or explained, and she needed to know that Hawkwing would find rest beneath the trees.

A long, heavy silence answered her question. "When your strength faltered, so did the shadow warriors," Foxfire said at last. "More men came from the fortress, and we were forced to flee. A choice had to be made between the living and the dead. Do not grieve for Hawkwing: she is free."

* * * * *

But she was not.

The spirit of the elven girl wandered the battlefield. She was dazed and angry and confused, though the battle was long over. The call of Arvandor was sweet and strong; still more compelling were the rhythms of the forest, heard and felt and understood as never before.

Yet the child could respond to neither. She had been torn from life too soon, and though her existence had not often been easy or happy, she was not yet reconciled to leaving it behind.

Thus it was that the priest of Loviatar had an easy time finding the elf maid's wandering spirit. An unseen hand reached out, seized the girl, and pulled her into a shadowy gray realm.

Hawkwing's untamed spirit rebelled against this

captivity, but these were fetters that even a will as strong as hers could not break. The entity that imprisoned her was powerful but twisted; a cold, salacious soul that reveled in the wounds of the girl's discarded body and the frantic terror of her captive spirit. The ugly soul of this being—a human, a priest of some sort—was made all the more terrible for the impenetrable coating of smug piety that armored it.

"You must answer me what I ask you," his voice demanded, speaking in a language Hawkwing had never before heard but found that she could understand. "Behold this man's livid scar. Who is the elf whose mark this is?"

Hawkwing had no intention of responding, but the priest took the answer from her mind.

"Foxfire, an Elmanesse of the Talltrees clan," the priest's voice said aloud. "Where does this elf reside?"

Again the elven child refused. But it mattered not. The secrets of the hidden stronghold poured from her. She could no more stop them than she could command the wind or rain.

And so it went, for as long as the gray-souled priest desired to contain and compel her spirit. At last he was done with her. Hawkwing tore free and flung herself away from the inquisitor's casual cruelty. Nothing the elven girl had endured in life had marked or bruised her as deeply as this captivity of her essence and the plundering of her tribe's secrets. But though she was frantic and half mad, she set a true course for the elven woods and home.

There she had found solace before; in time, perhaps, it would come to her again.

* * * * *

Finding an agent of the Knights of the Shield was not so difficult a thing to do, provided one knew how and where to look. Hasheth suspected he could learn a great

deal of information in the clandestine shop of one of
Zazesspur's coin brokers.

A very profitable and unofficial market in Tethyr
dealt in the trading of the country's various coins. There
were many types of gold pieces used throughout the
land. Many of the larger cities and even some of the
more powerful guilds or noblemen minted their own
coins. The value of these rose and fell with the changing
tides of fortune. Predicting how a given currency might
fare, and trading coins in speculation of these changes,
was a thriving business in Tethyr.

Most merchants and makers of policy argued that
there was no real difference in these currencies. The
cities with more valuable currencies tended to pay
higher wages and charge higher prices that those whose
coins enjoyed a lesser reputation. In the end, they reasoned, the value of these coins in barter for goods and
services was about the same throughout Tethyr and its
neighboring lands. This was true enough, as far as it
went, but this argument ignored a simple and rather
obvious fact that occurred to remarkably few of Tethir's
coin brokers.

Many of these coins, though quite different in value
and purchasing power, contained about the same
amount of gold.

Thus it was that a bag of a hundred Zazesspurian
gulders, while nearly twice the value of a bag holding
an equal number of the zoth minted in Saradush,
weighed almost the same. There were in Zazesspur
two, perhaps three brokers who would buy up the
lesser coins, then melt and recast them as more valuable currency. The services of these enterprising souls
also came in handy when one had other reasons for
changing the shape of one's wealth. Prime among
these were the personal coins, either stolen or given in
payment, that were extremely difficult to pass in common trade. At times, possession of such a coin could be
deadly.

The Knights of the Shield often ordered gold coins to be placed on the eyelids of those slain by their agents. So difficult was it to spend these coins that beggars and pickpockets would often pass such a corpse and leave the treasure untouched, rather than risk the Knights' retribution. There were, however, some people who hoarded these coins and used them in a specialized system of barter. To an assassin or a hired sword, a cache of Knights' coins was a mark of prestige that brought in other lucrative assignments. Such a coin could also be redeemed for favors or information that far surpassed the value of the gold it contained. And from time to time, assassins incurred expenses—such as the need for a new identity or a swift departure to a distant port—that demanded that such coins be melted down and made into more widely accepted currency.

During his time in the assassins' guildhouse, Hasheth had learned the name of a woman who provided such services. He went to her now, riding one of his lesser steeds so as not to attract undue attention in the trades quarter of the city.

The establishment he sought, unaccountably named the Smiling Smithy, was the sort of shabby place that replaced cast-off horseshoes and reattached the broken prongs of pitchforks. The sole proprietor and craftsperson did not exactly meet the expectations suggested by the sign outside her shop. Melissa Miningshaft was a short, squat woman singularly lacking in either physical beauty or social graces. She was half-dwarven, or perhaps a quarter-breed, yet she was nearly as stout and heavily muscled as any full-blooded dwarven smith. Her features brought to mind a dried apple, her graying brown hair was scraped back into a tight bun, and to call the lumpy, ample form that strained the seams of her brown linsey gown "shapeless" would be erring on the side of compassion.

At the moment, the smithy's thick and sculpted arms were bared to the elbows and glowing red from the warmth of the forge and from the effort of pumping the bellows which fanned and coaxed the blazing fire.

Melissa glanced up when Hasheth entered, scanned him quickly from head to foot, and then harumphed.

"I would like to trade some coin," he said, placing a leather bag on a stout trestle table that held some of her tongs and hammers.

"Fer what?" she demanded gruffly. "Yer horse throw a shoe?"

Hasheth had expected this response. Melissa was extremely particular about those to whom she sold her finer skills. The dwarf woman was capable of making shrewd, clandestine deals and forging incredibly accurate counterfeit coin molds, but if this were to become widely known, she'd be forced to spend too much time and effort guarding the wealth hidden in the walls and cellars of her humble shop and home.

But Hasheth had credentials of a sort. He pulled his sand-hue sash from its hiding place in his sleeve and placed it beside the bag of coins.

"I wish to trade standard Amn danters for other coins," he said. "And nothing so common as gulders or moleans. I will pay twice the trade weight for any coin you possess that bears the mark of the Knights of the Shield."

Melissa let loose a burst of sardonic laughter in much the same way that an irascible dragon might blow forth a puff of smoke. "Yer actually looking for the Knights? Poor sod! I give you three days afore they come looking for *you*."

Actually, Hasheth was rather hoping to make contact before nightfall. "Have you any such coin?"

"A couple," she admitted, squinting at the young man as she weighed and measured the worth of his personal metal. "But that'll cost you four times trade weight."

"I said two; that is more than fair."

"Fair? That ring on yer little finger's worth more Amn danters than you could stuff in yonder coin bag, and me living here in this sorry excuse for a shack. You call *that* fair? Three times trade weight."

"Two and a half."

"Done," she said and spat into the fire. Hasheth was not certain whether this gesture was meant to punctuate the closure of their deal or to show contempt, but he was willing to let it pass.

Melissa pushed past him and disappeared into a back room. She returned promptly and tossed two large gold coins on the table. "Yer in luck. I was gonna melt these down for moleans come morning."

Hasheth picked up the first coin and examined the markings. It was definitely a Knight's coin, but he could not place it to any particular individual. The second coin yielded a bit more information.

"These will do. You'll find slightly more than two and a half times the trade weight in that bag."

The coin broker dumped Hasheth's danters onto the table and counted them twice, then nodded. "Good to do business with you, boy, but truth be told, I don't expect to again. Baby assassin or no, you might as well stuff a fireball in yer pants as travel with them coins in yer pockets. You won't be coming back."

"I thank you for your concern," he said coldly. "I'll be certain to mention you, should anyone give me trouble about these coins."

Melissa snorted, for the young man's threatening retort was no more than bluster, and they both knew it. The smithy had clients who held an interest in protecting her privacy. Anyone who attempted to betray her was likely to become a notch on an assassin's blade, or to be discovered with large gold coins, very much like the ones Hasheth had slipped into his bag, weighing down his eyelids.

Hasheth left the smithy, reclaimed his horse, and set off at a brisk pace for the stables. He would change to a more suitable mount, and then he would pay a visit to the gentleman whose coin he had purchased.

But first, he had to devise some pretense. It would be fairly easy, as Lord Hhune's apprentice, to be granted an audience. But first, Hasheth wanted to figure out some way to insinuate himself into the society of the Knights, something that would buy him membership into this exclusive and powerful group.

The Harpers were all fine and well, and they seemed to come up with coin when they required it, but from what Hasheth had observed, most of their agents were not concerned with amassing personal wealth or power. All told, the Knights of the Shield was a society far more suited to his ambitions. Hasheth was determined to find a way in, and he would count the cost—whatever it might be—a bargain.

Eighteen

Nearly two days passed. The forest elves seemed quietly impressed with Kendel Leafbower, for the moon elf had picked up considerable skill at woods lore during his four centuries of life. He walked nearly as silently as a forest elf, and he hunted game for the small group while the others stayed at their camp to guard their moon-elven battle leader.

Jill spent much of the time teasing Ferret, much to the amusement of Arilyn and Foxfire. It quickly became apparent to everyone but Ferret that the dwarf was flirting outrageously with her. As she watched Jill's avid pursuit of the elf woman, Arilyn was reminded of a question that often occurred to her when she saw a farm dog chasing a horse-drawn cart: what would he do if, by chance, he succeeded in catching it?

She read in Foxfire's twinkling eyes thoughts similar to her own. And behind the laughter in his eyes lurked the memories of their own times together. This made the course before Arilyn even more difficult, yet it steeled her resolution to follow it. Foxfire was dear to her; she would do what she must for him and the People.

And so, as soon as Arilyn felt strong enough to travel, she announced her intention of returning to Zazesspur.

"It was your idea," she retorted when Foxfire tried to dissuade her. "You brought up the fact that this Bunlap and his men are a matter for the humans to deal with. Let me find out who holds this hound's leash, and then let the humans take care of their own problems."

"I'm going with you," Ferret declared, her black eyes daring the half-elf to argue.

Arilyn didn't bother to try. For what she had in mind, two people would be needed. And she was certain Ferret would give her enthusiastic support to the plan Arilyn had in mind.

She was going to bring Soora Thea back to the wild elves.

Jill, however, had already divined her purpose. "Yer not thinkin' to go back into that pink prison, are you? Yer plannin' on bringin' out that sleeping elf woman, aren't you? You are," he added with disgust. "I kin see it in yer face. Well, I'm not fer goin' with you."

"I wouldn't ask it of you," Arilyn said gently. "You spent ten years in that palace. That is enough."

"You think I'm owing you fer springin' me outta that trap," the dwarf continued ranting, as if he hadn't heard a word she said. "You and this scrawny female can't fight yer way outta there alone, and you can't be totin' that liddle sleeping elf woman back to the forest, jest the two of you. Now, I'm not wantin' to speak for Kendel, here—"

"I will come, too," the moon elf said quietly.

"Never said I was goin', now did I?" Jill grumbled. "But since this ding-blasted elf here has gone and signed hisself up, I suppose I gotta go along and look out fer him. Gets into fights, he does, without never once stoppin' to think on whether or not he can win 'em!"

"I'd be happy to have you both," Arilyn said. "And you needn't enter that palace. You two can wait for us outside and hold the horses."

"Horses! I rode me a donkey this far, and I'll be a one-headed ettin if'n I'll trade him in fer one o' them long-legged hay-eaters," Jill said darkly.

"In that case, we'd better leave at once," Ferret observed, not recognizing the bluster behind the dwarf's gruff arguments.

But at Foxfire's insistence, Arilyn agreed to wait until morning before setting out. They settled down to rest for the journey ahead. Soon Jill was snoring lustily, and the practical elves Ferret and Kendel were deep in reverie. But to Arilyn's eyes, the usually serene Foxfire seemed restless, preoccupied. When the first flickering lights of the firebugs announced the coming night, he asked Arilyn to walk with him.

"The People face many battles ahead," he said somberly. "Within the forest, I am an able commander. The Elmanesse have not suffered raids by other tribes for many years, and even the orcs know to keep a wide berth from our hunting lands. But these new troubles are beyond me. You are needed here. Do not stay long from the forest."

"A few days, no more," she promised him. "But there are things I must do that can be accomplished only in the city. As I said before, we must know why Bunlap does what he does. In Zazesspur I have contacts; I'll get to the bottom of this problem."

"I believe you will. We work well together, you and I," he agreed.

Suddenly Foxfire stopped and faced the half-elf, taking both her hands in his. "There is something I must say before you go. We do well as we are, but I would make our partnership deeper. How much more could we accomplish if we could speak mind to mind, sense the other's thoughts and plans without words? Enter with me into rapport, Arilyn, and when you return from the city, stay with me in the forest for all time!"

Arilyn stared at the elf, too dumbfounded to speak. Rapport was the most intimate bond between elves, one that would last for the remainder of their mortal lives. It was uncommon even among the People, and almost unheard of for an elf to establish rapport with a human. She was not even certain that she, who was only half-elven, was capable of this mystic elven bond.

And to her astonishment, Arilyn realized she did not really want to try. Foxfire was a noble elf, admirable in all the ways that she valued. He was also a good and true friend, and she cared deeply for him. But though she loved the elf, the idea of entering into such a bond with him seemed wrong. It was not in her to do. Foxfire was everything Arilyn had ever thought she wanted, but for some reason it was not enough.

There were no soft words to explain these things to the elf. The only alternative method of responding was considerably less noble, but it was all that came into the half-elf's mind. And so Arilyn prepared to do what many another decent woman had done under similar circumstances: lie through her teeth.

"You do me more honor than you know," she began, starting with words she could speak in all sincerity. "I admire how deep your devotion to your tribe runs. And you are right. We would do much better as battle leaders if we could know each other's minds without words."

"Do not for a moment think I suggest rapport only for the benefit of the tribe," Foxfire said with a little smile. "It would be no hardship for me to enter such a bond."

"Nor to me," she told him. "But I cannot. I . . . I have already joined with another."

Foxfire stared at her for a long moment. "But how is this possible? Until midsummer's eve, you were a maiden still!"

"Well then, what of the twin-born?" she countered. "They form rapport from birth. There are many means of establishing bonds. As precious as midsummer was to me, there are other things in life equally worth sharing."

Understanding came in bleak waves into his eyes. "I see. Forgive me," he murmured.

She placed one hand on his shoulder. "There is nothing to forgive, only thanks to be spoken for the honor you have shown me."

He nodded and covered her hand with one of his, accepting her decision with grace. "It is late, and the morning will come all too soon. You must rest if you are to travel," he said.

They made their way back to the place were Ferret and Kendel rested in reverie. But Arilyn did not sleep, nor, she suspected, did Foxfire find his way into the fey repose of the elves.

*   *   *   *   *

The two elf women and their odd escorts traveled east along the forest's line—a longer path, but Arilyn wanted to put as much space as possible between them and Bunlap's fortress before entering open terrain. They traveled on foot the first day. Then Arilyn, in her guise of human lad, slipped into a farming village and bartered some of her emergency coin for a trio of sturdy horses—and a donkey for Jill.

Arilyn set a fast pace through the foothills, heading for Tinkersdam's hidden lair. The task ahead was tailor-made for the special skills of the eccentric alchemist. There were times that called for subtlety and finesse; this was not one of them.

They pressed their mounts as fast as Arilyn dared—and Ferret would allow—and they reached the entrance to Tinkersdam's cavern in the middle of the night. Arilyn led the way through the curtain of pines into the cavern and then down the winding passages toward the lair.

Tinkersdam was awake and at work, as Arilyn had anticipated he would be. The alchemist had little regard for schedules of any sort. Here, in a cavern deep within the hills where there was no natural light to mark the passing of time, he was even saved from the minor annoyance of day and night.

When the four travelers entered the alchemist's lair, they found him lying on his back under a large wooden contraption that had the size and appearance of a carriage. His plump, bowed legs stuck out from under it, and his feet were dangerously close to a simmering kettle.

Arilyn reflexively reached out to move the hazard away, but two things quickly occurred to her: Tinkersdam might appear preoccupied, but he was always incredibly aware of his surroundings. He would be less likely to kick over the kettle than a halfling would be to skip dinner. Secondly, there was no apparent reason why the kettle *should* be simmering. It hung on a tripod over the bare stone of the cave. There was no fire beneath it, not even a pile of glowing coals. Ergo, whatever was in that kettle was better left alone.

"So you're back," Tinkersdam announced, not bothering to come out from under his current invention. "Brought friends, I see."

The half-elf stooped down and peered at the alchemist, who was busily connecting an odd network of tubes and vials. Arilyn did not want to think about what explosive force he might have in mind to power this strange conveyance. "I've got a job for you," she said.

"As you can see, I've got one at the moment," Tinkersdam pointed out.

Words danced ready on Arilyn's tongue: the importance and urgency of the task ahead, the impact it would have on the elven folk, her own desperate need to free her Harper partner, if not herself, from the servitude demanded by the sword she carried. But none of this, she knew, would have the slightest impact on the alchemist.

"How would you like to blow up a palace?" Arilyn asked casually.

Tinkersdam looked at her at last with the expression

of one who hardly dared to hope he might have heard aright. "*How* would I like to? As in, what method would I prefer to use?"

"Bad choice of words," the Harper agreed dryly. "You can use any method you like, but there must be enough of an explosion to throw all who are within the palace walls into confusion. The explosion must come from inside, and it must happen quickly, so as not to alert whatever passes for a city guard in Zazesspur these days."

The alchemist scooted out from under the carriage, bounded to his feet, and bustled over to a table. Muttering all the while, he began to toss odd-smelling powders and tip flasks of liquid into a large caldron, working with apparently indiscriminate haste.

"I've been wanting to try this for years," he said happily, briskly stirring all the while like a goodwife beating a batch of biscuits. "Oh, I've run the odd small test or two, but nothing truly substantial."

"That mansion you rendered into rubble in Suzail— that wouldn't by any chance have been one of those small tests?" Arilyn asked cautiously.

"Oh, yes, indeed. I'm looking forward to seeing what this can do when given a bit of time and space. What palace are we destroying, if I might ask?"

"The home of Abrum Assante."

"Not the master assassin?" demanded Ferret, speaking for the first time since they had entered the cavern. "Are you utterly moon-mad?"

Arilyn turned to the incredulous elf. "Assante has something we need. You remember the story you told of the Soora Thea, the hero who will return? Well, she can and will, but first we have to get her from her resting place—in Assante's treasure chamber."

The elf's eyes lit with hope and then blazed at this sacrilege. "So that is what the dwarf has been blathering about! 'The liddle blue-haired elf woman,' indeed! Of course I will help. But you said the explosion must come from within the compound. How is this possible? Its defenses are nearly proverbial!"

Arilyn quickly outlined the story of her previous mission and described the water-filled tunnel they would need to swim to get in. "But we cannot take her out the same way. We will have to go out by the front door. And the only way to do that is to create enough chaos to convince Assante that he must use his escape tunnel. We will await him there and persuade him to see us safely out of the complex."

"And then he will die," Ferret added. "I can think of no man who would be more dangerous if left alive to nurse such a grievance. Even within the safety of Tethir, I would be ever looking over my shoulder! But what then? How are we to carry the sleeping hero into Tethir?"

"As luck would have it," Arilyn said dryly, "I have a friend working in the shipping guild. He will help make the arrangements."

"Here you are," the alchemist said, handing each of the elf women a small bowl. Arilyn glanced at hers. It appeared to be fine Shou porcelain, and around its rim was painted a ring of fire-breathing serpent dragons. A clear, waxy substance, still somewhat pliable, filled the bowl, and a cotton wick thrust up from it. At the bottom of the bowl was a layer of multicolored crystals.

"To all appearances, a candle," Arilyn said with admiration. "How long before the fire burns down?"

Tinkersdam shrugged. "An hour. Perhaps a bit less. Just be sure you are well away from it when it ignites. And put the bowls so that the fuchsia dragon—see that one over on the side?—points in the direction in which you want to direct the most damage."

"Assante's palace is fashioned of Halruaan marble, and the walls are a good foot thick. Are you sure these two will be enough?"

The alchemist's face took on a pinched, peevish expression. "Five of them would destroy a good part of the city! Why is it that the ignorant and the uninformed insist that anything of Halruaan make has an edge on the rest of the world? Bah!"

An idea, one that Arilyn would have dismissed as insane in less desperate times, leaped into her mind. The rivalry between Lantan's priests of Gond and the artificers of Halruaa was legendary.

"How would a Halruaan wizard prepare a fortress for attack?" she asked.

"Badly," Tinkersdam said with a sniff of professional disdain. "An artificer might do somewhat better, but even so!"

"You could anticipate such traps and dispel them? Of course you could," Arilyn said quickly. "All right then, here's what we're going to do. We four must go to Zazesspur to tend to Assante's palace. We will then return here, pick you up, and take you to the battle. Can you have ready the things you'll need?"

"I expect so," the alchemist said absently, his attention turning back to the wooden conveyance. "You might pick up a few things for me in the city. Some coal, some powdered sulphur, a good-sized bag of alum, and a jar of pickled herring. Lunch, you know," he added by way of explanation.

Arilyn swallowed a smile and led the way out of the caves. If it was herring that Tinkersdam wanted, she'd see that the Harpers and Amlaruil bought the alchemist his own fleet of fishing vessels! Provided, of course, that any of them survived the mission ahead.

* * * * *

By early morning they were in Zazesspur. Jill and Kendel took off to the parts of the city where non-humans would be less conspicuous. The two elf women made their way to Hasheth's home. Before they'd reached the outskirts of the city, Ferret had paused to don the disguise she used to walk among the humans.

For some reason, in her face paint and jewelry and silken clothes Ferret looked even more feral and deadly than the elven hunter and warrior that she truly was.

"Who is this friend of yours?" the wild elf asked in a low voice as they strolled along the broad streets, to all appearances, two elegantly clad women out for a morning promenade.

"Hasheth. A son of Pasha Balik."

"Ah. The Harpers have many threads in their webs," Ferret said approvingly. "But I have seen this human; he is very young, is he not? Not quite a man."

"He is not quite a friend, either," said Arilyn with a rueful smile. "But he hears many things and passes most of them along. And he is becoming skilled in the sort of intrigues such as we might need."

She opened the gate to a small marble town house and led the way through the small garden that fronted it. They were met at the door by one liveried manservant and ushered into a sitting room by another, who advised them that the young master had recently arisen and would be with them shortly. Apparently, Arilyn noted, Hasheth's fortunes were on the rise.

After a few moments the young prince joined them. He greeted Arilyn with a bow and slid an appraising gaze over the silk-clad Ferret.

"Your business in the east is completed? This visit is, I hope, a celebration of your success?"

"Not quite yet. We need some information. But first, how goes your apprenticeship?"

"Very well, actually," Hasheth said in a smug tone. "Hhune is an ambitious man who carries out some rather audacious plans."

"Just remember that one of those plans was the attempt to oust your father," Arilyn said, hoping to temper the young man's admiration of the lord. From what she had seen of Hhune, he was not particularly worthy of such adulation.

"I will remember and be on my guard," he said in a

conciliatory tone. "But tell me what you need to know, and I will begin the search."

"I need anything you can get on a man who goes by the name of Bunlap. He has a fortress on the northern branch of the Sulduskoon."

"The name is already known to me," Hasheth said with satisfaction, delighted to be a step ahead of the Harper. "He is a mercenary captain from the northern lands. There is much demand for his services. His men are well trained and as loyal to their captain as is reasonable. My Lord Hhune occasionally employs his men as personal or caravan guards."

"What is Bunlap doing in the Forest of Tethir?"

"That, I cannot tell you. He is not supposed to be in the forest proper. His men are supposed to guard the logging camp from attacks."

Ferret leaped to her feet as if she'd been shot from a balista. "A logging camp? Where is this place?"

"In truth, I do not know. The records say the logs are shipped from southern lands."

The elf woman shook with repressed fury—and something deeper than rage. "I would see something that was built of these logs. Now!"

Hasheth scowled, unaccustomed to being spoken to in such a tone. But Arilyn nodded, and the young man walked from the room. He returned with a polished circle of wood, some three feet across, that was in the process of being made into a small gaming table. This he placed on the floor; then he shot an inquiring glare at Ferret.

The female paid him no heed. She let out a small, strangled cry and fell to her knees beside the wooden circle. Her fingers traced the narrow rings, lingering at the pattern of tiny eyes that peppered the intricate grain. Finally she lifted grimly furious eyes to Arilyn.

"This tree was ancient when the hills of Tethyr were populated only by wolves and wild sheep! There are few trees of this age in the southern lands. This has to have been taken from the elven forest!"

A heavy silence fell over the room. "I'm no expert in local ordinance, but I know that's hideously illegal," Arilyn said. "Why would Hhune take such chances?"

"It may be that he does not know the origin of the lumber," Hasheth suggested quickly.

"I doubt that. Well, Ferret, it's not hard to guess what your next target will be," Arilyn said grimly.

"Hhune," agreed the elven assassin.

"But first we need your planning expertise," Arilyn said, turning to the tense young man. She described the mission and what they needed of him. Hasheth agreed to all, but there was a distracted, mechanical quality to his responses that Arilyn heard and mistrusted.

When their planning was complete, the young man walked the women to the front gate. On impulse, Arilyn turned to Hasheth and said softly, "Listen, I don't particularly like Hhune, but as long as he keeps away from the forest and the elves I'm content to let him live. Do this: find out why Hhune is taking such a risk and who might be at the head of it. If there's a way to stop this without killing your new employer, we'll do it."

"I will do what I can," Hasheth agreed at once.

He stood at the gate for a long time after the half-elf and the exotic courtesan had left, pondering how best to handle this new wrinkle. Of course, he could arrange matters so that Arilyn and her associate never found their way out of Assante's stronghold. That would be simple. A few words from him, describing the plans of a Harper within their midst, would surely buy him his coveted membership into the Knights of the Shield.

But there was no knowing what Arilyn had told her superiors, or whether the Harpers would send agents to replace her. Hasheth did not want any meddling northerners digging into Hhune's affairs or taking his place as Harper informant. No, Arilyn must be protected.

But he could not allow her to harm Lord Hhune. The merchant was too pivotal a part of the plans Hasheth had made for his own future. Certain sacrifices must be

made, and the plans made a bit more complex, but
surely, Hasheth concluded comfortably, such was not
beyond a man of his abilities.

*   *   *   *   *

The lythari slipped from his den through an eastern
door in the Forest of Tethir, one he had not used for
many years.

This door took him to the easternmost reaches of the
Suldusk hunting grounds, near the edge of the forest's
boundaries. Ganamede seldom came here, for the wild
elves who lived among these ancient trees had little use
for anyone outside their tribe. There were few wild elves
as hostile and reclusive as the Suldusk.

Even so, Ganamede had promised to look out after the
interests of all the green elves. In his wolflike form, he
padded silently southward to the Suldusk settlement.

The terrain here was more uneven and wild than in
the western parts of the forest. The trees grew upon tall
hills filled with caves and punctuated by rocky cliffs
and ravines. To Ganamede's eyes, it was more like the
forests of the far Northlands than those of most of
Tethyr. Indeed, here the first refugees from Cormanthor
had settled so many years ago. The trees they'd brought
from the elven forest still watched over the land.

The Suldusk, however, had lived beneath the trees of
Tethir for time out of memory. Their tribe had been there
to greet the refugees from Cormanthor—the elves who,
in time, had become the Elmanesse tribe—and they had
received the gift of seedling trees from the northern forest. But relationships did not remain cordial between
the tribes. There had been centuries of raiding, followed
by an uneasy truce. For many years there had been no
contact between the tribes at all. Even the lythari clans
did not hunt Suldusk lands.

Ganamede's sharp ears caught a distant sound—
faint, but alien to the forest and therefore keenly

audible. The lythari climbed a large hill that led toward the settlement. From there he would have a view of the valley below. Although it was heavily forested, he might catch a glimpse of the source of the disturbance.

Running lightly, the elf in wolf form crested the hill and came to a stop at the edge of a cliff. He stood, stunned, gazing out over the valley. What had once been a wondrous elven forest was ravaged and stripped of life and magic. Massive tree stumps dotted the land. The thick foliage had been burned away so that the dead trees could be more easily dragged to the river for transport.

Ganamede shook his silver head in denial. How could this be? The fierce Suldusk elves would never allow their home to be ravaged. Not while they lived, at least.

The lythari spun and ran for the elven settlement, which was hidden in a valley not far from the devastated forest. He stopped long before he reached it, halted by the scent of sorrow and death and despair. He crested the hill that overlooked the Suldusk valley, finding what scant cover remained. Cautiously he crept closer, for he had to know what had become of the Suldusk folk.

For a long time Ganamede stood gazing upon the ravaged Suldusk land. Then his silver form shimmered and disappeared, and he stood on the charred circle on two legs, a solemn, silver-haired elf. This he did without thought, driven by a deep and compelling need.

In his wolf form, Ganamede could not weep.

Nineteen

Bound together at the wrist with Arilyn's amulet of water breathing, the two elven females entered the well that was Abrum Assante's escape tunnel. While the giant shrimp went into a feeding frenzy over the ham hock Arilyn had thrown them, she and Ferret swam quickly upward. They bobbed to the surface of the water, cautiously scanned the pink-marbled tunnels for guards, and then climbed out.

As soon as Arilyn unfastened the amulet from around their wrists, Ferret toweled the water from her hair and then bound it up in a turban. She shook out a number of veils from her pack and draped them over her nearly naked form. Her role was to place Tinkersdam's candles in the upper palace. Dressed as a Calishite courtesan, she could do so without attracting much attention. A new face among Assante's women would be nothing unusual; his harem was extensive, and the women apparently came and went quickly enough. After all, the guardian shrimp must be fed!

And while Ferret set Tinkersdam's destructive candles in place, Arilyn would go about the task of stealing the slumbering Zoastria from Assante's treasure rooms.

When Ferret was safely away, following the palace map Jill had drawn for her, the Harper drew her sword and strode toward the door to the first treasure room. As before, three guards barred the way. Arilyn didn't slow her pace, but came on with deadly intent.

Two of the guards rushed her. Arilyn ducked under the first swing of the scimitar, and came up, twisting into a lunge at the second man. He parried her attack and shoved hard enough with his sword to send the much smaller female reeling back. Instinctively, Arilyn raised her blade overhead to meet his next slashing blow. She did not stop it so much as catch the blade with her own and press its attack slightly to one side.

The wicked scimitar continued its descent, cutting deep into the first man's shoulder. His scimitar clattered to the floor, his sword arm ruined, and his life's blood flooding the pink marble of the floor.

Arilyn continued her turn, slashing across the wounded man's throat as she went. She then whirled upon the dumbfounded swordsman who had helped to fell his own comrade. In three strokes, her sword found his heart. Yanking her blade free, she advanced upon the final man.

"Open the door or die," she said succinctly.

The guard did not need time to ponder his choices. He pulled a ring of keys from his belt and tossed it to Arilyn. She caught it and tossed it back.

"No. You." She remembered all too well the laborious task of disabling the devices that trapped the lock. There was no time for such precautions this time.

Fortunately for her, the guard did not know of the magical traps. He slipped a huge iron key into the latch and turned it. As he did so, Arilyn stepped back.

A flare of arcane light ripped through the halls.

Arilyn shielded her eyes, but not before she caught a glimpse of the guard's bones, gleaming weirdly through his flesh as his body jolted and shook. Finally he fell, charred beyond recognition, his skeletal fingers still clutching the white-hot key. The door swung open as he fell.

Arilyn stepped over the body, ignoring the dry, brittle crunch as she accidently trod on what had once been a human hand.

She made her way directly to Zoastria's resting place and lifted the dusty lid of the glass tomb. As she gathered the tiny elf woman in her arms, as one might hold a sleeping child, the first of Tinkersdam's explosions ripped through the palace.

"An hour, maybe less," Arilyn muttered sarcastically, quoting Tinkersdam and wishing the alchemist possessed a more precise awareness of time's passing.

She headed toward the door with Zoastria cradled against her chest, dodging a gauntlet of falling treasures as she went. All around her, statues toppled, and shelves laden with treasures rocked and crashed to the floor. As Arilyn ducked out of the path of a falling suit of armor, the second explosion hit, this one more powerful than the first. The tremors knocked Arilyn to her knees, but somehow she kept her hold on the sleeping elf woman. As she staggered to her feet, she blessed the fact that Zoastria had been small and slight.

Dust and small rocks rained down on her as she hurried back to the well. Ferret was already there, her knife pressed to the throat of an elderly Tethyrian man. As they had anticipated, Assante realized that explosions of this magnitude would destroy many of his defenses, and he had come to the lower levels of his palace to avail himself of his escape tunnel.

"The palace is coming down," Ferret lied fiercely. "Those explosions were but the first of many. Take the fastest way out, and take us with you, and you have a chance of living through this. When we are beyond the

palace grounds, you will be set free. If you call out for
help or try to attack us, I will kill you at once, and we
will take our chances without you as hostage. Do you
understand?"

The former assassin nodded slightly; even so small a
movement sent a thin line of blood running down into
his shirt. Assante set a course through the halls and up
sweeping marble stairs. The noise that assaulted them
as they entered the main hall reminded Arilyn of a cavalry charge at the heat of battle.

Screaming, dragging wounded friends or gathering
up armloads of possessions, Assante's retainers frantically sought escape from the burning building. Since so
much emphasis had been given to keeping unwanted
visitors out, the doors leading in and out of the palace
were few. In the confused rush for these exits, many
people had been knocked down and were now being
trampled underfoot. Those who retained their balance
surged toward the doors, too frantic to notice that their
feared master was among them.

Ferret gave the knife at Assante's throat an encouraging twitch, and the master assassin waded out into
the chaos and confusion. To Arilyn's disgust, the assassin did not hesitate to use his knife on his own people.
Indeed, Assante cut a way for them through the milling
throng, killing with brutal efficiency and then climbing
coldly over the bodies. He would certainly have tried to
turn his blade upon his captors, old as he was, but for
one precaution Arilyn had insisted upon: both she and
Ferret openly wore their Shadow Sashes, flaunting
their rank among Zazesspur's professional assassins.
Only a fool would challenge two such seasoned killers,
and Assante was no fool. He would wait for his chance
and then strike. She only hoped Ferret had gained
enough experience to realize this and to strike first.

Once outside, they made for one of the bridges that
spanned the reflecting pool. Unfortunately, so did most
of the survivors. At Ferret's urging, Assante shouted

repeatedly for his people to make way, and they did so.
Now that they were beyond the crumbling palace, their
panic was lesser than their deep-seated fear of their
master.

But the danger to the escaping elf women was all the
greater. Within the walls of the palace, the screams and
cries had reverberated into a deafening cacophony. Now
that Assante could be heard, now that the crush was
lessened somewhat, his plight would not go unnoticed.
Surely some of his guards would move to his rescue, and
neither Arilyn nor Ferret had hands free for such a
fight.

Ferret, apparently, had come to the same conclusion.
As soon as they neared the pool, she shoved Assante
viciously away from her, pulling the knife at his throat
back toward her as he fell. His body splashed into the
"water" with a sickening hiss, and blood rose to bubble
and pop on the surface of the acid pool.

Arilyn grimaced, for Ferret's action was shortsighted.
Without Assante to use as a shield, they were virtually
defenseless.

The Harper turned back toward the palace just in
time to see a guard rushing at them, his scimitar lifted
high overhead in preparation for swift retribution. She
leaped forward, twisted to one side, and kicked out as
hard and as high as she could considering the precious
burden in her arms. The kick landed firmly in his chest.
It was not much, but it stunned him and halted his
momentum long enough for Ferret to join the fray.

The green elf leaped forward and thrust her knife
into the guard's throat. She twisted the blade, yanked it
free, and then hurled it at a second guard.

"Run!" she demanded as she tore the sword from the
dead man's hands.

Arilyn did so. Ferret held the curved blade before her,
waving it menacingly at those who'd halted at the far
edge of the bridge. Then she lifted the sword high and
hurled it—not at the guards, but into the deadly pool. A

spray of acid splashed up into the crowds, droplets that would tunnel through flesh and sinew and bone, causing incredible agony as they left behind indelible scars, or blindness, or death.

Ignoring the screams, Ferret turned and ran after Arilyn.

It was not difficult to leave the compound's gardens. The gate had been shattered by the first rush to escape, and the panic within was nothing compared to the confusion outside Assante's complex. It seemed as if all of Zazesspur had come to see the excitement.

Arilyn pressed her way through the milling crowd to the carriage Hasheth had arranged for them, which waited three streets east and away from much of the turmoil. Kendel Leafbower sat in the driver's box, cloaked and cowled to conceal his elven nature.

Jill leaned out of the carriage and took the slumbering elf woman from Arilyn's arms. The Harper snatched up a cloak, draped it over herself, and then climbed onto the box beside Kendel. She took the reins from his hands and shook them briskly over the horses' back.

The dwarf, meanwhile, had deposited Zoastria gently onto the carriage seat and extended a brawny hand to Ferret. The wild elf hesitated only a moment, then grasped the offered wrist as the carriage lurched off. Jill tugged the wild elf inside with an ease that nearly pulled her arm from her shoulders, and brought her tumbling into his lap.

"Well, now," the dwarf said happily. "I knowed you'd come around to my way of thinking sooner or later!"

* * * * *

They were an odd company, these six travelers to the Forest of Tethir. There was a priest of Gond, who was a bit grumpy over having been persuaded to abandon his traditional yellow tunic for the more practical browns and greens of forest garb. There was a moon elven male, who walked as silent as a shadow, and a dwarf whose small boots thumped and cracked with every step. Then there were two elven females, one of the forest folk and one of the moon people, and the slumbering elven hero whom they carried between them on a litter.

Four days' travel lay between them and Talltrees, and Arilyn made good use of the time laying plans for the battle to come. All had a part to play, even the dwarf. Arilyn was past worrying what the forest elves would make of such strange allies. All that mattered was winning freedom—for them, and also for Danilo. How she would accomplish both these goals was not yet clear to the Harper, and these thoughts weighed heavily on her as they made their way eastward.

At last they neared the elven settlement. Arilyn and Ferret placed the litter on the ground to rest for a moment, but Ferret stopped in midstretch and let out a strangled cry. She set out for the settlement at a run.

"Stay here," Arilyn informed the others, and then she sprinted off after the frantic elf.

It was not long before she saw what the green elf had envisioned. Where the elven community had been was only a barren, blasted circle, too eerily precise to be anything but the result of a wizard's fire. The destruction had been swift and terrible. Although most of the circle had been reduced to gray ash, here and there bits of charred trees and the remnants of elven dwellings lay in tumbled piles, little more than glowing coals that Arilyn knew could not be quenched until they had burned all they touched into oblivion. Here and there wisps of smoke still rose from the rubble as the wizard's fire completed its grim work.

Talltrees was no more.

Twenty

For several anguished moments the elven females regarded the smoking ruins of the forest stronghold

"They are not all dead, my clan," Ferret said in a dazed voice. "Somehow most of them escaped, and they are even now nearby."

Arilyn did not need to ask how she knew. In times of great stress, even those elves who were not joined in special mystic bonds sensed things that their eyes and ears could not possibly have told them.

The green elf lifted her hands to her mouth and sent a high, ringing call out into the ruined forest.

The survivors of the Talltrees clan came quickly, but their eyes were glazed with the pain of their loss, and they moved as if their limbs were heavy and numbed by grief and exhaustion.

Ferret ran to her brother and fell into his arms. Rhothomir enfolded her to him, but he looked over her head, his eyes seeking out Arilyn.

"How did this happen? How did the humans find this place?" he demanded.

The answer came to Arilyn quickly, painfully, like the stab of a knife. "Probably they had a cleric," she admitted. "Some priests can force the spirit of the slain to answer questions. Hawkwing fell near the human fortress; we could not bring her back into the forest. All that she knew, they now know."

The elves stared at Arilyn in horrified silence. What she described was an unspeakable abomination. No elf would willingly disturb the course of another's afterlife.

"You have brought this violation upon Hawkwing, and this loss upon us all," one of the females said in a low voice.

"You led Hawkwing and the other elves from the forest," added another. "If you had not, this would not have occurred."

Dark murmurs rippled through the elven assemblage. Arilyn could not fault them. The forest folk were battered and beleaguered, and in times of peril they would naturally fall back into old ways. As an outsider, a moon elf, she was an object of suspicion. Arilyn wondered, briefly, what they would think when they met Jill and Tinkersdam.

"We followed your plans; we listened to your words," the Speaker said solemnly. "And in doing so, we have suffered. You must leave this forest at once and never return."

"You would let her go?" one of the elves demanded incredulously. "What is to keep her from leading still more humans to us? She must not leave; she must not *live!* The time has come for the clan to protect our own!"

"The time has come," announced a ringing voice, "for the children of Tethir to unite, and to fight. You will not harm Arilyn Moonblade."

The elves turned as one toward the source of this pronouncement. At the edge of the blasted clearing stood Ganamede, his silvery fur nearly the shade of the ash that drifted through the air. Even now, in their grief and loss and anger, the sight of one of the elusive lythari cast a spell of wonder over the forest elves.

As soon as all eyes were upon him, the lythari lifted his silver muzzle and sent a long, undulating call into the forest. Then he walked to Arilyn's side. His wolflike body shimmered briefly with silvery light as he shifted into his elven form.

As if from one throat, a gasp of wonder and astonishment rose from the elven clan. None of them had ever seen a lythari in elven form. Ganamede stood tall and proud at Arilyn's side, one hand resting on her shoulder in a gesture of friendship and support. In his other hand he held an elven bow. His silver hair was bound back, his angular face painted for battle in the custom of the forest elves.

One marvel followed another. In swift response to his call, a dozen enormous silvery wolves slipped into the clearing and formed a semicircle around the moon elf and her lythari protector. These did not transform, but their strange blue eyes met those of the forest elves with firm purpose. The message was clear: no one would move against Arilyn unless they were willing first to fight the silver shadows.

"I have come from the Suldusk lands," Ganamede said, speaking into a deep and profound silence. "Their settlement has also been destroyed, but they did not fare as well as you. Those elves that yet live are wretched captives, held in cages at the edges of the ravaged forest. Beyond that, near the banks of the river, is the human camp." He turned to Arilyn. "You know the ways of humans better than any among us. If you will lead us, we will follow, and we will attack."

"The Elmanesse have troubles enough of our own," Rhothomir protested angrily. "We cannot be expected to go to the aid of the Suldusk!"

Ganamede turned a steady gaze upon the Speaker. After a moment, Rhothomir dropped his eyes, visibly

shamed. If the lythari were willing to leave the forest to
aid the Suldusk, how could they do less?

"There is more," the lythari said. "The humans have
been cutting the ancient trees, burning large sections of
the forest lands. This threatens all the children of
Tethir. Once before our tribes united to stop a great evil.
This we must do again."

Ferret came to the center of the blasted clearing, her
eyes blazing with fervor. "And so we shall! Some of our
elders remember the battle of which this lythari speaks.
They must also remember Soora Thea, who led us to
victory! Today will legend be given life. Come, all of you,
and see the hero who has returned."

Cautious hope began to dawn in the eyes of the elven
folk. But Arilyn did not miss the fact that many of them
still regarded her with distrust, even hatred. They
would not soon forget the destruction of their home. Nor
were they in any frame of mind to accept a human and
a dwarf into their midst.

She tapped Ganamede's arm, jerked her head to indi-
cate that he and the other lythari should follow, and
then took off at a run for the place where Jill and
Tinkersdam waited. The lythari shimmered into wolf
form as he followed her, his clan hard behind him.

They found the alchemist seated on a log, his head in
his hands and a forlorn expression on his plump, sallow
face. If there was no work to be done and no property
waiting to be destroyed, Tinkersdam was utterly at odds
with himself. Jill was seated beside him, sipping experi-
mentally at a flask of summer mead he'd managed to talk
away from Ferret. Kendel was nowhere in sight. The
dwarf and the Gondsman looked up as Arilyn approached.
Both did an astonished double take at the sight of the
enormous wolves running silently at her heels.

"No time to explain," she said. "Tinkersdam, climb
onto this lythari's back. One of the others must take the
dwarf, and some of you go into the forest to look for a
moon elf male with red-gold hair and blue eyes. He's

probably hunting. Take all three of them near to the place where the battle will be. Await us there. But I swear by Gond's gears, Tinkersdam, if you blow up something before we join you, you're on your own from now on!"

The alchemist rose, shrugged, and shouldered on his massive pack. He clambered awkwardly onto the lythari's back. Jill followed suit, albeit with a string of grumbled curses. The two lythari disappeared into the forest, stumbling a bit beneath their loads.

They disappeared not a moment too soon. Ferret burst into the clearing, the People of Talltrees close behind her.

The elf woman stopped and pointed to the sleeping figure of Zoastria. "Ysaltry, Nimmetar, you fought under Soora Thea's command. Come forward and say whether or not this is she."

Two elderly elves came forward. They gazed for quite some time at the elf woman's still face, remembering ancient times and long-ago battles. Finally, they nodded.

Ferret looked to the half-elf. "Begin," she said urgently.

Arilyn slowly drew her moonblade and held it up high before her. Faint blue light dawned in the moonstone in its hilt and spread down the shining length of the blade. Those elves who had never seen the magic sword in battle exclaimed softly.

The significance of it was lost on none of them. All had heard the story of Soora Thea, the hero who slept. All of them knew Arilyn carried a moonblade. Slowly, the realization came upon them that the sword in her hand was the very one their ancient hero had carried.

The knowledge of this, and the wonder of it, burned bright in the eyes of the survivors of Talltrees. Even so, Ferret spoke the words aloud in the ringing tones of a lore-talker.

"For hundreds of years, it has been said among us that for as long as the magic fire of Myth Drannor burns within this sword, a hero will return in times of greatest

need. Once before Soora Thea led our tribe in battle. She
will come again, now, this day, in response to the call of
her clans-daughter."

Taking the cue Ferret provided, Arilyn moved to
stand behind the slumbering elf woman. The light from
the moonblade fell upon the still face and set the sapphire braid sparkling. The half-elf took a deep breath
and then spoke into the expectant silence.

"Come forth, you who were once Zoastria, known to
the people of Tethir as Soora Thea. Your time has come
again."

Mist rose from the blade and swirled over the form of
the slumbering elf. Zoastria's elfshadow, pale and insubstantial and wraithlike, stood before the forest folk.

As all eyes clung to the spiritlike form, the essence of
the elf woman slowly began to take on substance. The
ghostly outline filled in, gradually becoming as solid
and mortal as any of the forest folk. Yet she stood like
one caught in a trance. Her eyes were closed, her body
still. Her face warmed, changing from the color of snow
to that of pearl. At last her eyes opened and settled
upon the people of Tethir.

Zoastria's gaze swept the assembled elves, coming at
last to rest upon the wizened faces of the two elders.
She strode forward and clasped the wrist of the aged
Ysaltry in a warrior's greeting.

"I remember you well, Ysaltry, daughter of Aman-
cathara. And you, also, although your name comes not
readily to my tongue. You both fought bravely in a time
long past. Your wisdom and your memories are needed
now. We have much to teach your people before battle,"
she announced in a firm, commanding voice.

The eyes of the forest folk darted toward the place
where the elf woman's slumbering form had rested but
moments before. Arilyn stood there with a quenched
and silent moonblade held in her two hands, but the litter before her was empty. Shadow and substance had
again become one.

Silence, complete and profound, gripped the elven people. Then Rhothomir went down on one knee before the tiny moon elf warrior. As one, the people of Talltrees dropped to kneel upon the forest floor, pledging to follow the hero who had returned.

*   *   *   *   *

The rest of the day passed in council meetings and frantic preparation as the elves prepared to march on the logging camp. Even the lythari clan lingered nearby, listening to the planning. Each person had a role, and all sensed the need to mesh their actions with those of their new allies.

Finally, with the coming of night, Arilyn and Ferret at last had a chance to learn more about the destruction that had taken place in their absence. They sought out Foxfire, and the three withdrew to the shadows of the elves' makeshift camp. The elf women shared a roast haunch of rabbit—the first food either of them had eaten that day—as they listened to his grim story.

"The humans came upon us more suddenly than I would have thought possible," Foxfire said quietly. "They knew the way, and they had been forewarned of all our defenses. Their wizard killed our scouts, even blasted the dryads' trees! There were spells of silence about them, I think. If not for the warnings of the birds, they might have come upon us, as well. We were able to retreat into the forest before the wizard's fire was unleashed upon Talltrees, but barely."

"How did you escape pursuit?" Ferret asked.

"They did not pursue."

Arilyn caught the note in Foxfire's voice, the unspoken fear in his eyes. "You believe that we are being baited, drawn into a battle of their choosing."

The war leader met her gaze. "That is so. The humans did this once before. They laid waste to Council Glade and left some of my own arrows among the slain. They let us know where they could be found, and they waited in ambush for us." He paused. "There is a matter that lies between me and the human leader. This attack has his stamp upon it."

"What this time?" she asked softly.

For a long moment the wild elf did not respond. "I have told you that I carved my mark upon the face of the human known as Bunlap. The body of one of our scouts—Uleeya Morningsong—was left just beyond the circle of ash. My mark had been cut into her cheek."

Arilyn leaned forward and placed both hands on the wild elf's shoulders. "If the gods are kind to you, you will never come to understand evil men as well as I do. But you may believe what I'm about to say to you."

The male nodded for her to continue.

"When in Zazesspur, I learned that this man, Bunlap, was hired to guard a logging camp from the Suldusk. It would not surprise me if this task proved to be far more difficult than he had anticipated. It is likely that the early battles with the Suldusk tribes ignited his hatred of all elves. You see only the part of the flame he turns toward your clan. No doubt there are others in the forest who wonder what they might have done to deserve such hatred.

"I have known many men like Bunlap. There is never a single, simple explanation for the evil they do. So please, my friend, do not take more of this upon you than you need to carry," she concluded softly.

Foxfire lifted a hand to touch her cheek. "Thank you. I will think on what you have said. But come—we should join the others at council."

The Harper nodded and rose to her feet, moving with her customary decision toward the council fire. But Ferret caught the male's arm before he could follow.

"When last midsummer was upon the forest, we were pledged to one another," she said softly. "Have you forgotten this so soon?"

Puzzled, Foxfire gazed down into the elf woman's black eyes. "We were very young when we spoke our pledge, and since that day our feet have taken us down different paths. It was you who asked to be released, before you went among the humans."

"I cannot regret what was done for the clan," Ferret said. "But you forget the reasons why we pledged to each other, so many years past. I am lore-talker and sister to the Speaker; you are war leader. Together we would have brought strong children to the clan, elves who would in turn lead the People. If you do not soon choose a suitable mate and produce heirs, you will not remain long as war leader. You are needed, and you must think of the clan."

"Ah." At last Foxfire understood the elf woman's concern. "And you fear that if I were to choose Arilyn, the clan would not accept the children of a moon elf in our midst."

Ferret nodded. "That is part of it. There are things about our new battle leader that you do not know. She and I have met before, in the humans' city. You must believe me when I tell you she is not what she appears to be."

"I see," the male said slowly. He studied the elf woman for a moment, marveling that she, too, had long known and kept Arilyn's secret. But then, as he considered the matter, it was not so surprising after all. Ferret was utterly single-sighted in her desire to serve the good of the forest elves, even if that meant allowing a half-elf into the elven stronghold and keeping that secret from her own brother.

"So you know Arilyn is half-elven," he said bluntly. "And knowing this, now that you have also come to know *her*, does it truly make any difference?"

A startled expression crossed Ferret's face, once when she realized that Foxfire already understood Arilyn's true nature, and then a second time as she gave consideration to his question.

"No," she said in a wondering tone. "No, I suppose that it does not."

Then her face softened, and she placed a hand on Foxfire's arm. "There is one thing more, something I had
not thought to tell you. For all the truth in what you say,
the half-elf is not for you. She loves another. A human."

"This I also know," the male said softly. "But I thank
you for your concern. Come. We should join the others."

The elves drew near the circle and entered into a
heated debate concerning the best strategy for dealing
with a human wizard.

Arilyn nodded to her friend and then turned back to
the discussion, for in it, she saw an opportunity to
explain Tinkersdam's presence at the coming battle.
"You have all witnessed the damage the human wizard
inflicted. Not only the destruction of Talltrees, but the
way he could turn elven arrows back against their
archers. Imagine what such could do if he had time to
prepare for battle in a place of his choosing! The spells
he could cast, the traps he could lay?"

Several of the elves nodded grimly. None who had
fought that first battle would forget the sight of their
kindred burned to cinder in the span of a heartbeat.

"I know someone who can spring these traps and best
the wizard in battle. He is a human, a scholar, and a
priest of a goodly god. He has been an ally of mine for
many years. Even the lythari accept him. They have
taken him ahead to the battle site, along with two warriors to protect him, so he can scout and prepare."

"A wise precaution," Foxfire said quickly, seeing the
grimaces on the faces of most present. "Even in the days
of Cormanthor, humans fought beside the People
against a common evil."

"I will speak truly. This man is nothing like the
humans of ancient Myth Drannor. He has no love for
the elven people or our way of life," Arilyn said with all
candor. "But neither does he bear us any ill will. He *does*
hate all things Halruaan, and you can be assured that
he will make this fight against the wizard his own!"

"So be it," Zoastria said, and the others, still awed by

the return of their ancient hero, were content to accept her word as final.

The elves debated briefly about the best way to approach the Suldusk lands. Less than two days' march to the east lay the valley known as the Swanmay's Glade. Here was the largest lake in the forest, and from it a small river wound its way toward Suldusk territory. They could build rafts and float downstream more rapidly than they could walk. It was agreed that they would leave at first light, after a night spent in reverie, meditation, and prayers to the Seldarine.

When the chorus of morning birdsong began with the first few tentative, somnolent chirps, the elves were already on the move. They followed the trails the retreating humans had left, not a difficult thing to do.

As usual, Tamsin had gone up ahead to scout. He had not cried back a warning, but none of the elves doubted that he had come to grief, for his sister Tamara suddenly stopped walking and cringed, and placed both hands over her eyes.

A silence fell over the elves, for what could the fey female have seen that would cast such desolation over her, but the death of her twin-born brother?

Tamara's shoulders rose and fell in a long, steadying breath, and she lifted her eyes to Foxfire's face. "It is as you have said. The humans are luring us to them. They will be waiting for us, and for you. Come. You will not want to see this, but you must."

Several hundred paces down the trail, a sapling had been stripped of its branches and turned into a post. To it was tied the body of an elf. Not Tamsin—this one was a stranger, a Suldusk elf, dead for perhaps three days. Flies buzzed about the body, lingering on the shape of a flower that had been cut into one of the dead elf's cheeks.

"How many more elves mark the trail south?" Tamsin murmured in a despairing voice. "How many more will die in captivity before we reach the southern forest?"

Ganamede, who had returned to the Elmanesse with
the dawn, padded over to Zoastria's side. "I have seen
the human camp," the wolflike lythari said. "Their numbers are far greater than ours, and they have had time
to set up defenses. Our only hope of prevailing—and
freeing those elves who have not yet been slain—is surprise. I have spoken with my clan. The lythari will take
you between the worlds to a place much nearer the
camp than the Swanmay's Glade—a day's walk, no
more."

"The humans have had more than three days' head
start," Rhothomir observed. "Even so, they will not
arrive at their camp long before we do and will surely
not expect us so soon. They will no doubt have scouts
watching for our passage. With what you suggest, we
could slip past unseen and catch the humans utterly
unaware! If your clan is willing to take us, we accept
most gratefully."

The elves set about dividing into small groups so they
could travel with the dozen or so lythari through the
gates to the battle site. Foxfire was among the first to
go, as was Rhothomir. It seemed best to send the leaders first, but Zoastria waved aside her turn and
motioned for Arilyn to come with her.

The two elven females walked away from the others.
When they came to a small clearing beneath the shade
of some ancient oaks, Zoastria came to a halt. "The
battle comes sooner than I had expected," she said
abruptly. "It is time."

Arilyn gazed down at the smaller elf, not understanding. She followed the elf woman's gaze to the
moonblade on her hip.

"You have worn it well, for a half-elf," Zoastria admitted. "But my time has come again. I will have my moonblade returned to me."

Twenty-one

Arilyn stared at her ancestor, dumbfounded by this demand. She had not foreseen this result of raising the sleeping warrior!

"The moonblade has accepted me as its wielder. The sword and I are joined!" she protested. "I cannot turn it over to another as if it were no more than a common weapon!"

"Only one can wield the sword," Zoastria said sternly. "If you have another weapon, draw it, and we will let skill decide the matter."

The half-elf rejected this notion at once. As much as she admired the elf woman's skill at arms, Arilyn suspected she could best Zoastria in battle. And she had not restored this ancient elven hero to the demoralized Elmanesse only to destroy her now. Nor had she ever once thrown a fight. This Arilyn simply could not do, not even for the sake of the forest folk.

Zoastria must have seen some of this in the half-elf's eyes, for she quickly offered another suggestion. "Or follow your heart's desire. Give the sword to me willingly and be free of the moonblade once and for all. In relinquishing the sword to a former wielder—and its rightful owner—your duty to the People would be honorably fulfilled, and your pledge to the moonblade's service would be returned to you."

As the half-elf pondered this unexpected solution, an enormous weight lifted from her heart—and the void was filled at once with a strange sense of sadness and loss. "And the power with which I endowed the sword?" she asked tentatively.

"It would be removed. If this is your wish, we will proceed."

"One moment," Arilyn murmured. She drew the sword and held it, savoring for a moment the only link she had ever had with her elven heritage. As much as she feared the moonblade, and resented and at times even hated it, she never thought she would be called upon to give it up. Yet this she would do, for the good of the elven People, and for sake of the beloved spirit that would otherwise be trapped within.

Arilyn squared her shoulders and lifted the moonblade high one last time. She envisioned her eldritch double, and also the second shadow that she had unwittingly consigned to the service of the blade. Then she commanded them to come forth.

The paired elfshadows poured from the blade and took shape before her. Arilyn's throat tightened as she looked upon Danilo's mirror image. She wondered, briefly, if her friend would have any knowledge of what had transpired in the woodlands of Tethir. Before she had learned of her own elfshadow, and when the entity of the sword was under the control of her teacher, Arilyn had often been beset by dreams whenever the elfshadow was called forth to do Kymil Nimesin's bidding. She only hoped that in his dreams Danilo understood what she was about to do and why.

Taking strength from the warmth in his gray eyes,

Arilyn thrust the moonblade back into its sheath and unbuckled her swordbelt. She handed it to her ancestor.

Zoastria drew the sword in a smooth, familiar movement. The blue fire in the enspelled moonstone flared high and then subsided. The sword had accepted anew its former wielder. And one of the runes magically engraved upon the blade—that which marked the power that Arilyn had added to the sword—began to blur.

As Zoastria murmured the bonding ritual that Arilyn had never been taught, the half-elf watched as her mark upon the elven sword faded utterly away—and as her elfshadow and Danilo's, hands entwined, dissipated like mist.

* * * * *

"Thank you for seeing me, Duke Hembreon," Hasheth said as he settled into the chair the great man had offered him. It was a heady experience, being in the presence of so powerful a man, and Hasheth did not mind very much that another man's worth had purchased this privilege for him. It would not always be so.

"You said you have word from Hhune. Is there trouble in Waterdeep?"

"Nothing beyond the ordinary," Hasheth replied, sincerely hoping this would prove to be true. "As you know, Lord Hhune has taken upon himself the burden of finding a solution to the problem presented by the forest elves."

At least, Hasheth added silently, that is what I would do in his position. The young man doubted the other Knights of the Shield knew of Hhune's illegal activities in the elven forest, or that they would condone them. How better for Hhune to keep such knowledge from their eyes than to offer to handle the matter himself?

"It seems Hhune has confided in you," Duke Hembreon observed, testing the boundaries of the young man's knowledge.

"I am his apprentice," Hasheth said simply. "I wish to learn all he has to teach."

There. It would be impossible to say more plainly—unless he abandoned any attempt at subtlety—that he was being initiated into the secrets of the Knights.

The Duke nodded thoughtfully. "And what has Hhune learned of the elven troubles?"

"The elves of Tethir are being despoiled. Their ancient trees are cut for lumber, their people slain. This is the work of a petty warlord, a mercenary captain by the name of Bunlap. The elves have sworn a blood oath against him. They will not cease their retaliatory strikes until this man lies dead."

"And this lumber?"

"It has been shipped to Port Kir through a most ingeniously twisted route. The mercenary realizes an enormous profit. This he uses to raise an ever-bigger army to bring against the forest elves and perhaps for other uses, as well. Much of the lumber has made its way to a shipyard, where it is made into swift and well-armed ships. This Bunlap is a dangerously ambitious man."

Hasheth leaned forward, his eyes wide and earnest. "I am young, Duke Hembreon, and perhaps not ready to trace the path of such a man without leaving marks that betray my own passing. It may be that Bunlap has learned of my efforts. He may make some attempt to implicate my lord in this, as retaliation. I have reason to fear he has found an accomplice in this work—someone close to Hhune. I have not yet learned the name of this villain. But I pray you, let me continue to seek his identity. If the Knights look too closely into Hhune's affairs, this traitor may fear discovery and take flight."

The Duke regarded him somberly. "There is wisdom in what you say, as well as a modesty becoming to a man of your years. You do well to bring this matter so openly before me. It will be as you have asked. The Knights will leave Hhune's traitor in your hands. But as for this Bunlap—where can this man be found?"

"He has a fortress near the mouth of the Sulduskoon's northern branch. The logging camp is much farther to the east, where the river and the forest touch."

A frustrated grimace twisted the Duke's face. "The Knights of the Shield do not have an army to send against him over such distances!"

"An assassin, then," the young man suggested. "I know of one who will do the task well and take word of its completion to the elves. She is half-elven, and eager to see that peace is made between her mother's folk and her father's. To this end, she has received assurances from the forest folk that the death of Bunlap will end the troubles."

This was, of course, an utter fabrication, but Hasheth assured himself that the end result would bear out his words as true. After all, Arilyn had set her sights on the destruction of the logging operations. To do so, she would have to remove Bunlap from the picture.

"See to it and report to me when all is done," the Duke said.

Hearing the dismissal, Hasheth rose and walked from Duke Hembreon's chambers, doing his best to hide his elation.

The interview had gone far better than he'd hoped. Just a few more steps and he would be firmly in the graces of Hhune, Hembreon, and the Knights. And the only cost would be Hhune's fleet of ships.

A bargain, by Hasheth's eyes.

* * * * *

The following day, the forest elves and the lythari gathered in the hills beyond the Suldusk settlement. They would attack with the dawn, and there were still many preparations to make, and plans to lay, for the battle ahead.

The most difficult of the tasks before them would be

rescuing the captured elves. By the best estimates of their lythari scouts, perhaps fifty elves of the Suldusk tribe remained alive. It was hard to judge their numbers with any certainty, for they were huddled together in cages built upon the ruined ground, from branches torn from the pillaged trees. The human camp was split, with some men guarding the captives, and others camped near the river. Accordingly, the elven forces would have to be divided.

Despite the grim nature of the task before them, the elven folk could not help but look with bemused wonder upon the strangers in their midst. Kendel Leafbower they accepted readily enough, though his obvious friendship with a dwarf was beyond their understanding. It was the human who most fascinated them.

Tinkersdam kept to himself, muttering and fussing with the collection of pots and vials and powders that he'd carried with him. The elves had all heard Ferret's story of the destruction his concoctions had unleashed among the humans in Zazesspur, and even Tamsin, perhaps the most xenophobic elf among them, was more than willing to let Tinkersdam go about his business unhindered.

Arilyn felt rather useless amid the quietly intense preparations. In many ways her part in this battle was over. Through her efforts the lythari had joined the forest elves, and Zoastria had returned. The half elf had also secretly sent Ganamede into the forest, seeking allies among the fey forest creatures—those folk who were so reclusive that even the elves could find them only if they wished to be found. The lythari knew all the secrets of the forest. Even so, Arilyn felt little hope that Ganamede would succeed in gaining recruits.

She also felt oddly incomplete without the elven sword at her hip, for she had not been without the moonblade since her fifteenth year. Nor did she have a sword with which to replace it. Such weapons were scarce among the forest folk.

This lack did not escape Foxfire's notice. "You cannot go into battle without a sword," he insisted.

Arilyn shrugged. "I've got a dagger. That'll do long enough for me to disarm one of the humans." She attempted a smile. "I'll try out a few of their swords and keep the one I like best."

"But even so, you must have a blade. If not for yourself, for the good you might do the tribe—the People," he corrected himself. There were now three elven races uniting in preparation for battle, and the once reclusive Elmanesse were learning to expand their concept of community. "Not one among us can match your skill, not even Soora Thea!"

Foxfire nodded toward the tiny moon elf female, who was demonstrating an attack sequence to a small group of young adult elves.

But Arilyn shook her head. "No, her technique is far cleaner and more polished than mine could ever hope to become. If there is any lack, it is because the moonblade has grown in power since she last wielded it. At least four elves have carried the moonblade since Zoastria passed it on, and each added a power to the sword's store of magic. Truth be told, moonblades are becoming pretty damned hard to handle," she concluded. "I doubt there are many left that still hold their magic."

"And fewer still who can manage such magic," Foxfire reasoned. "The tales say such a sword will consume anyone unworthy who draws the blade. It must take great courage to accept a moonblade."

The half-elf merely shrugged. She was not being modest. She had first drawn the sword without knowing any of the implications.

"I have often wondered about the power you gave to your sword. They say this gift is not a deliberate choice, but rather the true reflection of the wielder's needs and talents," he observed.

"Or mission," Arilyn added. "Sometimes the magic comes in response to a sudden challenge. One of my

ancestors found himself in a disagreement with a red
dragon and ended up endowing the sword with fire
resistance. Imagine his surprise when he woke up and
found himself alive after *that* battle!"

The green elf chuckled. "So that was how you endured
the wizard's fire bolts. I have seen the sword cast a
glamour over you, and I have seen the uncanny speed
with which it moves. Which of these was your gift?"

"Neither. A moonblade can be handled by only one
person," Arilyn explained, "and that can cause problems
if you've got a partner. My gift was to share the blade
and its magic, should he have need of it."

"Ah. This explains much," Foxfire said.

Arilyn cast him a quizzical look.

"During the battle at the river, I was hard pressed by
the human fighters," he began. "Yet I saw the shadow
warriors come forth from your moonblade, and I noticed
that one among them was not elven, though he quickly
chose to appear so. I did not understand how this could
be, until you told me you had joined with another in
rapport.

"Do not look so startled," he said, smiling a bit at the
stunned expression on the half-elf's face. "As you yourself told me, there are many kinds of sharing. The gift of
your moonblade to this human was the deepest bonding
of any you could have offered him. It reflected, as you
have said, your deepest wish. And perhaps it was a
needed thing, that the moonblade should do this. You
were not able to see your need for this human or to find
your own way to him."

The half-elf stared at her friend, utterly dumbfounded by his words—and by the realization that she
could not dispute them. The power she had given the
moonblade was one of rapport, and her heart—and her
sword—had chosen Danilo to share this most elven gift!
How strange, that the well-intentioned lie she had
offered as a balm to Foxfire's pride should turn out to be
simple truth!

Foxfire's smile was slight and rueful. "You are not the first to bond with a human in one way or another. There is something about them that draws many of the People. There was a song sung among the elves of Trademeet about this very thing. I do not remember the words, but for the last line."

"How brief their flame, yet how bright they burn!" Arilyn recited. "Yes, I have heard it sung."

"And you know the words of this song to be true, as did your mother before you," he added softly.

Arilyn jolted as his meaning struck her. "You know. You know I am half-elven. You have known for some time!"

"Almost from the beginning," the elf agreed. "At first I did not speak for the same reason that Ferret held her silence: it seemed the best way to serve the clan. You were needed. Then I kept silent for your sake, and for my own. Very soon I realized your being half-elven was not important to me, nor should it matter to any of the People. Your soul is elven, else you could never have wielded a moonblade or sought another in rapport. That you have chosen to share that bond with a human does not change your elven nature or belittle it."

For the first time in her life, Arilyn truly understood the dichotomy of her own nature. "Thank you," she whispered.

Foxfire placed both hands on her shoulders. "These were things which needed to be said. We go into battle tomorrow. You know what faces us, and you also know I myself must face Bunlap. He will die, or he will be avenged. Either way, this matter must end."

A slight rustle from the forest beyond caught the ears of both elves. They looked up into the bearded face of a centaur.

Arilyn remembered him from the elves' midsummer celebration. He carried a long spear and wore an expression of grim determination. Apparently Ganamede had been convincing when he carried her message to the other peoples of the forest!

"We came as soon as we could," the centaur announced, speaking the Elvish language in a deep, grave voice. "I am Nesstiss, and there are ten centaur warriors with me. It may be that the fauns will come as well, but do not expect to see them until battle. To whom do we report?"

* * * * *

The appearance of the elusive centaurs galvanized the army of forest people. Their grim, quiet determination shifted toward fierce glee, even exhilaration. Shortly before dawn, they gathered for the attack, hiding among the trees that lay just beyond the portion of the forest devastated by loggers.

The scene before them was like something from the most desolate reaches of the Abyss. The rich undergrowth of the forest had been burned to ash, from which blackened tree stumps rose like giant mushrooms. An oppressive aura of despair hung like a shroud over the land. Yet even this stirred the children of Tethir. The ruined forest was a grim reminder to all of why they fought.

Arilyn took her place with those who would make the first surprise charge. Their numbers looked pitifully few to her eyes, and she imagined how their attack would appear to the mercenaries. On impulse, she reached into her pack for the vial Tinkersdam had given her more than a month before—the concoction he'd made from the shrieker mushrooms.

She shook the vial and unstoppered it, shook a few drops onto a square of linen, and hurried over to the centaur captain.

"Nesstiss, give me your hoof," she demanded. The centaur looked surprised, but he obligingly bent one leg. Arilyn stooped and wiped a bit of the potion on the hoof. "Now put it down, as gently as possible."

Nesstiss eased down his hoof. The crunch of a pebble beneath it was magnified to a startling rattle. He looked at Arilyn with wonder.

"Five centaurs, charging the camp from either flank," she said with a grin. "It'll sound like a cavalry charge. That ought to wake up the mercenaries!"

She caught Zoastria's eyes upon her. The elf woman nodded in solemn approval. "Anoint the hoofs of the others, quickly," she said. "Centaurs, do as Arilyn suggests. Attack from both sides, startle the humans, and send them toward us. Then circle around to the back of their camp and continue to press them."

Arilyn motioned for the centaurs to get into position; then she handed another bit of linen to the nearest elf and indicated that he should help. When the centaurs were ready, she went over to Zoastria.

"There's a drop or two left in the vial. You have heard how it increases sound. Drink it, and your commands will be heard over any battle," Arilyn said softly.

The tiny elven warrior took the potion without hesitation and tipped back her head. Arilyn reclaimed the empty vial and stepped back into the ranks of elves.

Zoastria faced the assembled forces. Her eyes blazed as they swept the lines, connecting briefly but intensely with each one there. Then she drew the moonblade with a slow, deliberate flourish. The centaurs lifted their long spears into position, each looking very much like a lance-bearing knight and fearful warhorse, combined into one being.

The elven battle leader spun toward the encampment and whipped the sword forward, signaling the attack with a battle cry that rang over the hills like a dragon's roar.

Immediately the centaurs kicked into a charge. Hooves pounding, the two small bands swept out wide and descended upon the camp like summer thunder. The ground shook beneath them, magnifying their charge into that of a vast army.

In response, the mercenaries poured from their tents, half dressed and fumbling for their weapons. Again Zoastria shouted, and the first wave of elves ran through the deforested grounds toward the still-bemused humans.

As he ran, Foxfire fitted an arrow to his bow and sighted down the nearest and most deadly target. Two hideous orc-human hybrids charged forward to meet the elves. Their speed was astonishing, their battle-axes held high. Foxfire aimed for the slower runner. His arrow took the creature through the throat. The half-orc plunged to the ground, and as he fell his up-held axe bit deep into the back of his comrade.

"One arrow, two half-orcs," Arilyn commended him as she passed, her hands empty but for a single long dagger.

The half-elf was not skilled enough with the bow to shoot while running, but she was the only one there who knew of that lack. Every member of the Elmanesse tribe was a hunter trained to shoot with deadly accuracy while running down prey. Black arrows rained down upon the mercenaries, sending them fleeing for cover.

But there was none to be found. Already the centaurs had circled around to the back of the camp and were pressing the humans forward. The cries of men who died on the ends of centaur spears mingled with the clash of swords against the oak-staffed spears as their comrades sparred against the centaur warriors.

A tall human stalked through the encampment, his dark cloak flowing behind him and a large, broad-bladed sword in his hand. He smacked a retreating fighter with the flat of his blade, roaring out orders until the chaos settled into some semblance of order. His mercenaries formed into ranks and raced forward to meet the elves hand to hand.

Arilyn picked her first opponent, a large man who was equipped with a fine Cormyran sword and very little else. Shirtless from slumber and clad only in woolen trews, he had managed to pull on only his boots before battle. She charged straight at him, her dagger held level before her. The man saw the charge and the gleaming hilt in her hand, but he could not judge the length of the weapon. Ten inches of steel, held at just the right angle, could give the illusion of a sword.

The man parried with an upward sweep—one that fell several inches short of Arilyn's oncoming blade. She hurled herself at him, thrust the dagger into his belly with one hand, and grabbed the wrist of his sword arm with the other. Tearing the dagger free, she twisted her body toward him. She yanked his arm down, bringing her knee up hard to meet it just behind the wrist. The bones of his forearm gave way with a brutal crack.

Arilyn rolled clear of the falling man and came up with his sword in her hand. She whirled and lifted the sword high to meet the downward sweep of a battle-axe. At the last moment she remembered that the weapon in her hands was not elven steel. She pushed the direction of the parry closer in toward her opponent, so that she blocked the wooden haft of the axe, rather than its blade.

It was a well-done impulse, for surely the axe would have shattered the slender Cormyran sword. As it was, the force of the blow pushed her borrowed blade to the ground. Before the axeman could lift his weapon for another sword-shattering blow, Arilyn kicked out hard over their joined blades and caught him just above the belt. The man folded; she danced aside and finished him with a quick stroke.

Nearby, one of the elves was fighting toe-to-toe with a much larger human, a rough street fighter who wielded two long knives. One of the blades slashed through the elf's defenses and tore open his shoulder. The human grinned wildly and drew back his other knife for a killing stroke.

Arilyn's first lunge knocked the attacking knife out wide. She body-blocked the wounded and much smaller elf, sending him reeling out of the line of battle so that she might take his place. Facing the street fighter, she feinted high. He crossed his blades before his face to

ward off the blow. Arilyn continued the attack, her borrowed sword diving in over the joined blades, pinning
them into place, and pressing them down. The man
jerked his knives free of the sword with a shriek of
metal, a movement that sent both arms out wide and
left his torso unprotected. The half-elf's sword plunged
deep between his ribs. She lifted one foot high and
kicked the impaled fighter off her blade, then turned to
find another foe.

Not all the forest people were faring so well. Some of
the humans had broken through their ranks and were
forming a line between the elves and the cover of the
forest. They had apparently learned the danger of
engaging the forest folk amid the trees and did not
intend to be pressed that far northward.

Seeing this, Foxfire looked about for the mercenary
captain. He caught a glimpse of a swirling dark cloak.
The human was battling one of the centaurs who,
although bleeding from several wounds and bereft of
half his spear, still parried the man's broadsword with
a broken length of oaken shaft.

The elven archer lifted his bow for the shot. The black
bolt skimmed between the combatants and grazed Bunlap's face—as Foxfire had intended for it to do. The
human let out a roar of anger and pain. He clapped one
hand to his bleeding, scarred cheek.

The centaur made use of this opportunity to clobber
the man across the shoulders with his staff. Unfortunately, the creature's wounds had stolen most of his
strength. Bunlap whirled back toward the centaur,
swinging his sword viciously as he went. The blade sank
deep into the centaur's body, cutting a deep and deadly
furrow between his manlike torso and his equine body.
Seeing that this particular battle was over, the mercenary turned to search for his elven tormenter—and his
long-sought prey.

Foxfire was easy to pick out from among the forest
elves. He had deliberately left his auburn hair unbound,

and for once its bright color was not dimmed by the usual ornaments of feathers and woven reeds that helped him blend with the forest.

The elf met the human's coldly furious gaze and then began to back into the forest. On his signal, the elven warriors slipped away from their individual battles and began the retreat.

The mercenaries pressed them through the razed ground but came to a stop at the tree line, as they had been ordered and drilled to do. Their eyes turned to their captain, who stood over the body of the centaur, his black beard sticky with his own blood and his hate-filled eyes fixed upon the forest.

Bunlap did not need long to decide. "Pursue," he said, and then he himself strode toward the forest in search of the elf who had marked him . . . and revenge.

Twenty-two

Tinkersdam had never considered himself in the role of war leader, and he found he did not much like it. The elves with him, twenty or so, had been ordered to follow his instructions, and they were quick to do so. That much was fine. But he had no gift for stealth, no love for the insects that ignored the elves to buzz around his coppery hair, and a remarkable lack of tolerance for something in the forest air. His nose itched, and he felt distressingly as if he might sneeze at any moment.

At least his little band had surprise on their side. The mercenaries wouldn't expect them for another day or so. Tinkersdam hoped this also meant that their damnable Halruaan wizard would have no more than the rudimentary defenses in place.

The Gondsman called a halt, spat out a tiny flying insect, and squinted in the direction of the captured elves. He could see no evidence of mechanical traps or triggered devices. Probably the idiot wizard relied on his fire magic spells to form a defensive perimeter.

Tinkersdam smiled slyly. So be it. Such spells were like a door—and a door meant to shut intruders out could also be used to close the mercenaries in.

He took a coil of twine from his belt—the thin, almost transparent "spider silk" ropes Arilyn had used to good effect for many years. It was one of his earlier inventions. The thought of testing it himself was actually rather pleasant.

"See that tree, right by the edge, the one marked with yellow paint for cutting? Affix this twine to an arrow, and on my mark shoot it over that branch. It should fall into that cage, just short of the captives. Shoot high; the angle of the rope has to be steep. Can you do that?" he demanded of one of the elves.

The archer nodded and did as he was bade. His arrow streaked into the lofty tree, a shimmering thread trailing behind it, and traced an arc down toward the captive elves. The captive elves acted as if they did not even notice, but one of them surreptitiously fastened the end of the line firmly to the bars of the cage.

"Oh, fine. Well done all around," Tinkersdam said happily. He took from his bag several small wood-and-metal devices and a jar of cream. "You know what to do with these. Get up the tree, hook the top wheel over the rope, and grab the handle. You'll slide down the rope fast. This ointment is for the return trip. Sticky hands. You'll be able to climb the rope better. Take it with you, and get those folk up the rope. You, you, and you four—climb that tree and help get the captives away into the forest. The rest of you, wait. When the others attack the camp, we also attack."

The elves nodded. They had not long to wait for the signal. A pealing elven battle cry undulated through the forest, followed by a thunderous, rolling charge.

"Essence of Shrieker Mushroom," the alchemist muttered thoughtfully. "Yes, indeed—an excellent result."

As planned, his band leaped to their feet and began

hurling the small, hard pellets Tinkersdam had given them: small, fetid missiles of sulfur and bat guano mixed with substances that were particularly sensitive to the presence of Halruaan fire magic. Some of these pellets fell to the ground, as harmless as pebbles. Others struck unseen barriers. These exploded into walls of arcane fire, walls that rippled about to encircle the encampment in a flaming palisade.

Through the licking flames they could see the silhouettes of frantic guards milling about in search of some escape. Some tried to rush through the fire. The walls merely bulged, and then snapped back into place.

"Oh, splendid," Tinkersdam said delightedly. "Neatly penned. Very tidy. A fine result!"

He watched as six elves, one after another, rapidly slid down the steep rope and into the flaming enclosure. There came a splintering crash as they broke through the top of the wooden cage, and then the clash of sword on sword as some of the elven warriors held back the guard.

After a few moments the first of the captured elves came into view, climbing up the rope hand-over-hand into the trees. Tinkersdam counted as they came. One after another, forty-seven bedraggled elves made their way up into the safety of the trees. Fierce yells and the sound of intensified battle within the fiery enclosure suggested that some of the Suldusk elves remained behind to aid their rescuers and perhaps to avenge their captivity. By Tinkersdam's estimation, the operation would soon be over.

"Oh yes indeed, an excellent result," he said with satisfaction.

*　*　*　*　*

Foxfire raced off into the forest, leaping lightly over fallen trees and dodging low branches. He had already chosen his ground: a small level clearing not far from the ravaged logging site. It was a good place for battle. His people could take to the trees and fight from cover, and he could at last face the human who pursued him.

When he reached the clearing, he stepped behind a thick cedar and waited. He could hear Bunlap's approach—heavy iron boots crunching the foliage, his breath coming in short, furious bursts that whistled out from between his clenched teeth. Foxfire tensed in readiness. His would be the advantage of first attack.

But some instinct, perhaps born of hatred, sharpened the human's senses. When Foxfire leaped out from his hiding place, Bunlap did not so much as blink, but instead hurled the knife he had back and ready.

Foxfire leaned aside with elven speed and agility. The knife that would have found his heart buried itself instead in the muscles of his arm. For a moment the elf felt nothing but the thump of impact. Then pain, white-hot in its intensity, seared up his arm. He swayed and reached for the tree to steady himself.

The human came on, sword in hand.

* * * * *

The Elmanesse fled into the forest, the humans following them like hounds nipping at the heels of a hare. Indeed, the mercenaries had little choice in the matter. Eight of the centaur warriors still stood, and their spears pressed the humans relentlessly northward. And loath though they were to fight the elves amid the trees, they were less eager to face the wrath of their captain.

Vhenlar, his loaded bow ready in his hand, was one of the last to pass the tree line. He was less afraid of Bunlap than the others, and in some ways he would have preferred to take his chances with those deadly horsemen than to face the elven archers again. The prospect of venturing into Tethir's deep, cool shadows, every one of which might hide a wild elf, chilled him to the soul.

He did not get quite that far.

A stand of ferns exploded into movement, and from it
leaped the most astonishing creature Vhenlar had ever
seen. Shorter than a halfling, the creature had a naked,
manlike torso atop hindquarters rather like those of a
stout, two-legged goat. Wild brown hair erupted from
the creature's head and fell to his shoulders, where it
mingled with an equally rampant beard.

A faun, Vhenlar realized with awe. He lifted his bow
and took aim. The arrow—a stolen elven bolt—streaked
toward the creature's throat.

The faun snorted and made a lightning-fast grab for
the arrow. He fielded it without blinking. Before the
stunned Vhenlar could absorb this astonishing parry,
the faun leaped at him.

The Zhentish archer went down, his hands flailing
as he tried to push the small warrior off. A sudden
bright pain exploded in his gut and seared its way up
into his chest. The faun leaped up and danced away
into the forest.

Vhenlar looked down at the black shaft protruding
from his body. A wry, bitter smile twisted his lips.
Although this was not quite the end he'd imagined for
himself, somehow he'd known from the first that one of
those elven bolts would turn on him. There was a certain perverse satisfaction in being proved right.

Darkness, deep and swift and compelling, surged up
from somewhere within the mercenary's soul, drawing
him down toward oblivion.

* * * * *

Beneath the shadows of Tethir's trees, Zoastria faced
off against a pair of swordsmen. The moonblade in her
hand flashed and darted and thrust with astonishing
speed. Terrifying speed, and a power that lay on the outermost boundaries of the elf woman's skill and
strength.

The force behind each stoke, each lunge, nearly tore

the sword from Zoastria's hand. Keeping her balance
was difficult. More than once she had overextended and
presented an opening to the humans' blades. Her arms
and shoulders bled from several small wounds. If not for
the uncanny speed of the moonblade's strike, which
allowed her to quickly cover such lapses, she likely
would have been slain.

The half-elf had admonished her to hold the sword in
a two-handed grip, else it would be too difficult to control. Zoastria, in her pride, had ignored the warning.

From the corner of her eye she caught a glimpse of
the half-elf just as she ran a half-orc fighter through.
Not bothering to retrieve the blade from his chest, she
ripped the sword from his hand and turned to meet the
next attack.

The tiny moon elf darted between the two men, duck-
ing below the instinctive sweep of their blades and
whirling back to lunge at the man to her right. She got
in below his guard; the moonblade sank easily between
his ribs.

But the man was not through just yet. As he fell, he
lashed out with his sword. Zoastria was in too close for
the edge to find her, but the hilt and crosspiece struck
her hard across the face. Her head snapped painfully to
one side.

The elf threw herself sideways so that her continued
motion would absorb some of the force of the blow. She
hit the ground hard, spat teeth, and rolled to her feet.
Dragging the increasingly heavy moonblade up into
guard position, she faced down her second opponent.

Before she could strike, a stunning jolt tore through
her from behind. She glanced down at the bloody arrow
protruding from her body.

With a yelp of triumph, the swordsman hauled his
blade up and across his body for a backhanded slash.
Zoastria raised her head and prepared to meet death.

A sword flashed in over her shoulder and dove toward
the swordsman. It pierced his leather gauntlet, plunging

deeply between the twin bones of his forearm and pinning his arm to his chest.

Thin but strong arms gathered up the elf woman and bore her away from the fighting. Zoastria looked up into the eyes of her half-elven descendent.

"That arrow has to come out," Arilyn said, placing her hand on the crimson shaft.

"Do not," the elf woman replied as fiercely as she could in her fading voice. "It has pierced a lung. If you remove it, I will die all the faster, and there are things that must be said. I name you blade heir. Take up the moonblade once again and finish this fight."

With those words, Zoastria seized the arrow and tore it free. Blood bubbled from the corner of her lips, and her head slid limply to one side.

Arilyn stood, staring down at the elf woman. Zoastria had sped her own death so that her blade heir could claim the sword. A moonblade could have but one wielder.

The half-elf turned and strode to the place where the moonblade had fallen. Indecision shimmered over her, for neither of her choices looked promising. To take up the blade was to willingly embrace untold centuries of servitude—perhaps an eternity's imprisonment—to the moonblade's magic. There was also the very real possibility that the sword would not accept her this time, for she had rejected it and turned aside from the elven sacrifice it required.

The sounds of battle tore Arilyn's gaze from the sword. All around her, the forest folk fought fiercely for their home. Yet the humans were many, and the outcome of the conflict by no means certain.

Instant death, or eternal servitude.

Arilyn stooped and seized the blade.

Twenty-three

A flash of vivid azure magic burst from the moonblade, enveloping Arilyn in a flair of arcane energy. And then it was gone, as quickly as it had come.

The moonblade had reclaimed her.

Without pause for reflection or regret, the half-elf flung herself toward the nearest battle. A dozen or so mercenaries had surrounded a pair of elven females, who stood back to back and held off the taunting blades of the humans as best they could. The humans were toying with their captives. The females' clothing hung about them in ribbons, and their coppery skin was marked by many shallow cuts. More painful to the proud elves than these wounds was the indignity of their situation. Arilyn saw this in her elf-sisters' eyes, and she burned with wrath at the lewd, taunting comments that the captive elves, mercifully, could not fully understand.

Arilyn stalked in, her moonblade held high over her right shoulder. Without breaking step, she slashed into the

neck of the man to her left, cutting him nearly to the bone.
She pivoted with the backswing and knocked the sword
from the hand of the man on her right-hand side, then
ran him through before the surprise of the attack could
wipe the lascivious sneer from his bearded face. She
heaved him off her blade and into the reflexive grasp of
the man behind him—a short, slight youth who staggered under the weight of his dying comrade.

For a moment the young mercenary could not use his
sword. One of the elf women seized the opportunity. She
darted forward and drew her bone dagger across his
windpipe.

"Down!" Arilyn shouted in Elvish as she slashed forward. The elf woman dropped and rolled as the magic
blade whistled in over the young man's head—and cut
a deep and bloody path through the eyes of the mercenary who approached from behind.

Eight men still stood, eight against three elven
females. No longer were the mercenaries quite so cocky.
There was an element of vindictive fury to their fighting
that brought to mind wicked children, outraged when
the puppies they tormented nipped at their fingers.

Arilyn winced as one of the elf women was disarmed,
almost literally, by the brutal stoke of a broadsword
wielded by a man nearly thrice her weight. Two of the
men leaped at the wounded female and wrestled her
down. One of them pinned her arms, and the other opened
her belly. Grinning fiendishly, they left her there to die
slowly.

Arilyn's first thought was to end the elf woman's agony
as quickly as possible. Yet she could not. Pressed as she
was by the remaining swordsmen, she could not get
through with the merciful gift of death. And the elf
woman who still fought at Arilyn's side was not much better off than her kin. She bled freely from many wounds,
and her face was nearly gray under its coppery tints. Arilyn noted with sudden sharp horror the softly rounded
swell of the elf's belly. The female carried her unborn child

into battle; there were two more lives soon to be lost.

The half-elf nudged the swaying female sharply. "To the trees, while you still can!"

"I will not leave you alone," the elf insisted.

Arilyn hesitated for only a moment. The warning that Danilo's shadow-double had sent her rang loudly in her mind: she could not call forth the elfshadows again without grave danger to herself. Yet in truth, what risk was this, to one whose life was already forfeit to the service of the moonblade?

"Come forth, all of you!" Arilyn shouted.

She parried an attack even as the mists that presaged the elfshadow entities poured from the sword. Then the startled humans fell back as they regarded the eerie manifestation taking shape before them.

Eight elfshadow warriors, apparently as solid as life and armed with elven blades, stalked toward the dumbfounded humans. One of them, a tiny, blue-haired female, slipped an arm around the pregnant elf and helped her toward the safety of the trees. Arilyn saw this and took comfort in the knowledge that Zoastria was still watching over the forest People.

Then the moonblade's mists seemed to close in around Arilyn, and the blood-soaked earth wavered and tilted strangely as it floated up to meet her. Arilyn scanned the entities of the moonblade and then turned her rapidly failing gaze on the sword in her hands. As she slid inexorably into the darkness, a tiny smile lifted the corners of her lips. Danilo's double was not among the warriors, nor had her rune of rapport reappeared on the sword.

Whatever her fate, Danilo had been freed.

* * * * *

The appearance of the elfshadow warriors brought new strength to the weary and outnumbered elves. From his corner of the battle, Kendel Leafbower looked with awe upon the white-haired mage who bore down upon a pair of half-orc mercenaries, his outstretched hands crackling with eldritch energy and the many braids of his hair swirling like the snakes of a vengeful medusa. At the sight of this new and fearsome warrior, one of the burly creatures let out a strangled whimper of fear, dropped his sword, and ran for the trees.

It was not among his more intelligent decisions. Roaring out an oath to Morodin, the dwarven god of battle, Jill leaped into the half-orc's path—and onto the high, thick stump of what had until recently been an ancient tree. This brought him nearly eye-to-eye with the larger fighter. Jill evened the score completely by lifting his axe high overhead. It plunged in deep between the fleeing half-orc's eyes, cleaving his skull as easily as a goodwife might slice through a summer melon.

"Hee hee!" exulted the dwarf as he hopped down from his perch. His battle glee quickly turned to frustration, however, for his axe refused to come free of the thick skull. Jill planted one booted foot on the fallen half-orc's chest, the other on his ruined forehead, and tugged and grunted for all he was worth. None of this availed.

Before Kendel could call out a warning, a spear-wielding human closed in on the preoccupied dwarf. He thrust the tip of the spear deep into the thicket of pale brown beard, forcing the dwarf's head up and back.

For a moment Jill froze. His eyes sought his elven friend, and he made his farewells with an apologetic little shrug.

But Kendel was not prepared to lose his odd companion. Inspiration struck; he pointed toward the captive dwarf. "Jill!" he shouted desperately. "The dwarf's name is Jill!"

A smirk crossed the mercenary's face. "And what of it?" he said, misunderstanding the elf's ploy. "I've nothing more against killing me a female dwarf than a male, though may Cyric take me if I can tell the difference one from t'other!"

Storm clouds began to gather on Jill's craggy face. "I

ain't no ding-blasted female!" he roared in a voice that plumbed depths no human male could reach. "You human men got the eyesight of a mole and the git-up of a gelding—no wonder yer wimmenfolk is takin' up more common with the likes of elves and halflings!"

The insult seemed to strike the mercenary in a sensitive spot. "Jill?" he repeated, this time in a cruel taunt.

The single, sneering word at last had the desired effect. Galvanized by the familiar insult, the dwarf reached forward and seized the shaft of the spear. He leaned back and then ripped the weapon to one side, ignoring the strands of dun-colored beard that were torn out by the V-shaped prongs of the iron point. Then he lunged at the weapon and bit clear through the shaft.

Before the man could recover from the surprise of this unusual counterattack, Jill chewed lustily and then spat a mouthful of oak splinters into the man's face. He leaped at him, the broken spear head held like a dagger. The man stumbled and went down under the fury of the attack, and found himself securely pinned to the ground by nearly two hundred pounds of irate dwarf.

"Jill was me mother's name," the stout little warrior growled and then drove the spear home.

The dwarf hopped to his feet and wiped his blood-stained hands on his tunic. Still in the throes of his own peculiar battle frenzy, he stomped a couple of times on the dead half-orc's head. The skull gave way completely, and the axe slid free with ease.

Kendel made his way quickly to his friend's side. "The battle is not yet over," he said with a grin. "Come . . . there are many introductions yet to be made."

Understanding—and a touch of wry humor—flooded the dwarf's slate-gray eyes. He responded with a deep-throated chuckle and fell in beside the elf.

"Oh, but that were a smart one," he said admiringly as they trotted toward the nearest skirmish. "Yer a quick-thinkin' one in battle, scrawny elf though you might be. Me kin's gonna love hearin' this tale, once we finish this

business and get us under the Earthfast Mountains.
Come to think on it," the dwarf added, a speculative tone
entering his voice, "I got me a right pretty little cousin
you might like to meet."

Kendel blinked, astounded by the dwarf's invitation to
accompany him to his ancestral home, by the cozy welcome Jill obviously anticipated for them both, and by the
somewhat daunting prospect of being expected to court a
dwarf maid. And oddly enough, to the homeless and dis-
enfranchised elf, there was an odd appeal in all of it.

"Her name wouldn't happen to be Jill, would it?" he
asked casually as he raised a sword to meet an onrushing mercenary.

The dwarf scowled and stepped into the path of the
charging human. "Yeah," he said in a belligerent growl.
"And what of it?"

* * * * *

Bunlap advanced on the wounded elf, his bearded
face twisted in a hideous parody of glee and his sword
held high and back. Foxfire's torn and bleeding sword
arm refused to respond. He seized his sword in his other
hand and managed to bring it up. The parry was weak,
but it turned aside the first blow.

The man thrust in again, high, with a quick, stabbing
movement. Foxfire parried again, this time more surely.
For several minutes they fought, the blows ringing
harder and coming faster.

But the loss of blood was beginning to take a toll on
the elf. His vision swam, and the human's sword darted
in over his guard to cut a deep line across his chest. Foxfire lunged at his opponent; Bunlap danced back, and
the elf fell facedown onto the ground.

The expected killing stroke did not come. A heavy, iron-
shod boot stamped hard on the elf's lower back, sending
waves of agony shimmering along every nerve. Dimly
Foxfire felt the man's sword cutting deep and burning

lines upon his skin. Apparently Bunlap intended to mark
the elf as he himself had been marked. He took his time,
cutting his signature with painstaking care and a sadistic pleasure as tangible to the fading elf as his own pain.

Suddenly Foxfire heard a startled oath. The heavy
boot that pinned him to the ground was gone.

The elf lifted his head, shook away the haze of pain and
blood. To his astonishment, Arilyn stood between him and
the human, an elven sword held in a two-handed grip.

"You again," Bunlap said in a low, ominous voice. "Get
out of my way. This elf is mine."

"I think not," the elf woman said coolly. She met the
mercenary's first vicious stroke and parried it with a
circular sweep that sent his sword arm out wide.

Bunlap stepped in close and delivered a bare-knuckled
punch to the elf's beautiful face. She reeled back, shaking
her head as if to clear her vision. Then she ducked as he
brought his sword whistling down and across. It was a
near miss. A thick lock of her wavy sapphire hair fell to
the ground.

The elf woman straightened to her full height and got
her moonblade back out in front of her. She lunged,
turned the lunge into a feint, and then lunged again,
the moves coming so close together that Bunlap was
forced to retreat.

He responded by landing a brutal kick to Foxfire's ribs.

The beautiful face of his elven opponent darkened with
outrage. She slammed her sword into its ancient sheath
and leaped forward, her hands reaching for Bunlap's wrist.

The attack was unexpected. Surprising, too, was the
female's next move. Holding fast to the man's sword
arm, she pivoted so that her back was pressed against
him. Then she leaned forward at the waist, yanking
down hard on his arm as she did so. Bunlap somersaulted over her and landed heavily on his back. His
sword clattered to the ground.

Growling like an enraged bear, Bunlap rolled onto his
stomach and seized the elf woman's ankles. With a

quick jerk, he pulled both feet out from under her.

With elven agility she twisted and managed to get her hands under her as she fell. This broke her fall somewhat, but did nothing to free her from the vengeful human's grasp.

Bunlap rose to his knees. With a quick, vicious movement, he twisted the elf woman so that she slammed down onto her back. He jerked her toward him and then fell forward to pin her body to the ground.

He was a large man, well over six feet tall, and his heavy-muscled bulk weighed closer to three hundred pounds than two. No female, no matter what her skills in battle, could free herself from such bonds.

Bunlap propped himself up on one elbow. With his free hand, he struck the woman across the face again and again. He took his time, leaving livid red welts on the pale skin but never hitting with enough force to break bones. This was vengeance of another sort, and one best taken slowly.

At first the elf woman struggled beneath him, her hands pushing at his chest. Gradually, the fight went out of her and her eyes—odd, gold-flecked blue eyes—became distant and unfocused. Bunlap had seen such things happen before. Terror did odd things to women. Such withdrawal was not all that unusual. And so he did not wonder when her lips began to move in a soft elven chant, or notice that her hands, which had fallen limply to her sides, moved in slight, subtle gestures. Arcane gestures.

Bunlap noticed none of this. His thirst for vengeance had given way to a darker emotion. He tore aside the elf woman's outer tunic, grimacing as he gathered up in both fists the fluid, silvery mesh of the elven chain mail that lay beneath.

It was at that moment that the elf woman finished her chant. Eldritch energy poured from her, and the metal of her sword and her armor glowed with white heat. Bunlap screamed with agony and rage as the waves of power jolted through him, yet try though he might he could not release his grip on the deadly elven mail.

He was not aware of the moment when the killing surge stopped, nor did he know how the elf woman managed to get out from under him. When he came to, he was on his knees, his blackened hands held before him like the claws of a charred bird.

"Arm yourself," the elf woman said in a low, musical voice. "If you've any honor, stand and fight."

Bunlap looked up into the eyes of the elf woman and at the point of her sword. Both glowed with angry, arcane blue fire. He found he had no desire to fight. "With these?" he demanded as he held up his ruined hands. "How can you speak of honor?"

"I give you the opportunity to die on your feet with your sword in your hands," she said. "It is more than you deserve. Refuse, and I will cut you down where you grovel."

The utter contempt in her tone stirred the proud man into action. He seized his sword, accepted the searing pain of contact, and rolled to his feet.

Bunlap was a hardened mercenary. He'd killed his first man at the age of thirteen and since then had won his living by the sword. But in his nearly forty years of constant fighting, never had he faced a swordmaster to match the one before him.

Cold, grim, inexorable, the elf woman worked his sword down with each stroke and parry and thrust. Finally she forced the point of his blade to the ground. With a quick move of her booted foot, she stomped on the blade and tore it from his blasted hand.

Holding his gaze, she ran him through the heart.

All this Foxfire witnessed as if he were watching through smoked glass. He could not move, could do nothing to stop his enemy from harming the elf woman he loved above all others. Unreal, too, were the moon elf's ministrations when she turned and stooped beside him.

Gentle hands helped Foxfire to sit against a tree,

probed his bruised ribs and pronounced them whole,
bound his wounds, and held a water flask as he drank.
When at last the haze of pain began to dim, the elf
woman took his face between her hands and turned it
toward her.

With a start of wonder, Foxfire realized that this was
not Arilyn at all, but someone like enough to her to be a
twin. Only the hair—the rare color of spun sapphires—
and the slightly more angular lines of her face, distinguished her from her half-elven descendent.

"For all you have done for my daughter, I thank you,"
the elf woman said in a voice like wind and music. "You
have shown Arilyn that she possesses an elven soul. Tell
her that her mother is proud. Tell her she and I will be
together again, in service to the People for as long as we
are needed, and in Arvandor when our task is completed. Tell her this! I would speak to her myself," the elf
said with obvious longing, "but to come to her again
would hasten our reunion, and that I must not do. Arilyn is needed by the People. You will tell her these
things?"

Foxfire nodded, and the beautiful moon elf dissipated
like mist at highsun.

Fear filled the green elf's heart; once before he had
seen the shadow warriors disappear during battle, after
the fall of the moonblade's mistress. He struggled to his
feet and staggered toward the glowing light that her-
alded Arilyn's sword.

The moonblade lay on the blood-soaked earth, its
arcane blue fire dimming rapidly. Its wielder had fallen
nearby. Oddly enough, Ferret knelt beside the fallen
warrior, cradling her raven head in an oddly protective
gesture. Around them stood a circle of exulting warriors: green elves, both Elmanesse and Suldusk, centaurs, fauns, lythari, even a battered and broadly
grinning dwarf.

Ferret looked up and met his gaze. "The battle has
been won, and Arilyn lives!"

Twenty-four

After the wounded were tended and the dead returned to the forest, the sylvan folk began the northward trek. By common agreement, they would rebuild, forming a settlement at the Swanmay's Glade that would embrace Elmanesse and Suldusk alike. After the battle, the wisdom of joining together had been clear to them all.

Arilyn and Ganamede walked together. The half-elf was still weak from her ordeal and thinner than ever, yet she was strengthened by the success of her mission and the sweetness of the message Foxfire had given her.

Neither she nor the lythari were much given to talk at any time, and each had a heartful of matters to treasure and contemplate.

Once again, Arilyn found she had to ask her friend for help. This was becoming easier for her to do. In the community that had developed among the forest people, it did not seem intrusive to ask for or to offer assistance. Especially now, when all the fey folk were united as never before.

"Before I take my leave of the forest elves, there is one more thing I must do," Arilyn said. "You told me once that a time would come when I must walk between my two worlds. For this, I need your help."

Ganamede stared at her for a moment; then he nodded in understanding and approval. "I will take you to Evermeet," he agreed.

* * * * *

Queen Amlaruil started as the ring on her small finger emitted a silent alarm. She had worn the ring for many years; it warned her when someone entered the magical gate on the far side of the palace grounds. It also would transport her there, instantly, along with whoever happened to be at hand. But even if she went alone, the elven queen did not fear. She was no fragile figurehead to be cozened and protected; she herself was one of the powerful safeguards that kept Evermeet secure. Amlaruil knew the ancient high magic of the elves and carried the special power of the Seldarine. Few were the forces that could get beyond Evermeet's formidable queen.

She nodded to her scribe and her honor guard and then touched the ring. The four elves emerged at once in a deep, forested glade. There were two figures waiting there: a large, silver-furred lythari, and a tall and slender moon elven female. As yet, neither had perceived the queen's arrival.

Arilyn looked with wonder at her ancestral home. A few butterflies fed upon the flowers that dotted the meadow grasses, and the ancient oaks that surrounded the glade were robed in the deep emerald hues of late summer. It was a scene such as might have been found in the virgin forest of many a land, except for an aura of eldritch energy as pervasive as sunlight.

"Evermeet," Arilyn whispered.

"I will leave you here and return when you are ready

for me," Ganamede said, vanishing from sight almost as soon as the words were spoken.

Arilyn felt the tingle of magic at her side and glanced down at her moonblade. A faint blue mist rose from the blade.

Her eyes followed it, then widened in astonishment. The mist reached out like reverent fingers to touch a shimmering oval gate. Arilyn had seen it only once before, but she knew it well. It was the power that her mother had inadvertently given the moonblade—a link between the worlds of elves and humankind.

"Who are you, who dares trespass upon this place?"

The question might have seemed harsh, but for the sheer beauty of the voice that spoke it. Arilyn's throat tightened. The voice reached deep into her memory, recalled the lullabies her mother had crooned to her as a child. Liquid starlight—for some reason that was how Arilyn remembered her mother's voice. This one had the same limpid, shimmering tones.

Arilyn turned to face Amlaruil Moonflower, Queen of Evermeet.

It was the elven ruler's turn to jolt in astonishment. "Amnestria?" she whispered in a voice filled with longing and awe.

This startled Arilyn, for she did not think she looked much like her mother. Indeed, the queen quickly realized her mistake and composed her features back into the mask of regal serenity. Nor was Amlaruil much like Amnestria, Arilyn noted. The queen's features were more delicate, her hair like silk and flame. She was tall, taller even than Arilyn, with a pale, otherworldly beauty that reminded Arilyn of the lythari females. And although Amnestria's inclination had been to be nearly as solitary as her daughter, the queen was accompanied by a pair of gold elven guards and an elderly moon elf male—no doubt an advisor or a scribe.

At least they had one thing in common, Arilyn mused: each had seen Amnestria in the other. She herself would

never have believed it possible, and she doubted the
elven queen would ever accept the link between them.
So be it. She herself had matters to tend.

The Harper drew the moonblade and fell to one knee.
She placed the elven sword on the grass at Amlaruil's
feet.

"I am Arilyn Moonblade, daughter and blade heir of
Amnestria of Evermeet. As long as the fires of Myth
Drannor burn within this sword, it will serve the People
and their rightful queen."

There was a long silence. The elven monarch stood like
a statue of marble and moonstone. Arilyn understood. All
moonblades were pledged to the People, yet the queen
could hardly accept the sword without acknowledging its
wielder. With her next words, however, Arilyn gave the
proud queen a way out. She took Amlaruil's commission,
given her by the hand of Captain Carreigh Macumail,
and placed it beside the sword.

"I have fulfilled my duties as ambassador of Evermeet and have come to give my report."

"Rise, and speak," the queen said at last. She waved
the guards back and bid the elderly scribe to take a seat
on a fallen log.

Arilyn gave a concise but thorough accounting of the
events in the Forest of Tethir. When she fell silent,
Amlaruil asked her a number of questions. Finally the
queen nodded.

"It is not the task I gave you, but nonetheless you
have done well."

"Then permit me to name my fee," Arilyn said evenly.
"Carreigh Macumail indicated that he'd been empowered
to approve any request I might make. I certainly have no
objection to such generosity, but in the future, you might
want to fill in a figure before signing the note."

This seemed to amuse the queen. "You are definitely
Amnestria's daughter," she said wryly. "She was ever
one to speak her mind. Yet I see that there is much of
your father in you, as well."

"What you see before you is my doing," Arilyn said in a calm, even tone. "I am not a soup, made by tossing a little of this and that into a pot. As for my father, we met for the first time but three winters past." She paused and touched the gem in her restored moonblade. "You and yours made certain of that."

There was no accusation in her voice, just a statement of fact. By the decree of Amlaruil, the moonblade had been dismantled and the sword and stone divided between Arilyn's mother and father. This had kept the dangerous elfgate from becoming as powerful as it might have been, but it had also robbed Arilyn of her family and the knowledge of the sword's true power.

The queen's gaze did not falter. "I suppose you've wondered why we never sought you out after Amnestria's death."

"No."

Amlaruil raised one brow. "You're not going to make this easy, I take it. Very well—nor would I in your position. It is known that those of mixed blood are banned from the island kingdom. You must understand. Evermeet is the last retreat, our only secure refuge from the incursions of humanity. Many of the People, particularly the high elves, fear our culture is giving way to that of the humans. Half-elves may in themselves be no threat, but the symbolism is too powerful. We cannot make exceptions, not even in your case. Perhaps *especially* in your case."

"Yet here I am," Arilyn pointed out.

"Yes." The queen was silent for a long moment, and the gaze she turned upon the half-elf grew more searching. For the first time the queen's features showed a touch of regret. "You have done remarkably well. To my knowledge, no one has ever before had to discover a moonblade's powers alone. Had we known you possessed the potential to wield the moonblade, we would have taken another course. We knew, of course, that Amnestria's blade would pass to you, but we never expected you to . . ."

"Survive?" Arilyn finished dryly.

"Few elves are up to the demands of an ancient moon-blade," the queen pointed out. "Most have lain dormant for centuries, and only a handful of the swords retain their power. Many elves refuse their inheritance, with no dishonor. It was not unreasonable for us to assume that a half-elven child would be unequal to the challenge."

"But you let me try, fully expecting that I would be slain. I drew the moonblade that first time knowing nothing of this, or of the hidden requirements of the sword."

"And had you known all, would you have done differently?"

The question was shrewd, and Arilyn was momentarily startled by the queen's insight. Obviously, she could not deny the truth in Amlaruil's words, and she responded with the gesture of a fencer acknowledging a hit.

"What was done is done, and I am content to leave it so," Arilyn said. "But there is a reason why I speak of these matters now. My mother spoke often and fondly of her youngest brother, and so I have named Prince Lamruil as my blade heir. Will you tell him of his inheritance and see that he is properly prepared to receive it? I took up the sword unprepared. I would not see another do likewise."

The queen stood in silence for a long moment. "It will be done. On behalf of my son, I thank you for showing him this honor." She paused, as if considering what to say next. "You were speaking of your fee," the queen prompted, clearly eager to once again put the conversation, and the extraordinary half-elf, in terms she could understand and control.

Arilyn met her gaze squarely. "I want a vast tract of land to the east of the Forest of Tethir, stretching from the borders of Castle Spulzeer to the origins of the Sulduskoon River. Have your agents—or the Harpers, or whoever you please—obtain the land."

"Your fees are high," the queen commented.

"The wealth of Evermeet is fabled to be beyond reckoning. And you did say that I could name my price."

The queen gave her a searching look. "And what will you do with these lands?"

In response, Arilyn dug one hand into her bag and drew out a handful of seeds: winged maple seeds, pine cones, acorns.

For a long moment, the queen and the half-elf held each other's gaze. "It will be as you have requested. The lands will be ceded to you to do with as you see fit."

Arilyn bowed and walked to the place where Ganamede had disappeared.

"One more thing," Amlaruil said softly. "In behalf of the People, I accept your fealty and your sword. May you always serve them as well as you have today."

The half-elf turned to face the queen. She drew her moonblade and saluted in a uniquely elven gesture of respect.

The two elf women stood for a moment gazing upon one another, but there was nothing more that either could say. They were unlikely to meet again, and Amlaruil could in truth give the half-elf no more acknowledgment than this. Yet it was more than Arilyn had anticipated, and she was content.

As if sensing that her task was done, the silver wolf appeared. Arilyn slipped with him back into his veiled world, and to Tethir beyond.

And behind her, the elven queen stared thoughtfully at the shimmering gate that had brought the half-elf to Evermeet. Since she was ever the queen, part of her mind dealt with practical matters. It had never occurred to her that the lythari might be able to access this particular gate. Although no lythari had ever proven traitorous, safeguards must be taken.

Amlaruil stooped and picked up the commission the half-elf had left behind. She absently unrolled it and glanced at the elegant script. Her eye settled on a

certain curving rune, and a jolt of astonishment shook
her. A subtle, skillful turn of the quill had transformed
the half-elf's chosen name "Moonblade" to "Moonflower,"
the clan name of the royal moon elf family.

"Captain Macumail," Amlaruil murmured, recognizing at once the source of this forgery.

The outrage she expected to feel at this sacrilege simply did not come. Amnestria was lost to her, but her
daughter's daughter was a credit to the People . . . and
the clan.

"Arilyn Moonflower," the queen repeated softly.
Although she realized no elf on Evermeet could ever
hear her speak these words, they felt right and good
upon her lips.

* * * * *

At dawn, several days hence, the survivors of Zoastria's Stand stood together at the eastern boundaries of
Tethir. They all came: the green elves—both Elmanesse
and Suldusk—the lythari, even the fauns and centaurs.
Only Jill and Kendel Leafbower were missing, for now
that his self-assigned task had been completed, the
dwarf was eager to see his kinfolk once again, and the
two had departed the evening before.

All who gathered carried the grandchildren of Cormanthor—seedlings from the ancient trees that in centuries to come would extend the wondrous forest for
miles. It was a small thing, perhaps, in the face of all
that the sylvan folk had lost and all that they would continue to endure. But each tree was a living link to their
beloved forest and a symbol of the new coalition between
the tribes, the lythari, and the other sylvan creatures.
They who had merely endured, would now rebuild.

And so they worked together throughout that long
day, with a harmony rare among the forest folk. With
the coming of night, they retreated to the familiar
haven of the trees.

When the evening meal was over and the songs and tales fell silent, Foxfire sought out Arilyn and asked her to walk with him. They walked in silence until they found themselves back in the seedling forest. It was an oddly appropriate place, one that mingled new beginnings with ancient and cherished memories.

"I have a message for you from Rhothomir," he began. "It is not one he could easily give himself, so I offered to speak for him. This I do with all my heart."

"Speaker for the Speaker now, are you?" she teased him. The elf smiled faintly, but he would not be deterred.

"The People of Tethir offer you a home in their midst. Join the tribe and live beneath the trees your own hands planted. This is your place," he concluded softly.

"There is a part of me that would like to accept," she said with complete honesty. "There is a part of me that *will* remain. But look around you," she said, sweeping a hand toward the fledgling trees and the little mounds of soft earth where the sylvan folk had planted seeds of hope.

"You will live to see these trees grow. I am half-elven, Foxfire, and I will be gone before the branches of these two oaklings meet overhead. There are things I must do elsewhere. Like the lythari, it is given to me to walk between two worlds. You have shown me that my soul is elven and have helped me to know that my path and my heart lie with the humans. But I can promise you this," she vowed as she drew her moonblade from its ancient scabbard. "As long as the fires of Myth Drannor burn within this sword, a hero will return to the Forest of Tethir in time of need."

She showed him the blade, and the bright new rune that blazed upon it, and then she slid the moonblade carefully back into its place. "It is given to me to add a power to the sword. This is it: when the people of Tethir are in need, the wielder of this blade will come. But most likely, it won't be me. My life will not be that long, and I wish you to have peace long after I have joined my ancestors."

Foxfire nodded and then gathered her into his arms. Arilyn went to him, remembering everything, and regretting nothing. Her elven soul would always be linked to this forest. Perhaps, in some future age, she *would* return, her essence giving strength to the elven sword. But as she had said to her dear friend, her heart lay elsewhere, and so did her path.

Twenty-five

It was after midsummer when Lord Hhune's carriage rolled through the northern gates of Zazesspur. He had enjoyed a very eventful interlude in Waterdeep, the rival city to the north. Granted, some of his plots and plans had withered on the vine. It did not appear as if the northern outposts of Zazesspur's thieves and assassins guilds would take hold—a pity, for these were favored tools of the Knights of the Shield. And he, Hhune, had been labeled as a member of this hostile group and barred from Waterdeep. The Knights had also lost their capable agent in Waterdeep. The Lady Lucia Thione had been unmasked and exiled. It would be many long years before the Knights of the Shield again managed to place an informant so high in Waterdhavian society.

Even so, Hhune felt certain he could turn these losses into personal gain. Although he could not enter the northern city again, there was to be no disruption of shipping between Zazesspur and the north. And Waterdeep was still reeling from a series of disasters: crop failure, incursions of monsters stripping the forests of game and the fields of cattle, political uncertainty. Zazesspur's goods and surplus crops would find an eager, almost desperate market. Finally, he had with him the deposed agent, and he had spent much of the trip southward mentally devising various uses for her.

Lucia Thione, formerly the ranking agent of the Knights of the Shield in the north, was a rarity in Tethyr: a surviving member of the old royal family, albeit a very distant relation. The tide of royalist sentiment in Zazesspur was swelling, and who knew what heights an ambitious man might reach with such a consort at his side? In addition to her purple blood, she was a woman of rare beauty and keen business acumen. At one time, Hhune would have counted himself lucky merely to spend time in her company. He was ecstatic to find her utterly in his power!

Of course he had said nothing of this to her. Lady Thione fully expected to meet her death in the land of her forebears, and she had spent the trip trying to subtly insinuate herself into Hhune's good graces. It was gratifying to him to have this beautiful, nobly bred woman pursuing his favor, and he intended to allow her to work for it!

Eager though he was to install his "guest" in his country estate, Lord Hhune set a brisk pace for his town offices. Business must always come before pleasure. He strode in, nodded to the clerks, and called for his scribe.

To his surprise, the young Calishite brat—the royal apprentice Balik's men had saddled him with—came to his bidding.

"Good day, Lord Hhune," Hasheth said. "I trust that your business in the Northlands went well?"

"Where is Achnib?" Hhune demanded.

The lad's face darkened. "He is dead, my lord," he said bluntly. "May all traitors and thieves meet the same end. But you need not hear of this from my lips. Word of

your approach reached us this morn. Duke Hembreon
awaits you in your office."

Hhune's boots suddenly seemed rooted to the floor.
Amid the changeful winds of Zazesspurian power, the
Duke stood as unbending as a sycamore. His was an
ancient family with vast wealth, and he himself was a
grave, distinguished man whose impeccable sense of
honor and duty extended to all he did. Therefore, Hembreon tended to view his position in the Knights of the
Shield as noblesse oblige. He was also one of the most
important leaders of the group, Hhune reminded himself as he shook off his immobility.

The duke stood as Hhune entered the room and gave
him his hand. "You have performed a great service to
the people of the city."

"I live to serve," Hhune said smoothly, but he cast a
quick sidelong glare at his young apprentice. Hasheth
gave him a subtle nod, as if encouraging him to play along.

"As you requested, Lord Hhune," Hasheth began, "in
your absence I strove to ferret out who among your men
might be in league with the Nelanther pirates. It was
Achnib, as you suspected. Two of these pirates are even
now in the city's dungeons—men who have sworn that
Achnib hired them, paying with information of shipping
schedules and routes.

"Nor was that his only crime. He was stealing from
you, skimming the profit from the caravans and hoarding coin. What he planned to do with such is beyond
belief."

"Achnib was always ambitious," Hhune said in a sage
tone, hoping this would fit into the incredible scenario
the younger man was weaving.

"The scribe was not content with selling information
to the pirates. He began to traffic in armed ships with a
warlord known as Bunlap. Worse, there is a faint trail
which attempts to place this crime at your door."

"Indeed?" Hhune managed, marveling at the young
man's audacity.

Incredibly, Duke Hembreon seemed to swallow the absurd recitation. He rose and extended a hand to Hhune.

"By your efforts, the city has gained use of a fleet of some fifteen ships. All Zazesspur owes you thanks."

Hhune murmured a response and saw the duke on his way. Then he turned an ominous, narrowed gaze on his apprentice.

"Much of what I told the duke was true," Hasheth said earnestly. "Achnib was skimming, and he was in league with the mercenary captain. But he lost his nerve and hoped to scuttle away in the confusion after your involvement with Bunlap and his logging operation became known. He attempted to buy passage to Lantan. To protect your interests, I had both Achnib and Bunlap killed, and turned the ships over to the Lords' Council as confiscated goods. They would have found out about them, regardless. Better this way, and be a hero rather than a culprit."

"You seem to be unusually loyal," Lord Hhune pointed out suspiciously.

"What good would have come to me had you been brought low?" the young man said, reasonably enough. "Besides, the Knights were pleased by my initiative and permitted me to enter their ranks, and so, in protecting your interests, I served my own."

Hhune shook his head, apparently stunned by all this. "What of Duke Hembreon? How did you learn the identity of such a powerful man among the Knights?"

"Palace intrigue," Hasheth lied, thinking of the coin in his pocket. He wanted to impress Hhune with his many connections and his own importance. "One of the few benefits of being born a pasha's son. There is more that you should know. The Harpers have been inquiring into your affairs. I thought it best that this matter was concluded, and quickly. The Harpers would not be contented as easily as Duke Hembreon."

"Well done," exclaimed an amused feminine voice. Hhune looked up; he had almost forgotten about Lucia

Thione. "You have a talented new ally, my lord. Perhaps you would consider another? With three such minds, what could we not accomplish in Tethyr?"

Hhune regarded the beautiful woman and the hawk-nosed youth and decided that he could do worse.

"Meet my new apprentice, my dear," he said to Lucia. "And Hasheth, this is Lucia Thione. Surely you recognize her family's name and realize that it must not be spoken outside of these walls—at least, not until the mention of it can advance the fortunes of us all."

For a moment the trio regarded each other intently. Relief was bright in Lucia's beautiful eyes, now that she knew what Hhune had in mind for her. The lord saw also that she understood his purpose in making this introduction. The knowledge of her identity offered both potential power and grave danger—and the secret bound them together. It was a subtle way of accepting her offer, while reminding her that her fortune was bound indelibly with his. Hhune also noted the soft, warm look the woman cast over the impressed lad; this amused him. If Lucia was willing to use her charm to advance her position in Tethyr, so much the better for him.

"You should not have killed Achnib," he told Hasheth mildly. "He was not terribly intelligent, but neither was he personally ambitious. He carried out his duties well enough, with loyalty usually found only in retainers with four legs and fleas. Such men are hard to find. I thought you might kill him, but I'd hoped otherwise. That is the only part of the test you failed, however. Overall you have done well."

"T-test?" faltered Hasheth.

"Of course," the lord returned in an amused tone. "You do not think I would allow you to give away my entire fleet, do you? Mark me, I am not happy about the ship you gave to the pirates, but you shall pay for it from your earnings. And other than that lapse, you did precisely as I had anticipated. The fleet is now in the hands of the Council of Lords. I could not keep it—the risks of

discovery were too great. But the merchants of Tethyr
will continue to benefit from the protection the fleet
offers, while the Council pays for its upkeep. And who, I
ask you, is both head of the shipping guild and a ranking member of the council? Who will control this fleet?"

Understanding—and fear—began to enter the young
man's eyes as he realized he was not quite as clever as
he had thought himself. The realization that he had
been acting according to Hhune's design—and no doubt
with the lord in full knowledge of his activities—both
humbled and horrified him.

"But how—" he began.

"How?" repeated Hhune coolly. "That is what you are
here to learn. You have made a good start. If you wish
to become a ranking member of the Knights of the
Shield, you will have to do better. You may start by
telling me about this pretty Harper of yours and her
plans for Zazesspur."

* * * * *

Arilyn said her good-byes to Hasheth several days
after the final battle. The Harper listened to his explanation of the situation, doubting most of it but willing
to let the matter rest. She reclaimed her horse from the
young man, glad to be done with her sojourn in the
southern city.

She had not particularly wished to return to
Zazesspur, but Tinkersdam had elected to stay behind.
He had acquired a taste for battle and decided that
tumultuous Tethyr was as good a place as any to test his
toys. Ferret, too, had traveled with her to the city, intending to even a score with Lord Hhune. Strangely enough,
after a long and private conversation with young
Hasheth, she seemed willing to abandon that notion.

But that very night, at the hands of an unknown and
unseen assassin, the reign of Pasha Balik came to an
abrupt and bloody end. It was rumored that he had

been betrayed from within, for no one saw the assassin come or go. The only sign left behind was a long, jewel-colored scarf, such as that which might be used to fashion a lady's turban.

And the next morning, Hasheth became a full member of the Knights of the Shield, having proved his loyalty by purchasing Hhune's safety at a cost many men might consider too high.

* * * * *

Arilyn left before dawn, unaware of the events of the night just past and the changes that would soon sweep Zazesspur. Her heart was light as she rode swiftly toward the north—and home. For the first time in her life, she truly knew where she belonged.

The Harper had not gone far beyond the city walls when the she heard the sounds of battle on the road ahead. Incredibly, a familiar tenor voice was lifted over the clash of swords. She nudged her horse into a run.

The words of the song became clear as she neared the battle. Set to a rollicking tune, it was the sort of ditty she had come to expect—and had learned to endure.

> "We've come to mourn the paladin,
> The best and noblest sort of man.
> His way was clear, his will was strong,
> But he's just as dead as if he'd been wrong!
>
> "Alone he faced the orcish hoard,
> And, dauntless, drew his mighty sword.
> He did not flinch, he did not blink.
> He surely did not stop and think!"

A familiar mixture of exasperation and elation flooded the half-elf's heart. The irreverent song could have come from only one person. Arilyn flung herself from her horse and raced toward the fighting, her moonblade in hand.

But the battle on the road ahead was more comic than life-threatening. In the center of the conflict stood Danilo, his arms crossed as he observed the fight between his small band of hired escorts and a group of would-be brigands. For his part, he sang his battle song, which was probably meant to spur on the fighting in classic bardic tradition. Although how this particular song might have inspired anyone was beyond Arilyn's comprehension.

Unaware of the amused half-elf's presence, Danilo continued to sing:

> "The halls of Tempus opened wide;
> Our paladin was led inside.
> He shares with all his noble creed,
> And frowns on wenching, feasts, and mead.
>
> "We cannot mourn this hero's death,
> Though of his strength we are bereft.
> If you must weep, weep for the god
> Who now endures this tiresome sod!"

Danilo did not content himself with his bardic endeavors. Between stanzas he cast small cantrips that threw confusion into the enemy ranks. Arilyn chuckled as a brigand fell facedown on the dirt path, his boot laces suddenly tied together.

The young mage looked up sharply at the rich, rare sound of elven laughter. When his gaze settled on Arilyn, joy broke, like a sunrise, over his face. He drew his sword and started fighting in earnest as he worked his way through the circle of fighters toward her.

Arilyn sighed. Danilo could handle a blade well enough, but he was no swordmaster. At the moment she had no patience for prolonged battle. So she drew the moonblade, held it high, and let out a ringing battle cry in the Elvish tongue.

The brigands looked up, startled by the fearsome

sound. The addition of an elven warrior to their foe was too much for their faltering resolve. The band scattered and made for the hills to the east—where, Arilyn noted with a touch of dark humor, a certain alchemist awaited them, all too eager for opportunities to try out his latest lethal devices.

The nobleman put away his sword and came swiftly toward her. Arilyn noted that Danilo's face had been deeply bronzed by the summer sun, and he seemed leaner, hardened by life on the road. He looked considerably older, too, as if time had touched him in a way that a few months' absence could not explain. Arilyn had no love for magic, but she recognized the mark that powerful spells left upon those who cast them. Apparently Danilo had not been idle during their time apart. It seemed that when tales were told, they would be spoken both ways!

There was something else about him that was different as well. Arilyn, who had recently come into a knowledge of herself and her path, recognized the peace of a similar understanding that lingered about him. Nor was there a hint of pretense on his face. For once the mask he held to the world was utterly gone and his heart was entirely in his eyes.

Danilo took her hands in his; this time Arilyn did not pull away.

"We meet as we parted," he said quietly.

"Pretty much," she agreed in a wry tone. "Why is it that I so often find you surrounded by people who'd dearly love to see you dead?"

A fleeting smile touched his face. "The curse of charm, wealth, and fame, I suppose," he said dryly. "But enough jests. I have sorely missed you."

With these words, he released her hands and reached out to touch the enspelled moonstone that was set into the hilt of her sword. It was a gesture he had often made during the past two years. Suddenly Arilyn recognized it for what it was. It was the only caress she had permitted him, his only tangible proof of the bond that lay between them. She wondered, briefly, how much Danilo understood of her magical gift of rapport, or how he would feel when he learned it was no longer there. But she must tell him, and at once. No one could touch a moonblade but its wielder, upon pain of death.

So she caught his wrist firmly before he could touch the moonblade. "You cannot," she said firmly. "The power that enabled you to share my blade is no more."

The bleak, empty look that filled his eyes smote Arilyn's heart. "It is no more, because it is not needed," she said quickly. "For what I can do myself, I do not need the moonblade's magic." Other explanations could come later; this much she owed him now.

"Is it possible?" he murmured with wonderment. "Arilyn, I have waited two years and more for you to know your heart. Mine you already know—it is yours, along with my life and my soul."

"Your heart I will take into my keeping, and gladly. But your soul," she added with deep satisfaction, "is once again entirely your own."

FROM BELOVED AUTHOR
ELAINE CUNNINGHAM...

FOR THE FIRST TIME TOGETHER AS A SET!
SONGS AND SWORDS

Follow the adventures of bard Danilo Thann and his beautiful
half-elf companion Arilyn Moonblade in these attractive new
editions from Elaine Cunningham. These two daring Harpers
face trials that bring them together and then tear them apart.

Elfsong
Elfshadow
Silver Shadows (JANUARY 2001)
Thornhold (FEBRUARY 2001)
The Dream Spheres

AND DON'T MISS...
STARLIGHT AND SHADOWS

Daughter of the Drow
In the aftermath of war in Menzoberranzan, free-
spirited drow princess Liriel Baenre sets off on a
hazardous quest. Pursued by enemies from her
homeland, her best hope of an ally is one who may
also be her deadliest rival.

Tangled Webs
Continuing on her quest, drow princess Liriel Baenre
learns the price of power and must confront her
dark drow nature.

Counselors and Kings
ELAINE CUNNINGHAM

Under the blazing sun of Halruaa, intrigue stalks the land.
Skilled wizards compete for power and wealth, threatening to
destroy any who interfere. Only the society of Counselors,
impervious to the effects of magic, can maintain balance and order.

Book I: THE MAGEHOUND

Matteo is a rising counselor, intent on
serving his wizardly masters well. Yet when
a spark of magic is discovered within him,
he must flee the wrath of one sworn to root
out such talents: the magehound.

Book II: THE FLOODGATE

As Matteo and his companion Tzigone
search for clues to their mysterious pasts,
Kiva the magehound, now fallen into
disgrace, plots in secrecy to destroy those
who opposed her. To accomplish her ends,
she plans to unleash a power that could
sweep away all Halruaa.

April 2001

FROM THE DARKEST REACHES OF FAERÛN'S PAST COMES A NEW ENEMY.

Return of the Archwizards
AN EXCITING NEW FORGOTTEN REALMS EPIC

BOOK I: *The Summoning*
TROY DENNING
A new evil returns to Faerûn after millennia spent in a shadowy hell.
March 2001

BOOK II: *The Siege*
TROY DENNING
The world-spanning schemes of Shade begin to take shape,
along with a new empire in the heart of the Great Desert.
December 2001

THREE OF THE MOST POPULAR
FORGOTTEN REALMS
AUTHORS TELL THE STORY
OF FAERÛN'S GREATEST KINGDOM
— AND ITS GREATEST KING.

The Cormyr Saga

CORMYR: A NOVEL
Ed Greenwood & Jeff Grubb
A plot to poison King Azoun IV brings the kingdom to
the brink of disaster.

BEYOND THE HIGH ROAD
Troy Denning
With the threat from within at an end, Cormyr faces an even
greater threat from the barbaric Stonelands, and a princess begins
to understand what it means to rule a kingdom.

DEATH OF THE DRAGON
Ed Greenwood & Troy Denning
Plague, madness, and war sweep through Cormyr and the people
look to their king for salvation. Only the mighty Azoun has
the chance to defeat the horror that will change Cormyr forever.